BY STARLIGHT

A Post-Modern Fairy Tale

by Vivian Call

To my great friend Nancy,
otherwise well named for
her boundless charisma as
- The Nance-meister.
'Gorgeous' and 'larger-than-life'
only live in hearts big enough.
Over the last few years, I've
dealt with impossible odds
because of my dearest L.
You believed in me and in
everything I have become.

- V.G.C.

PART ONE

The Truth

CHAPTER ONE
THE STAGE

When something is never supposed to happen, it typically does. Accidents happen. Caca happens. The word 'never' is a doormat - a welcome mat.

In the town of Ashvale Plains, the night sky SHOULD have been completely black. It wasn't. Instead, millions of tiny lights peeked through. They were cracks in the infinite wall of nothing. They proved that beauty was meant to be. It was destined; it was written by starlight.

Ashvale Plains was almost a city, but it gave up half-way. Its flat, boring, concrete sidewalks were well travelled by people going through the motions of success or happiness. The upper class were big fish in this puddle of muck.

In Ashvale, weddings were like slow, dumb birds with their ritual mating dance. A proper man found a woman who wouldn't argue. They got married. Love might be mentioned a few times in the wedding vows, but that was it. Romance was just a section in the bookstore. No-one really believed in fairy tales.

Life was simple by design. Everything was squared and ruled, just like the sidewalks. Everyone had a straight path set in concrete stone, and that was the foundation of Ashvale Plains. No-one ever broke these rules. Ever.

Riley was a bright girl and a gifted artist. She was always doodling in high school, even in art class. Her textbooks bloomed with quirky wit. When her caricatures got her in trouble, she defended herself; she had a black belt in smart-ass comebacks. She was also notorious for going off script. If Ashvale Plains was a marching band, she was Charlie Parker in the back, playing bebop.

Riley was dark haired and dark eyed. Her hair was straight, and it was long enough that it reached all the way down her back. Her bangs were short, however, and she puffed them away from her eyes when she was drawing. She had a few small, cute moles as finishing touches to her smirky face. She wasn't athletic, and boys only noticed her curves when her back was turned. She was always hanging off the arm of her disinterested boyfriend, Jeff.

Jeff Anders was Golden Boy. He had the looks. He had the style. Mainly, he had rich parents. His family owned land, but acted like they owned the town. Even in school, Jeff was known as 'Mr Real

Estate' because of his promising future.

He was assured a football scholarship whether he earned it or not. He'd go to a great college and then continue the family habit of wealth. He knew this. He made sure everyone else knew it.

Jeff was probably among the Top Five Most Popular Kids in school. He had smart, short brown hair and quick blue eyes. Everyone knew he could have any girl he wanted. For some reason, he hung out with Riley. In truth, he chose her because her family wasn't well off... and he enjoyed a social advantage, that way. He could dump her at any time and no-one would ask why. To him, it was power. Jeff Anders was on top of it all. He was Da Bomb.

No-one said this more than Clark.

That prick, Clark thought. Jeff keeps ticking away, and someday it'll fall. Everything'll blow apart, and he'll be nothing but a crater. Man, I'd love to be there, just to see it. He does NOT deserve to be with Riley. I hope he frickin' chokes... preferably when Riley isn't there to Heimlich him, and save his wormy, whiny ass.

Clark was the weird guy in the corner. Tall, handsome, but odd. He was the guy who kept trying to invent stuff that nobody else heard about. He looked stressed most of the time. He was focused on other things, and winged through school without much trouble.

Someone said Clark's mom was a verified psychopath, but this was high school gossip. They also said he was experimented on, when he was a baby, and that his internal organs were sold on the Russian black market. Strangely, no-one ever mentioned his father.

In high school, Clark started reading about aeronautics. He fit in a chapter or two during lunch hour, and he burned through five text books in a semester. His science teacher wouldn't explain things to him, because she had no idea what he was talking about. That fact offended her. She called him an arrogant kook, and graded him harshly afterward. It vexed him when he only got a 93% in physics.

In math class, someone joked that Clark was secretly building a UFO.

"No," Clark explained. "Just a couple ideas I have about airfoils and efficiency."

Mr Gray leaned aside to his students and chuckled, "Airy-fairy stuff. Little wings. Heh heh."

He grinned with his big, macho beard.

"That's fine, little Clarkie. I'm sure they got places for people like you… somewhere. You and your wingy-things."

The students laughed. Most of them, anyway.

Clark wasn't little; he was very tall, and quite strongly built. He was just younger than Mr Gray by thirty years.

A short, freckled kid called out from the back of the class, "Oh, so maybe them flyin' lights ain't UFOs, after all. Maybe they're fairies… like CLARK."

The class tittered, and then fell into hooting laughter, like monkeys: "Hoo-hoo… a-haa-haa-haa!"

Timmy scored big. Everyone was proud of him.

"Look at him!" Timmy pointed. "Fairy-boy's blushing!"

It was true. Clark was angry and turning red. Everyone loved it until a pretty, dark-eyed brunette looked up from her drawings. It was Riley. She wore a straight face.

"Timmy? Whatever latent, homophobic self-shame you're carrying around, you don't have to worry. You can relax, now. Okay?"

The class stopped dead. Her poker face didn't budge.

"Everyone likes you, Timmy. Everyone accepts you. I do. Mr Gray does. The rest of the class does. I bet even Clark, here, does. But he isn't carrying around psychological baggage and projecting it on other people. So… dude? You can just relax. You're gonna be okay."

Mr Gray stood speechless. He recognized a few of those words from marriage counseling. Jeff Anders sneered and turned his head.

Timmy took a few seconds to reply: "Wahh?"

"Never mind," she said. "It's just coming-of-age stuff. Maybe it'll make sense in your 40s."

Riley focused on her drawing book again. She started squiggling her pencil.

Mr Gray widened his stance. He couldn't allow this. He decided to 'assert' - yeah, that was an important word. It was his class, after all, and he was the teacher. He crossed his arms over his big chest.

"I think somebody wants some time in detention hall."

Riley stopped. Her pencil halted mid-stroke. She froze in place.

No way, she thought. He's coming after me, now? What the? Aww, what in the actual…? Man, I hate this school.

"Yeah, I think so," Mr Gray drawled. "Young Ms Henway? Maybe you'd better pack up your little art studio, there, and just waltz on down to detent-"

"FINE," Riley sighed. "I'll concentrate better. Maybe I'll get some work done." She picked herself up from her desk.

The whole class gave a final one-liner: "BUSTED!"

Colleen Dietrich hissed at her, "Takin' out the trash."

Normally, Riley would turn on them. She'd let out a crack that would level them all. Unfortunately, Mr Gray was still watching her. Her marks depended on his ego.

She gave a friendly salute to Clark on her way out. "Seeya, dude."

Hmm, she smiled. Yeah… WORTH IT.

It was springtime. Outside, it was sunny and warm - but she was in detention hall again. When she was late for class, she went to detention. When she'd been absent without excuse, she went to detention.

She was in detention a lot more whenever her dad was drinking.

Whenever she had to pick up the pieces of her home life, her grades suffered. Naturally, none of the teachers could respect such a slacker.

Detention hall was especially quiet, that day. Riley flopped into a chair, unzipped her pack, and had her lunch. It didn't take long to finish a chocolate bar, three small bags of peanuts, and a can of root beer.

She hesitated, but flipped open her sketchbook.

She'd started drawing a college stairwell. It was a monument to ascension. Its outside railings spread like wings, and they were adorned with baroque ivy. It didn't look aged; it looked sacred. She thought that sketch was okay.

Another drawing was a fountain in a park, but it looked more like jubilant fireworks. It was joy, and freedom, and dazzling light. Water leapt upward, naked and shining. She thought that drawing was alright. Her dad saw it, and called it "a wine glass taking a piss."

She stopped for a moment. She listened. No-one else was in detention hall. No-one else was nearby. She looked around, just in case. Then, she carefully lifted the pages till she uncovered the last drawing. And it was him… Clark.

He looked like a pioneer. They always had courage, and a keen mind, and old school salt. He was like one of those men who wasn't a cowboy, but tried to bring civility and class to the old west: a man who talked about treaties, and who didn't spit tobacco. He was the scholar in the fine coat; the total gentleman; the inventor who'd start with iron, but create electricity.

In her drawing, he was right there. He wore his clever glasses and stood with his tall, strong physique. He didn't invent things, he invented time. Men like him invented new eras. He was that kind of man. She always knew he was different. He wasn't just another teenage boy; he was genuine beyond his years.

Clark? she thought to herself. Can I come with you?

She looked at her drawing. She wished he could answer.

Nah, she smiled, dropping her head. No. Of course not. Who is he, really? Who is Clark David Benjamin? Look at him - so handsome, and pure. And powerful. My God... those EYES.

There were eraser marks all over his broad shoulders. She tried again and again to get them right. She always smiled a little more when she made progress. She loved touching those shoulders, if only on paper. Those shoulders? They really lifted things. Like... anything.

She sighed and added some touches with her pencil.

Clark wore his white dress shirt - always pressed and tidy. It was like the cloth draped over a beast's cage; an afterthought hiding what was really inside. His hair was a tossing mane on his wild intellect. His grey eyes: gemstones mined from steel. His shining glasses fit his look perfectly.

His face belonged on a coin. Clark would change the world, someday. He'd go far, but on a completely different path from hers. It didn't matter how much she liked him.

She also knew there was 'real life.' Jeff Anders was still the right choice, or so she thought. She knew Clark was different, and fascinating, and kind of incredibly beautiful in his own obscure way… but Jeff assuredly had a future. That was something she needed. She needed to leave Ashvale Plains behind her. This town bled your soul. Everyone who lived here, died here.

She'd hoped to pursue her art, but there were setbacks. Riley's art teacher once looked at her with tired eyes, and grumbled, "No-one cares, kid. The best you can do is look pretty, and maybe someone will let you tag along. 'Wanna study art? Start with lipstick."

Riley snapped out of her reverie. She discovered that she'd been tracing Clark's profile with her fingertip.

My dear, dear Clark, she thought. I'm so sorry to let you go. But I have to.

She opened her mouth, then closed it again. She couldn't ever tell him. She couldn't say a thing. She knew her heart, and she knew the truth… but she had to live in reality.

CHAPTER TWO

UNDER THE RADAR

Riley called out to him in the school corridor. "Hey, Clark?"

She walked over to him, chewed her gum once, then held it.

"Dude, why aren't you coming to Lisa's party? I know it's Thursday, but Lisa's parents are gone. Isn't, like… isn't Tracey gonna be there? and Jenny?"

Clark's glasses shone in the light. He swept back his hair; he had a prominent forelock of blond hair swinging down like a Tarzan-vine. The trained strength of his arm tested the creases in his shirt.

Along with physics, Clark knew biology and biochemistry. He was a fitness nerd. He would've excelled in wrestling, but the gym teacher was a little too friendly with his thigh, once. He missed a few practices on purpose. The next year, Mr Lester moved to another town.

Clark was strong enough to gracefully overpower most men. With Riley, though, he stood perfectly straight and perfectly still. He was careful with everything around him. It was like he'd just discovered a little brown fox in a grassy field: Ohh! he thought. Well hello, there, Pretty!

"Uh… yeah," he puzzled, looking briefly in her eyes. "Yeah… Jenny. And, uh… uhhh, Tracey. Right."

It took him a while to visualize them. He wanted to look at Riley, but tried not to. He didn't want Jeff to get suspicious.

"Yeah," he continued, idly, "They'll be there, I guess. I got a bit of extra stuff I'm doing, though - just some projects. The usual. You know."

"Jeez, man, you're always working!" Riley gave a light swat to his arm. "What - 'you gonna be a millionaire, or something?"

She hugged her books tight to her chest. She breathed in, held it, and waited for his answer.

"Nah. Life's too twisty, if you have a net worth in the millions bracket. I can probably snag something around $270K, though. That's my target salary."

Riley shifted her books, took a thoughtful chew of her gum, and stared at him.

"So… you'll be frickin' flying, but still under the radar?"

He paused.

"…Yeah. 'Good way of describing it."

He smiled back at her - she always understood. Talking with Riley was like a warm handshake. And such lovely hands.

"Yeah," he concluded. "Under the radar. It's like the old saying goes: *An eagle may soar, but a weasel will never get sucked through a jet engine.*"

"AHH," she nodded. She raised her pointer finger. "Confucius, again."

Sparks danced in their eyes. His eyes called out, 'Hi, Riley! I'm right here!' Her eyes glimmered back, singing, 'Hel-LLOOO, Handsome!'

She graced him with her sweeter-than-music smile. That smile killed him, because he couldn't smile back. Not with Jeff around.

"Yes. Confucius," he closed his eyes and dipped his head respectfully. "You are most learnèd, my friend."

She snorted with laughter.

"But how about you, Riley? You're going to Lisa's? Mm - going with Jeff, right?" He tried to look indifferent.

"Yeah..." Her eyes opened - they invited him in. "Yeah, I'll be there. I'll be there." She nodded to him vaguely. Her smile said it all: Please? I'd love to see you.

"Cool," he said. He pursed his lips, but bobbed his head agreeably. He hated Jeff oh-so-very much.

She turned to face him. "Clark? What are you always working on, anyway?"

She gave another chew to her gum. She tilted her

head to look up at him. He was so tall, she had to crane her neck. She felt like a tiny forest nymph meeting a noble prince.

He explained things with sudden kindness in his eyes.

"I got this feeling, once. It made me think of what flying would be like, without wings. I guess there isn't a word for it. It's wind, when it meets energy. I know, it sounds airy - just like Mr Gray said. But right now, I'm trying to expand the natural fields of magnetism as a comparative model. I'm reading lots about Euclid and Tesla."

Riley's eyes bugged out.

Oh my GOD, she thought. He's going to do it. He's going to be that GUY. I knew it. I knew it!

Clark noticed her astonishment, but saw it as shock. He stepped backward.

She thinks I'm a freak, he thought. Like everyone else, she thinks I'm a weirdo. She's so tense right now. I can see it.

Jeff Anders sang down the hallway.

"RI-LEY!" he called her, like calling a dog. "Uh - we're LEAVING...?"

Jeff spanned out his arms impatiently. Two girls scoffed at Riley's inattention. Riley Henway obviously didn't deserve Jeff Anders. He was from a rich family, and everyone knew Riley was trash. Really - Jeff even had a sportscar.

She glanced back at Clark. "Well, I'll seeya later? Maybe? Always good chatting with you."

Yeah, right, he thought. You're polite, even after recoiling in fear. And you're the only one who even talks to me.

"Y'know, Riley," he began meekly, "You're the only one who ever, like… gets me."

He stood tall and well dressed in the corridor, with his strong, square shoulders, tidy sleeves and smart glasses. Her brow knit for a second, thinking. Clark saw it as irritation; she probably couldn't associate with nerds like him.

She walked back to Jeff. Jeff yanked her by the hand. Clark's insides crawled.

That bastard, he thought. He should NEVER take her hand like that. How do they let him? Why is it acceptable to treat her so roughly? so rudely?

He felt thunder building. He wanted to fight Jeff, right then and there, but he knew what the Anders clan would do to him. They'd destroy him. Their money outweighed everything.

He turned his back and walked away. He swept his hair from his eyes. He couldn't bear to see her being handled like that. It ground his guts like rusted metal.

He didn't turn back, so he couldn't see Riley glancing at him.

Riley saw his strong shoulders. She saw his purposeful stride. Clark was walking away, and it looked like he really meant it.

Oh no, she thought. Does he hate me? I'm over here with Jeff… is that why he's stalking away, like that? Because I'm trying to mingle? Now he hates me?

Jeff tugged her along like a handbag - like an accessory.

"Hey. Who were you talking to?"

"Sorry. Just a friend." She paused for a second.

Jeff leaned in close. "Riley, if you had friends, you'd know by now."

"I, uhh..." She walked next to him, trying to keep pace. She knew she was lucky to have Jeff. Jeff had it all; that had to count for something. Of course it did.

He pressed his mouth up to her head. "You belong with ME... right?"

He talked loudly with his other friends and pulled her along. She faked a smile. She went back to the role of Golden Boy's Girlfriend. Everyone expected her to do this; it was supposedly a great honor. It wasn't the worst lie in Ashvale, but she lived it.

I'm sorry, she thought. I'm really sorry, Clark. I wish I wasn't such a screwup. I wish we could just... just you and I, we'd... we could leave.

Clark? I wish I was a better person.

CHAPTER THREE

SELF-DISCOVERY

Riley was doing her makeup for the party. She had her mirror, and she had time to think.

Sometimes, she wished there was a grand ball. She'd have a dress of shining silk, and then he'd arrive: perfect, in his tuxedo, like a modern-day knight. Clark... the true gentleman. And he'd ask her to dance.

His glasses would shine in the dim light. He'd walk past all the other gawking girls, with their skewed glances and open mouths. He'd stride confidently toward her, and he'd smile at her, and he'd reach out for her hand. He was so tall... He was a great man, and he was meant to be tall. He'd ask for this dance, and then he wouldn't dance with anyone else, that night. Despite everything, he'd still like her, and they'd dance together.

That would be the perfect dance, with her perfect knight, on a grand ballroom floor, slowly circling each other. His great, firm arms would lead her, but if his eyes would follow her? If his eyes would follow only her, that night? all night? She'd be in bliss. He'd look at her, and wouldn't stop. They'd hold each other, and look to each other, and that dance would be everything.

Riley was still doing her makeup, and she saw herself blush. A lot. She realized how much she cared about Clark. She DID think of him fairly often… well, every day. Probably a few times a day. Maybe more than ten or twenty.

Huh… she thought. This is like the stuff grandma talked about. Granny Faye. 'The beauty of still rivers.'

Granny Faye was wise about things, so it didn't matter if she sounded nutty. True wisdom doesn't follow the same tracks as grammatically correct sentences. Truth runs underneath, so it won't match what you see on the surface.

Granny Faye confirmed that True Love is real… and once it kindles, it never goes out. She said that stars were hope, and there were more than enough for everybody.

She also had three cats, which probably meant something. They perched on her overfed bookshelves like tubby, furry owls. If she was the good witch, they were her minions.

Riley daydreamed about Clark. Still rivers, indeed. Maybe he'd come to this party anyway? She'd see his powerful smile, and his firm, dimpled cheek.

She listened, hesitated, then practiced kissing her own hand.

Her heart was a waterslide. Everything rushed the right way. Her arms and belly swept along like leaves in a flood - naturally. Her breath drained out of her, then dragged back in greedily. It was undeniable - her breath was an unstoppable tide. She had to kiss more… press her lips deeper, and to the sides of his mouth, and she had to reach around to hold the back of his head. Had to. Her eyelids fell limp, then closed fully. She was listening to his warmth.

She felt through his hair, like sifting fine grain. She could sense his face close to hers. His eyes were intimately close. His soul was so close, she could kiss her secrets into him. All her secrets. Everything. And he took everything. He was the only man strong enough to carry his secrets AND hers. He was the only man strong enough to hold her world.

He held her, and she locked. CLICK. Everything came together and fit. The world was beautiful. Time was magnificent.

Her breath wafted into nothing, like a phantom. The moment faded.

When she returned to the real world, she realized this was the greatest kiss she'd ever had. She was eighteen, soon to graduate, and she'd had plenty of boyfriends in the past. This wasn't even an actual kiss, and it was phenomenal.

She buried this in her memory, and would never

admit it to anyone. Never to her friends, never to her mother, and not even to Granny Faye. And she'd never, ever let Jeff find out. Of course not.

The truth frightened her. She hid it within, so that she could also hide.

CHAPTER FOUR
NET WORTH

At the party, Tracey was so drunk she fell over, Jenny slapped Todd for being gross, and Rob laughed so hard he spilled his drink on the couch and got bitched at. This was the party. Nothing new.

Riley was there. She secretly hoped Clark would show up. She held her drink and stood near the front window. The music pounded behind her, and drunken teens hooted or laughed. Jeff was busy somewhere, acting cool, and Colleen Dietrich was on the back balcony, having a smoke with all her friends.

Where was Clark? Riley pictured him alone, in the dark, over a lit workbench. He was in his creative space, building things that no-one else could understand. He was a great guy, but distant. He was like music that you couldn't quite hear. His ideas would probably make him rich, someday.

Of all the people she knew, Clark was the worst fit in Ashvale Plains. Was that why she liked him? Because he wasn't another chummy, beer-guzzling guy? No. It wasn't about popularity. Clark took command of his future. Sadly, she knew she'd never be part of it.

"What, are you watching the weather?" Lisa yelled. Lisa's music thumped from her dad's stereo. Everyone had to yell louder.

"Nah," Riley answered. "Just keeping track, in case more people show up. I'll tell 'em who's where."

"Well, Jeff's down in the den. 'Got a few cases, down there, if you want something more to drink." Lisa popped up her brows and flicked her eyes toward the den. "You know - being social?"

The girls knew the plan: get drunk, get Jeff interested, take him someplace private... and maybe get him attached, for the long term.

Of course, Riley thought. Yeah. Of course. Sell yourself, for a meagre chance of snagging a guy. Babies equal marriage.

"Hmm," Riley thought. She tapped her chin. Lisa took it as playful, sly scheming, and chuckled.

Yeah, Riley thought to herself. That should shut her up. Nobody needs help getting one of those horn-dogs to jump on them. They're just walking boners.

She decided to check on Jeff anyway. Maybe keep him out of trouble. She took the stairs down to the den, just as two other girls bustled past her. They were leaving, and they had angry scowls burned onto their faces.

Yeesh, Riley thought. Someone said SOMETHING, and it was ugly.

Riley walked carefully, with quiet steps. She heard the boys talking. She stayed in the hallway and listened.

"Ya, but it's not like she has boobs, anyway. And moles? I guess she was born with those? They don't help."

He was corrected by a deeper, sarcastic voice.

"Naw. 'Beauty marks.' It's what artists call them. So she's a BE-EAU-tiful artist…"

Dubious chuckling.

Jeff Anders sneered: "Pff. Who says she's an artist? 'Can't be a cheerleader, and she walks tall when she shouldn't… and it's not like her family's got anything worth… anything."

The deeper voice added, "Not in terms of daughters, anyway."

Riley's jaw dropped.

"WELL," Jeff slurped his can of beer, "Riley's like all the other chicks: good for something, if nothin' else. Except, Timmy here doesn't know what we're talking about. Do ya, Tiny Tim?"

"Hey, SHUT UP," Timmy whined. "I just haven't found the right… like… nobody I actually LIKE."

The deeper voice blurted out, "And you think Jeff likes Riley? Huh? No curves, no family advantages. She's a whole lotta nothing… and, at best, a four-out-of-ten for looks. She's kinda girl-next-door, if you live on Homely Street. Dude, you have to be with someone who's at least an eight. A man needs self-respect."

It was John Malick with the deeper voice. He was known as 'Jonno.' He was huge, heavy, and flat-faced. He shook his head at Jeff in disapproval.

Jeff leaned forward, glaring. "Self-resp...? Respect? I GOT respect, Jonno. So, WHATEVER..."

Jonno mumbled, "I bet it's a real 'whatever' relationship. 'Sounds like it."

Jeff sucked on his beer. "Well, who needs to date, if you know what you want? It all ends up the same thing. She's just some chick with a half-decent ass. And you don't have to try too hard, to 'know her better.' Jesus, I could get her drunk some night, blindfold her, and even Timmy could finally man up. Hell, Timmy - you could jump on top of her, and then stop whining all the damn time."

Tim squawked, "Wait, what? W-...? Your GIRLFRIEND?"

"Yeah," Jeff continued. "Girlfriend. Right. 'Girlfriend' is loosely put... 'kinda like SHE is... little tramp. Timmy, you could buy the liquor for her and me, pay me fifty bucks, and we'd call it an evening."

Riley's hand clamped over her face. She could hardly believe what she was hearing. A tear wobbled in her eye. Rage or shock, she couldn't tell.

Jeff opened another can of beer.

"It's all the same. They're good for something, if nothin' else," he concluded. "I mean, most chicks are good for nothing. You gotta admit that much. Sports teams, academic awards, frickin' school administration… you see the trend, right? It's all guys. It's been like this for centuries. It's ALWAYS been like this. So it's Darwinism. In the end, women are basically good for one thing… having sons."

Timmy stuttered. "Y-yeah, I guess. I mean, that's where all great men came from. Right? Like in history class. We don't ever hear about Abraham Lincoln's mom, do we? 'Makes sense, if-"

"OH," Jonno interrupted, "but WAIT… Riley's an ARTIST. Don't forget that. That'll change the world."

The boys chuckled, then went quiet.

One of them muttered: "Is somebody out there…?"

Riley left as quickly as she could, but she stayed silent. She climbed the stairs with trembling legs, then grabbed a beer. She looked at it, scowled, then smacked it down on a tabletop. Someone else was using pineapple juice for mixes; she poured herself a glass. Pineapple juice. Straight. She went back to the front window. She wasn't even searching for Clark, right now. She was looking at the glassy image of her town, outside. This… place. Her own reflection was weak and ghostly against the black.

Her heart reached out to that emptiness.

Clark? Will you just take me away from here? Could you? I'd love you forever, if you'd come, right now, and take me away. Please? You're the only good guy I know. PLEASE? And could you love me, also, the way I love you? Dammit… Why do we even have these stupid friggin' fairy tales? Why do we even tell ourselves these lies? Things like 'hope?'

Riley stared outward, hoping to see her friend. She didn't pay attention to the booming music. She didn't hear the people on the back balcony, on the other side of the house.

This was Lisa's party, but everyone followed Colleen. They followed her out to the balcony, where the 'real people' talked. Riley knew not to trail after them, because they'd stop talking. They'd all stop and stare at her coldly until she left. Colleen never liked her big words, or all that 'stuff' she was interested in. Art was for weird people.

"What is she even DOING?" Colleen snarled. She peered through the glass doors of the balcony. She watched Riley's back.

"Is she, like, leaving? Or is she waiting for someone? Maybe Cinderella needs a reality check."

A few chuckles.

"Isn't Jeff down in the den? Like, HELLO? Earth-to-Riley?"

Colleen's friends flopped out on lawn chairs or leaned against the balcony railing. They milled about like teenage philosophers. They talked about important things and passed around cigarettes.

Someone told Colleen about the boys in the den. The boys had gone through a case of beer already, and their conversation drove everyone else away.

"But - they're just being GUYS, right? Boys'll be boys?"

Someone agreed, and assured Colleen that filthy, disgusting swine can be female OR male. These complete pigs were most certainly male.

Colleen had a brief flicker of a smile. A plan came to mind. It ping-ponged between the sides of her brain for a minute, and then she took action.

"Be right back," she chirped. She nipped over to the glass doors, slid through, and closed them behind her with a wink. Riley didn't see her sneak downstairs to where the boys were drinking.

"No, nothing," the deep voice said. "Lisa throws a good party, and lotsa beer, but she's a peasant. There's nothing here worth a buck. Actually, 'can't think of anybody who's got it good, here in Ashvale. 'Cept you, and maybe the Dietrich family."

Colleen strode in. Light caught her blonde hair like a crooked halo.

"Well, WELL... speak of the devil, and... like... here I am. My ears were burning, I guess. What was this about my family?"

Jonno rolled his head toward her and drawled, "You're loaded."

She scoffed. "Pshh. You're one to talk." She rolled her eyes playfully.

The boys chuckled. Colleen looked them over, making Timmy turn pink. When she focused on Jeff, he sat up straight.

"But yeah - Jeff? You're fairly well off, too, right?

You even have a two-seater sportscar. Why ARE you dating someone like… like that girl, Riley?"

"Why do you ask?"

"Well, I honestly wanted to talk to you about something. That's why I came down here. See, I noticed Sonia wasn't here tonight. You know - Sonia? from, like, Poland or whatever?"

"Hmm," the boys nodded. No-one had anything bad to say about Sonia.

"Yeah," Colleen flapped her hand in the air. "Sonia. Tall Sonia. I'm surprised she's not here."

"Why's that?" Jeff tilted his head.

"Well… I can't be totally sure, but… I think she was talking about you in math class. I figured she'd be here, just to meet you. Like, just to say 'hi.' Right? Just meet you at a party - that kind of thing.

"See, someone mentioned football, and then she started whispering. She was blushing and smiling a lot, and it was easy to tell that it was about you. It was a had-to-be-there thing. Now, I don't know what was said, exactly, but it got me thinking. This was Sonia. She's, uh… quite a catch, Jeff."

"What, you think Sonia was talking about me, in math class?"

"The honest truth? I didn't hear everything. But hand-on-my-heart, I got a strong impression."

Jeff went quiet.

"Hmm," he mused.

"And Jeff? I realized something. Our best years go to waste, if we don't aim high enough. Some people don't give themselves enough credit. 'Just my humble opinion."

The boys all stared at Colleen's performance.

"Haha - I'm not suggesting you chase after Sonia 'cuz she's tall. Aiming high, right? Ha! Haha...!"

They nodded politely at her joke. Then, Colleen stood at attention.

"But, like... where's your girlfriend, Jeff? Sorry to ask." She shrugged at him.

It was obvious that this den was occupied by cave-dudes with their beer, and their rotten farting, and their endless dirty jokes. No girls wanted to be near this place without a compelling reason.

Something strong clicked in the boys' heads. Riley wasn't with Jeff. She was his girlfriend, too, and for some reason she wasn't by his side.

"That girl?" Colleen prompted. "Riley?"

"Yeah, Jeff." Jonno held the air with his deep voice. "So where is your little girlie?"

Another silence.

"Oh," Colleen stepped backward. "Uh... if you can't answer that one? Look, I'm sorry to bring it up. I don't mean to be a buzzkill. But honestly, though? I don't think Riley should get away with treating you like that. 'Not the kinda girl you want to bring home to your parents."

Jeff's ears perked up. "What?"

She turned away, shaking her head.

"I dunno. Disrespectful, isn't it?"

"What do you mean?" Jeff asked. He sniffed and

gave closer attention. "Yeah, Colleen, she's met my parents. She talked with my mom about the museum. My dad thought she was polite enough. It's fine."

"Well, if she's really your GIRLFRIEND, then... I mean...?" She lifted her palms at Jeff. "Like, where is she? The LEAST she can do is sit with you."

No-one wanted to be around these drunken thugs. They were so slow witted, they didn't even notice their own stench. They had heavy-lidded expressions and slack jaws.

Colleen prompted, "What kind of girl ISN'T with her boyfriend, at a party?"

There was a brief silence.

Jonno growled, "Maybe the artsy prudish type."

Colleen lowered her head.

"Look, I'm prob'ly not the best at couples counseling. But this is Lisa's house, and everyone's here... and everyone sees this, Jeff. At least Sonia has a sense of class, like from Europe. Poland's in Europe."

Jeff squirmed. His ears turned red. He flexed his knuckles like he always did before a football game.

"Sorry to bring it up," Colleen lied. "Uh, I gotta get back to the balcony. Someone's holding my drink. Ta, darlings..."

She waved and walked back upstairs.

In the den, it was just Jeff, Jonno, and Timmy. Their heads spun after Colleen's speech.

Jonno leaned back in his chair. He had a thick, boxy head on top of his bulky frame. He was Jeff's buddy from football. His hair jutted from his brow like flattened sod. He had the dull, vacant eyes of an attack dog. He licked his lips before asking serious questions.

"So. Jeff. Your family - they know people." His voice was deep and rumbly.

Jeff released a sudden hiccup of laughter.

"Well, YEAH... of course we do."

"Do you know cops? or gangs? or people with power?"

Jeff sat forward and glared at him. He licked his top teeth.

"I AM a person with power, Jonno. I mean, what are you even thinking about? Something legal? Something illegal? Do you want better 'roids, or something? 'Cuz that's not my game."

"Actually," Jonno started, "I'm thinking something like... not everyday street drugs, or 'roids. Maybe a little 'time out' for somebody. Look, your family has lots of land, here, right?"

"We control rents," Jeff nodded. "We control the pulse of this town. Damn straight, we got land. That's why they joke about me being 'Mr Real Estate' in Ashvale."

Jonno nodded. "We should pull a prank. We need a place, and something other than street drugs. We need some kinda sedative. Just something to put in somebody's drink, and then they're knocked out. They gotta be knocked out for a couple hours while we prank 'em."

"Oh yeah," Jeff rolled his eyes. "I know, I know… yeah, my uncle used to be a pharmacist, right? He told me there's the type of pill where you drug someone, and you could steal all their stuff, or completely humiliate them. Or worse. Pfft - 'heard all about that."

Jonno closed his eyes and nodded.

"I bet your uncle has all the details. It's hard to trace, right?"

Jeff dismissed him with his hand.

"Ya, ya. Small-time crap. He even showed me some of them, once."

Jonno leaned toward him. "I'll go get some better 'roids from your uncle, and maybe a special request. You go find a quiet place. You wanna get some respect back? Knock down anyone who disrespects you. Like your little friend Riley. If she wants to be at a party with other guys, FINE - let her have 'other guys'… lots of it. See how she likes it."

Timmy's eyes flicked back and forth. Something stirred up his anxiety. He squirmed in his seat.

Jeff looked squarely at Jonno.

"You can't be serious," he said quietly.

Jonno was motionless.

"The fact is, I'M serious but YOU'RE NOT. Maybe that's why people don't take you seriously, Jeff. They only JOKE about you as Mr Real Estate. You might talk like a man, but you never act."

Temperatures rose in that room. Jeff tried to sit as tall as Jonno. He felt his knuckles.

"You'd do this? Y'think WE'D do this? We'd drug her?"

Jeff challenged him, at first. Then his focus changed.

"Well, it's hard to trace, right? And we put it in a stiff drink, she wouldn't even know the difference… yeah, let's see her try to be snooty, after that."

"Main thing is," Jonno added, "she won't know what hit her. Look - you heard what Colleen said. EVERYONE sees Riley treating you like crap. Are you gonna let her walk all over you?"

Jeff stared straight ahead. He had no expression. Gears were turning, somewhere.

"Naw," Jeff said. "I'LL go talk to my uncle. I'LL make sure it isn't traced, not you. And it can't be some obvious place, so none of our Anders properties. I dunno - somewhere she doesn't recognize right away."

Timmy squirmed again. "Are…? Your girlfriend's gonna get-"

"She's NOT my damned girlfriend, Timmy. She insulted me. And she's not getting away with it." Jeff cracked his knuckles. "Naw, this isn't just revenge. We're gonna make it worthwhile."

Timmy's face turned pink. He sat stiff and straight. Jonno sat back, nodding slowly. He was thinking of everything he could do to a girl like Riley.

Jeff shook his head. "This is just natural order, boys. Everyone knows she's trash. It's like the food chain: the king of the jungle is master of the hunt - the lion, not the lioness. Everybody knows that."

A few hours plodded by. Upstairs, Riley smiled and chatted with two or three people. The night was loud music and sweaty air. The party came and went. No Clark.

CHAPTER FIVE
Two Lights

On the night of Lisa's party, Clark was lying in bed. He looked out his window and watched the stars. There were so many of them out there, but he only needed one. He needed one of them to listen. He held his hand over his heart and prayed like every other night.

"My dear Riley - somewhere in this world, you're... I just hope you're..."

He stopped. Today, her eyes bugged out in fear. He talked about his stupid projects, and she shrank away.

"You don't know how I feel. You can't know. Everything would change. Also, Jeff Anders would hurt you, if he thought about 'us' together. He'd hurt you, because of how I feel. I can't let that happen.

"I see you almost every day, but I MISS YOU

constantly. Can you understand? I wish I could just look at you, and catch your eyes, and then you could see INTO ME… and just KNOW.

"You're so far away, but maybe you'll feel this. Maybe I can reach you, somehow? Just know, somehow, that I'm in this world, too. There's at least one heart, a living heart, right here…"

He stopped. He closed his eyes.

"…and this heart will dream of you forever."

He smiled sadly.

"Forever, Riley."

He looked sternly up at the night sky. He needed one little light to tell her. The stars stayed up till dawn; perhaps they were considering what he'd said.

Late that night, in another part of town, there was a run-down, two-bedroom flat. The floors were linoleum, and they curled at the edges. The walls smelled like insulation because of the drafts. Riley tried to sleep on the couch. The couch was the farthest place from the bedrooms, where her mother cried and her father yelled.

Riley had returned late from the party and her father lit into her. He knew she was out at some party somewhere, and there was drinking, and something about this triggered him. His face turned red up to his receding hairline. First he snapped at her, then he yelled at her for throwing her life away.

"You just squander EVERYTHING, don't you? After all I've done to support you, you flush it down the toilet. God, you're selfish. You're so damned selfish, and cheap, and lazy…! Damn it, girl, it's no wonder you're unlovable."

Riley crunched over with tears growing in her eyes. Her mother saw how that stung. Her father hesitated. He almost apologized.

Her mother tried to de-escalate, but her father's anger only shifted gears… as always.

"Kim? You're just a bad mother. This whole house is a failure, and it starts with you. You… DON'T you walk away from me! Who do you think keeps a roof over your head, Kim? HUH?"

It all went downhill from there. Riley's mom hid in the bedroom, but her father followed.

As he screamed at her, she whimpered, "Morley…! Morley… PLEASE…!" Strands of her long brown hair stuck to her chin and cheek.

After he was sweaty from screaming, her father finally passed out. Her mom stifled sobs for another half an hour. Riley got to sleep around 2am. She didn't get up from the couch.

At seven in the morning, she grabbed a few packs of peanuts. Her dad brought these home from 'work.' She did her homework before he got up, then hustled to school after five hours of sleep.

Woohoo, she thought. Another lovely day in the town of Ashvale Plains. Maybe I'll trip over a suitcase full of money… and not sprain my ankle. Maybe Colleen will trip over something, and break her stupid face. Maybe Jeff will actually start to like me today? Maybe he'll even kiss me back?

Underneath her wry humor, she kept something precious. It kept her smiling, no matter what the world threw at her. She had a dream. It was her secret.

Hmm, she smiled. Maybe I'll see Clark again.

She had no idea what was about to happen. It would destroy her life.

That evening, three teenage boys met outside the gym: Timmy, Jonno and Jeff. They lurked by the steel door at the back. It was about 6pm. They spoke in low, furtive tones. They ducked into the evening shadows.

"Dinner and a movie," Jonno nodded to Jeff. "But you're getting her a stiff drink with a little somethin' extra. And then she looks real drunk, and Timmy's got his car waiting outside. We need Tim's four-seater, here…"

Jonno nudged his head at Timmy's beige sedan.

"…and not your little sports car, Jeff. Right?"

Jeff nodded grimly. The boys glanced at each other like preparing for war. Fire lit their eyes.

Jeff chewed his lip.

"It's not like she didn't have it coming. She's gonna snub me? insult me in front of everyone? even in front of Colleen? and she's gonna disrespect ME, never mind what SHE is…? She'll pay for that. Hell yeah, she has it coming."

"She's always acted like this, Jeff." Jonno shook his head at him, like making him admit a fact.

Jeff squinted and snarled, "So she wants to hang

around other guys, at Lisa's? Sure. She can have 'other guys.' We're just making it happen. It's what she wants, so it's what she deserves."

He smirked meanly. This was how Jeff justified his plan.

Timmy Karnes was more anxious than usual. He blinked frequently. Jonno was perfectly relaxed.

"So," Jonno bobbed his head agreeably. "When?"

Jeff raised his head. "It's set up tonight. It's a dinner date. I told her I'd been thinking, and I wanted to make a change - 'for us.' Girls always fall for that crap. 'Shoulda seen the starry-eyed look on her face. Pathetic."

Someone in the gym finished their reps. A heavy clang announced the end. It was the sudden ring of hundreds of pounds of metal.

"Now - we have Timmy's car," Jeff considered, "but where are we actually going, huh? It's Friday, and everyone's gonna be out. It'll be hard to find a quiet place."

The other two were stumped. Jeff shifted his weight impatiently.

"Boys, we're not doing this in Timmy's frickin' car. We're taking her somewhere safe. I mean, safe from cops, or whoever."

Timmy swallowed, then made a suggestion.

"I got the keys for my aunt and uncle's warehouse. They store lawn supplies there. They got an office upstairs, and a door that locks. There's a bed in the back room. My cousin used to crash there. Is that…? What about that?"

The silence closed around them like a final seal.

Jonno grunted: "Works."

Jeff agreed. "Yeah."

Timmy checked left and right. "H-How long does it last? Like, h-how long… do we…?"

Jonno bobbed his head. "How long's our party tonight, Jeff?"

Timmy squeaked, "Is she unconscious for, like, forty-five minutes, maybe?"

Jeff grinned broadly.

"My uncle? The guy who used to be a pharmacist? He gave me these pills."

He rattled a little plastic pillbox.

"Just one of 'em knocks her out for twelve hours."

Their minds raced. They didn't notice the sudden quiet in the gym.

"T-… Twelve hours?" Timmy's eyes widened. "W-… how… what are we DOING with her, in all that time?"

"Well," Jonno drawled. "Two of us are gonna wander around the building. Enjoy the night air. Have some drinks. Maybe do some target practice on beer cans. Meanwhile, the third guy keeps her company. Each of you has your bit of time… what is that, four hours, or so?"

"…Four hours?" Timmy squinted incredulously. "Four hours ALONE? with a girl?"

"YES, Timmy," Jeff rolled his eyes. "Congratulations."

Jonno drawled low, "Whatever. You both have your playtime. I want her at the end. Save the best for last."

He stared off into the distance and chewed his jaw.

"I'm gonna want her when she's just waking up. You know… confused and mumbling? Can't even cry right? They're so cute."

The gym was especially quiet. Usually, someone would hit the showers after lifting weights. Someone had just been lifting, and it was hundreds of pounds. Whoever was in there, it was no amateur… and they were weirdly quiet.

Jonno leaned up against the doorframe.

"It's short notice, but I'm in. It starts with a dinner date, tonight? When?"

Jeff's lips twisted into a half-smile. His voice was sly.

"I figured we should do this quick, before anyone catches on. I'm meeting her at eight. Yeah. Two hours from now. We'll be having dinner at eight-thirty, with a few glasses of 'wine.' It's a late dinner; it'll look like she's drunk on an empty stomach. We'll leave the restaurant early. She'll be out by nine or so."

Jeff let out a huge sigh.

"And then, Tiny Tim, I'll introduce you to Riley. She's ours till the morning."

"LIKE HELL, SHE IS."

Timmy squeaked and jumped from the door. Jeff staggered back and waved to Jonno.

"Get… get away from the door, Jonno!" he hissed. They all stared at the back entrance to the gym.

Jonno stepped clear. Then, the steel door boomed open and smacked the outside wall. Something massive, like a glacier, filled the doorframe.

"W-… What the hell?" Jeff sputtered. "Clark BENJAMIN? What? What do you want?"

His sweaty, white T-shirt stuck to his chest. He stared back at Jeff. He wouldn't answer.

Jeff looked left and right. Jonno stood like an ape with his arms dangling. Timmy made frightened, quivering sounds in his neck.

Jeff assumed command: "There's two ways this goes, Clark. Either you're in on this, and you have a little fun with the boys… or I have Jonno, here, beat you to death with his bare hands."

Clark shook his head. His blood pounded inside. He stared at Jeff.

"Look," Jeff snarled, "Some snotty piece of trash is gettin' what she deserves. It's gonna happen. Choose smart, here, 'cuz… 'cuz your own bodily health depends on it."

Timmy glanced back and forth between Jeff and Clark. He spoke aside, to Jeff. He could barely enunciate.

"Naw, J-… Jeff? I-I-I don't think he's really okay. Look at him."

Jeff pretended to be in control.

"Make a call, Clark. Are you a man? or are you dead meat?"

More silence. The door hinges whimpered after being blasted open. They'd peeled metal out of the doorframe. Clark just stared. He wasn't thinking much like a man. He was death with giant steel arms.

"What are you staring at?" Jeff blustered. Sweat glinted on his temple.

Timmy pleaded, "Jeff, no... look at him. There's something really wrong with him." Timmy edged away, digging for his car keys.

Jeff huffed, shook his head, and pointed at Clark. "Jonno? Hell with it - beat this retard into the ground. Frickin' KILL him."

Something clicked in Jonno's head and his dull eyes engaged. He leaned forward to charge. His meaty legs thumped on the ground like a bull's. Clark stood waiting for him - unmoving. All Jonno's mass hurtled toward him, but Clark didn't budge. Jeff smiled coldly. Clark glared back at him.

As Jonno barreled into him, Clark somehow turned. His hands found a grip and steered Jonno's shoulders, just like a steering wheel. Jonno's head swung to the side and smacked the doorframe; he collided face first. He fell backward with his arms extended like a mummy. Then Clark stepped out to meet them.

Timmy danced backward. His hand grabbed at his keys.

"He's not even… I told you, he's… NO. I'm out, Jeff! No way! NO WAY…!"

Timmy's keys tumbled from his hand and fell to the ground. His fingers shook in the air. He kept his eyes on Clark and edged farther backward.

Jonno rose up with an angry grunt. His nose was cracked at the bridge. A sudden red dribble streaked his face. He wrapped his arms around Clark like a bear and tried to drag him to the ground. Clark grasped him, stepped confidently, and planted his legs where Jonno would trip. He stared straight at Jeff and let Jonno lose balance. The thug pitched down and sprawled helplessly into the dirt.

Clark just stared at Jeff. He held onto Jonno's arm, but never broke eye contact. He even started to twist Jonno's arm, but he kept staring at Jeff.

Jonno struggled, and then growled, then gave short yelps. Clark wouldn't let go. He braced his foot on him, and the yelps pinched into a tight scream… because Jonno was bending the wrong way. Something that shouldn't have snapped, snapped. His shoulder popped out with a dull, meaty "pukk."

Jeff took a step backward. The whites of his eyes were huge. He swallowed in his throat. His breath was shallow panting.

"I WANT YOU TO PAY ATTENTION, JEFF ANDERS."

Jeff took another step backward. He watched Jonno, the strongest guy he ever knew, being chewed up by that sick weirdo… Clark Benjamin.

Clark pulled the arm up and Jonno gasped several times. That arm wasn't attached right. Jonno kicked and flailed, but Clark continued. He dropped it, and lifted Jonno's OTHER arm, as if it were a demonstration.

He made Jeff watch; he stared straight at him without blinking. His eyes were almost metallic... cold. Unyielding. Jonno writhed, crawled, and screamed an odd, painful, cat-like squawk. And again, a deep SNAP that was close to a 'thud.' Jonno grunted and sobbed into the ground.

Clark held the arm up to show Jeff. He still didn't break eye contact.

"NOW... NO DISTRACTIONS, JEFF."

Clark let the arm fall like a sack of meat. He opened his palms, and Jeff raised his own hands innocently. He saw Clark's eyes: two hidden suns.

Timmy withered on the spot. His little eyes peeked up, hoping he might survive. Jeff stood only a little bit taller.

"W-We didn't do anything. And... You even come near me, and the cops are all over your ass!"

"OH... FOR PREVENTING A RAPE?" Clark still hadn't blinked.

"For... for..."

Jeff remembered the pills. He got them from his uncle. They were illegal to possess, and his uncle would be guilty of distribution. Jeff would be charged, and his uncle would be charged, and Jeff's friends would be accessories. They all knew about the pills, and what they could do, and made plans to use them. This would ruin all of them. It would ruin their families. It would ruin their names.

"D-Don't hurt me," Jeff begged. "Please don't hurt me."

"CANCEL YOUR DATE. YOU DON'T DESERVE HER. AND GIVE ME THOSE GODDAMNED PILLS."

Timmy Karnes wilted down to nothing. He was on his knees, but still cringing lower. Jonno had no use of his arms. He lay there, gurgling, with his face grinding in the dirt. Jeff was suddenly powerless.

Jeff swore he'd give Riley distance. He promised. He swore on his mother's soul.

"IF I EVER SEE THIS AGAIN, JEFF… IT WON'T BE A WARNING."

"P-Please don't say anything. You can't. C'mon. You can't tell…"

"NO. OF COURSE NOT. I WON'T TELL ANYONE ANYTHING."

Something terrible formed in Clark's mind.

"THE POLICE WON'T KNOW. NOT EVEN RILEY WILL KNOW. CAN YOU GUESS WHY?"

Jeff searched for an answer.

"Uhh… you need favors? You want money? Is it money?"

"NO, JEFF.

"NO-ONE WILL EVER KNOW ABOUT THIS.

"NO-ONE WILL INVESTIGATE MOTIVES… AFTER YOUR… SUDDEN DISAPPEARANCE.

"I COULD GET AWAY WITH HOMICIDE, AND YOU KNOW IT."

He was right; no-one would talk. Three well established families would cover everything up.

Clark stepped over Jonno's body. He retrieved the pills from Jeff so he could destroy them safely. He clicked on his smartphone, swept a video capture around the scene, and gave a few final words.

"UNDERSTAND THIS: YOU AREN'T SAFE. YOU WILL NEVER BE SAFE, EVER AGAIN… RAPIST."

Jeff couldn't sleep that night. He wasn't worried about the law, anymore. He wasn't even worried about his family's reputation. He faced something very, very real. He feared for his life, and he couldn't ask for help.

He had to do something.

CHAPTER SIX

EXPOSURE

It was springtime in Ashvale Plains. Flowers happened, just like last year, and green things struggled to get out of bed.

In May, a star student died. People didn't notice that she was avoiding school, but she'd been away for two weeks... and then she died. People said she killed herself, and maybe from bullying - maybe because of her cleft lip. Surprisingly, Colleen was silent on the matter.

Timmy told everyone that he wasn't supposed to say anything, but big Jonno had a grievous accident. Jonno would be stuck in the hospital for months. It was his shoulder: a 'backward total dislocation,' he said. Every class in the school sent him a get-well-soon card. Clark signed, "I hope it's not too painful. Maybe a good stiff drink will help?"

One day, Colleen's friends made fun of Riley's shirt. It was long sleeved and the weather was warmer. Riley wasn't exposing enough neck, or enough shoulder, or any bare midriff.

"Nothing worth showing?" a girl said.

"Oh, SERIOUSLY," Colleen recoiled, "No-one wants to puke right now. God - cover up the ugly before it hurts someone."

These were grade twelve girls. The school hallway was their hunting ground; they roamed in packs. They claimed territory wherever they could gather in numbers.

Riley only stopped, turned, and made a face. Her lip drew up like a curtain, unveiling her mocking sneer.

"Oh look," a girl said to her companions, "she's got hick-green teeth."

Riley knew what was happening. She was being baited into a very unfair fight. The best she could do was walk down the hallway toward the exit.

Colleen scowled at her, "Ya... go run and hide your face, ugly girl."

One of her friends grimaced.

"Ugh," the friend added. "They should have rules to keep that away from children. It's, like, damaging."

Colleen spat, "Someone should put her out of everyone's misery."

Surprisingly, Jeff had little to say.

He added, with a weak voice, "Well, uh... I guess Colleen can't be best friends with everybody."

He hesitated, because Clark was nearby and probably listening.

Everyone watched Colleen picking at Riley. Everyone saw the jackals circling, then saw Riley walk away. The girls sent their remarks after her. Clark waited a bit, and then he followed her, himself.

"Hey, wait a sec."

He walked up behind her. His hand floated toward her shoulder. When it lit there, she flinched.

He softened his voice. "Uhh - 'you okay?'"

"Yeah," she turned to him. "Yeah. I'm fine; I'm outta this place in a few months, anyway. No big deal."

He looked at her skeptically. He glanced at her long-sleeved shirt.

"You know what? Wear whatever the heck you want. You don't need to be a fashion groupie. Trends are what people do when they can't think of anything better. But you, running out of ideas? Nah, that doesn't sound like you at all."

He shook his head. A dimple was shining on his cheek.

She couldn't help but smile. He thought she was different? Smart? Did he LIKE her, maybe?

"Clark, can I tell you something?"

He bent his brow. "Of course. Of course."

Riley led him outside. The sky was marbled with clouds. The sun seemed hesitant to show its face.

"Clark, can I trust you?"

He looked at her strangely. He was startled and

hopeful. He focused on her, but she lowered her eyes. She worried that he was getting impatient.

She continued, quietly, "I just want to be able to trust you. Is that okay?"

His voice was warm, like sunlight. "Yeah. Always."

She hesitated. She looked left and right. Finally, she lifted her eyes and told him.

"This is why. Alright? This is why."

Riley rolled up her sleeve. Clark saw her pale skin darkened with bruising. Hot breath fumed from Clark's nostrils.

"...Jeff?"

"No," she said quietly. "My dad."

Clark bowed his head. His jaw set in place and clenched hard. Riley rolled her sleeve down again.

"I can't actually tell people. I just... with you, I..." She gave a meek little shrug.

He growled low, "Did you contact anyone for help? Like, police?"

"NO," she slinked backward. "No. Hell no. No, I just need to make it through this spring, and then a bit of June. Then I graduate, right? And then I'm outta here. Yeah. Then, I can leave-"

"-Leave Ashvale Plains," he said, summing it up. He stood tall and nodded with her.

She exhaled. She closed her eyes. HE KNEW.

Thank you, she thought. Thank you, my dear Clark. Thank you for understanding.

He paced. "Riley, I can't. This can't happen. Not

to you. No." He couldn't look at her.

"No, you need to be my friend, here, okay?" She looked up at him sweetly. She pleaded to him. "You know what'll happen, if word gets out? and then someone tells him? You know what he'll do, right?"

Clark was silent.

"He'll friggin' kill me. No, he might actually kill me - get it? Me AND my mom. You get it, right? The system DOESN'T WORK. Otherwise, it would've worked for people by now. You gotta keep a secret for me. Can you do that? Please? I really wanted to tell someone, and trust someone. So, I... I need you."

Clark's hand went to his chest.

Riley tipped her head. "Crap, dude - are you okay?"

He said nothing.

She poked him. "Huh? 'You havin' a heart attack?"

"Of sorts," he grumbled angrily. "How long has this been going on?"

She stayed quiet, then shook her head.

"He's just my dad."

Clark seethed inside his level grey eyes. "You want me to do NOTHING while this happens to you?"

"Ya," she nodded assuredly. "I'm gonna trust you with the truth. You're good for it, right?"

A minute passed. He struggled to breathe normally.

"If it's a secret, why are you telling me? Why are

you doing this to m-... why are you trusting me, Riley?"

Her eyes looked about aimlessly. Inside, she felt around in her head, trying to find the right word. She finally settled on one, and looked up at him.

"Understanding," she said. She didn't mean sympathy. She meant connection.

His breathing sounded close to weeping. His hands stiffened into fists.

"I won't tell anyone." He steeled himself. "I hate it... but I promise."

Riley watched his face. It looked like there was an elevator inside him, and cables broke, and it fell all the way down and shattered at the bottom. Broken pieces rattled in his face. His steady grey eyes weighed heavily with a new gloss.

"It's a big promise, man. Thank you."

His voice crept forward. "I, uh... it's because I..."

He what? He understood? What, his dad, too?

"I'll keep your secret. For you. But if anything else happens, we're gonna do something. Can YOU promise?" His eyes lifted up through mountains of pain. They searched for hers.

She thought for a few seconds. Her mouth opened and closed. Her lips pouted slightly, then pressed tight. In the end, she couldn't answer him.

The rest of the day blurred by meaninglessly. Clark shuffled home, found his mom, and helped her sort the mail. She took things literally, so junk mail was a problem for her. Then Clark headed upstairs to polish off his homework.

"Look, I know I don't notice stuff," his mother said, "but you look distraught. What's happened?"

"Nothing, Mom. Teenager emotion-stuff. I bet that must've been tough for you, right?"

"Ugh," she rolled her eyes. She flapped her hand to dismiss the topic. "I could tell you, but you don't have all night."

Clark's mom, Bernita, had undiagnosed Asperger's Syndrome for most of her life. She was quirky, and maybe a little flakey, but she knew everything about ancient mythology. She could've been a professor, if the college took her seriously. She was a private tutor.

After having Clark, the stresses of raising a child uncovered a bitter edge in Bernita. Her marriage suffered. Clark's father eventually turned his back on the family.

Clark never forgot that evening. His dad came home and met his mother in the kitchen. Young Clark was in the front hallway near the door. Clark heard brief fighting.

He heard his mom snap angrily. She was defensive because of her books. Sometimes she'd bury herself in a new book for days.

His dad spoke something low and vicious, and ended by yelling two words: "...WITH FREAKS!"

Clark heard his mother gasp, choke, then start to cry. He heard his father's striding footsteps as he stormed out the front hallway. Clark dodged backward, and his shoulders bumped against the coat closet. The sliding doors rumbled behind him.

His father bent down with his red beard glinting. He smelled his father's body odor.

"And you? Just end yourself. Sooner or later, you'll be a psycho like your mother. Either she'll kill you, or you'll kill her." He tipped his head left and right, like sing-song sweetness. "Or maybe you'll go on a little SPREE with the neighbors.

"You aren't meant to be alive; you're a human mistake. You're just 'wrong.' If you're any man at all, cut the world's losses. Kill yourself. Save the rest of us from suffering.

"You're a psycho, kid. Do what you have to do."

Alexander F Benjamin swooped out the front door. He didn't even close it. He revved up his car and spun off, ripping through the flower bed beside the driveway.

The door was left open. Clark stood there, watching, looking out at the world. The tire tracks were brown, muddy wounds across the lawn. He could smell the dampness of the soil.

His father was gone, and his mother was behind him, crying. He heard her lean on the kitchen table and drop down on the floor.

So, he thought, my mom and I are wrong? But not 'fixable' wrong? Why am I wrong? I'm sorry for it - can't I be okay? When's dad coming back?

It was Clark who cooked dinner, that night. His mother couldn't stand from the floor. She was there for four hours. Clark made her a dinner of salad sandwiches with a side of buttered toast. He sat with her on the floor. She ate a few bites, but mostly stared off into space. He realized that adults did 'home' things better than he could.

After a while, Clark stopped looking at the front door. He didn't want to close it, but he did. Even then, he kept hoping to hear his father. Maybe he'd knock? Maybe he'd still sit with them for dinner, even though it was Clark cooking.

He and his mother sat on the floor. His eyes settled on their shoes, as they both leaned against the kitchen cabinet. Soon, he found himself staring at his own hands.

"Mom? I'm gonna fix things."

He didn't know how he could. He touched her arm. She didn't respond.

"Mom, I promise. Don't be sad. I can fix things."

Years later, he helped her sort the mail. He didn't tell her about school, or the bullying, or Riley's bruises. He made a quick stir-fry for dinner: soy sauce and brown sugar, mixed vegetables, but no mushrooms. His mother couldn't eat those. She still checked the bowl for mushrooms anyway, because she always did. She went to eat dinner alone in her study.

He had a lot of time to think, that night. He thought of Riley's home. It weighed on him. He thought the stars were vain, to be so bright. They should've bowed their heads.

"Riley…" he whispered. His hand pressed to his heart. "Someday, I will. I swear to God, I will. Somehow, I'll do it - I'll find you, and we'll LEAVE. The two of us will just leave. Those stars? They're soulless, tonight. They're uncaring. They shouldn't be lit. But I don't care about those stars - not anymore. They can't stop me. They can smile all they want."

He thought of where she was. She was home, but not safe. Her father would hurt her. There'd be yelling, and fighting, and physical violence.

"No," he shook his head. "No, at least understand this…"

He begged to her, wherever she was.

"I need you to know just one small glimmer of truth. Just so you know. Please, Riley… just know that I'm here."

Across town, in a run-down two-bedroom house, Riley's dad swore about something. Her mom tried to ask a small question. It was like a mouse beside an angry bear. The bear roared back. That was just the beginning.

Riley hid behind her bed, next to the wall. Her mom whimpered as her dad sneered mean, cutting insults. Kim's brows bent up, and her head tucked down, and her shoulders drew together. She somehow bore the weight of her husband's words. He never let up.

"Yeah, this household's broken… an' you let it happen. You're still just a secretary? You're flittin' around, pretending to look for a better job? Some of us have real-life obligations. Some of us have to actually TRY, Kim!"

He kicked a chair across the room.

"I mean, I wish I could just flop in someone else's house, while they took care of everything. It must be a pretty sweet deal, right? RIGHT? While you do JACK-ALL?"

Kim had nothing to say.

Morley spat aside, "FINE." He grabbed his coat. "When I come back, it's because I OWN this place. 'Cuz I WORKED for it. I have that right, and I damn-well EARNED it."

He strode out. When he slammed the front door, the walls boomed.

Kim stifled her crying, then sobbed into a pillow on the couch. The air was quiet; it was still in shock.

Riley's footsteps were slow, like she was at a funeral. She wore pink hippo pajamas that she had since she was fourteen, and she wore two pairs of socks. Her hand settled on her mother's shoulder blade. Her mom was still wearing dark slacks and a light, silky blouse. She hadn't changed since the office.

Her mom cried, and Riley rubbed her shoulders.

"You, uh…" she sniffled. She turned a little toward Riley. "You wouldn't by chance know how to change locks, would you? You're the smart one."

"Naw," Riley shook her head. "If I'm the smart one, I should stay beside you right now. Locks can wait. I'm taking care of what matters."

"Baby? I'm not the Queen of all Mothers, you

know. I shouldn't... I shouldn't... keep a home like this, for my child."

Kim's lips shook. Her eyebrows crawled inward. Her head lowered in shame.

Riley looked at her straight. "Mom? I'm graduating. And I'm eighteen. So I'm an adult. We got this far. We're good. We're gonna make it."

"I know, I know..." She almost smiled. "I ache for you, Riley. You try so hard. God, you're tough." She touched Riley's arm.

"Mom, do you want my room? I can take the couch. Then, later tonight, you're in a safer place. Kinda."

Her mom didn't answer. Riley sat with her, rubbing her shoulder, not knowing what else to do. She decided to stay quiet. The clock in the hallway ticked. The refrigerator hummed in the kitchen.

Without words, her mom wiped her nose, tidied herself up, kissed Riley on the head, and turned in. She closed her bedroom door gently.

Riley was in her own bed when her father returned. He somehow opened the front door and stumbled in. He thumped his way into the main bedroom. He tried to kick off his boots, but he fell on the floor. He stayed there. In minutes, he was snoring.

Riley stood and opened her window. The moon was a bright mother, still watching over this broken cradle.

She took a deep breath. The fresh air was nice. It was different. It smelled better than this house. She turned and cuddled back in bed.

In the corner of her room, there was a shelf with a picture she drew when she was ten. Also there was Louis, her stuffed rabbit. He was white, still somewhat fluffy, and wore a little necktie. She pronounced his name as "LOO-ee," quite affectionately, ever since she was small. She dragged him everywhere. On weekends, she'd stuff Louis into her little pink backpack, jump on her bike, and go searching for shadows of magic. Louis was a time wizard, of course, and she was the heiress to The Hidden Kingdoms. Her mom agreed, as long as Riley wore her bike helmet.

So many wild adventures began with the fateful words of a little girl: "C'MON, Louis!" She'd grab him and whisk out the door, and his necktie would flap like a tiny cape. Where there was sunshine, there could be ANYTHING!

Louis stayed on that shelf for the last five years. It felt like his magic was shelved with him. He was pale, sitting there in the darkness. He was pale like the moon or the brooding clouds.

"What next, Louis?" she asked wistfully. "Do I get failed, 'cuz Mr Gray feels like being a jerk? Does Colleen get her friends to beat me up?"

Louis answered with silence.

"Well, you're optimistic. Clear roads ahead, then?"

Louis confirmed with total quiet.

"Thanks, man." She nodded to her childhood

friend, Louis-the-Stuffed-Rabbit.

She looked up past the clouds. She saw the stars wink back at her. They kept a secret, like an in-joke.

She felt a sudden wave pass over her shoulders. It was warm and smooth down her back. She felt something pure and beautiful cleanse her heart.

What was THAT? she thought. Uh… is it 'cuz I'm going to graduate? be a professional artist? No. Maybe Mom's getting promoted tomorrow? That'd rock. Or maybe she's getting out. But what the heck WAS that?

This wasn't hope; it was deeper, and it was powerful. She'd just felt something warm reach down and hold her. It was a sixth sense of overwhelming kindness.

One star, somewhere, was a dimpled smile for her. Something felt like home. A real one. Her real home, somewhere… and it was waiting for her. It wanted to find her, and it wanted to take her away from all this. It wanted HER to get out. It was a strange moment, like an epiphany. Sure, Louis was a cuddly old treasure, and the moon and stars were really pretty, tonight… but this?

This loved her.

CHAPTER SEVEN

THE FALL

Mr Gray ambled up to Riley's desk. He had a heavy arrogance, like a cop who'd just flashed his lights and pulled her over for no reason.

"Well, well… lookit little Ms Henway. I can tell what kinda math YOU'RE doing: zero-sum. 'Cuz those are some real zeroes, you're producing down there."

Riley put down her pencil. She'd plotted her graph of exponential growth, and the curve was suddenly and drastically tall. There was nothing wrong with it, but she'd added spots and drawn it to resemble a giraffe. She titled it 'exponential G-raph.'

Mr Gray shook his head. "Why do we even try to teach you?"

"It's, uhh," she stalled, "It's math AND art. It's both. 'Graphic' arts, if you will."

He gaped vacantly at her, then grunted, "Just do the work, ya flake."

Someone else slapped down their pencil. Angry breath steamed out.

"What is it, Mr Benjamin?"

Clark fumed. He stared down at his paper. He wanted to say, 'It's art and math, sir - both. It's because she's a polymath. Haha. Get it? She's a Renaissance woman.' However, he couldn't risk embarrassing the teacher. Clark remained silent.

Mr Gray scratched at his beard and curled his lip. "What is it? Huh, Clark? What are you goin' through?"

My list of reasons to kick your ass, Clark thought.

"Clarkie-boy, I'd hate to start knocking percentages off your term..." Mr Gray flexed his big, thick-jawed smile. He stood tall with authority.

"Well," Clark grinned back, "Thankfully the marks add up, and that's it. Math isn't totally subjective, right? Not something based on personal opinion, like... oh, I dunno... art."

Mr Gray nudged up his head. "Yeah, 'cuz art's just a bunch of made-up, abstract crap." He looked half-way to Riley, but not directly at her.

Clark nodded. "Well, yeah. And math's just representation by Arabic numerals."

The air thickened like cement.

"What?" Mr Gray was shocked stiff. He craned his neck to look at him. "No, Clark, it's NUMBERS.

It's numbers, and it's ENGLISH."

Clark didn't blink. "Fibonacci brought them from northern Africa. Arabic numerals are just representations. They're concepts. They're not reality. So they're made up."

It was like he'd dropped a huge, iron gauntlet in the room, and Mr Gray wasn't ready to be challenged.

"…Whah?" Mr Gray's jaw dropped. The whole class saw bags under his eyes.

Clark raised his brows and prompted him, "The Arabic numeral set?"

Mr Gray spoke as if addressing an alien creature: "We talk in English here. Not Arabic, not African, and it ain't the Fibonacci sequence. We got numbers, and we speak English. That's reality. No abstracts."

Mr Gray stared at Clark to avoid his other students' gaze. Clark stared back, then opened his hands and admitted, "Okay. 'Just something I read somewhere."

Mr Gray shrugged. "Pff! Whatever. Snooty BOOKWORMS…" His eyes were fat, white globes of irritation. "And I guess ya don't have a dad around to teach ya manners. Weirdo."

Clark remained silent.

Mr Gray turned his back and muttered. "I bet I can guess why."

Clark said nothing. His face flushed pink. Something silver beaded in his eye. Riley's two eyes stabbed at Mr Gray like ice and death.

Mr Gray scratched his beard and sighed. His ex-wife was another mouthy bookworm - another pretty, brunette smart-ass, just like Riley. Too much like her.

Mr Gray strolled around the classroom like a security guard doing his rounds.

After Clark spoke, Timmy Karnes had to excuse himself to the washroom. He walked around the far side of the room to avoid Clark.

Jeff Anders hunched low over his workbook.

He sneered quietly, "Freak."

Clark ducked his head down and whispered back to him, "Hey, what's YOUR graph like, Jeff? You're really smart when it comes to PLOTTING things."

The class kept silent. It sounded like the inside of a coffin, except for Mr Gray's manly boots and the scratching of pencils.

What was Clark saying? thought Riley. Math's just a bunch of symbols? They're made up, like representations? So numbers are just practical art. Was Clark defending me?

Her eyes lit. She looked up at him. She couldn't reach him until she discreetly waved. When she finally caught Clark's eye, she mouthed two words: "Thank you!"

He nodded back to her graciously. That silent nod spoke for him: "But of course, milady." She hid a smile, but her cheeks bunched up tight on her face.

Mr Gray continued parading around his class. He was oblivious to the communication between students. He deliberately avoided Riley and Clark for the rest of the day.

Jeff dumped Riley only three days before the prom. He decided to go with Sonia, instead. Sonia was from Poland and had amazing legs, so Jeff's move was either congratulated or quietly scorned. The key moment was by his locker. That was where he dumped Riley, and where he crushed her soul. He made sure lots of people were there to see it happen.

"Yeah, well," Jeff shrugged, playing it up, "I'm moving on with my career. Things change. What else do you want me to say?"

"Maybe give me a reason for breaking up? You don't even know where I'm going. I could be moving to your city, near your university campus, and I-"

"No. This high school thing is done, arright? We're not little kids anymore. All this holding-hands-at-recess crap is dead. It's childish. So, like… GROW UP."

"Oh, right, so you're going to date Sonia, now? Go to the prom? Run off to college together, as high school sweethearts?"

"Well, maybe I have a taste for sweet," he said.

Everyone remembered Riley and her spicy wit.

Jeff squared his shoulders. "Or maybe I just have taste."

The gathering crowd let out a satisfied "Ooh…"

Riley was unfazed. "And our two years, together, Jeff? What did they mean to you?"

"I dunno. The folly of youth." Jeff rolled his eyes. His friends chuckled. "But if you wanna be nostalgic, you're on your own. I'm moving forward. It's time for real life."

She dropped her hands to her sides. "I've been there for you… for two whole years. That IS a relationship, Jeff. That IS real. Things can work. It's workable. I know we could-"

"Riley, give up. You're not even relationship material. 'Kay? Give up."

Riley stifled a sob. "-but…?"

He stared at her. He said nothing. The air was empty like the long, hollow boom of a drum.

A few of the popular girls sang a dramatic "ooOOOoooh." Colleen Dietrich had a swaggering smile on her glossy lips. They all witnessed Riley Henway getting slammed down hard. What was even juicier was this: it was Jeff's locker, so SHE had to walk away. She had to be the loser, slinking away with her tail between her legs.

She tried to keep things together. She stood tall. She kept her dignity. She still heard them giggling behind her.

Colleen wore her crocodile's smile. She tossed her golden hair, flashed her perfect lashes, and taunted, "Run along, little tramp…" She pursed her poofy lips with satisfaction.

Riley spun on her. "SCREW YOU, fake-faced SKANK!"

Students snorted and laughed out loud. Colleen couldn't respond to 'fake face,' and everyone laughed at her. Riley actually had backup, this time. This meant she couldn't be beaten up afterward.

Riley strode off. Someone gave a single clap-clap of approval, and it almost looked like she'd won. Jeff watched his credibility drop. He didn't have full authority, here, and it disgraced him.

He squinted his eyes down to black slits, like a snake's. Behind them, there was a new, seething venom - a grudge, like 'enemy-for-life.'

No, he thought. No, little Riley, you don't get to win. Ashvale's in my pocket, and it's gonna ruin you.

CHAPTER EIGHT
Just So You Know

Riley's mom worked part-time as a secretary, but she often looked for a better job. She was actually looking for an escape route.

"Kid? I gotta head out for a few days. Can you hold down the fort, this weekend?"

"Uh-huh." Riley's gaze was numb. She lay across the couch with her head on the armrest. As soon as she'd gotten home, she dropped her books and collapsed.

"Hey. Don't you have a prom to look forward to?"

Riley's neck twitched. Her mouth twisted. She held everything in.

"Riley, Honey - we all have to try, here. Our family's struggling, sure, but we're still a family. We survive. We have to hold things together. Okay?"

Riley mumbled to her, "So it's the weekend, and you'll be back in a few days?"

Her mother nodded vaguely. She didn't make eye contact.

"So like what, Tuesday? Business, till next week?"

Kim took a moment to respond.

"Yeah. And just… go easy on your dad, okay? Things are rough with him, right now. We all have our struggles."

Riley heard this all before. She watched, and listened, and her mom said 'you only get one family, in life. Make the best of what you have.' Her dad was trying, and her mom was trying, and everyone hoped Riley would try really hard too.

She saw through it all. Her mom was just as scared as she was. That was what Riley respected the most; her mom was terrified, and human, and that's how they could relate. Her brave face was paper thin. Riley loved the woman underneath. They both tried to be strong for the sake of the other.

"Okay, well, I'm back in a few. Business stuff, right? I got that portfolio for the Fentons. They're looking good, so… I gotta secure us a deal."

"Mmm," Riley turned over. "Can you take me with you?"

"Y'know, I'd love to, but…" Kim laughed nervously. "Yeah, I honestly wish I could take you along with us… with me. You could win the whole deal. But I'll need you here, alright? I'll bring home some real bread. I hope." She smiled with pretty lipstick, and her shoulder-length brown hair had a lovely shine.

"So you packed your black, sleeveless dress for business?"

Kim McEwen-Henway froze. Her kid was too damned smart. Riley's brain was a trap made of steel, and it snapped shut. Kim's head rolled down guiltily. Her voice dropped like a rock.

"You can't say, like… Please don't say anything," she muttered. She stood there, unable to move. She glanced at the door, and then her daughter. She looked back and forth, like a quick decision.

"Mom?"

Kim slowly turned her head.

"Mom, you'll look like a fox. You'll be absolutely gorgeous. You and I both know it." Riley smiled a little. It was the first time she smiled that day.

"But you can't-"

"I won't. And he won't notice a thing. Jeez, Mom… how much attention DOES he give you? Right?"

"But," she whispered, "I'm embarrassed. You can't do this kinda stuff when you're older."

Riley corrected her with playful sternness: "You're not 'older,' Mother. You're just foxy. There's a difference."

Her mother huffed a quick laugh.

"How do I deserve you, Sweetheart?" She stepped forward and kissed Riley on the head. "I'm gonna try to sort some stuff out, and maybe… you know, in a couple weeks, you and I can, like...?"

Kim looked to the front door again. The way she flicked her eyes, she meant go THROUGH the front door, and not come back.

"Okay? I don't want you in this kind of situation, ever. Just-"

"Stay strong. Gotcha. I'm on it."

Riley was the perfect figure of strength. She lay across the couch like roadkill.

"Well," Kim paced uncomfortably, "I mean, call Granny if you want to talk to someone. Okay? I'll be right back. I will. 'Promise you. Okay?"

Jeez, Riley thought. How many times does she have to ask me if I'm 'okay?'

"I know," Riley said. "I've got the prom to look forward to. 'Got dumped, lost my date, and no-one wants me, but I can look forward to it anyway."

"WHAT?" Kim's arms flapped to her sides. "Aww, HONEY...! Oh, no! We need a Girls' Night, as soon as I'm back. I'm so sorry, Baby!"

Riley stiffened her brow and pouted firmly.

"Ya, but look at me. I've got it under control." She shrugged. "I'm just gonna watch some movies or something. Maybe binge on junk food. Effective therapy. I'm on the up-and-up. Been here, done that. I've got half-a-dozen T-shirts already."

Kim's head tipped sadly. "Riley? You're one helluva woman. And I love you."

"Hmm. Good luck on your business trip, Mom. I mean it."

Riley didn't even look at her. They both knew what she meant.

"Ya, and you give Granny Faye a ring, okay? She loves you as much as I do. I gotta run. I'll… I'll seeya soon."

I gotta run, Riley thought. Yeah. 'Okay.' Run, Mom. Run.

She'd be gone for more than a few days.

This was shaping up to be the worst weekend of Riley's life. Thankfully, her father was away. He was weekending in the city. She dreaded when he'd come home, though, when he'd be hungover. He'd be worse than usual.

She heard some pre-prom celebrations that evening. She heard hooting, and breaking bottles, and squealing car tires. A few blocks over, someone screamed angrily. Ten minutes later, she heard police sirens.

She got up to check the door, to be sure things were locked. She had a weekend alone, nowhere else to go, and nothing left to study for. But she'd made it. She'd graduated. She was still waiting to hear back about bursaries and a few art colleges in the city. Then… she'd finally leave Ashvale behind her.

For the prom, she would've gotten that dress from the bridal shop. It was a second-hand bridesmaid's dress. Riley had it held for her since April. When she pinned her hair back, and stood straight, she looked like a spirit from an enchanted forest. Even if Jeff still treated her like crap, she'd look positively fantastic. She'd feel good about herself, regardless. Maybe she'd even catch Clark's eye if it was a special night.

Yeah, she thought. THAT special night. The night when he finds me, and dances with me... our dance together. And we'd hold each other, and look to each other.

But now? No prom, no dance... no need for that dress, anymore.

"Hmm," she realized. "No prom dress? Extra money? Yyyes!" She snarled brilliant white teeth. Her eyes shone wickedly. She'd have her own night, in spite of being dumped by Jeff. 'Heck with the prom! She'd find a movie, wrap up in blankets, and get delivery food.

"I am TOTALLY ordering Szechuan. I'm getting those little ribs in spicy gooey stuff, and the smoky rice! Yeah! Take THAT, Anders... you prissy, spoiled snot!"

She stood tall like a soldier and strode to her room. She'd saved so much money for that dress, but now it'd be put to good-

"Why's my door open...?"

Her mother always closed doors behind herself, respectfully. Her father didn't. He owned the house and made sure everyone knew it. He only used doors for slamming, during his fits. Who opened her bedroom door? Who'd been in her room? And why were they in there?

Riley gritted her teeth. "Louis?" she called to her

little stuffed rabbit. He was perched on a corner shelf at the far end of her bedroom. He guarded the picture she drew when she was ten… and he also sat on a tiny, pink change purse. She kept priceless things in there, when she was a little girl - pretty stones and plastic jewelry. She found a piece of quartz, once, and she thought it was a diamond. More recently, she'd stashed dollar bills in there, saving for her prom dress. She was so proud of finding that dress. She'd saved up for months.

"Louis." She stopped. "Why are you looking at me sideways?"

She stepped forward. She reached for Louis, lifted him up, and retrieved the change purse. The tab on the zipper dangled loosely. It was open. The purse was empty.

She dropped it on the ground and held Louis to her chest. Her stomach grumbled. Her arms shook.

Mom? she wondered. Did you run off with my money?

She paced out to the kitchen and checked the top cabinet. Sure enough, the booze was all still there… bottles and bottles of it. Aged scotch, vodka, and rum. Her father probably took the money. Her money. He'd have a wild weekend with it. He probably kept the rest of the alcohol here, for when he returned.

He'd left a note on the table: "Back Monday."

Monday would've been her prom night - should've been her prom night. Instead, that was when her father would return. Her mom would still be away. Monday was going to be rough, and she had all weekend to worry about it.

Riley slumped out of the kitchen. Her head hung down onto her chest where she cuddled Louis. She fell back onto the couch.

Her mom and dad both knew about the prom dress. They knew when she'd use that money.

"Louis? Did my mom stab me in the back? Did she have more anxiety than usual, tonight? or did my dad rob me for liquor money?

"Is it horrible that I'm second-guessing BOTH of my parents? 'Cuz I lost Jeff, and I'm alone, and I have nowhere to go, and now my family's out, and all my savings are gone. It's just you and me. Two nothings."

She really needed Louis. It didn't matter that he was just fabric. He was a representation, and he meant comfort. He was a reverse voodoo doll. To children, dolls are still a presence; children can love them, and trust them, and not be judged. To adults, they're reminders of childhood magic. They're mementos from a different world.

Louis always listened to her. He heard all about her dreams. His ears poked up attentively. His eyes were wide open. His necktie flopped flat onto his belly.

"Hey, Louis? I'm hungry, man."

She heard someone yelling a few blocks away. Car tires screeched.

"In a word, how would you describe this stupid

town? Is it 'wretched,' or more like 'abysmal?' If you don't want to comment, that's fair too."

Louis said nothing. He stared straight ahead. He had a flat, empty expression.

"Yeah, that's what I thought. Hey, Louis? If I paid some mafia guy to break Jeff's kneecaps… you wouldn't say anything, right?"

Louis held an ominous silence. Riley gave him a crooked smile.

"Ay. You's a real stand-up guy, Lou." She squeezed him lovingly.

She was reminded of being ten years old, and entering a drop-in art show at the library. She thought it was her big break. She'd drawn sketch after sketch for two weeks, and finally had three great pieces. Each of them surpassed anything she'd ever done.

On the day of the show, her mother was away unexpectedly. Her dad couldn't help her get there because he was in no shape to drive. The only way Riley could get her art to the library was by rolling her sketches into cardboard tubes, and then taping those into her little pink backpack. She'd jumped on her bike and pedaled for an hour-and-a-half. By the time she finally arrived, it was too late to enter her art with the other submissions. It was just a bunch of adults eating cheeses and laughing at unfunny jokes. One of them pointed at her when she arrived. His friend sniggered.

Riley's jaw dropped. Her eyes went blank. She felt like she'd just been punched on the inside. Her little feet stood on a floor that was for other people... this whole library was for those other people. Not her. And definitely not her art.

"Hello? Miss?" Professor Piersen called to her. He saw her come in. "Miss, are you here for the art?" He reached out his hand. "Did you also bring someth-...?"

Riley turned and ran out. Professor Piersen slouched as he watched her bang the outside door. It flung open abruptly and then slowly drifted shut.

Once again, her art didn't matter.

"Louis? Look around, buddy." She indicated the empty house. "I guess this is who I am. This is my glory. My prom. WELL... now we know. Now we know.

"Enough of this Cinderella crap. I might snag one of those liquor bottles MYSELF, before Dad gets back. I mean... who cares? This is the most promising time of my life, and I know that NOBODY gives a damn about me. Not even Jeff. I'm stuck at home with a stuffed rabbit."

Louis isn't even alive, she considered. Maybe I should be more like him. Maybe that's how I 'get out.' The future doesn't look like anything. Maybe this is it?

Riley shut her eyes. She tried to block out the world. She still heard distant yells, and laughter, and car engines. If she could block out the whole world to permanent black, it'd be really peaceful. She already knew no-one would miss her when she was gone.

The doorbell rang. Riley was startled and sat up straight. Who the heck? Maybe her mom called Granny right away? But… there wouldn't have been time.

A kind old delivery man in a blue suit came to her door. The man was tall, but hunched over at the shoulders. It looked like his arms were poles for lifting things. He had little round spectacles, twinkling green eyes, and silver hair that tried not to be baldness. He had tufty eyebrows that waved like the whiskers of a sniffy, friendly old dog. Even his voice was threadbare.

"Uhh - delivery? For… is it Mr Riles Hangey? Sorry, things got humid on the packages, here. The lettering got all smudgy." He adjusted his glasses and still couldn't see.

"Nah, I got it," she said. "Bad handwriting, sir. It's just kids and their computer keyboards." She gave him a sweet smile and made his week.

"Oh. Okay, well, this big one's for R-"

"Yeah, Riley Henway. That's for me… I guess."

She received a hefty package. It weighed down her arms. She was startled by how heavy it was.

"And, uh, this one too. You'll have to sign for these, if I can find my pen…"

"Ahh - okay, ya," she stalled, hustling the packages. She had no idea what they were. The big one was the size of a dresser drawer, and it was HEAVY. Another one was lighter, but almost the same size. Then there was a third, which was clearly a fancy bottle.

"Hunhh," she stopped, surprised. "Granny never sends me that kind of… ah well."

"And I think that's about all of it," he said, patting his pockets. He produced a shiny brass pen for her. She signed on the old fellow's clipboard, thanked him, and gave him another blushy smile. It was quick, but she knew he'd like it.

"Oh…!" he exclaimed happily. He gave a shy nod and left. Fifty years ago, women smiled at him like that.

Riley gawked at the packages. What was all this? Was Granny off her medication, or something? She settled down to unwrapping things. There were no notes. No instructions.

The lighter parcel was stuffed with glossy, sensationalist magazines. Everything was about Hollywood, celebrity gossip, pop music, women's sexual health, astrology, and all the juicy literature from the supermarket lineup. One magazine was packed with photos of hunky male models from Iceland. Another magazine's feature story was about a coven of mermaids… mermaids who were making secret pacts with the ghosts inside the Titanic.

Riley's nose crinkled and she laughed out loud. "Aww, Granny! You rock."

The heavier parcel was twenty-four tubs of gourmet ice cream.

"GRANNY! Are you NUTS?"

Was it Granny? Riley stared, breathless. She saw

Mocha-Cashew Galaxy, Rembrandt Caramel-Fudge, and two others she'd never even heard of, as well as…

"…nnnNO!" Her eyes widened; there it was. It was right there:

The Chocolate-That-Is-Unspoken.

She'd only caught rumors about this legendary ice cream. She knew someone who'd had it, five years ago, but they wouldn't discuss it. They moved to Austria later that year. They never said why.

The bottle was a sweet champagne. It came with a 'CashVale' local-dining gift card. The card was redeemable at high-end restaurants in Ashvale Plains.

She sat back on the couch, breathless.

"Well. Uh… Louis?" Her eyes were huge and bright with stars. "Louis, my man… we're ordering in tonight. And it's gonna be awesome."

She turned to Louis and nodded. A powerful grin was building in her face.

"What, Louis? What's that you say? You think I should gain ten pounds?"

There was a knock at the door. Then the doorbell rang merrily. The old man stood there on her step. He stood taller and straighter than before.

"Sorry, Miss - there was one more thing, and I nearly overlooked it! Oof… 'would've been criminal, if I had."

He bowed slightly, and with two outstretched hands he passed her a long, sealed cylinder. It was black like a limousine with silver trim.

The man smiled funny and waved off her

signature. His eyes flashed at her.

"Naw, I won't trouble you with the signing. It's for you, Miss. Definitely you." He nodded, winked happily, and left wearing a big, mischievous smile.

She stood in the doorway for a moment and puzzled. She knit her brow. This was all very surprising; Gran certainly took care of her this weekend.

But Gran couldn't have sent this. None of it was sent "express." Someone must've heard about what happened in school. This couldn't be an apology from Jeff, that was certain.

Riley stepped back inside and closed the door.

She uncapped the cylinder and carefully shook out the contents: one immaculate, long-stemmed, vibrant red rose. There was a tiny card attached. The card was lightly perfumed. The inscription was golden ink, and it was penned with great care:

"Just So You Know - YOU ARE LOVED."

Hunnh, she thought. If this wasn't Mom, or Granny… who the heck was it?

She looked over at Louis. She blinked, then scowled lightly.

"You're a stuffed rabbit. You didn't do any of this."

Her eyes drifted. For a moment, she let herself dream it was Clark.

CHAPTER NINE
FORGET-ME-NOT

Just before graduation, Clark applied for a patent. It was rejected. Boeing had just secured the rights to something very similar. Clark's passive electro-conductive airfoil was a fantastic idea, but a team of European engineers beat him by five months.

Clark was still heartbroken several days later, but he went to his prom anyway. He was supposed to go with Tracey, but she snuck away early in the evening. She ran off with Mark, and they made out behind the school. Tall Mark, that is - not Geeky Mark. Tracey's plan was to use Clark as a disposable ticket, just to get to the prom. They didn't dance. She barely looked at him. She smiled once or twice with excitement, but only when she saw someone else. When Clark went to get her a drink, she disappeared. He'd barely turned his back, over at the punch bowl, and she vanished.

Without a date, Clark left. He went walking through the open lands of Ashvale Plains. This was Ashvale Field. Of any place in the whole county, Ashvale Field had the most stars.

Out here, it was mostly sky, and he could forget about the rest of the town. He blocked it all out, till he saw someone lurching - staggering - struggling down the path.

He ran up to try to help them, and he ran into Riley. She was drunk.

"Uhh... damn. Riley? Are you okay? Hey, are you alright?"

"Never better, big guy," she joked. She leaned against him and patted his chest. "Never better. 'Cept my mom left again, and my dad's back, and he's way drunker than I am right now. You? What, you're not with your date?"

She poked him with her finger. "So. Have ya had any?" Her eyes shone up to meet his.

She smiled cryptically. By 'had any,' she meant 'drinks'... and not 'intimate encounters.' The way she smiled, though, Clark really wondered.

She certainly didn't mean 'had any perfect dreams-come-true, like kissing Riley Henway in Ashvale Field, when the moon was a tilting bowl spilling its stars across a velvet sky.'

"CLARK, dude..." She thumped his chest. "Had any DRINKS, I mean? 'You want to get a drink with me, man? A fond farewell to our last night of youth? Our blessèd, innocent youth?"

"Nah, I don't drink."

"You don't...? WAIT. Y'know what, buddy?" She threw her arm around him. "I can respect that. Some people stay dry; they smile, wave their hand, and drive their friends home, afterward. It's still cool. You're still cool, Clark. At least, you're cool by me."

He could smell how cool her evening had been. Probably rum.

"But d'you know what that means, dude?" She suddenly brightened and swayed around to look at him.

"Uh... what?" He was caught in angelic light.

"You graduated with COOL. It's like graduating with honors!"

Hmm, he thought. Thanks, but I already graduated with honors.

"Clark! You earned the COOL Award, and nobody even knows it!" Her cheeks bunched up with glee. "Aww, I'm so proud of you, man!" She staggered and almost fell into a bush. He caught her and held her steady.

"I should probably get you home," he said flatly.

She righted herself, but then she felt his arms. She slid her hands up his stony muscle.

"Mmf - Clark? You can take me home."

Her voice was low, but hopeful. She nodded slowly.

"You can take me home, Clark."
She smiled subtly.
"And, if you want?" she swayed closer, "you can

read me Confucius, for pillow talk. I really love your voice."

Her hand rested against his tight belly. She gazed up at him. Her legs wobbled and almost gave out.

"No, I just," He struggled to keep her upright. "I just want you… I just want you… safe."

"Mmm," she grinned hotly, teasing him. "You WANT me… oooh-hoo!" Her eyes were wide and bright with glee.

"Riley?" he spoke with a smooth voice.

"Yeah, big guy?" She answered with her eyes: beautiful, dark pools.

He tried to step back. She clung to him and followed.

She leaned closer. "You know, Clark, I should tell you something. I've kept a secret buried for a long time. So… you take me home, and I'll finally tell-"

"Riley?" he cautioned her, sternly.

"Myeah?" she smiled up at him.

"Shut up. Seriously."

Her face fell. She looked sad and afraid, like a puppy that had just been disowned.

"Don't joke about this, okay? You're drunk. I really, REALLY like you. Always liked you. REALLY liked you. Always. But this?" His finger drew a circle around their heads. "THIS? Here? Us? It doesn't happen. Okay? 'US?' No. Not when you're blitzed out of your frickin' tree. And-"

She lifted her hand. Her finger crossed his lips. He stopped dead. Terror seized him. Her voice mesmerized him like an enchantment.

"What if I want you, Clark?"

Adrenaline. His damage-control instincts kicked in hard.

"You don't."

He looked into her eyes firmly. She recoiled a little.

"Tomorrow, we'd wake up, and you'd wonder how it all happened, and you'd have terrible regrets. You'd regret being with me. It wouldn't be what you wanted. You were just drunk, and that'd make it rape. You can say, 'Oh, I love you, Clark, I love you and want to sleep with you,' and then tomorrow you could say I raped you, because you were drunk out of your frickin' skull."

She watched him with a mixture of panic and pain.

"No!" she replied. "No, you wouldn't ever do that! You'd never rape me... JESUS... Clark, I know you. You're quiet, but you're a really great guy. You're sweet, and gentle, and..." She swayed closer. Her voice was an angel's feather. "You're sweet, and gentle, and kind. You'd never do that to anyone."

He stopped, stood away from her, and spanned out his arms.

"Ya. EXACTLY. You'd better believe it. There's no discussion. I can't take you home."

She still didn't understand.

He tried to be clear: "Look, tomorrow is something we both have to live with. This 'now' thing is a lot smaller than the rest of our lives."

They stood facing each other. He nodded to her slowly, making sure the message clicked. He stepped forward, took her hands, and squeezed them. He held her around the shoulders and steered her back on their path. They walked together in silence.

Her voice was gentle. "So, YOU… won't have sex with ME… because you really like me." She pieced it together. "And to protect me, so I don't regret stuff, later."

A gust of breath came from his nose. It was a discreet laugh.

"Yeah," he smiled to her. "Thank you for hearing me."

Riley's face turned ashen. She was smart enough to regret drinking, that night. Clark saw her eyes turn downward.

"I love your mind," he reassured her, "and how quick it is. I sincerely do. Being with you feels like real company. I don't know how else to say it. You understand me, Riley. Even NOW. You're such a great friend. I really want to keep that. It means a lot to me."

Again, he looked over to her with admiration. Even while drunk, she made more sense than the rest of the world.

She didn't look up. She spoke to their feet.

"Y'know… once? No wait - more than once." She chuckled privately. "I, uh… I was with Jeff, and I wanted to call him 'Clark.' Like… y'know… when it really mattered."

She squeezed her eyes shut. "I'm sorry I said that. But I'm sorry for pretty much everything, right now."

Of course, he thought. You'll say things that are absolutely ridiculous. You're so drunk, you even talk about spending the night with me. You don't know it, but that really is cruel and unusual punishment. Can you understand this pain?

They walked a few more steps. Clark swallowed. His head rumbled. His blood pounded. He'd never have another chance.

"Fine. Riley? Stand with me. Right here. Now, look up."

They were walking in Ashvale Field. They were two tiny morsels on a flat plate, served to the giant midnight sky. Silver dreams hung above them in the black. There were so, so many. There were so many stars, they all looked tiny… like fine sand made of light.

Riley and Clark were together. They were utterly lost, floating in the cosmos. Lost… together. Looking up was like looking down into a bottomless pit, and there were trillions of gems beyond their reach. They both looked over this edge, into an unknown future. They were young, and alone, and had no idea what was going to happen. They stood side-by-side. They only had each other.

"Okay. You're drunk. You won't remember much. So… what I'm about to say is like one of those little stars. Just one. I'll say it tonight, and it'll fade tomorrow. And you won't remember."

She turned sadly. "I'd want to." Her breath swam with alcohol. The odds were stacked against her.

I really hate myself, she decided. I am so, so stupid.

"Arright. Riley, I remember you from grade three, and up to grade six, when you left for a different school. I remember that multicultural Christmas thing, in grade five, where you had to sing that Ukrainian folk song. I LOVED that song, when you sang it. I remembered it, years later, because I wanted to remember you. I just… I took it with me. I kept it in my heart, from childhood to this very day.

"Then in grade six, you moved. When you moved back, I thought it was fate! Then you went on a date with Jordan Swanson, and I wanted to die."

He waited for a moment. There was distance and pain in his face. Then he chuckled.

"I always thought about you. Even when I was a seven- or eight-year-old kid. I had dreams that I could save you… from, like, Darth Vader. Your house was a castle, and I was going to climb it, and I think your dad was actually Darth Vader. That's how I dreamed, as an eight-year-old. I wanted to be your prince, or your champion, or your knight. And I really, really wanted to be the one to save you. You were the princess of my world.

"So - THANK YOU for getting totally drunk, Riley. 'Cuz now, I can tell you something. It'll be a blur for you, but I have to say it for me."

He was shaking. The shaking wouldn't stop. He smiled at her ironically. His jaw trembled. He fought the tears. He took a breath, held it, and told her:

"I... am... HORRIBLY... in love with you."

His chin shook. His words towered over them both.

"I UTTERLY ADORE YOU, Riley Ann Henway."

All the stars stopped to look at them. The moon turned pale. The night air went silent.

He took another quivering breath. "God, I adore you. So much, I can't even tell you. And I don't want you to remember this, because... I'm pretty vulnerable, here." He huffed out a small, nervous laugh. He knit his brow a little, to emphasize. "You're a dream, walking through my life. That's how I feel. Not 'know,' but what I feel. And a person feels things like truth, right? I think you're... The only thing that's real in this world is you."

He took a huge breath.

"Days pass. And nights pass. Flames today, then flicker, then dim light, and then cold. That's what things really are. You won't remember this, tomorrow."

"Wait. Clark?" she began. "Clark, for YEARS I've felt like-"

"NO, Riley; you're really drunk. So we can't even talk about this, now. I'm sorry for telling you to shut up, but this is really serious for me. I just need you safe... like, even safe from me. I just want to take care of you. Not use you, not sleep with you, not ever hurt you, EVER... but keep you safe."

He dropped his head and shook it slowly.

"So, I am NOT taking you h..."

He swallowed. He had to wait a few seconds to settle.

"How are things with you and your dad?"

She replied weakly, "Whaddya think? Here I am, no date for the prom, wandering around drunk, alone... 'cuz I can't go home. Nuh-uh. Not home. Not tonight. My dad's in 'drunk-incredible-hulk' mode. You know. Turnin' green. Smashing stuff. Yelling a lot. I can't be around the house, and my mom's away on business." She waved her arm at the horizon.

He nodded to her and held her around the shoulder. He held her lightly, in case she had bruises.

"I'll take care of you. I'm going to make sure you're safe, tonight."

Clark walked her to his house. They walked together in a protective silence, like carrying something precious and fragile. At his place, he brought her around to a side door and led her downstairs. His workshop was in his basement.

Occasionally, he worked all night, so he kept a cot down here. It was quiet and protected. He led her through the darkness, sat her on the cot, and settled her in. She lay there and breathed - still drunk, still confused. He stepped up to his kitchen, and then quickly returned.

"Okay, um… quilts are here, and the window's open for some fresh air. I got you a glass of water, and… well, a few granola bars, in case you get hungry. And this blanket's heavy, but really soft. Here…"

He knelt down by the cot. He was barely visible from the upstairs light. He lifted the blanket around her. He made sure it covered her feet, and then up around her shoulders. He brought the glass of water and granola bars within her reach. He tried not to look at her pretty eyes. Her head rested easily on his pillow.

It was so quiet, she was safe from everything.

He kept the stairwell light on, but the rest of his workshop was cloaked in darkness. She could barely make out his table with its pencils, strange blocky devices, and sheets of graph paper.

"Riley, are you alright? 'You good?"

He knelt beside her. She was bundled in tight - so warm, and so cozy, her face was beaming. She was so happy, she glowed.

He paused. He took a terrible chance and reached down to touch her cheek. His hand felt bliss. He hoped she wouldn't hate him tomorrow. He hoped she'd forget everything. He knew she didn't care about him, so touching her cheek was really wrong.

He withdrew his hand.

"Clark? Dude, no-one's ever tucked me in since… not since I was really little."

She turned clumsily to face him. Her eyes didn't focus.

"Wait… I gotta ask an important thing. How come you're like this? Why are you always so nice to me?"

He sighed. Drunkenness numbed her mind. He'd just told her everything - all about his feelings for her. He turned to her and shrugged.

"I'm not. This is how you should be treated. You should be loved. I've always known that."

He turned his head away. He pushed up his glasses again, then surreptitiously wiped a tear that was forming on his cheek.

"Hey. Tomorrow, I'll make something greasy for breakfast. Sausages, ham, eggs, bacon, hash browns… good for hangovers." He avoided her eyes, but nodded for encouragement.

Then he looked at her again. She took hold of his hand and returned it to her cheek. She held it there and pressed it in place. She made him look into her eyes. She still had rum on her breath.

He balanced at the edge of a cliff. He fought like hell, clinging to his personal code. He somehow managed to NOT kiss her. Cheek? No. Brow? No. Lips? Absolutely not. Every instant stabbed him through the heart. He held his ground.

Her eyes finally weighed, lower and lower, until they closed. He listened and waited. He knelt beside her until her breathing was relaxed. When he knew she was asleep, he carefully removed his hand.

His lips made words for her:

"Goodnight, Riley."

He stood up from her cot. He backed away from her. He hated every footstep as he climbed the stairs. He wanted to stay beside her. Guard her, maybe. He wanted to care for her, but he couldn't be such a creep. Hovering over her, and guarding her, while she slept? No, she'd wake up and she'd be terrified. She'd probably scream.

Upstairs, in the hallway, his mother whispered: "HOW WAS THE PROM?"

"Uneventful," he moaned. He paused. "Look, I've got a friend crashing down in the shop. She, uh… she had a few nasty guys coming after her. Can she be safe here? I just want to take care of her. Just tonight."

"Ooh, my big boy's got LADY company!" His mom blushed with pride.

"No, mom," he sighed. "Seeya tomorrow."

CHAPTER TEN

THINGS UNSAID

The kitchen table was well lit. The plastic tablecloth was so orange, it might've glowed in the dark. The stove was close by. Riley felt its heat on her cheeks. She smelled a sweet and spicy haze.

This was a strange comfort to her. She was awake, but had no idea how she got here. She played it cool, even if she was startled out of her hangover.

How was she in Clark's kitchen? She was surprised to be here, but she was baffled that she didn't wake up beside him. Did she NOT throw herself at him, the previous night?

Right now, Clark was a circus ringmaster - he stood proudly, wearing his apron and wielding his spatula. Lots of sizzling, greasy things flipped or did tricks. They dazzled Riley, who watched from the table. They were served on large, white plates as their final prestige. Poof! Hot, greasy, home-cooked comfort food. It was a humble breakfast, but there was a lot of it. Riley had more breakfast, here, than she'd eaten in the last three days.

Her stomach glowed with warmth, but her heart stretched to the point of bursting. It was really him… and he was cooking for her. Why was she here? The question was building in the air, higher and higher, and soon it would have to drop.

Presently, she was busy with blueberry pancakes, sausages, eggs, bacon, hash browns, toast with jam, and a big spill of maple syrup. She dabbled in a bowl of green grapes and slices of apple and mango. She watched this man working hard with honeys and batters, so that every sweet, buttery, and crispy mouthful was loving perfection. The food baked her insides until she was golden.

"Oh, so YOU'RE Riley," Clark's mother sang out. Her eyes were huge, white, and ecstatic, like a cartoon. She wore a thick sweater and wide, permanent-pressed mom pants.

"Mm-… Hi, Ms Benjamin. Does, umm… [munch, munch] …does Clark always cook you breakfast?"

Riley slurped at her second glass of orange juice. The orange juice was just a chaser to Clark's famous Secret Olympic Breakfast Smoothie; all she knew was, it had kiwi, and wheatgrass, and who-knows-what else.

Clark's mother, Bernita Hale-Benjamin, stood still

and tried to think of the most accurate answer. Clark stepped in for her.

"Breakfasts? Occasionally," he grumbled. "Weekends, and… well, summer vacation." He glanced at his mom, shrugged, and went back to work. "I mean, there's not much better to do, weekend mornings."

"PSHH! Yaaa!" Riley corrected him. "Yeah, sleep in! Sleep in till NOON! Or watch cartoons in your pajamas, eating a couple bowls of Frosty Sugar-Smacks! Or - or maybe…" She looked over at Clark.

What would she do, this morning? Easy. She'd start by taking his shirt off.

She stuffed another mouthful into her cheek.

She summed up: "You'd get better ideas, Clark. You should indulge, if you… HAD ANY." She crunched her toast.

Clark hesitated. The words rang through his head. 'Indulge, if he HAD ANY.' Like if he 'had any' drinks last night? or 'had any' intimate encounters?

Hmm, he peered at Riley. Indulge, huh?

She sucked back her orange juice. Her eyelashes flicked.

Nah, he thought. She's really smart, but she's not sending those messages. No way. She must've forgotten last night.

"Oh, Clark's a real idea-man!" his mom beamed.

Riley looked him up-and-down and grinned naughtily into her glass.

"Oh, I BET he is…"

Something on the stove clanked awkwardly.

Riley lifted her brow. "Yeah, I saw his workshop. Seriously, man?!" She crunched her eyes shut. She widened them again with amazement. "What's with all that crazy sh-... I mean, what's all that stuff on your workbench? A buncha cylinder things? Some real' heavy magnets?"

His mother sighed. "He can never explain it to me, dear; I just can't follow. And the man doesn't ever slow down."

Clark needed to remove the 'mom' element from this conversation.

"Want a tour?" He bridged his eyebrows.

Riley scarfed down her toast. "Yeah! Sure, yeah!"

"Grab a tray. Bring breakfast. I'll show you."

He wiped his hands in his apron, tossed it aside, and extended his arm toward the stairway.

Riley was intrigued. She set her plates on a TV tray and followed him downstairs. This was Clark; these were his projects. These were his creations!

He led her toward some dubious-looking prototypes on his workbench. There were a few miniature metal wings, some modified battery testers, and a leaf blower held in a vice grip. All these were scattered at the base of a dark, vertical-looking engine.

"Arright," he muttered absently. He unceremoniously swept things aside, and one or two metal bits clattered on the floor. He gestured to the space - that could be her breakfast table.

"So this is sorta personal, okay? These are a few of my ideas. Umm… don't laugh."

He stepped beside the tall, black-tubed engine.

"You might have seen this thing last night. This ring of tubes? Columns, like big vertical pistons? They ARE pistons. And these magnets, inside? They are serious frickin' magnets. I haven't fine-tuned things, yet. Someday, this might be as tidy as a Swiss watch. Or as big as a locomotive.

"So y'know engines? their pistons? Fuel ignites inside them. When the fire flares, pistons start pumping…"

Riley watched. She tried to avoid making Freudian jokes, even if fires flared and things started pumping.

"Yeah, these magnets ALWAYS repel each other. Always. They always repel away, like firing pistons; that's just how they are. It's their nature. But I've made a flat, iron shield that fits in between them. The iron blocks the magnetic forces between those magnets. Then, the magnets relax and come together.

"With this iron shield in between, the magnet pistons come together like pistons NOT firing. Look: from the side, it looks like a magnet-and-iron sandwich." He pointed at a piston. It had a heavy magnet resting above, another heavy magnet braced below, and the iron shield set between them.

"So this shield is round like a dinner plate - see? And there's an open area in the shield, here… like a piece of cake missing. The magnets DO repel each other, in that place. Just those pistons work - boof! THOSE magnets pump up. They repel.

"The shield revolves whenever pistons pump. The shield is on an axle, and there's a slide, here, on the axle. Whenever pistons repel, they turn the axle and turn the whole shield. A spinning, iron dinner plate.

"So the shield turns, and the open area moves to another set of pistons. See? Then THOSE pistons repel, and the shield moves again, and the NEXT pistons repel, and the shield moves again, and so on. The magnets fall back together whenever there's iron in between."

Riley watched pairs of magnets reacting, then falling back into place. Clark tried to sum up.

"Yeah... so when there's iron, or ironic... no, wait. It's 'ferrous,' right? Yeah, like in chemistry class."

"Heh heh," she pointed. "So it's like a ferrous wheel." Her eyes twinkled at him.

He stopped, then laughed out loud.

"m-HAH! Haha! Yeah!" He grinned hard. "Aww, man - I hadn't thought of that!"

Clark was quiet for a moment, like he was trying to say something. He looked at her kindly.

"So, anyway..." He waved off his machine. "It's like a gas engine, but with no gas. I'm just tricking magnets with iron. Magnets push away from each other, but everything spins and they get together again. That's how everything works."

Riley stared thoughtfully, chewing a hunk of

bacon. "Is that… like, one of those impossible machines? perpetual?"

"I hope so. Bye-bye gas crisis."

"Wait. Isn't there some thermodynamic law against that? from physics? like in physics class? I think I saw it in a mad-scientist movie."

"Yeah. The second law of thermodynamics. Entropy; tendency toward disorder. It's a constant. That's why all the other machines never work. And these magnets will eventually wear out, too. But then again, the moon will stop orbiting the Earth someday, and tidal power won't work anymore. For us, it'll keep circling. It's more of a 'big picture' thing. It's relative."

He raised his finger to make a point.

"So, are these magnets strong enough to keep the engine spinning? Can it be efficient enough - slick enough - that the pistons keep pumping? 'Cuz then, I make it a power generator."

"Mmm-hmm," she smirked. "Pretty slick, dude. Uhh… why wouldn't the magnets just stick, when they're close to the iron?"

He hesitated to answer her.

"Because they interact with each other. Their nature, as pairs, is stronger than when they're separate. That's my theory. Normally, one of 'em would just flip, polarity would line up, and they'd be inseparable."

He scratched his jaw and bobbed his head back and forth.

"Meh. Maybe it's mad-scientist stuff. Maybe it should be in a movie."

She looked up. "I gotta ask something…"

"Yeah?" He turned to her brightly. He knew how smart she was.

"Clark, what-in-the-sweet-hell happened last night?"

He sighed. His face fell. She saw this and stepped back fearfully.

Oh, no, she cringed. I did something. And to CLARK. What did I do? On prom night, no less! What did I do to him?

She raised her hands and tried to recap what she knew.

"Look. I woke up this morning, down here in this workshop. And you just made me breakfast." She lifted another piece of bacon to her mouth and chewed. "Thanks for all that, but… last night? How did I get here? What happened?"

He stepped up.

"Prom night sucked. I found you out by Ashvale Field, and we went for a walk. You were real upset about Jeff. You talked to me about him. You mentioned your dad was in a bad state, too, so I invited you to crash over here."

Riley's feet crunched together. "Did I say anything else?" she asked meekly. She needed to know, but she knew it would cripple her.

What did I say to him? What did I tell him? Does Clark know, now? And he doesn't feel the same way?

Of course, I told him. That's why he's so quiet. I told him I loved him, and now he's quiet about it...

"Nah," Clark waved her off. "You were kinda drunk. You mumbled, and didn't say much. 'Cept, that Jeff was a total dick-head. And he deserved to fall in a hole, and never be heard from again."

"Did anything... like... between us, did anything...?"

The moment of truth.

"No," he reassured her. He smiled like the warming sun. "Nah, nothing weird happened. You didn't do anything or say anything - at least, not when I found you."

She exhaled. Her shoulders fell with relief.

She chewed on her bacon. She nodded again, and looked up to him.

"Thanks for helping me. You're a really good friend, man."

He shrugged at her. "You needed a place to crash. It's all good."

She chewed, swallowed, and kept thinking. HOW could she ever keep her hands off him? Alone, at night, after so many drinks?

Ha, she thought. That's classic Clark behavior. He finds some drunk girl wandering alone, at night, and he doesn't take advantage of her. He doesn't shame her. He doesn't hurt her. No, he takes her under his big wing, and invites her to stay over at his house. And then to have breakfast with him, and meet his MOM, for God's sake...

Did I try to kiss him? Is he hiding something? He is. He totally is. He's hiding something, so I won't be embarrassed… Damn. If he's hiding something, then… he knows. And now he isn't saying anything. I must've told him, and this beautiful man is just preserving my dignity. So he can't feel the same way. He's so good to me. I'd never deserve him in a million years.

"Thanks, Clark." She smiled sadly. "I guess I gotta… umm… I gotta get home, so no-one worries about me."

"Yeah. 'Kay." He smiled gently.

I worry about you, he thought. Does that make me your real home? I'M the one who worries about you. I'm the place where you're loved. I'll always miss you, and always wait for you. Forever.

Riley had to face an ugly fact. To know the truth, she had to challenge him.

"Well, thanks for breakfast, man. Thanks for taking care of me, last night. And, uh… thanks for being so… 'understanding.' Of everything. You know."

"No problem," he replied.

Oh no, she thought. I told him I loved him. Now he's just being kind. What a sweet, sweet guy, to not break my heart.

Hmm, he thought. Yeah. 'Thanks for being so understanding,' she says, because she was drunk out of her skull, and babbling about love. I can be understanding. I can forgive her. It killed me, to hear it, but she was just drunk. Yeah, Riley, I can forgive you... since you didn't mean it.

Neither of them really understood.

Riley couldn't remember anything. She didn't remember the workshop last night, when the smell of his blanket enveloped her. She lay in his cot, in the dark, and love's intoxication spun her senses. She felt smooth, endless circles. She was pulled down in an undertow of need. She grabbed his pillow and growled for him:

"Oh, GOD... Clark... nggh... Kiss me...!"

She squirmed around in his blanket. Her breath surged... his cologne swelled fully into her lungs. It was like planting her face onto his bare chest, breathing with her open mouth, and tasting him. Then, unexpectedly, it flooded over her tongue - his true scent. She found the animal part of him; the signature of his naked body: his sweat.

She wrestled under his blanket, kicking and thumping. Her blood drummed. His scent made a roar through her body like an ocean swell. It was just a moment, but it felt like he'd been with her, right there. She was alone, yet so close to Clark. His heavy blanket felt like his warm arms around her. It was as close to him as she'd ever get.

Riley thought of two stars. They could be so close to each other, but separated by so much night. So much loneliness between them. They were separated by the cold reality of never. And never was infinite.

This all happened, but she wouldn't remember.

Clark remembered everything. He lay in bed that night with his mind reeling. She was right there in his workshop... Riley Henway. She was nestled in sweetly, like a pearl. It was torture. She dreamed, there, on his pillow.

Everything about him was drawn tight - tense, like an archer. He glanced at his bedroom door. He was so close to her.

He was so close, right now - so close.

Too close.

Tension pulled in his chest. His pulse was leaping fire. He lay in his bed as quietly as he could. He rolled his eyes, turned over, and tried to sleep.

Yeah, his teachers said blah blah blah, something-something about teenage hormones. They were too afraid to talk about the reality: it was raw, untempered love coursing through innocent blood.

Clark looked out his window at the distant stars... light-years away. Riley was just as far away. He couldn't lie beside her. He couldn't hold her. He could never kiss her.

God... she was right there, in his stupid shop. He could just sneak downstairs, lock his workshop door... kneel by HIS cot, in HIS private space... and he'd actually be with her. He'd have time. He could. He could kiss the sweet lips of Riley Ann Henway, the heart of his world. That moment could tell her everything.

Instead, Clark lay still. He watched the distant stars.

I hate life, he thought to himself. I hate life, and I hate this, and I hate myself, and I frickin' DESPISE Jeff Anders... but she's worth it. She... is worth all of this.

Love her? Of course. RESPECT her? I must. Unquestionably. I would die before I ever mistreated her. I love her, so I won't kiss her goodnight.

Riley? I love you so, so much.

As he lay in bed, Clark's chest felt like it had caved in. It didn't matter; he knew what he did was right.

That was 'prom night' for young Riley Ann Henway and her strange friend, Clark.

CHAPTER ELEVEN

APART

After high school, Clark went to a college overseas. Riley had to stay in Ashvale to work a few entry-level jobs. She was still trying to save up money.

Jeff and Sonia were together for less than a month. When he broke up with her, Jeff accidentally called Sonia a dirty little sleaze. Sonia stood tall and proud and laughed in his face.

That summer, Jeff managed one of his father's real estate offices. He lost his temper a few weeks in, and subsequently lost a client. Jeff fired two low-level employees and felt better afterward.

There were complications with Jonno's recovery, and he got fatter and more embittered. He didn't get out of Ashvale; he ended up living with his dad and not doing much at all. Even when he recovered, he wouldn't go back to football.

During college, Clark vacationed in Italy. He spent time in Florence, because he wanted to see where the Renaissance happened. He sent his mother dozens of digital photos of classical art, and made sure they were in ultra-high resolution. When he returned, he had an office job waiting for him.

Riley worked in catering for two years. Then, there was an anonymous complaint against her. No-one would discuss it. She was dismissed. That same week, the boss's daughter graduated from high school. She took over Riley's job. People were quiet about that, also. Riley scrambled to pay rent and ended up waiting tables at a café.

Her mother Kim met a man named Roger. Riley immediately helped her move out of their old home. She brought workmen to her old house, grabbed her mom's stuff, and left her father bewildered on the kitchen floor. He was drunk, and sweaty, and hazy eyed. In the end, Riley stepped over him and checked her bedroom one last time. Bad memories. All of it. So much hiding.

She gasped softly when she spotted Louis the Rabbit. She grabbed him and left. She pitched the house keys on the kitchen table and closed the door behind her.

Clark heard about this through social media gossip: Kim McEwen-Henway had been unfaithful, and she'd run off with another man! Such scandal in Ashvale! When he read this in his office, Clark pumped his fist.

"YES! Yeah, Riley's Mom! You GO, girl!" His colleagues looked at him funny.

That night, Clark celebrated. He bought a bottle of sparkling non-alcoholic pear cider. He ate dinner alone, but he raised his glass high and toasted her.

"To Love, and to A Home Without Bruises. May his kisses make up the balance."

He smiled with steamy eyes and drank deep.

Clark and Riley didn't stay in touch. It was a shock to both of them when they met at a Christmas party.

"Hey! CLARK! Aww, how've you BEEN, man?" She clunked down her can of root beer, ran to him, and hugged him. His heart leapt up in his throat and he choked on it.

"Oh, hi - hi Riley."

His brow warped with agony. She squeezed him and tugged side-to-side. She wouldn't let go; she only squeezed him tighter.

Dear GOD, he thought. Do you have to be so sweet? Do you understand what this does to me? Why are you doing this?

Clark was her dear friend; the true heart; the one good man. She couldn't tell him how much she missed him. She noticed how distant he seemed, in that hug. The discomfort showed in his face.

"Aww, I really missed you, Clark! How's your... like... ANYTHING?"

She still had her arms around him. He held back from truly embracing her.

"Pretty much the same," he confessed. "And you? It's really, uh… really nice to see you."

She only broke away from that hug to tell him about art colleges, and saving up for tuition, and her mom remarrying. She also mentioned her dad's convictions - now he was doing time.

"So, at the moment I'm doing little jobs and living in apartments with monthly leases. Sometimes I do a bit of couch-surfing… but y'know, you've gotta hunker down when you set your sights high. There's this college that specifically has courses on charcoal drawing. Ooh - I'm totally going after THAT one." The gleam in her eye was bright and hungry.

She mentioned that she was catching a bus out of town, the next day. Clark wanted to ask for her number, but he couldn't. He knew that her characteristic, sweet friendliness would only change to polite boundaries. He knew what those boundaries would be. He accepted them. He wouldn't embarrass her, by making her state them out loud.

Of course, crossing boundaries was EXACTLY what she wanted. Then, maybe, things might develop to, "Hey, uh, Riley? Do you wanna go on a date?" or "My Lovely, would you have dinner with me? and then, perhaps, an evening of dancing?"

She dreamed of his steady voice, just like his warm blanket, saying, "Riley? Let's run away together. All I need is you." She had these girlish dreams that he'd love her, somehow, and they could just be together.

Dreams, she thought. He was so polite with that hug. He always is. Polite, and keeping his boundaries.

They talked at that party and preserved the space in between. She tried not to make him uncomfortable with giant, tackling hugs. She only smiled, chatted with him, and played with her hair.

The next morning, he sat bolt upright in bed. No - he'd ask for her number. He'd go straight to the bus station.

"Yeah," he said to himself. "Emails are too impersonal. Actual phone numbers? They mean something."

If he caught up with her at the bus station, it'd be a real gesture. Then, if she felt like it, maybe he could take her to lunch sometime…?

He drove to the bus station and checked his watch. 7:52am. Most of the outbound buses left in the early afternoon. Clark didn't care; he'd wait for her. Hell, he'd drive her to wherever she was going, if she'd let him.

The floors were cold and dusty. Echoes bounced everywhere. Parents herded their excited children and teenagers loped along with bulky packs. The holidays made everyone scramble; it was a beehive that had been whacked with a big, festive stick.

Hours dragged till 10:20am. Clark sighed, and wondered about breakfast. He thought about getting something at the café, inside the station, but he didn't want to miss her. He waited till a little past 11am, when there was a lull in traffic. He picked up a greasy egg sandwich on an English muffin. It dripped melted cheese.

"Wait, can I get two of these?" he asked. The young server with the nose-ring looked up at him and shrugged. A second egg sandwich plunked onto the countertop.

Yeah, Clark thought. She might be hungry. She might want something. And she likes root beer, doesn't she?

"And uhh… a root beer? Great. Thanks."

"Happy to be of service," the kid moaned.

By 2:28pm, the second egg sandwich wasn't even warm anymore. Its melted cheese went back to its natural plastic consistency.

Clark paced when his legs felt stiff, but otherwise he watched from the corner of the station. It was near the janitor's closet, and it had a view of the entire floor.

At 4:13pm, he realized that her egg sandwich wasn't appealing in the least. It became Clark's dinner. Clark caved and bought a newspaper. He watched for Riley for another few hours, looking up if anyone arrived. 5 o'clock? Nothing. 6, and then 7? No. She hadn't come.

About 9pm, a janitor arrived. He was bald, paunchy, and looked like his entire career had been in maintenance. He started his night shift by tidying up. He tossed a big cardboard box out from his closet. It was full of assorted junk. He nudged it over against the wall with his boot.

"Uhh," Clark rubbed his temples. "Excuse me, umm... have you seen a young woman here... twenty-two years old, maybe five-foot-six, with LONG, long brown hair?"

The janitor cocked his head to the side and stared at Clark.

"She was traveling. She was heading out today."

"Yeah," the man joked, "Traveling. Along with a couple others, y'know..."

"OKAY," Clark tried to keep patient. He stood tall. "Yeah, she's a friend, and-"

"Oh, you KNOW her? Oh, okay, then." He handled his broom and held back a smirk.

"Yeah, through high school."

"High school," the janitor noted.

"From frickin' GRADE THREE, man, and I need... to get a message to her. Wait, what's this box of stuff?"

"Lost an' found," he dipped his head. "Free, an' up for grabs. Every month, we toss whatever ain't been claimed. It's the end of the month, right? December? And I ain't in, for the next couple nights. Even I got holidays."

Clark noticed a little pink backpack with sparkles on it. He peered closer, and sure enough, the little pink backpack had "Riley Henway" scribbled on the front.

Clark staggered, recovered his feet, and plucked it from the box. She'd left already... but she'd forgotten something.

"Oh yeah," the old man mused. He bulged his cheek out with his tongue. His eyes were distant. "Yeah. Her. Pretty girl. 'Couple cute moles, like them fancy white-wig movies? Long brown hair, but short in the front? Dark eyes, bright sparkle?"

Clark paused. "SIR! Yes, that's who I'm looking for! When did you see her?"

"Ehh," he leaned on his broom handle, "She came in real late last night. She just slept on a bench, there. Over there."

He pointed with his finger. Clark's head swiveled.

"An' she got the first bus outta Ashvale at 5 in the mornin'. She woke up just in time. She jumped up, grabbed most of her things, and ran off. She was no hobo, or nothin'… she just…"

His face clouded over. Clark listened in agony.

"She just had nowhere to go. 'Shame for a nice girl like her to be alone. Especially during the holidays."

Clark slid his hand up past his brow. He clenched his fist and pulled his own hair.

"Yeah," the old guy continued. "Friend of yours? She was off and runnin' before I noticed her pink bag, here. She woulda went to Metro Station, I think. But after that, Lord only knows." He shrugged, and resumed sweeping.

Clark lifted the bag with gentle hands. It was an old pack, and her name was scribbled on the front in permanent marker. She must have written it when she was a kid.

Ahh, to heck with being proper, he thought. I'll open this, and I'll find out where she's going. Then I'll drop it off. It won't look too 'stalky,' will it?

He unzipped the little pink backpack and found a few essentials: a hair-dryer, a brush, and a little stuffed rabbit wearing a necktie. There was nothing else.

"Thanks," he called to the janitor.

"Yeh," the man dismissed him. He kept sweeping.

Clark went out to his car. After a day of waiting, it was now dark and the air had turned chilly. He got in his car and thumped the door shut. He flicked on the overhead light. He held up the pack to study it.

"There's nothing here," he thought out loud. "Nothing obvious enough. If I find some way to track her down, it'd just be creepy."

He started zipping up the pack. He gave a last look to the stuffed rabbit.

"Sorry, little guy. You're probably missed. But I promise: I won't lose you."

He carefully zipped the pack shut.

A few weeks went by. Clark couldn't think of any way to return her belongings without seeming creepy. He could've hired a private investigator, or checked academic records, or maybe designed a computer program to gather her digital footprints. He didn't want some stranger to follow her around, though, and he didn't know what school she went to. Her digital footprints would have been on the internet, but that was 'data mining.' That was for social media empires or government spooks.

A year passed. Clark kept her backpack safe, just in case he met her somewhere. After another year, he just kept it safer, and felt worse about it. At that time, he worked in a technical institute, designing prototypes. Riley was back in Ashvale, waiting tables.

Clark's work was becoming important enough that it needed security. He had a personal consultant: Matteo Landucci. Matteo's voice was smooth and smoky. He had a lean face and strong eyes. He was calm and easy-going, like a young lion relaxing in the shade… handsome; dangerous. He was well kept with dark hair slicked back. He wore tailored suits in a dark maroon color. They were dark enough that they wouldn't show sweat, or grime, or sometimes dried blood.

Elsewhere, Matteo was known as Agent Landucci. He was a government liaison. For Clark, he was security. For Clark's enemies, he was the shadow of death. Matteo was the next best thing to secret service. He truly WAS the 'man in the dark suit.'

One day, Clark got a surprising email. His morning coffee was still too hot to drink, so he was reading memos at his desk and sipping tentatively. He sipped, scrolled down through his email, read the usual boring legal stuff, and then there it was: Henway, Riley A.

He lurched forward and made a sound like "MBULP!" His hot coffee jumped down his throat and burned his chest on the inside. He breathed rapidly, trying to cool it, but remembered the email.

He shoved the pain aside. An email? From Riley?!

His world lit up like a Christmas tree. He panted through a giant, ecstatic smile. The thrill was wings to his soul. His sweet Riley... she wrote to him!

He read the email. The subject line killed him. He had a hard time with the rest.

She was getting married.

Everything fell. His whole life wore a terrible, dark fog. He saw nothing but grey.

"Hey - Clark...?"

It was his friend, Matteo.

"What the...? You look like crap, man."

Clark said nothing.

"Clark. 'The hell happened? You look like your house just burned down." He spoke in a dead-pan voice, but then reached out to him with quiet, genuine concern.

"Seriously. What just happened?"

"Uhh... just... an event I can't go to. A friend's getting, umm... married. And I won't be able to attend."

"Yeah, but you're even paler than usual. 'Close friend?"

"...Yeah," he whispered. He tried to cover by bending his brow and scowling: "Dammit. I wanted to go. It just sucks, when things..." His voice drifted away. "When... when things don't work out."

"Bull," Matt challenged him. "What is this? There's more happening here, and you're not saying. You don't lie, Clark, 'cuz you're a good man. But you

SHOULDN'T lie, 'cuz you suck at it. Is someone actually getting married?"

He sighed faintly. "…Yeah."

"Okay, so it's someone important. Wait, is it that GIRL? THAT one? Your 'closest non-relation,' for our Aegis contract? The… the brunette you try not to talk about?"

"YEAH, Matt. It's her. Okay? And she's getting married."

Matteo took a step backward. His heart broke clean in half. His eyes searched his friend as he shook his head in disbelief.

"Oh, man… I'm so sorry. Oh my God, I'm sorry." He stepped forward and carefully put his hand on Clark's shoulder. "Are you gonna be alright?"

Clark said nothing. He stared past his computer screen. His emails were a forgotten blur in front of him, but they felt like a distant echo behind him.

Matteo slowly pulled back his hand. He stood beside his friend and remained silent. He was security - the man in the dark suit - but he couldn't protect Clark this time. This one slipped through and wounded deep.

Oh no, Matteo thought. What the hell is gonna happen to him? Are we gonna lose him? Will he quit? Will he leave?

"Matteo?" came a weak voice. Clark hadn't moved. "It's over. All of it. It's just… nah, it's over."

Matteo's head dropped.

Clark spoke in quiet, measured words. "Look. I know you have friends in high places. You know people; you know military brass. I wanna work on something new. I want them in on it. Soon. Next week, maybe. Can you help me?"

"Ya," Matt confirmed eagerly. "Absolutely. But are you in any shape to do this?"

Clark ran his tongue through his cheek and nodded at the floor.

"Yeah," he decided. "Right now it's all I've got."

CHAPTER TWELVE
So Far Away

The wedding was gorgeous: roses and white streamers everywhere. Trellises had climbing flowers along the walls and archways. Everything entwined together like a lacework enchantment. The DJ was the groom's brother.

Riley braided-up her hair like a fairytale princess. Her gown had sashes pinned by tiny, silken, white roses. Her bridesmaids were three close friends from school and art class. Sadly, her mom and her new stepfather, Roger, couldn't attend. There was a conflict with Roger's schedule. The only true family there, for Riley, was her grandmother Faye.

The groom had many, many friends attending; he introduced more than twenty of his best college buddies. The evening was all frat handshakes, and then wild stories from college years. Gran waved politely at the boys, and went to sit with Riley. The boys were occupied with themselves.

No-one saw Clark. He hadn't responded, and he didn't attend. Two of the bridesmaids joked about it. Riley was strangely flattered.

Clark, she thought. He couldn't come. But he WOULD go to a friend's wedding. He'd even go to an acquaintance's wedding. I know him; he would. He's honest; he's loyal; he... he avoided my wedding? He didn't even reply. Did I upset him? Was it awkward, somehow? Was it that night? Was it prom night? or maybe... did he have some kind of attachment to me?

She had one more secret locked inside - another secret about her love for Clark. This was the last day she'd worry about it. Today was the first day of the rest of her life. She was married.

Clark... She smiled faintly, during the reception. Ohh, Clark, Sweetheart. I guess you'll never know. WE'LL never know, will we? The candle has flickered, and now it's gone.

She kept her secret hidden. It was safe there, inside her. She'd keep it safe forever. Nobody would ever know.

Granny Faye sat beside her. She was tiny, and darker-faced, and sweet. And she knew everything.

"It's okay, Sweetie." She patted Riley's arm with an air-light touch. Her hands were feathers of kindness.

"Yeah, it's a big day, today." Riley tried to smile back. "But I'll be alright. It's a beginning."

"No, I mean… it's okay. It's okay, Wee Riley." She smiled up to her, sadly.

"I know." Riley stated this flatly. "Today means a lot to my life. I'm just…"

Gran was still looking at her.

"Yeah, Gran? I kinda feel like I'm saying goodbye to my past…? It scares me a little."

Gran smiled. "Things have a way of working out, me dear. It's true. There's no difference, Honeysweet, between the things that are meant to be and the things that happen."

Riley didn't completely follow, but was glad to have her company. Granny Faye meant well.

She looked up at Riley with a new smile.

"Me dear? You know why I keep the company of cats?"

Riley grinned back with big, moony eyes.

"Uhh… maybe 'cuz you're the cover girl for *Crazy-Cat-Lady Illustrated?*"

Gran cuffed Riley on the shoulder. It was a wedding, otherwise it would've been the back of her head.

"You listen, you cheeky little imp!" Her eyes and wrinkles tightened. They knew things. "You listen. Listening is what this is all about. My cats know things. They hear it on the wind. They're like weathervanes for intuition - for spirit and wind. This is a skill that people forgot. Really. Now, more than ever."

Riley watched. She couldn't blink.

"You keep listening, Wee Riley. Listen to the wind. There's life in everything, always, like the coals beneath the ash. Like the stars, after daylight. You be sure to listen, and you'll be sure to learn."

Riley's eyes were lonely.

"BREATHING is wind, too, you know... so there are subtle things with you, every moment of your life. It's in the flow of things. It's the beauty of still rivers."

No, her breath felt more like a habit.

"Your wedding is a weighty affair. But don't forget to enjoy TODAY. You only live it once."

Granny was either nodding subtly, or her Parkinson's was acting up again. She had Parkinsonian side effects from her medications.

"And I know your heart, me dear. You're a bright light. The right things will come to you. They have to; they will. That's how truth works. Otherwise, there wouldn't be truth AT ALL in this world."

"Yeah. I guess so." Life hadn't been fabulous yet.

"You'll need to take my word, until you get to my age. I've seen enough years, I've learned to read them."

She looked at Riley with kindness and confidence.

"Yeah," she replied. "Gran? I'm married, now. This is my happy wedding. I'm fine."

Granny Faye leaned in beside her.

"I know," she smiled closely. "I know."

Granny Faye knew things, as if she'd dug a well right down to the truth... or whatever was running deep. She tried to explain what was real, despite the limitations of words. She sounded like a crazy old cat lady. Still, Riley's new step-father always kissed Faye's hand, and her mom would always touch her shoulder, while walking by. It was a respect like superstition; Granny knew things.

Granny Faye shared an apartment with three cats: Muriel, Angus, and Vincent. They always perched somewhere nearby, and watched things... a lot. They were like the three ravens at the witch's house - watchers, roosting in the eaves.

A few weeks after the wedding, Gran was in her apartment sorting her bookshelves. Vincent suddenly looked up at her. He stared intently.

"What is it, Sugar Plum?"

"Mraak," he squawked at her. Immediately, the phone rang. Granny answered quickly. It was Riley.

"Oh!" Gran started. "Hello there, me dear! Very nice to hear from you!"

"Hi, Gran? Do you have a few minutes to talk?"

"Aww, I've had too many idle years, Sweetie. Of course. Let's talk. For as long as you like. Oh, I think Vincent says 'Hello.' He's smiling at the sound of your voice."

In the background, Vincent yapped loudly.

"Granny... you know how good things are supposed to happen?" Her voice twisted tight. "They're supposed to, right?"

"They do. They do. And it's good to believe in them, along the way. 'Makes life easier.'" She smiled thoughtfully.

Riley explained the tension with her new husband. Twice in the last week, he was late coming home from work. According to him, he 'lost track of time.' That was why he came in the door after ten o'clock... smelling like perfume. He gave no other explanation.

"Well, Honeysweet, you're a beautiful, charming young woman. It's better for HIM if he notices that." Gran was firm on that point.

Riley wasn't as sure: "I'm worried that I'm just not... Like, we met at work, and he asked for my number, and things began fast. But I want this to live, Gran. I want this whole marriage to survive."

Granny Faye went quiet, then she spoke plainly.

"Riley? You want to be loved. By all rights, you absolutely should be. Anyone with brains would know they're blessed to have you. I'M here for you. You know that."

"Thanks, Gran. I, uh... It's pretty hard sometimes, y'know?"

Riley's breath quickened, then jerked. She held the phone away, but Gran heard her sniffle on the other end.

Granny Faye took a moment. "You're what, twenty-one years old?"

"Twenty-FOUR, Grandma..."

"OH, dear me! We could be roommates, then! Two retired old bitties, in an old folks' home?"

Riley sniffed, then grumbled at her. "Ya - sorry, Gran. I don't have the qualifications, yet. And I've got this social event… it's called 'My Life.' I still gotta attend that."

Gran tipped her head.

"You're not late to the party YET, Bright-Eyes. YOU. Riley. You, with the lovely hair, and the fresh pink in the cheeks. There's a simple thing to remember, Honeysweet. When the prize is still ahead of you, how can you say you've lost?"

Riley took a step back for perspective.

"Granny?" She sniffled again. "Gran, I think I messed up. Y'know at my wedding, when you talked with me? And I was nervous about the day? Like something from the past was still inside me? Well, something's still troubled, in there."

Her voice trembled.

"Someone got lost, Granny Faye. It's like hope - a little light, still alive inside, and… and I miss it… and I…"

Granny Faye listened.

"And," Riley struggled. "And I think I really miss him!"

"I know, Sweetie." Gran's smile was unmistakable.

"You don't even…" Riley's face twisted. "Wait, do you even know who I'm talking about?"

"Not by name, Sweetheart. But I know."

The two women shared an unspoken moment. They sat together and listened. The phone recorded dead air over a distance, but they heard it for what it was: understanding.

"Granny Faye?"

"Mmm-hmm?"

"…His name is Clark. I've known him all my life, but I WANT to know him for the rest of it. It's that kind of thing."

Gran waited and let the seconds fall in silence, one after the other. They were footsteps taking Riley where she needed to go.

"Gran? It's like he's always beside me, even when he's gone. He always felt that way, to me."

Gran nodded. She smiled sadly. "I know, Sweetie."

Riley stayed true to her course. She trusted her new husband, even if her smiles were staged. It was more Riley's nature to go completely off script; she'd be boldly honest, and run to Clark, and throw herself down at his feet. She'd declare to him, 'I LOVE you, Clark! I've ALWAYS loved you, and I need you to know! Clark Benjamin, my heart belongs to you. This is my life, and you are my dream, and I LOVE YOU!'

Then, when Clark lifted her from the ground, she would rise into his kiss. Her feet would dangle beneath her, and he'd just hold her there, because she belonged. They'd kiss, and they'd kiss, and time would bow its head in respect. He'd hold her hands, and look to her. Their eyes would dance in that perfect moment.

She thought of this often. This was how she survived kissing her husband, and she spent a few years this way. She convinced herself that "honesty" meant being faithful. In truth, it meant something else entirely.

After those long years, Clark saw her on the sidewalk. He was driving through their hometown of Ashvale. She was right there, on those plain concrete squares. She was walking with her four-year-old son.

Clark was visiting Ashvale to see his mom. He was thinking of moving back to take better care of her. When he saw Riley, he quickly changed his mind. He turned a corner, drove numbly up the street, and stopped at a traffic light. He lowered his eyes. Darkness closed around him.

His thoughts circled like ominous black birds. She had her own life; she chose her life; this was her choice. She was married, and now she had a son. She'd never leave or betray a marriage. She'd be devoted to her son, unlike some parents. Unlike certain fathers, that is.

Riley had made her choice. It was clear that she hadn't chosen him.

Behind him, a car blared its horn. Clark looked up; the light was a green-eyed cyclops. It cheerfully told him to move on. Move on! Move on, Clark! Past this crossroads! Move on!

He drove straight through.

Never in his whole life had Clark seen roads so grey. They looked like they'd died. Color was gone, like the blood from a corpse. The yellow dashed lines were an afterthought, like pale thread holding a seam.

He left Ashvale Plains.

CHAPTER THIRTEEN
STRANGE MEN IN SUITS

Riley didn't hear about the attempt on Clark's life. His research had attracted powerful investors and even government interest. Some investors were more scrupulous than others.

He'd been working on experimental containment for energy. It wasn't meant for power grids or batteries. It was an idea he'd had when he was much younger: a science fiction movie had soldiers in special armor, but the armor was actually a robotic suit. It made the soldiers nearly invincible and frighteningly strong.

At the time, Clark didn't acknowledge his own vulnerability. His ruthless work ethic often kept him up past 4am. Co-workers said he was obsessed.

Who cares? he thought. I'm not good enough for her; I'll focus on whatever I have left.

He earned his first million in his late twenties. When he realized he was a millionaire, he laughed bitterly. It was all delusion.

One weekend, he locked himself in his laboratory. He secured the back-up power for the building so he couldn't be interrupted. He brewed pot after pot of coffee and worked for two-and-a-half days straight. He finished late on Monday morning. After he crashed and slept for six hours, he called his lawyer. He'd just changed the value of his company's stock. He'd taken electrodynamic engineering to a new level.

Then, a week later, he was walking back to his car. The parking garage smelled like motor oil. Quick footsteps echoed on cold cement. Clark had his briefcase in one hand and picked through his keychain in the other.

"Clark Benjamin? Hey... Mr Benjamin?" Two young men in blazers walked toward him, smiling. Their blazers didn't fit well. Their black ties were knotted hastily.

Clark couldn't recognize them. "Uhh... sorry?"

The taller man asked plainly: "Are you Clark Benjamin? Y'know, the...?"

Clark tightened his hold on his briefcase.

"Mr Benjamin, we're representatives from..." and he extended his hand to shake.

Clark saw himself at a disadvantage. One hand would be held in place, and his other hand would be full. The shorter man was already pacing around to his side. Clark watched what was actually happening.

He knew they were taking position. Unfortunately, his eyes gave him away.

Their shoes scuffed the gritty pavement. Shorty flicked open a knife and shot it at Clark's chest. The briefcase whipped upward, and the knife only pierced leather and wood. Clark bent his briefcase, twisting the knife away, and beat it down against Shorty's hand. The knife swayed loose and dropped to the ground. It hit the cement with a tinny clatter.

Mr Taller was fast. He planted his hand over Clark's throat, crowded inward, and put his knife through Clark's belt-line.

Clark grunted and winced. When he staggered, he kicked the other loose knife under the car.

No, Clark thought. I'm built better than that.

Mr Taller pulled the knife free. Clark's feet shifted. He fumbled again for his keys.

Shorty stepped up to grab him. "You friggin' gook-eyed piece of..."

He'd hold Clark down so Mr Taller could get the job done.

Instead, Clark grabbed his keys, swung his briefcase in a wide arc, and turned with it. His alarm honked. He yanked the door open.

Again, feet scratched against the ground, and Mr Taller cursed. Clark barely dropped into the car and pulled up his legs - and thumped the door shut. He squeezed his key-fob, and the doors locked with a loud thud. The two attackers loomed darkly against the window.

Clark clutched his abdomen, where he'd been cut… no, stabbed. Stabbed deep. Blood dribbled on his keys when he slotted them in the ignition. He twisted. The engine chattered and hummed to life.

BOOM… Mr Taller elbowed against his window. He reached back to strike again.

BOOMTKT, the window crunched.

Clark moaned, revved the car and squealed off. He left them behind, chasing and swearing. Their blazers rattled loosely on their shoulders.

Clark's voice was a broken squawk. "911," he wheezed into his smartphone.

"I'm sorry," said his voice recognition. "Could you repeat that?"

"NO," Clark snarled bitterly. He thumbed his cell while he drove.

"911? I need medical attention… no, I can't say where I am. I'm en route to the… Metro Central Hospital… It's a stab wound. What? LOOK, if I start to pass out, I'll pull over, but not before! Just bring some damn gauze!"

Since that incident, his work received better attention. Government interests snatched him up. He was immediately enrolled in a witness protection program, and Matteo Landucci was assigned as his personal security advisor.

He had no idea who'd tried to murder him. He had a quiet social life. He assumed his work upset a balance… or someone's balance book.

"What? W-W-… HOW?" Jeff Anders screamed

into his smartphone. "But there were TWO of you, and you had frickin' KNIVES! Wait, I bet he even saw your faces, right? And then he got away with EVERYTHING..." Jeff paced. He clenched his empty fist.

"What? No, I was kidding. Did he actually see your faces? Wh... Oh, right. Of course. Because you had to get in CLOSE. With knives. So he definitely saw you."

Jeff huffed into his phone.

"Did you get anything at ALL? ...Nothing?" He bunched up his lips. "No, there's no pardon, or reduced sentences, or anything. You get paid bare minimum, because you FAILED. Really - two goons with knives can't take down one nerd?"

His phone muttered something.

"No," he growled. "No family. Leave 'em alone for now."

Jeff blew out his lips.

"All you had to do was GUT that big sack of meat, and steal his research... but you got made, and you have nothing. For God's sake, he's just one guy."

The phone squawked weirdly, in protest.

"I don't give a damn if he was intense! You didn't keep your side of the deal. I'm destroying this phone, and I won't be talking to you again." Jeff bleeped his smartphone off. He watched until the screen went black.

He stopped, then rolled his eyes and tapped his smartwatch. He emailed a friend who was a jeweler, and asked to use her crucible again. His smartphone needed to be melted down.

Jeff Anders was running for public office. Unfortunately, Clark still knew about the conspiracy to rape Riley. Clark knew about the drug possession. He could ruin the Anders name.

Jeff used $60,000 of election funds to pay hired killers. Two men had been convicted of manslaughter and needed bail money. Jeff counted on Clark's research to recoup costs. The murder flopped, Jeff lost his money, and now Clark would be on guard.

In a fit of rage and frustration, Jeff went drinking. All night, he bullied his driver and stumbled through club after club. All he could remember was swatting waitresses on the behind and calling them "dirty tramps." He woke up in a messy hotel room with a young, brunette hooker.

He kicked 'Sera' out of his room and tried to find his clothes. Everything stank like vodka, even the blankets. He texted his driver with his watch, got dressed, and then slung his coat over his shoulders. Something clumped against his ribs.

"Wha…? Ya, 'kay, what the hell is this?"

In his inside pocket, he found a .38 caliber revolver. It still had four bullets loaded in it. He couldn't find its serial number.

Jeff spun on his heel and called after Sera. Where the…? Did he…? What ever possessed him to buy a damned gun, especially on the black market?

"Uhh… 'Kay, Sera? SERA!"

He stopped and clamped his mouth shut. The hooker said nothing, so she probably knew nothing.

He ducked down and sniffed the barrel.

No, he puzzled. Not fired recently. No smoky smell. Only four bullets? It's always two bullets per person, right? So, 'one-two,' for one person, and then 'one-two' for another.

Clark... is he married? Who's he with? or is there someone else I need to silence? Maybe Riley, herself? Well, yeah - anyone who dares to insult me. Maybe in her last moments, she'll finally give me respect.

Jeff stood straight. The revolver weighed heavily inside his coat, and he rather liked it. It was a big, metal hard-on that he could whip out and kill people with. Was he actually considering murder? Apparently, yes. He'd just made a down payment. If he was in this deep, he'd have to see it through.

In the past, one of Jeff's relatives mentioned a certain boardroom. It was a lesser known board that controlled business by managing people. Often, those people were never seen again.

Jeff knew this boardroom was in another state, and it was difficult to find, but that was intentional. He decided to find them. Maybe he'd join them.

"I shoulda gotten something nicer," he mused aloud. "Maybe a decorative handle? Maybe ivory, or whatever. This is such a peasant gun."

Jeff realized he could be stronger than Clark and better than Riley. He now had the power to make that final, and make it stay that way forever: BANG.

CHAPTER FOURTEEN
ASTROPHYSICS

After three more years, Clark was living in Ashvale Plains again. He wanted to help his mother, and he liked the quiet. The government even gave him a big, secure house to live in. He only hoped he could hide from HER.

One evening, he and Matteo sat in a tavern. They had a weathered, wooden table in the back. The whole place smelled like french fries and lager. The carpets were ancient; their pea-green color had faded over the decades.

Clark had his mineral water in a tall, skinny bottle, and Matteo had a beer. Clark wiped back his bangs whenever they went rogue in the sweaty air. Matteo's hair was slicked back cleanly. He looked young and neat.

The men talked about new security measures.

They talked vaguely about portfolios and completed contracts. They listened to clinking glasses around them; it helped with the silences.

After working together for eight years, Matteo finally asked a hard question.

"So. You never talk about her, ever. But she's really important to you, huh?"

Clark gave him a look, and Matteo respectfully backed off. He set his beer down gently.

"Yeah," he added. "I know. My girlfriend was pretty important to me, before we split. And yeah, I really missed her."

Clark shook his head. "You'll find someone, Matt. Don't even think about being lonely; lonely's not gonna happen to you. You're too young, and you look too good in a suit. You'll find someone. Even in Ashvale."

Matteo spread his fingers along the tabletop. He took a slow breath.

"Yeah. Well, I might've. Last weekend, in fact."

"Told ya," Clark chuckled darkly.

Matt fiddled with his bottle, turning it in circles. He spun it with his fingertips. His tongue ran through his teeth like he was counting them.

Clark nudged his head up. "So, Matt... what's she like?"

Matteo scratched his brow.

"Uhh... well," he began, "we just met on the weekend, totally by chance. It was a complete surprise, but we have serious chemistry. We totally do, and we both know it."

"Nice." Clark managed to smile at him.

Matteo blushed a little. "We almost kissed, man...! We only talked for an hour or two, and..." His eyes floated amongst stars.

Clark's smile lines grew. His face hardened around a grin.

"Awesome," he concluded. He stared at his friend.

There was a tense moment. Matteo's brow squeezed tight. He ducked down like he was making an apology.

"Yeah," Matteo admitted. "He's beautiful."

Clark didn't move. A quiet moment passed, and Matteo slowly looked up.

"Are you okay, Clark?"

Clark didn't blink. "Yeah. Fine. What's he like?"

Matteo spoke softly around a young, shy grin.

"Look, dude, this is new to me. And none of my friends know about this - certainly none of my family. You're, like, the first person I admitted this to, alright? There's you... and there's my bathroom mirror. That's it. And I still don't understand, myself."

Clark shrugged easily.

"W... you don't even seem fazed. Are you... do you know about stuff like this? I mean, you're not like most people, Clark."

"No, I'm average. Straight. So I don't understand much."

Matteo shook his head softly.

"Uhh... I don't know, either. I just know how I felt. How WE felt. It was sudden, and I... and it was real. And it really surprised me. We even planned... We're actually gonna have dinner together!" Matteo smiled brightly with a tiny gust of laughter. Then he swallowed tensely. His eyes dropped to the floor. He went quiet.

Clark reached for his arm and added, "I'm sorry, bro. There are some things I'll never understand. You're an awesome guy, Matt, and a great friend, and I professionally trust you with my life. I'm really sorry I can't understand this WITH you."

He looked at Matteo kindly. "I can't understand, but that means I sure-as-hell can't judge you."

Matteo chuckled and rattled his beer bottle against the table. He looked up with his strong eyes, and the men shared a brief smile.

"And here I was, thinking you knew everything," Matt joked.

"Naw, it's like stars, man. Astrophysics," Clark explained. "I'm no astrophysicist. I'm no authority on the subject. It's the same with gay love."

Clark sat up. "I mean, look at gravity. I dunno how gravity really works, in astrophysics. I have no idea. There's just something-something about heavenly bodies, and then there's this natural force of attraction..."

Matteo chortled and dropped his head.

Clark scowled a little. His dimple gleamed.

"Hey, don't laugh! I don't understand gravity! All

I know is, it's natural, it's invisible, but it's always been there." He spoke proudly, "And it's partly responsible for keeping this world together. People DO rely on it, without even knowing. 'Cuz it's everywhere. So I accept it.

"I don't know it, but it's part of everything. So I love it, just as I'd love Creation."

Matteo chuckled back.

"So gay love is everywhere, and holds everything together? and people rely on it, even if it's invisible to them? Whaddya you think this is, Clark? You think this is 'The Force,' or something?"

"No, dude," he leveled with him. "You protect me. You keep me alive. You're a pillar of my world, Matt, and you love someone out there. So, yeah… gay love is definitely a part of my life."

Clark stopped and looked at him gravely.

"And Matt? We're always making discoveries in astrophysics. Respect those people at the forefront. They're brave, and I respect them from the heart."

Matteo nodded happily. Then he shook his head.

"You're SO WEIRD, Clark…"

Clark held his head high and spoke dramatically, like from a soap-box, "And yet, my good man, you accept me. That is so very fair of you." He closed his eyes warmly.

Matteo scoffed. He gazed down at the tabletop for a while.

Glasses clinked around them. Waitresses carried drinks. A radio played country music or blues in the background; whichever it was, it was drowned out by the evening chatter.

The two men had a thoughtful moment.

"What am I gonna tell my mom, Clark? What do I tell my brother? or, like, other people who know me? the people I work with?"

Clark struggled. His head tossed side to side.

"Go out to dinner, man! Jeez! You have a date! Start with that, and maybe someday tell your family that you've found love, and that you're happy."

Matteo's eyebrows lifted. "I found WHAT, though? Am I 'this,' now? Will anyone accept it? It's not who they know. This new 'real me' is gonna look fake."

"Matt, there is no 'this.' You don't fit in any box. You're young, handsome, and your name is Matteo. And you LOVE someone out there. That's the greatest gift a human being can give."

They sat together in silence. Matteo tried to say something else, but stopped.

Clark spoke in a low, grave voice. "Trust me, Matteo. Love is your strong suit. You could lie, and live a lie, and live in misery for someone else's convenience... or you can be brave, and be real about it, and live real. It'll be hard, but believe me: love is bigger and stronger, anyway. It's way bigger than any of us."

"Yeah," Matteo licked his lips. "It'll be big news, alright. Maybe a dividing point. I don't want to lose my family, okay?"

"No," Clark said carefully. "Your family has to accept something, but it's easier for them. Your mom has a gay son. He's solid, and he's professional, and he's a fantastic guy, and he's in love with a man. She may not get it, but it all comes down to accepting what you don't know. It comes down to love, all over again. It's faith in the people you care about."

Matteo released a sigh of irritation. Clark tried to continue.

"Can your mom 'not know,' and still love you? 'Cuz that's all it is."

Matteo held his beer bottle. His fingernails pecked the glass. His head sank down.

"Okay. So what's the truth here, man? Am I really gay, and I never knew it? Or, like... did something just HAPPEN to me, somewhere along the line?"

Clark smirked, then laughed.

"I'd say so! You fell in love, you poor schmuck! THAT happened. That's as serious as it ever gets!"

Clark took a swig of his mineral water and Matteo lifted his head again. He looked aside and drummed his hands down on the tabletop.

"Psh..." he rolled his eyes. "Sure, Clark. Live real? Well, what about you? Are you gonna talk to her? like, EVER?" He blinked for emphasis.

Clark stopped. This question killed him. His chest caved in. He crawled across the lowest floors of loneliness. His eyes were old and tired; he closed them.

Matteo backed up. "I'm sorry, man. I just… we both…"

"We're both stuck here," Clark said. "But talk to her? Me? No. I won't. At least, I really hope not."

Matteo's eyes softened and wrinkles hugged up from his cheeks.

"I'm sorry, man. I didn't mean that. I'm just freakin' out. Last weekend, I learned something huge about myself. I'm still in shock. Sorry."

Clark waited, then came to his conclusion.

"In my case, she got married and had a kid with someone. I know I love her - and I always will - but my reality is, we're apart. I have to honor that. I have to protect that distance, BECAUSE I love her so much.

"I love her profoundly, Matteo, and it's why I can't tell her."

The men sat quietly. Other patrons clinked their glasses and talked. The music could've been country, blues or folk; it was difficult to tell. It was a heartfelt song, and it didn't matter what genre it was.

Clark finally nudged at his friend. "Hey, Matt?"

"Ya?"

"I really gotta ask you something, man."

"Yeah. Of course." Matteo sat straighter.

Clark chewed on his tongue, looked up to Matteo's eyes, and smiled curiously. He opened his palms.

He asked with a bright and eager grin:

"Bro - SERIOUSLY, what's he like?"

CHAPTER FIFTEEN
THE WIND SPEAKS

Then, Clark met her again. He met Riley again, completely by chance. It was early autumn. Something blew on the wind.

Her seven-year-old son was struggling with a toy plane in the park - it wouldn't fly, no matter how much he tried. Riley sat on a bench at the edge of the park, under a tree. She was scribbling in a balance book. She wiped the hair back from her brow. She checked over her book, and checked again. She hesitated, then crossed something out. And then something else.

She sighed.

She crossed out "Halloween Party?" followed by "new winter coat." She kept "Albert, Christmas."

Her balance book didn't care. It stared back at her blankly. Her mouth tightened - smiles were locked out. She was alone.

Clark didn't see her, at first.

A plastic yellow plane clattered and cartwheeled, and scuffed in the dirt. It scratched to a stop by Clark's feet. A young boy chased after it. He had unruly, curly brown hair.

"Dude. Kid. See those flap things?" Clark wore his dark longcoat and hat.

The child stopped and looked at him skeptically.

"Ailerons, man. They're called 'ailerons.' Arright?"

"Aliens?"

"NOooo - aww, I wish!" He grinned heartily at the boy. "Then it'd be flying saucers an' stuff. That'd be really cool... but naw. See these flaps on the wings? Ailerons. And the other flaps on the tail? Those are elevators. If you want your plane to climb, just bend 'em a little. And there's a negative pressure area, too. Air pulls the wings upward. It's complicated, but..."

He reached, picked up the plane in his hands, and adjusted its flaps.

"Lookit. See, if this is bent up like this... and the wing is curvy like this, right?"

The little boy peered over with fascination. Clark demonstrated how airfoils worked.

"See, the air just flowwwwwws..." He mimicked a hippie. "It flowwwws, mannn."

The kid snickered. Young laughter made Clark glow inside.

"It's all the same air, right? But when there's

negative air," he wafted his hand up, "WE swoop in, to fill the space. That's us."

He elbowed toward the kid. "We're the plane, dude. We go where we're meant to go. And that's how an airfoil works."

The kid tilted his head, and then he knew.

"It kinda…" he clinched his little eyebrows. "So maybe in… in AIR, it 'sucks,' but not the bad way." His little dark eye sparked. He was already joking about physics.

Clark waited, swelled, and then laughed out loud.

"Smartest kid ever! How old are you, big guy?"

"I'm seven. But I'm already in grade four."

"Waaaaaaat?" Clark eyeballed him with big, silly amazement.

"I skipped a grade," the kid explained proudly.

"You what? You did?" Clark leaned forward, "Well, no wonder you understand everything."

"Albert!" A weakened voice rang across the field.

"Hey, is that you, Mr Brain? Yeah, you better go check on your mum."

Clark's head lowered again. Then, as the boy pattered off, Clark turned and caught his attention.

"Ay. Kiddo. Grade FOUR? That's AWESOME. Y'know, there was an inventor, once, named Albert. I bet you'll be smarter than him." Clark looked down his glasses and arched his brows.

Albert called back proudly, "Sure, I could soar like an eagle - but I'd rather be quick, like a weasel!" He shot up his finger to make his point.

No, Clark thought. No. It couldn't be. How did he...? Is that...?

But sure enough, he watched the boy running back to his mum - to the most beautiful woman Clark had ever seen. It was her. Riley Henway.

Clark fumbled with his briefcase and got ready to leave. That was the end of his peaceful day at the park. All the stress returned, and then some. It piled onto him like a ton of nails, and now it was slowly, grindingly ripping him in half. He got up, turned, and started walking.

"Umm," said a fairy-soft voice. "Excuse me? So, you met my son?" Her voice was gentle, but protective.

Clark's face dropped. He shook his head and waved out his hand. He walked away. Behind him, she scoffed lightly.

"He knows about aliens," Albert pronounced happily. "He's kinda funny."

How funny? she thought. Goofy funny? Laughing funny? Or luring-kids-in-the-park kinda funny?

Her voice declared boldly: "HI... I don't think we've met."

Oh yes, said his heart. Yes we have.

She wouldn't move. He was trapped. She saw him, now, and she was going to recognize him. He teetered on the edge. He choked, like there was an angry bullfrog lodged half-way down his throat. He couldn't even look at her... but he had to. It would kill him, inside, but he had to.

He owed it to her - it was respect. He respected her, always.

Always.

He swallowed, took a deep breath... looked at his emotional cliff... and jumped.

"Riley?" he asked meekly.

"CLARK?" She walked up and took his arm. She faced him and spotted sudden tears. They were fresh tears running down, shivering as they fell from his jaw.

"Oh my GOD... Clark? What...?"

"He fixed my airplane," Albert squeaked.

She turned for half a second. "He what? Fix...? Yeah, he does that." She turned back again. "Clark, why won't you talk with-"

He nudged his head up: "Where's your husband."

Riley's shoulders fell. She curled her lip bitterly.

"I dunno. Ask Naomi, or Gigi, or Monique."

"Oh," Albert moaned. He looked away with disdain. "They're buncha filthy slots."

"ALB-...!" Riley spun at him. She pursed her lips and looked at Clark again. "Uhh, yeah. Well, what he means is..."

"Thanks, Albert," Clark nodded politely. "I get the picture. Are YOU okay, though? How do you feel about your dad? Are you alright?"

"He's just stupid," the kid replied.

Riley huffed. She corrected him, "He... Daddy left your mum, but he's not-"

"He's STUPID," Albert repeated, pouting with

finality. "He's stupid, and I don't even like him."

Clark listened attentively. Albert noticed this - an actual adult wanted to hear him! His little feet stepped around so he could face Clark.

"Teacher says not to lie, and Dad lied. All the time. ALL. THE. TIME." Albert shrugged right up to ears. "If he lies, he didn't even do school! So ya, that means he's STUPID. Ugh!" The kid rolled his eyes in a big, slow, wide orbit.

Clark watched him: huge, brown eyes; exaggerated expression; goofy humor in emotional hardship. Clark recognized this like an old friend.

Albert capped it off with a summary: "Ya. Stupid. So what." He fiddled with the ailerons on his plane, then paused and looked up. "Did he hurt you? Is that how come you're crying?"

Clark looked further downward. A deep, calm voice came to the surface.

"No, dude. Your dad didn't hurt me." He turned to Riley. "No. Not your dad."

Riley panicked. Inside her throat, she felt rumbling. A train was moments away from being a wreck. This was about prom night, and the wedding he avoided, and things that even Clark wouldn't tell the truth about.

"…Mom, why is the man crying? He fixed my airplane, an' it's fine. Did I do something wrong?"

Clark spoke immediately. "NO, Albert. You didn't do anything wrong. Not at all. You're a good kid. Never forget that, okay?"

Riley's lips tried to make sounds, but they couldn't. Her hand lit on her son's tiny shoulder. She gently pulled him back. She watched Clark change, like he'd given up somehow. She'd never seen him look so broken.

He looked at Albert candidly. "Albert? When I was about your age, I actually MET your mom. Yeah. I met your mom way back then. And now - she and I? We're both older than THIRTY. So that means I met her quite a while ago, don't you think?"

Albert could do the math, but he wouldn't understand. He didn't know what decades felt like. He couldn't, yet. Clark knew. Riley knew.

"Yeah, that was a long time ago, buddy. But I remember meeting her. I do. And I'll tell you the absolute truth, Albert: she was the most beautiful, beautiful woman I had ever seen - EVER - in my entire grade three class."

He nodded for emphasis. Albert listened carefully. Riley listened breathlessly. Sun-flares of panic and exhilaration flashed through her.

Clark bit his lip. He smiled sadly and looked down at the kid.

"And I fell in love with her, Albert."

"W-...Clark?" Riley's world turned upside down and shook. She fell off.

"Yeah. In grade three, and then grade four, and all the way up till..." Clark acted puzzled. He held his chin comically, like he was deep in thought. The kid started grinning.

He looked down to Albert, and concluded, "Till yesterday, even. Yup. I was in love with her yesterday."

Riley grit her teeth. "Clark, don't do this. Not around my kid. Could we, like, maybe, talk some-"

Clark cleared his throat and continued. He nodded to Albert.

"Your mom, you see, is a VERY special person."

"I know," he grinned. "An' I love her, and she loves me back." He twisted in place, spinning left and right, like getting a big hug.

"Kid? She's more special than angels, even. Why? Because, just like you, there's only ONE. Just one Albert... and only one Riley Ann Henway."

The kid stopped swinging and listened.

"There's only one in all of existence, and I'm blessed that I live in this world, and in this time. I got to meet her. So my life was blessed. Better than angels."

She was a bystander for this conversation, but she now she knew CLARK had been a bystander for her whole life.

"I know this," he continued. "I know it in my heart - in my safest place. I mean 'safe,' like... even like your own room, where you keep your superheroes."

"They're dinosaurs," he corrected.

"But I bet they're super-dinosaurs." Clark pointed his finger. "Right. Like Albert-osaurus, only it's Albert-osaurus Rex?"

Albert grinned white with big brown eyes. Clark made a mental note.

"I always miss her, Albert. Grade three, and graduation, and when your mom and dad got married. Every day. Even today. Even when I was fixing your airplane."

"My airplane? You even missed her then? Like, a minute ago?"

"Of course I did. Definitely."

Clark closed his eyes. His jaw set strong, even though he stood on the ruins of his heart.

"I miss her forever, Albert. That's kinda what love feels like. So that's why I might look a little sad."

Albert stayed quiet. He'd learned something very real.

"I'm glad you love her, and that she loves you back. That's very important."

Riley glimpsed years and years of pain. She felt her insides drop, like her gut splashed onto her shoes.

Clark smirked. "But I think I'm okay now. I got to see your mom again, which was nice. And I got to meet you, right? So I feel better, because… well, I think you understand me. You know why I'm a little sad."

Clark stood straight.

"You're a cool guy, Albert, and you understand me. That makes me feel a lot better." He gave his best smile. "Thanks. It was really nice meeting you."

Riley somehow managed to close her jaw. Clark still wouldn't make eye contact. He took a deep breath, nodded respectfully toward her, and turned to walk away.

I'll never have to face that again, he thought. At least now she knows.

She swatted her kid's back, jovially. "HEY, uh - Albert? C'n you go grab my pencil, back there?" She couldn't look away. She pointed aimlessly toward her bench at the edge of the park. The kid beetled off as fast as his little legs could carry him.

Clark handled his briefcase and shrugged. "Okay, well… sue me. I'm not going to lie to a good kid. I can try to keep it light, but I've felt strongly about you for the last-"

Riley grabbed his shirt and yanked. Her lips took him.

Finally, when they were in their thirties, they met.

Her lips were warm and true. They anchored him there, just for that moment. He couldn't run away. He couldn't turn his head. She made him wait, as she told HER SIDE of their story together. This kiss didn't say 'hello.' It said 'For All My Life, Clark Benjamin.'

She stood with him there, and taught him what her dreams felt like. Her dreams were tall, and brilliant, and powerful. That's who her dreams really were. Finally, she could tell him everything - so she kissed from the heart.

At last, after painting his lips, she stopped with a tiny, wet click. They held each other. They looked to each other. They slowly, silently nodded. Their eyes agreed about unspoken things. There were so many

things that could've been; things that should've
been... things that were meant to be, but never
happened. Granny Faye knew all about these things.
When you really know them, it's called "faith." To
Riley and Clark, it had just happened out loud.

He barely whispered, "Well, that was-"

"-unexpected," she smiled.

He breathed.

"...Yeah."

It took a while for his feet to touch ground again.
His voice was weak. It croaked, "Us?"

She closed her eyes and nodded.

Their arms looped together. She fell into his chest.
He wouldn't let her fall; she could count on him. He
was a castle. He was Clark, and she knew exactly
who that was. He was so damn solid, you could build
a church on him. Clark's words wrote themselves in
stone.

But he loved her? She always knew his heart was
strongest of all, but he really, actually loved her?
HOW?

Clark finally held her, and so SUDDENLY held
her. He only hugged her four times in his whole life,
and he treasured those brief moments, but this wasn't
just a hug. He didn't know what it was. He could
smell her hair, and the scent was different from years
before. He wanted to lie down in it, wrap himself in
it, and just dream the scent of her hair. Her slim arms
were like lace - so soft and beautiful... how could he
deserve them?

Oh, no, he thought. Oh God, no… I can feel her breathing. I can actually feel her breathing, against my chest. I can sense HER LIFE, here, in my arms.

"Mmph," she mumbled. She buried her face in his shirt, muffling her voice. "So, umm… what are you doing these days?" She nuzzled into him firmly. She wouldn't stop for small talk.

"Ahh, you know… research."

"No," she chuckled, pulling free, "Seriously, Clark, I really don't know." She looked up at him.

He was too busy looking at her to remember words.

"I… stuff," he mused happily. "Like - contract, something… Whatever. I don't even care, right now." He laughed. None of that mattered.

Her eyes were so close to him, he could admire their complexities and purity. He realized this: he could never be a greater man than in this moment. He glimpsed his reflection in her eyes.

"Well…" He posed tall, like a fine gentleman. "Might we have dinner, some evening, Miss Riley?"

Damn, he thought. Oh, damn… dammit, I said that? I called her 'Miss Riley,' like a little girl? Patronizing crap? Where'd that come from?

"I, uh… I can get a sitter. No prob. I will."

She couldn't afford a sitter for more than a few hours, but she had to find a way.

"Mmm… well," he stroked her hair, "We are NOT going dutch, on this. 'Wanna send him to the movies, with some friends? All good. I'll pay for admission; I'll pay for the trip. I dunno - wanna bring BRAINIAC along with us? That's fine too…"

She sighed. "He can be a handful… so, probably not with us. Kids, right? I'm guessing you don't know about that, personally?"

"Ah… no. But I get it. Moms are the steering wheel of the future. Societal engineering."

"And multi-tasking," she added. "That was invented by a mom."

He looked at her fondly. "No doubt. 'Tired yet?"

"Constantly."

He took her hand. "Okay, well… I know this guy? He's actually pretty good with kids, eh? At least, he might be able to help Albert, now and then. Science projects, or the museum… if you like."

"Yeah. I like." She grinned.

He kissed her hand. "And this guy? He really wants some time with you. More than anything."

"Mmm. Yeah," she purred. "Okay."

She scissored her ankles and crossed her legs a little.

"MOMMM - your PENCIL. Here's your pencil." Albert looked back and forth. "Wait… you guys knew each other a lot in school, didn't you?"

CHAPTER SIXTEEN
TABLE WITH A VIEW

Riley wore pearls, a rather low-cut dress of shining blue, and a pair of black, strapped heels. Clark had a very modern suit. It looked like it had been ironed with a diamond. She was an electric ribbon. He was crisp geometry. The evening skies wore navy and black.

The restaurant had an Italian name, and when they entered they were greeted by the owner, himself. Clark shook his hand, and quietly said something like "comb his tie." Something Italian, she figured.

The owner took them up a broad, winding staircase. He seated them on a private rooftop patio overlooking the city. Riley had a hard time sitting down, at first, because of the endless view. The city was a jeweled garden at her feet.

Their patio was bordered by classical sculpture

and climbing ivy. Tiny, pale lights shone through the leaves. A single candlelit table stood by the edge of the patio, where a stone border kept them from the five-storey drop. Somehow, it was quiet. It was a haven, here, right in the middle of the city.

The owner himself asked, "Some wine tonight, Miss?"

She was caught completely off guard.

"...Sure, sure. M-maybe some white?" She had no idea. "In a bit?"

The owner stalled, stunned. He stared at her with his lips parted, wondering where she came from. What tiny, unknown corner of the world did she call home?

Clark beckoned to the owner. Then he leaned toward him, intently, like a wolf lowering his neck. He spoke quietly so she couldn't hear.

"Amico mio? Dai alla signora tutto quello che vuole."

(My friend? Give this lady everything she wants.)

Clark smiled politely, but also to remind the owner that he had teeth. The owner promptly vanished. A new waiter adjusted the lights. Riley and Clark were left in a pool of darkness, with faint ripples of sparks around them. The candles made their faces glow like beautiful ghosts.

A few minutes passed before they began asking questions.

"Clark? What do you do, these days?"

With her fingers, she held the world's skinniest

fork. She used it to eat tiny pastries that were stuffed with grilled herbs and toasted cheeses. She guessed that the pastry dough, itself, was somehow made with honey.

Clark stopped. "I have to ask you a few things, first. I'm sorry."

She paused, chewed, and sat straight. She nodded to him.

When he asked, he meant to ask kindly: "What do YOU do?"

Her eyes lowered. She tightened her lips for a second.

"I wait tables, Clark." She smiled sadly. "Actually, I work at a diner a few blocks away. My boss is probably part of a Mediterranean mafia. Maybe one of the 'not-nice' ones. And I don't want to see another black olive, ever again, for the rest of my life."

Clark nodded gravely. "I'm guessing it's not perfect?"

"It's a balancing act, with bills. I, uh... well, you know, my art never took off."

His eyes narrowed like a dangerous Clint Eastwood.

"Your art?" he growled quietly. "It should. You're great. You're visionary. You're living TALENT."

Her teeth shone in a sweet smile.

"You don't need to butter me up, big guy."

"I absolutely am not," he argued. "I've seen your

work. You HAVE something. You have a line, on something, like you found a vein of gold. It's like you reached in and grabbed it out of a river. You have a firm grip on artistic greatness. Nobody else has what you have."

He leaned closer. "I can see it… but I can't do it. Only you can."

She shook her head.

Lost dreams, she thought. Things of the past.

He scowled back at her, jokingly. "What, you don't think pure talent counts for anything?"

"Sad to say, but people prefer Greek salad. If you compare my art to Mediterranean fast food? Grub is where the money is."

He stared at her like he'd witnessed sacrilege.

"I love your art. YOU love your art. You should…"

He stopped. His eyes could've grown tears.

She offered kind words. "It's more like 'do what you gotta do.' It's not about how I feel. Overall, I'm pretty happy, if I can keep feeding my kid. It's tough, sometimes, but it's worth it."

Clark quietly fumed. Then, he slowly lifted his eyes. He caught hers. Their gaze held evenly. He spoke in a calm, level voice:

"Do you want out, Riley?"

She blanched. Her mouth wouldn't speak.

He took her hand and then he chuckled a little.

"Riley… can I say this? Can I call you 'My Love?' Is that okay?"

From her hand, he felt her tremble inside. She turned her head tensely, shrugged, and laughed under her breath. Her eyes lit.

She admitted, "Y-yeah… umm… yeah, I think we both bring that. To the table. Clark."

She squeezed his hand. Clark's world spun loops and danced in madness.

She ducked with shyness and smiled tightly.

"Umm… I love you," she told him. She FINALLY told him. There was a blushing teenager inside her who was very alive.

His light met her light. They shared a breathless moment.

"WELL… Riley… My Love… I can't talk about it. That's where I work."

He was silent for a few seconds.

Her eyebrows bunched downward. She looked at him sideways. She nipped the last edge of a pastry from her fork. She chewed quickly and furtively, like a rabbit. She listened as he spoke again.

"Look, I… remember the 'kids' thing? I can't have kids. Sorry to be so candid, but I had that guy operation. The not-having-kids one. It was part of the hereditary non-transference clause of my contract. I know, that's ridiculous, but I have a SERIOUS gag order. It's a lifetime contract."

She chewed, then held her napkin over her mouth.

"Holy CRAP, man! What'd you do? Are you okay?"

He nodded back gravely. "Oh yeah. Yeah, I'm okay, but..."

They listened to the traffic of the city, far below. Their words huddled close on this lofty balcony.

"I sold some patents to the United States Military. There are some strings attached. I got roped into some 'intellectual copyright' stuff."

She slowly folded her napkin and set it on her lap. She rested her hand on it. She didn't know what she was hearing.

"Riley, you remember the workshop? Where you crashed, on prom night? Well, it's been appropriated. They moved my mom, and everything. They cover tracks."

She spoke in deadpan humor: "You're scarin' me, dude."

"Nah, I have personal security staff. His name's Matt. We have things wrapped up - inclusively.

"Personally, I'm living well off royalties. I am a very SECURE millionaire. My net-worth, anyway, is about fourteen-and-a-half. Umm... probably seventeen, by now.

"So. Sometimes I do research, and a bit of consulting... but otherwise, I'm retired."

She chirped: "At thirty-two?"

He nodded: "At thirty-two."

"A millionaire. You're a millionaire, Clark." She snorted and laughed. "You don't act like one. You don't dress like one. You're... you look like YOU." She grinned beautifully.

"Mmm," he rolled his eyes. "Ya. 'Like my disguise? I'm dressed up as an egghead researcher in a suit. But I asked you, Riley…"

He very slowly squeezed her hand. He held it firm, and then held it tight. She could not escape this question.

"Are you tired? Do you want out?"

He held her hand, but it tried to draw back. He kept a firm, warm hold. His voice was low and gentle, but strong.

"Riley? COME WITH ME."

She recoiled a little. "Clark, it's a little sudden."

"Is it?" he asked, without blinking.

Well no, she thought to herself. Not sudden for me. But how can he show up one day, and love me, and want to take me away with him?

She looked in his eyes.

Oh, those strong, grey eyes, she thought. So hopeful. And what if my doubts are wrong? They're sensible, but what if this isn't the time for sensible? This is my greatest dream, not my common sense.

"Riley, please. Please come with me…?"

She saw the steadiness of his eyes. All that Clark-strength now focused on her. It all waited on her next word. She couldn't think of what to say. She opened and closed her mouth several times, like the cat who couldn't decide whether it wanted to stay in, or go out, or stay in, or go out. Or whether it wanted to run wild under the moon, following the true song of its heart.

The waiter arrived as she remained quiet, still thinking. He brought her a tall bottle - white wine, as she'd requested. She absently grabbed the bottle in one hand, by the neck, and poured herself a full glass. The waiter's composure didn't budge. He didn't dare. He received the bottle again, in his white gloves, and poured Clark full - precisely as full as his ladyfriend. Clark flicked him a look, and the bottle was kept nearby.

White wine. She'd wanted something "maybe sweeter," and Clark suggested a 25-year-old Sauternes.

She sipped, and her brows popped up. She had a longer pull at her glass, and set it down slowly.

She paused. "Waaaait..."

She turned her head with a sly smirk. Clark knew she was up to something.

"You're that mysterious guy in the suit and longcoat, sitting in the PARK... aren't you? You're that government spook with the briefcase, sitting in the park! You receive intel from, like, 'dead drops.' I don't even know what dead drops are, but you're him! The guy in the suit! You're Agent Smith!"

She saw his face darken. Either he was insulted, or she struck a nerve somewhere.

"That's AWESOME!" Her mouth split into a euphoric smile. Her pupils swelled wide with adoration. "You're the BAD GUY, from a good thriller!"

"Don't even go there. I'm just a researcher." He

sighed and gave her a sideways look - a little playful scorn between old friends. He saw her blushy smile and was compelled to smile back.

She spoke with pride. "I knew you'd be something, given a couple years. Or twenty. God, look at you… you're important to this COUNTRY." She had a drink of wine, tipping her glass a bit to the side. She wouldn't break eye contact.

"AND, you're a staple of spy fiction." Her eyes twinkled.

He moaned. He bent to touch his brow.

She spanned her fingers wide in the air. "And probably the silent hand in the shadows, pulling the marionette strings of the world."

He raised a finger to interrupt her, but she leaned forward. She squeezed his arm.

"Kidding. I'm KIDDING, dude. I know you. You're the greatest man I've…" She exhaled carefully. Could she say? Her mouth struggled between smiles and crying shapes.

"…just like you've always been." Her cheeks flushed. Her fingers held tight, and her thumb rubbed his forearm.

Jesus, she thought. Why is he stiff? He looks great, but… what, is he all toned under there?

She patted his sleeve once. It was so tight, it clapped. She tried to ignore that.

"Riley, some things are different. Some ideas paid off." He seemed pensive. "And my life went straight, since then. Financially, anyway."

He chuckled. "My basement? Some of those projects worked out."

She shook her head.

"I wish I'd..." Her eyes danced around his face.

He waited. She didn't elaborate. She was thinking of prom night. So much had changed, but now her prince came for her. Now, she could run away with him.

She looked closely at him.

"Can you just take my word on this?" She lifted her hand up to her heart. "Some things, Clark - things you didn't know - they really didn't change." Her eyes pleaded to him. "Okay, big guy? You hear what I'm saying?"

How could she tell him about her greatest kiss, in high school? or how she dreamt of him? how she ached for him? No-one knew. Not her mother, not her grandmother, nor any of her friends. Nobody knew the whole truth, except Louis the Rabbit. He was just a memory, and he wasn't even real to begin with.

"There are things I haven't told you, Clark. Teenagers are mixed up, and they have a lot on their minds, but some things stayed straight-and-true."

She smiled with a twinkling eye.

"True, like a compass. True, like magnetic North. Somehow, it led me to where I was supposed to go. Just... it did. Truth did."

CHAPTER SEVENTEEN
WALK THE WALK

An hour passed. She tapped at her phone, confirmed a text, and Albert was sent to the post-movie slumber party. She sighed, fluttering her lips like a deflating balloon. She knew she'd hear about 'Rad Rangers' and ONLY 'Rad Rangers' for at least a week.

Her phone screen didn't want to turn off. She tapped the power button a few times, and it still wouldn't respond. She finally dunked it into her purse.

"Problems with your phone?" he asked.

"Nah. I think technology's your game, anyway."

They talked through the evening. The sky mellowed and darkened, like aged wine. Above them, stars gathered - silver fairies, all watching to see what might happen next.

"Could I take you home, Riley?"

She hesitated. "Uhh - REALLY sudden, man."

"-NO, no, I mean… can I accompany you, and get you home safe? I'll have a car here, whenever you're ready."

"Oh."

"Or, I could drive you home myself; whatever's comfortable."

She tipped her head sideways. "H-how are we gonna work this? I don't know where you live, but I can guess HOW you live. I'm just in my tiny apartment, twenty minutes from downtown." She waved her skinny fork aside.

He spoke gently. "I live in a rather secure building. It has a couple added security features. 'Guess you could call them that."

She twisted her lips skeptically. "Yeah. 'Sounds about right, Secret Agent Man." She winked at him.

"Riley?" he whispered softly, "I don't want to say goodbye. Not yet. Please, could we take a walk?"

"Mmm. Well, I'd love to take a really long walk with you, and I mean HOURS, holding hands and stealing kisses… but I'm wearing strapped heels."

"Ah. Right… uhh…" He went quiet. "Okay. Okay, then. Someday, though, I was thinking of just taking a stroll, and going back through Ashv-"

"-Ashvale Field!" Her eyes lit. "I'll go barefoot! I don't care!"

He laughed out loud. His smile gleamed.

"See, that's the Riley I know! That's a Riley

answer. 'Barefoot,' as opposed to fancy heels."

"What?" She twisted her expression. "What's so funny about that?"

"Look. Your shoes? They're the perfect point where 'Greek goddess' meets obsidian jewelry. They're positively dazzling. And your little feet are Michelangelo's masterpieces... I mean, if he ever worked with porcelain. Sorry to be weird, but I could look at your little shoes all night.

"But you? Nah! Barefoot, in the cool grass, on a starlit night, after a dinner with wine. That's so natural. So honest. So you."

Can I kiss your toes? he thought. I'll be gentle - I promise.

"Well, Clark," she nodded her head. "I'm just going barefoot, in the grass. Under the stars. But I'm going with you."

"You're such a romantic," he concluded.

"Maybe. Just take me with you." She nodded again, happily.

"Well, y'know what?" He grinned. "No problem. Forget the heels. I'll just carry you."

"Clark?"

"Mmm?" His brows bent upward.

"CLARK," she commanded.

"Yes? W-What?" he stuttered nervously.

"Take me with you, Clark. I'll even go barefoot. Just..."

It was the greatest moment of Clark's life.

"Take Me With You."

She didn't blink.

"You asked, 'Come With Me?' There's your answer. I'll go with you, My Love - even barefoot."

The waiter approached and offered choices of dessert. Clark was busy trying to contain an intense smile. He looked off in a few different directions. His joy was like steam trying to escape through a crack in his grin.

Riley saw the waiter and waved him off politely. She guessed at the costs of desserts.

"Ahh - no. Nope. Thanks anyway."

She was content. She gathered her things. She was ready to leave… to 'go with Clark,' wherever that led.

Clark leaned toward the waiter. "Umm - could we have the gluten-free, triple-chocolate cheesecake, and keep the vanilla gelato to the side? And could we have that express, and to go?" Clark kept to English so she'd hear every word.

The waiter ducked back into the shadows. He returned quickly with a discreet box. Inside was a four-hundred-dollar slice of cheesecake.

CHAPTER EIGHTEEN

GLOWING

"Has this happened WAY too fast?"

Riley rested her head on his shoulder. She gently swayed in his arms as he carried her. She cuddled her little package of cheesecake and looked up to his face.

The long grass whispered with every step. The crickets had vowed silence.

"Fast? No. Not too fast. We've had a flame that lived as embers. 'Smoldered,' right? like those romance books would say?" He winked at her.

She nodded up at him happily: "Ya! They totally say that!"

"And you and I? We loved each other. We didn't even know it, but we did. So… no. Not too sudden. We've had glowing embers for a long, long time, Miss Riley."

She purred, "Y'know, I love when you call me

that." She wore a curious smile. She added, "I'm actually divorced, in my thirties, with a kid, in a dead-end job... and you make me feel so pretty, and so young."

He stopped.

"Of course you are." He nodded to her with conviction. "You're young, and you're beautiful, and I know this very well. And I wasn't kidding about the grade three thing - what I told Albert, and you."

Riley listened closely.

"That's about twenty-five years, Riley. That's a quarter of a century, for measure. Yes. We measure this in centuries, now." He broke eye-contact, trying not to scare her.

"You're nuts," she blinked up at him.

He paused. "I am," he grinned back. "Whose fault is that, now?" He pecked a quick kiss on her cheek.

She stared hungrily at his lips. She coiled upward, like a rare kissing-snake, and tasted him again. She sucked at his lips and pulled his head closer. She made him stand still, and hold her, and accept this.

He stood in Ashvale Field, keeping her safe in his arms, while she bent herself around his mouth. He met her tongue carefully, stroking it with his own. He breathed steadily: out, in... out, in... and OUT. He told her, with a strong exhalation, that he needed her. She nodded loosely.

Her lips squeaked, and she released a tiny moan. His mouth pressed wetly and impatiently. His heat planted into her - a kiss that told her firmly, with no hesitation, that he would melt her. His chest was a growing furnace. His kiss promised that it would burn away everything that she wasn't. He'd burn stronger than the world; he was a crucible. He would only keep her. She was his pure gold, and to hell with everything else.

She mumbled plaintive sounds. She shifted, and he slowly pulled away. His sigh was another warm blanket over her cheek. She thought she heard his lips say 'need you.'

He swallowed. "Y'know, we could just eat cheesecake. That's good for a first date."

She shook her head with a wrinkly smile.

"No. No, man, I think our first date was our disaster prom. You found me when I was drunk, and lost, and you took me in and you cared for me. You kept me safe." She laughed. "And then you cooked me this MASSIVE breakfast, in the morning."

"Ha. Yeah. My mom absolutely adored you."

Her whole body went rigid.

"Clark - STOP... you said 'adore.' You said you adored me... you TOLD me that, didn't you?"

Twenty-five years of pain rose up like a huge, thundering wave... and it washed right by. He stood like he was tall, and naked, and brave.

He spoke with resolve, "Yes, Riley, I did. I adore you. I am absolutely, ruinously in love with you. I sincerely want my life... to be beside yours. Does that make sense? What I'm trying to say isn't just simple;

it's more like… fundamental."

He looked ashamed. "Am I creepy as all hell?"

She couldn't blink. "Yes, Clark, you're a total weirdo. But only because you don't belong in this ugly world. Weirdness makes you awesome. You're an advanced alien living in stone-age Ashvale. You're a complete space cadet."

He closed his eyes.

"And I discovered you," she continued. "I get to keep you. You're my mystery. MY miracle. Hah - you even make ME feel special, and that's gotta be magic, or something."

This pained him. She didn't notice.

"Wait," she said. "Look up there. See that one?"

She pointed upward. The night sky was tickled with silvery stars.

"See what? That's Libra."

"Naw - that one. The bright star. Brighter one. By my finger. See it?"

A moment of quiet. He focused.

"…Yes. I do."

"Yeah. Is that one close to your home planet?"

He laughed heartily. She shook in his arms. She just lay there, smiling at him proudly, bumping with his laughter. She reached her fingers around his ear and played with the hair at the back of his head. She crunched in close to him and kissed his ear once.

"Clark?" she whispered.

"Mmm-hmm?" He nuzzled her head.

"Make love to me."

CHAPTER NINETEEN
LEAVE THE LIGHT ON

He swished at the grass with his shoe. When he knew it was clear of stones, he set her down on her feet.

What is this? he asked himself. What is she doing?

His longcoat flapped onto the ground below them. It was a long, dark carpet. His blazer and shirt followed. Her eyes floated open.

"Hohh…!" she cried aloud, finally seeing this man in front of her. How did his shirt HOLD all that? His mass was like a boulder - several boulders, cobbled together to make the muscles of a man. Sure, he was an Olympic-style wrestler, but he looked better than those wrestlers on TV. If words could be a physique, he was what the word "pounding" looked like. A drum; a boom; strength rumbling from a giant, hidden heart.

She closed her lips just in time to catch a bit of drool. She swallowed. With her finger, she raised the side of her blue dress.

He gently kissed her cheek, skimmed his hands down her arms, and pulled her close to his chest.

He stopped her hands from moving.

"God, Clark... your skin's really... it's, like, really hot."

His kiss clicked, and patted, and squelched across her cheek. Every kiss was a button pressed in perfect sequence; her control was shutting down. Her eyes crossed and she moaned weakly.

"My skin," he replied, "I dunno. Maybe I'm a little excited?"

He cupped his hand behind her neck, pressed close, but held her wrist again. He stopped her firmly. He didn't let her undress.

He whispered to her: "Maybe we don't have to do everything...? You know, I can keep things on a leash, if you're more comfortable. It's been a couple of years, for us. I can hold on for another night. I just want that to be an option. Alright?"

She knit her brow for a moment, then her arms relaxed. She found herself hugging him. She sighed happily.

She almost thought aloud: WHY are you so good to me?

Her fingertips streaked down his back. They sensed all the strength that he kept at bay. He was hard like sculpture, yet somehow he held all that weight from falling on top of her.

Yeah, she thought. Things to look forward to. Other nights. With him.

"But you like this stuff, right? Mmm?" he teased her. His hands passed up and down her back, till one gripped around her waist, and the other fit firmly over her behind.

"Clark?" she panted. "Uh, Clark? I've never HAAAA-..."

She swelled in response.

"...h-had that attention before, from you, and OH-MY-GOD, your hands!"

"Mmm. Only if you're comfortable. With this."

"Oh ya," she agreed. "This. I love the 'this.' Definitely." Her eyes spun.

His chuckling was so deep, she felt it humming inside him. He smooched the back of her neck, drunkenly, and stopped beneath her ear. He left soft touches of his tongue, like cool dewdrops in the night. His cheek warmed her earlobe. Her neck felt the slow flood of his breath.

He whispered to her. "Look. I just want to be sure. If you're happier, we could just lie here together. I'm perfectly content with that. I mean, I'm with YOU." He smiled tightly.

She murmured, shyly. "Can we... can I still get rid of this dress? Maybe wear your coat? This isn't so comfortable. I just got it for tonight. Dinner, I mean."

"What?" He leaned back to look at her. He

scowled playfully. "You're ALWAYS gorgeous, you know. You could make a potato sack look adorable."

She swatted him playfully. "SHUT UP," she snickered. "Potato sack…? Look, I hate this thing, and with my paycheck it-"

"How much did it cost you? Can I ask?" His eyebrow perked up.

She dipped her head down. He tilted his own head to follow her.

"This… pinchy, scaly monster… was $550. And my credit card company? Ya, they just bought ME." She nodded. Acceptance.

"Oh," he replied. Then he had a sudden inspiration, and his eyes lit. "SHOPPING! 'Wanna go shopping tomorrow?"

He looked at her eagerly, like a dog hoping to play fetch. His arms dropped. Here he was: half naked, standing in this grassy field, at night, but his keen eyes desperately needed to know if he could take her shopping tomorrow.

She turned her head and blushed. She mumbled, "No-one's ever taken me shopping before, Clark."

Her brow darkened. If he was trying to win her over with gifts, this is how he'd try. Money. Clothes. Spoiling her with material wealth.

"Oh, we're going." He had iron resolve. He faced her with great earnest. "I'll take you, and you can pick Riley Fashions… forget costs. No, you should DEFINITELY express your beauty the way it needs to be expressed. No compromises.

"Otherwise," he beamed, "the world would be robbed of one of its greatest joys."

For a moment, she didn't follow. When she realized he meant her good looks, she scoffed lightly.

He looked in her face with pure hope.

"You know where to go. We'll go there. We'll find the right brands, or... or we'll get the right tailors to do things for you. Nothing's gonna stop you."

"Mmmf," she blushed. "Well, this dress puts up a stiff argument. I'd never buy it again."

He set his brow decisively. "If you don't feel amazing in it, then the DRESS... is wrong. It is a crime against you. Here. Uh... my coat." He retrieved it from the grass, brushed it clean, and held its inside lining around her.

"I'll hold this. It's a curtain for you, and then it's your robe. And we're going shopping soon. Okay? Just you and me."

She stared at him. Her eyes couldn't blink. NEED, they said. Her eyes wanted to eat him. But then, this was 'wanting.' He'd know about that. He'd use it, if he tried to charm her.

Still, there was something untempered about him... something raw and honest. Intense. Almost dangerously pure. Something powerful lived inside Clark, and there was no room for lies.

He looked away to offer her privacy. She tucked closer to his coat, slipped away her dress, and stood still. Here, she wore nothing but panties out in the middle of Ashvale Field. Then the warm wings of his coat swept around her. The coat's liner was sleek against her skin. His cologne was a faint, dark riddle, like the footprint of a mountain lion… traces of something rugged, and mighty, and brooding.

She felt his arms around her, folding her into his longcoat. His fingers fixed the buttons in front. She felt his chest pressing behind her; it was flexing and working. He tidied his coat till she fit. She only seemed to fit into his crevices, like a weed between stones. She paused. She didn't know how she could ever fit in his actual life.

"Clark? Can we have a life together? I mean, do I really have anything worth… like, anything I can offer you?"

She turned into him and rolled her brow across his chest. She was pressing her thoughts into his heart.

Please? her mind begged. I need to believe this. Please be real.

She waited for him.

I'm gonna die, her heart cried.

He petted her brow and kissed it. "Look - from all your struggle, you know about marriage. That's incredibly important," he nodded, "for US."

Holy, she thought. Marriage? Holy sweet mother of…

"And y'know, I haven't learned that in my life. So I'll learn about long-term relationships. The span of years; the balance of a household. You can teach me. You know these things."

She stayed quiet, and then looked up at him

sadly. "But, you know… Albert. You're okay with me being a mom?"

"No, I'm thrilled! It's YOU!" He braced her in his hands. "And if you accept me… well, you already have a child, and I can't have one. But if you accepted me," his lips bent around his next words, "if you BOTH accepted me, that is… maybe it could be like a family? Do you think that could work?" He laughed softly. She didn't see the quivering glint under his eyelid. His neck went tight.

"Uhh," he backtracked, "but that's way down the road. And it's a huge request, and it's totally open right now. Everything's openness. We're just talking, here."

She stopped him. "Wait a sec. I have a child from another marriage. That's not complicated? I mean, he and I ARE a family, already… or, we're like the last original members of the band; the ones who didn't split. And I also have some losses from that broken marriage."

Clark tried not to think of revenge.

"No you don't," he scowled.

"Ya I do."

"Riley? Quit your job. Forget about debts. You know how I feel, now… would you let me take care of you?"

She tried to keep her breath steady. "Are you talking about us, and a life together? and a home? and adopting my SON?"

"I'm thinking-" He looked like he'd just been

stabbed. "Maybe about that, yeah."

Ashvale Field disappeared for a few seconds. No crickets. Nothing.

"Okay, Riley. You know how I feel about you. You're very, very important to my life. So this is what I want." He faced her and held her cheek. "And your son? He's half you, but he's 100% Albert. How could he be more perfect?"

Riley's eyes widened and shone. He nodded with certainty.

"Yeah, that's the life I want. Strong, stable… uhh… marriage, someday. And offering support for a young life. That would be the greatest honor I could ever hope for."

His next words staggered out of him, like unsteady gears turning. "But YOU? No-one else can offer me 'you.' No-one else could make me so happy.

"I've seen how the world treats you. It hasn't been good enough. I want to give you better."

Her eyes rolled up to him. "But you said… marriage?"

"Mmm-… I mean, long-term relationship. You know. When you and I are in our seventies, and I'm still bringing you breakfast in bed, we could consider ourselves married. That's mostly what I meant."

She tried to process the last few days. She stood with him and swayed a little. "You STILL feel like this, after decades?"

He couldn't tell her everything. "Yeah," he nodded.

She was naked, but his coat was a cocoon. That night, her world would begin to change.

The crickets listened intently. In Ashvale Plains, this scene usually led to a pregnancy, and then a troubled year, and then indecision about the future. The darkness around them was chilly. It nipped her legs and bare neck. It goaded her toward physical intimacy. This was the stage, and the play always went on.

She looked at him flatly, like she just came in from the rain.

"Can I trust you? Could we lie down together, and just look at the sky? I know, it's lame. But I want to have someone to do that with. I'd really want to do that with you.

"Could we NOT do things we both expect, like lie here, naked, and have sex? Can we be ourselves? ask real questions? share things?"

He leaned his brow over to touch hers. They met... again.

She nodded slightly. "Clark, I really want to know you. Could we try that?"

His voice flooded over her, "You want to just lie here, together, and watch the universe happen?" Even in his throat, she could hear his smiling.

"YEAH." She hugged him.

This is perfect, she thought. We can just be TOGETHER, together!

She's so beautiful, he thought, but she actually wants to know me. How will this ever work?

He turned to her. "Y'know, I'm afraid, too. The trust thing is hard. I hope I can explain that to you, someday."

He wrapped her in his coat and kept her tight in his arms. He lay down with her carefully, like holding a pane of glass. She snaked around in his coat and lay upon his body. She tucked close and listened to his breathing - huge and calm, like a slow wind in the forest. This was her new home.

"Why are you always so good to me, Clark?"

"I'm not. No, this is all you. I'm just an honest man."

"W-... huh?"

He sighed. "I'm not good to you. I'm an honest man. I try to return the beauty that you've given to me. So, do I treat you well?"

She gave a deadpan reply. "You're taking me... shopping." She rolled her eyes up at him. "It's a first, dude. This is all totally new to me."

"Yeah? Well, every day, you're new to me. I'm grateful, and I try to do what's right. I don't do anything strange. I just honor you."

She chuckled once. "What are you? my very own, private, one-man, fanatical love cult?"

Silence tensed his brow. "Yeah. Sure. Cultist. Sorry, I forgot my antlers. And the only sacrificial offering I have is chocolate cheesecake."

He unclipped the package, mixed the gelato, and lifted the cheesecake over to her. He set it on his chest, a little below her face.

"Just let me know when you want a bite. I hear chocolate goes well with galaxies… and things that are unspoken. Just so you know." He kept the tiny fork close at hand.

She felt the warmth of his coat, smelled cologne on his chest, and watched the cheesecake swell with his breathing. When she looked up, it was diamonds as far as the eye could see.

Riley gazed. "When you see all those stars, do you ever ask yourself, 'what am I supposed to do?' Do you ever get that?"

"All the time."

She couldn't speak for a moment.

"Clark, I think you're the only person I can feel things with. The real things. You're not so much 'different' from everyone else. It's more like you and I are the same, somehow."

She lay still. She waited. Her nose gave a tiny puff of laughter.

"Just sometimes, that 'lost' feeling goes away. But only when we're together. Things start to make sense."

His arm tightened around her. "I know. Me too."

She ducked her head closer. "Why is that? Why do we feel like this?"

"I think we're two-of-a-kind," he said. "We're not like Ashvale. There are a lot of stars up there, but we're like two of them. Only two; just you and me. The rest of them go on forever; they're impossible to understand."

"How many of them are up there? How can there be so many?" she asked. She didn't expect a literal reply. Away from the city, without the pollution, they saw so many more.

"We'll never know," he sighed. "There are always more than we can see. And then we have no idea, when morning comes. They fade, in the-"

She interrupted: "…-light of day, like a candle going out. Flickering out. Going dim." Her eyes widened. "We're not finishing each other's sentences. You SAID something like that to me, years ago. Didn't you?"

"Yeah. Uh, it was kinda… it was right over there." He gestured at their path, behind them. "I made you look up at the stars. And what I said, that night, was like one star. Bright in that moment, but gone in the morning. And I counted on that; I counted on your memory to fade.

"That night, I confessed that I was horribly in love with you. But I couldn't tell you for real. You were drunk, and you forgot. You were 'friendly' that night, but I figured it was just the drink. I was convinced you never cared."

She reached out an arm and hugged him with it. "That star's not gone, is it? Huh? That star's still there, even after all these years."

He said nothing.

She grinned at him. "It is… isn't it, Clark? One little burning light, and it's been there this whole time." She sighed with satisfaction.

She lay bundled in his coat. He tightened his arms around her.

They shared a few gentle kisses of endearment, but otherwise they lay still. They watched all the 'everything' happen around them. They bravely did nothing else but listen to time.

Together, they saw the first wonders ever seen. They discovered the silence that had carried all things since the beginning. They lay together happily - a young couple enjoying evening theatre. They stayed for the whole performance, until the stars faded behind the curtain of dawn.

"Mmm," Riley mumbled, dreamily, "They're like little space fishies, flashing in the deep. And the great blue sky ocean swallows them up. But they'll be back tomorrow. Err... tonight."

"They will. We know that now."

She mused, "If there's aliens out there, do you think they look at the stars, too?"

"Definitely," he answered. "I think everybody does."

"So, do you think there's aliens, Clark?"

He swallowed. "I think that atoms are too small to comprehend, and the universe is way too big. We can't keep track of everything in between. Whether there are aliens or not, it's just a matter of what people know. Really, all that matters is fear. So I'm not really afraid of neighbors we haven't met. We're aliens to them, right?"

"I wish more people weren't afraid," she cuddled

closer.

"Yeah. Aliens are people too," he smirked and kissed her ear. "Speaking of little men, when do you expect Albert back?"

"Hmm - it's an over-nighter. Probably noon, or such. He'll text me. He's good with that. Plus, the McKinnleys love him."

Clark lay still, but a big grin was brewing under his surface.

"Riley?"

"Mmm," she replied.

"Can I ask why you named him Albert?"

She sniffed. She huffed a little, then started laughing. Her shoulders shook inside his arms. She buried her laughter in Clark's chest.

He turned to her, worried. "What? What did I do wrong?"

"Nothing… hah… haha…" She settled, took a breath, then tried to explain.

"My ex-husband wanted a son. Our deal was, if we had a daughter, he'd at least get to name her. So then, if we had a SON… well, I could pick a name. And I was perfectly happy with a son. Nah, I love Albert to the moon and back; he's noisy, brainy, hilarious, and pretty much fearless…"

"Well, yeah. 'Sounds like your son."

"But," she tapped his chest, "I had this secret, you see. And I didn't tell anybody, anywhere. I wanted to put it in a bank, or someplace where it could be safe."

She inhaled.

"The secret was, I missed you at my wedding, Clark." She inhaled again. "And I wished I'd kissed you in high school. And I wished we'd danced. And I shoulda shown you all my drawings - I have lots of drawings. I have so many drawings of you, creating and inventing and being gorgeous all the time."

Clark felt her warm exhalation on his chest.

"So my son is named 'Albert,' because Albert Einstein was a genius inventor... but you're the genius inventor in my life. I wanted to love you, just a little bit, in secret... safely... even if I couldn't be with you."

Clark kept silent. Riley pressed her cheek against his chest and finally told him:

"He's named Albert, after you."

She half-smiled.

"Albert carries my secret. He's my son, but he lets me love you just a little bit. Yeah. I buried my secret with my greatest treasure.

"I love you, Clark. I've always loved you."

She couldn't see Clark's face drain pale. She couldn't hear the droplets quivering down his cheek.

"But my husband? Nah, he didn't know anything. And ya, I guess HE was secretly in love with Naomi..."

The theatrics began; she sputtered out names. "Ya. Naomi. Ah, no, I mean Gigi. NO - no, I mean Monique!" She snorted and laughed.

By now, the crickets had fallen asleep. The first

songbird called across the field.

In the light of dawn, Riley and Clark were scruffy like drifters: he'd bedded in the long grass, and she was wearing an oversized coat. They'd hitched a ride with Everything, and it took them across the entire night sky.

"I missed you at my wedding, Clark. Now you know how much I missed you. 'Glad we finally got to catch up. And that thing about stars, fading? Ha. No they don't."

Riley smirked contently. She knew this meant 'happily ever after.' What could possibly go wrong?

PART TWO

THE LIE

CHAPTER TWENTY

The Empress and Her Clothes

They arrived at Clark's house. It stood braced in a firm foundation. It had pale stonework over concrete, tall windowpanes, and skylights in the roof. He didn't have neighbors.

There were a few low-lying shrubs and a thin lawn, because Clark was relatively new to the property. In the last few years, he'd grown thyme in the stone walkways. His paths had a sweet air.

Clark opened Riley's car door and helped her out. They were both exhausted, so he held her steady in his arm. He thumped the car door shut and slid his thumb across the print scanner. The car locked.

Her shoes clicked on the stonework path. The stones were broad, but he still steered her toward the safest ones for high heels.

"So, uh... I can have something delivered, if you

like. Something comfortable? A dress, your size?"

Clark opened his front door. Riley staggered into a hallway, wearing just her heels and his longcoat. Her heels echoed from white walls. The place was spartan and clean, like a hospital for one person.

"Actually, wait… I need you to speak your name, for a sample. It's government security stuff. Is that okay?"

"…What?" She craned up at him.

"I'll show you. Just speak your name, when I tell you. Hey, Athena? 'You up?'"

A quick beep responded from the wall.

"Athena? Grant access, Protocol One. New user and voiceprint. Userbase entry…"

He nudged her.

She looked up and spoke. "Uh… Riley?"

Athena replied in composite tones, like a spoken chorus: "Access granted, username: O'Reilly."

"NO, no, no, no…" Clark shook his head and grinned at her. "Hey, Athena? Do an identity search at Protocol X, and match her voiceprint with a new userbase entry. 'Riley Ann Henway.' Hey, Athena? Just help her with everything… she's set at Protocol One. Okay?"

Athena replied in several vocal tones: "Granted. Welcome, Miss Henway."

"Hi," she nodded back. "H-How are you?"

"Thrilled to meet you, ma'am."

Clark's arm hugged her. He mumbled, "She's helpful… sometimes."

Riley looked around, confused. "You really need a robot in your house? Does she do your floors and clean stuff?"

"Nah. Mostly, Athena just watches the door and lets people in. When she said 'Welcome, Miss Henway,' she meant it. It's a keyless entry. That can be handy, believe me."

Clark gestured vaguely in the house and shrugged. "Security. That's all."

"Yeah…" Riley pulled his coat closer around herself. "You said. Extra security features."

"Mmm. Y'know, I'll make breakfast, if you want. Do you want to settle in? We were up all night. Or, I was, anyway…" Something made his dimple shine.

She turned to him sharply. "Did I fall asleep?"

He tried to suppress a smile. "Mmm-hmm. Maybe for an hour or two, late at night. Just before dawn."

She cringed. Her eyes wrinkled with embarrassment.

"You didn't wake me?"

His voice rumbled like a hearth. "You slept. You lay on me peacefully. Sometimes you'd stir, but you'd smile. One time, you said you wanted to kiss me."

He mimicked her, with a soft brow and closed eyes: "Clark? Ohh - hi. Kiss you…? in a bit?"

He grinned hard and bowed his head.

"It was enchanting."

She pinched her eyes shut. "I can't believe I fell asleep! CLARK - I'm so embarrassed."

He shook his head emphatically. "No... No, it was precious."

"And you didn't have your shirt. You didn't have your coat, either."

"Ya I did." His dimple peeked at her. "You were in my coat, and I had you." He basked in the sight of her for a moment. He glowed with pride.

I had YOU, he thought. Impossible... incredible.

"Hey. C'mon." He led her further through the hallway and into his house.

"What does Athena do? Does she control other stuff? You told her to use my voiceprint? Now I'm a userbase?"

"She does security, but she also helps with investigation. She extrapolates data and then checks it. It's like predictive text, but with facts. So - she's heard of you, just because of me."

"You talked to her about me?"

"No. She knows my history, and you're very prominent in my life."

"What?" She faced him. "What do you mean? What does she know?"

He sighed. His brow pulled tight.

"She's like an obsessive scrapbooker, only she works at the speed of the digital age. Y'know, there are lesser versions being used by law enforcement, and some adaptations are used by the C.I.A.

"Athena knows about me and my interests, so she's heard of you. Distant connections. I'm sorry if that's a little weird, but she's just an information tool.

And she's thorough. That's all."

"Wait." Riley perked up. "Can she tell me stuff? Can she help me with things?"

Clark hugged her warmly. "Ya. Oh, ya." He squeezed her. "And you're Protocol One. There are only two people with clearance that high: you and me. You can ask her stuff, or order food, or order deliveries, or you can check city schedules. She'll fetch information from online, and even transmit things for you." He shrugged. "Think of her as a real-world, real-time encyclopedia. And personal secretary."

"Holy crap, man... Okay, hang on - Athena??"

The guardian voices returned. "Good morning, Miss Henway."

Riley bunched her brow, then looked up and asked, "What can you tell me, this morning?"

There was a minor pause. Clark shrank back.

"It is 8:28am," Athena announced. "Outside temperature is 13 degrees centigrade, with expected high of 24 by 2pm. Skies are scattered clouds, and a 40% chance of rain later tonight.

"Citywide traffic is suffering moderate congestion.

"Croissants from The Sunny Side Bakery are available, estimated delivery time fourteen minutes. Specials on..."

Riley reeled back. Her shoulders jerked. "Huh? WHAT? Wait a sec - I didn't tell ANYONE about those croissants! Dude, that was a... Athena? That was a private place! What, is she - is Athena spying...?"

The list continued, without stopping: "…tarts with lemon filling, and double-mochaccinos are half-price. The shelves at Pandora's Books have been fully restocked since 5:20 this morning."

Riley's jaw sagged open.

"At 3:30pm, the Metro Central Gallery hosts an opening of works inspired by Monet. The opening includes twenty pieces created by five local artists. Three tickets are reserved, as usual, via Benjamin Donations. Options for suggested attire are available through Renner and Scot Tailors."

She turned to him with lidded, darkened eyes. "She's yours, isn't she?"

He sighed and confessed. "Kinda. I helped create her, a little." He noticed Riley staring at him. "Is that alright?"

"Croissants. Art. New dresses. Okay - what is she?"

"Look, I'm sorry if it's weird. When some dude follows you, it's creepy, right? But when a computer identifies you, and catalogs what you've purchased for breakfast… it's actually harmless. Digital footprints. It's just information, acting on information."

"Uhh - could she NOT follow my footprints? Athena? No more stalking, please?"

The voices responded immediately: "Userbase Riley Ann Henway, 32 years old, 28 Addams Drive, Apartment 218: updates placed on standby."

Riley lowered her head. "Dude… no. Just 'no.' Alright?"

He rubbed her shoulders. "I'm sorry," he mumbled. "But, well… you shut her up. She won't follow you anymore."

He led her by the shoulders through his hall and into a washroom. He offered her his bathrobe and some oversize slippers.

"Here. Till we find you something comfortable. If you want to refresh yourself, I'll make you breakfast. 'That okay?"

She started to panic. "Clark, what is this? How do you live here? Why do you have some robo-chick living in your walls? And… how many bathrooms do you have, in a place like this?"

His head hung. "Could I cook you some breakfast, first? Let's just start there."

Oh, NO, she thought to herself. Is this completely wrong? Did I lose him? What happened to Clark? What is all this crap? What happened to the guy I knew?

His kitchen had an L-shaped work island in the centre. The room was dedicated to preparing cuisine. There were both passive and powered ventilation systems tucked into the ceiling, and he had a digital gas stove. There were floor-to-ceiling windows on the far side of the room. The kitchen table stood there, by the glass, looking down to gardens below. To the right of the table, the kitchen led away to another hall and to the bedroom.

The kitchen table had three chairs. Only one had been used recently; the others were tucked into the sides neatly. They looked like they were in storage.

When Riley joined him, wearing his bathrobe, Clark had pulled on his apron. His apron was magic: it took her back in time. She took a stool at the work island and cuddled inside his bathrobe. She watched him in his apron. The sounds of metal pans were like a favorite song from childhood.

He turned to her: "Breakfast panini? Latte?"

She nodded. She thought about hash-browns, sausages, toast, and big glasses of orange juice… but lattes were breakfast for grown-ups.

She stopped her reverie.

"Clark. You try too hard. You don't need to, with me. We could even have cold french fries for breakfast, and I'd fall in love with you all over again."

He slowed at those words, listened, then kept preparing things. A pan full of sweet, spicy things started crackling. They sizzled with the smells of salty bacon and fresh herbs. He sliced a loaf of bread into broad slabs.

Riley looked up. "See, I don't… like, I don't need all this. I'm not talking about deservedness, either. I don't have huge demands. I'll never ask you to make gourmet food. I just want you, Clark. The honest man."

"Well," he thought carefully. "This stuff? All these frills? I appreciated them, once. Now they're just a habit. But I like having them, for when I have company."

She turned her head. "Do you often have company?"

He stopped.

"Not for a while," he replied. He stepped away from the stove. He leaned on the counter and closed his eyes. "I tried to have a relationship, once. Her name was Danielle. It really didn't work out. She was a gold-digger, in a sense. A couple guys started floating around, and things got messy. Everything revolved around work, in the end. She was THAT kind of gold-digger. Yeah, it had more to do with extra-national interests. Politics. Betrayals. It turned out that she was from Belarus."

Riley reared back. "Danielle was about work? What exactly have you worked on, Clark? Can I even know about this stuff?"

His breath flooded from his nose. "I'm afraid not. Most of it, I can't talk about. Still, I know things that THEY don't. That's my nest egg.

"Look, you mean a lot to me. You're the closest person to me. So, if anyone ever approaches you, or anything weird happens, don't worry... but just call me."

Her eyes widened. "WHAT? What are you into? What do you mean, extra-national interests? That's not politics, it's frickin' SPIES... aren't you in some kinda protection? Like, don't they have better security for you?"

Clark passed her a plate. It was her breakfast sandwich with honeyed herbs, home-grown tomato, bacon, and melted cheese. It was pressed neatly in pan-toasted bread.

He nodded to her. "I have a good consultant, and I have Athena. This house. That's all the protection I need."

"The DOORMAN?" Riley glanced left and right. "But... wait, she's yours. Right? Isn't she? She's pretty serious, then."

"She is. Autonomous, High-Extrapolation Analysis. 'A-HE-Ana.' I went for a classic Greek name; I thought it was funny."

"No. Stop." She halted the conversation. "DID you. Invent. Spy technology. Clark." She stared at him.

A cloud passed over his face. "Effectively, yeah."

"Are you safe?" The whites of her eyes shone.

"As safe as anyone, in this country." He stood brave and tall, like awaiting judgement.

"Jeez, man. This is heavy stuff. Since when did all this happen?"

His coffee machine bubbled. It was preparing her latte. He stood still and wouldn't answer. He shook his head a little. He couldn't look at her. He paced over toward the kitchen window.

"Hey," she called. "Talk to me. This is scaring me, alright? And I care about y-... Ha. I frickin' LOVE you. I'm so happy I can finally say that. I LOVE YOU, Clark Benjamin. So could you help me understand? I don't want anything to hurt you. Ever. I want to be WITH you. So tell me what changed."

His coffee machine was frothing noisily.

He sighed. His hands clenched. He stood tall at the floor-to-ceiling window. He stared intensely. He looked far, far past his own reflection.

"Babe?" She knew she was stepping on something tender. She was treading on broken glass. "Where'd you go? I've never seen this shadow before. How did this start? What happened to you?"

"YOU GOT MARRIED." His lips tightened. He focused beyond the window, into his own past.

The latte was finishing. It began spitting hot froth.

The morning sun lit Clark like a display. The light couldn't compete with the pain burning on his face. His fist hovered at his side. It was loaded, hard as a cannonball. It wanted to blast the window to shards.

"Clark?"

He closed his eyes again and lowered his head. He'd sunken into something black. The coffee machine steamed down to silence.

Riley walked on eggshells in between landmines.

"I really, really hurt you, didn't I?"

He nodded imperceptibly.

"Yeah, Riley. You did. So I threw away my soul. Does that answer your question?"

His brow was hard when it turned at her.

"There was nothing left; my world died. I couldn't handle it. I needed to BE something - anything - and it didn't matter what it was. So I poured myself into my work. I put my soul into

THAT. That's why I had my career. For YEARS I wanted to reach out to you, but I couldn't. I was just-"

"-Afraid," she said. "I know. Me too."

He clamped his teeth together. He searched her face.

"But Clark, I was afraid of what would happen, and if I'd lose you. I didn't see you much, but I still didn't want to lose what we had. Our friendship? Occasional meetings? Christmas parties?"

He chuckled. "That hug, where you wouldn't let go."

Her shoulders dropped. "Oh, you noticed that!" She flipped her head left and right. "Well, GOOD! I hoped you'd get the idea. Only, I've always felt that. And the truth would've upset EVERYTHING."

Riley tilted her head down and closed her eyes.

"I'm sorry if you ever doubted, Clark. I'm sorry I took so long."

She bit into her sandwich. She chewed. The flavors came to life on her palette. She shrugged, realizing something.

"I'll tell ya one thing, for sure. Albert: he's gonna frickin' adopt you."

Clark chuckled quietly. His voice was level.

"And he's welcome here."

Riley crunched her sandwich. She bit down, stayed still, and thought about her son. He might have a great place to live.

"Really - how are we going to do this, Clark? You

still work now and then, but you'd be okay with me, like…" She sighed. "Am I visiting?"

He nodded. "Try visiting. See if you like it around here. See if you like me." He tried to stay calm. His chest thumped visibly.

"Uhh," she gazed up at him, "No, we're good, big guy. Oh ya. We're good. But…" She spun her fingers together, winding ahead to the future. "If things work, I might nix the diner, and just… be with you? 'Go With You,' sorta?"

"No," he replied coldly. "Nix the diner. Today."

She grinned, then started laughing. She shook her head back and forth and waved him off.

No, she waved. No, no.

Her hand wafted broadly in front of him. "NO… Nope. I've got rent. I've got bills. All that jazz. I got rhythm, I got music, I got my kid - who could ask for anything more? That whole song and dance? It's called 'real life.' I'm still in that production."

He smirked for an odd moment before he restated. "We'll have some things to talk about. Let's just say you have some new, long-overdue freedoms. Consider it like that, for now."

She chewed on her sandwich.

He mused quietly, "So we never spoke about mutual feelings for years? Wha-… how did that happen?" He looked down to her, looking for her insight.

"Y'mean, how did 'we' NOT happen? I can't answer that. Ashvale plays mean tricks on people. I dunno, big guy… but we're crazy about each other. I'll speak for myself, of course, but I think I hear the same from you." She reached for his hand. "Clark, I saved drawings of you. Like, maybe a dozen detailed portraits, over the years. This honesty has been a long time coming."

"Yeah," he said tentatively. He started rubbing her back. She sensed something unsettled in him.

"Hey," he started, "I wanna show you something."

Her eyes rolled up. "I have the weirdest déjà vu…" She chomped the last two bites. "Breakfast, and then something freaky-genius."

"Naw," he held up his hands. "This isn't some basement workshop. This is much better." He stood behind her with his hands gripping her shoulders, priming her. "I think you'll like it."

Riley lowered her head and chewed the last of her sandwich. She gulped down half of her latte.

I woke up in a dream, she thought. What's wrong, here? Nothing this perfect ever happens. It's never real… he can't really love me. What's he doing?

He led her away from the kitchen.

"C'mon. I think you'll like this."

He led her back through the hall and around a turn. Above his garage, there was a large, open area. The ceiling was all glass with sunlamps built along the framework. This was a greenhouse, and it was built to have good lighting at any hour of the day or night.

"I figured you'd want something to do. Ceiling?

Excellent light. And see all the floor tiles, here? They're modular. They're for planters, or irrigation systems, but really anything else you can dream up. You can do anything."

"Gardening, Clark? Well, my grandma has some window boxes, but otherwise it's not a big thing in our family. I don't think she even talks to her plants… just her cats."

"No, My Love. The LIGHT. The space. Heck, it's an environmentally controlled room."

She nodded politely. "I'm already busy, thanks. I have a little seven-year-old weed. Remember him?"

"I know. But I want this for YOU."

He drew her by the hands into the centre of the room.

"My garden got moved out back, with actual fresh air. And rain. And bees."

In the very centre of this room, he knelt down in front of her. He spanned out her arms and hands, like giving her wings.

"This is your studio. This is where you'd do your magic. I'd really love it… if you'd do art here."

She pulled back her hands and turned away from him. She tightened his bathrobe around her. This made no sense.

"Gotta clean up in the bathroom, for a sec. 'Kay?"

She found the bathroom again, where she'd gotten her robe. Her purse was nearby, along with her shoes. She closed the door.

This isn't possible, she thought. To be so nuts about me, he'd have to be… NUTS. It's insane.

Riley looked sadly into the mirror.

No, she thought. Maybe I should just get naked. Maybe I should just strip, and let him have his moment. Get this over with. Sleep with him, and then get back to working at the diner. I'm alone, I'm divorced, and I'm unwanted, so none of this can be real. He doesn't love me.

Riley scrubbed off her old makeup. She tidied her hair and pulled it back. When she looked in his mirror again, she planted her hands on the sink. She sighed in defeat. Even CLARK was ruined hope. Another guy trying to impress her. Another guy, just trying to make his play. He even pretended to love her dreams… cheap bastard.

Earlier, she'd switched her phone to vibrate; she was surprised to hear it ring loudly. She dug it out of her purse and read the caller I.D.

"What? *'Rosa della Città?'* Was that his restaurant? Maybe I forgot something…" She cleared her throat and answered it. "Hello?"

Silence on the other end.

"Hello?"

Still nothing. She waited, and heard nothing. She prompted a final time, then hung up.

Bad connection, she thought. Ah well. At least I didn't have to speak Italian. But now I gotta deal with THIS connection. I can't be another chick-of-the-week. I'll have to break it off with him. I can't believe

I'm actually gonna lose Clark, after all this time… God, this is gonna hurt.

She walked back to him. He waited for her, still kneeling.

"Clark, you can't buy me. You can't win me over with all your government money. I'd really hoped that we weren't like that. I, myself, have loved you for something very different. You're brilliant, but your heart's strongest of all. That's what I thought. That's what I always wanted from you. Not this. Not luxuries.

"I'm sorry, Clark. I can't do this."

He glanced around them vaguely. "All of this is meaningless. It's from a soulless part of my life."

"What?"

"Everything around you, here, was just…"

He huffed. He tried to compose himself.

"You got married, and I tried to cope. Nothing worked, no matter how hard I tried. All of this is loss. All of it is FAILURE. What you see around you is an unhealed broken heart. But if you ever want any of it, it's yours. Then it'd have meaning.

"Or if you want, I'll burn this house to the ground."

His eyes held her with a steely grip. They had no hesitation. There was no trace of a lie.

CHAPTER TWENTY-ONE
The Dark Table

Somewhere, there was a large building without a street address. It was more of an idea supported by metal and concrete. Concerned interests gathered there to discuss their investments.

The building had a secure meeting area where a large, black table stretched the entire length of the room. Twenty-four hands perched along that table's edges. A dozen men sat tense and impatient. They were businessmen; they were architects of bigger pictures.

A monitor at the head of the room lit brightly. It showed a figure wearing trim, prototype armor, standing alone in an enclosed test area. The armor was matched black-and-white pieces, more like the vanes of a mechanical wing. A narrator spoke in a flat, dark voice:

* * *

"The evolution of military power has always been empowerment of Man. The jet gave him flight and speed. The tank made him impervious. The gun let him cast stones at supersonic speeds. It was always man; man made tools, then man made war."

On the monitor, the figure lifted its arms from its sides. The air turned hazy and amber colored, and the figure itself dimmed. It seemed to create its own shadow. Then it levitated slowly. A low thunder emanated from the armor itself and static crackled across the video.

Men at the table gawked in astonishment.

"The arms race is for smaller, faster, and stronger; more efficient; more precise. Kill teams have better training. Drones have more effective armaments. The arms race grasps at power, itself."

The armor rose higher in the air. It wasn't connected to anything else. The camera cranked upward to follow.

"Icarus controls fundamental forces. It bends them to the will of man."

A mounted machine gun drummed out bullets. Muzzle flashes strobed the whole test area. The camera showed spinning metal droplets falling from the armor. There were no ricochets - only broken bullets sparkling down like spring water. The armor lifted even higher, close to the top of the test chamber. It was unmarked.

Some of the hands tensed upon the dark table. Old men sat up with startled grunts.

"Control of force allows man to strike harder and faster. Control of force allows him to be impervious, moreso than any tank. Control and mastery of force has even let him fly. THAT is the power of Icarus."

The figure dropped straight down and slammed into the floor. It didn't bend its knees or crouch; it didn't need to. It stood upright, like a gloomy statue that had been there the whole time. Cracks wrinkled the cement at its feet.

"The control of force, in the hand of man, becomes the control of nations. Icarus is the power to fall, and to always be the last man standing."

An armored fist clenched, lifted forward, and boomed with the sound of a cannon. The camera staggered wildly. Pale shards of concrete crackled down through a cloud of amber dust. As the air cleared, the armor stood behind a ten-foot crater. The armor lowered its fist, waited, then blinked back to normal lighting. The amber haze cleared. It stood motionless.

Hands fell flat on the dark table. Men stared.

"Within the United States military, independent researchers have advanced the electrodynamic sciences. Force itself can be shaped, because it is understood. It is in man's grasp. What you have just witnessed is pure power, and a glimpse of our world's future."

In that dark room, twenty-four hands lay motionless on the long, black table. Then, some rubbed tightly. Some knit their fingers.

"Clark Benjamin's research means EVERYTHING."

"It's either the end of the world, or total control of it."

"Gentlemen? We need him."

"Ohh, the U.S. Military has a big crush on him," said a bitter, whining voice. Hands made circles in the air. "He's their asset. They have him covered. He designed autonomous software that watches him like a hawk. Even Langley adopted that. Then there's his personal security advisor."

The voice sneered poison.

"Yeah, I'd say he's dug in. He's prepared. He's the world's biggest boy scout."

A deep voice rolled out a response. "And you're personally invested, Anders. Obviously. So we'll keep things quiet. No more direct action against him."

"NO. We take an angle," Jeff Anders snarled.

Blue eyes squinted meanly. Hands turned to fists.

"LEVERAGE, not force. He has a sweetheart, now. I know her. He's crazy about her. He'd do anything to protect her. And SHE… has a stupid little brat kid. So we hit the kid.

"We'll stir up trouble in paradise. Then she'll leave him forever, and he'll have nothing left. He'll be easy pickings - easily poached from the government. We NEED this man and his research; any profiteer knows this."

Another pair of hands drew together. Fingers steepled. A voice rumbled gravely.

"You'll have your shot at him, Mr Anders."

"Oh, rest assured," Jeff Anders snapped, "We'll own Clark Benjamin, or no-one will. The plan's in motion as we speak, gentlemen. It's money in the bank."

Black kings sat at that dark table. They focused on three pawns: Clark David Benjamin, Riley Ann Henway, and Albert Noble Henway.

CHAPTER TWENTY-TWO
TAP, TAP

Clark stepped close to her. "Sweetheart?" he asked. "Should we get you back to see your son?"

"Naw, I just texted. He'd be happy to spend ALL his time at Larsen's, anyway. And Larsen's family loves him. Albert's a total whiz in school."

"Ya," Clark rubbed his chin. "I figured that much. Grade 4."

Riley looked skeptical: "Y-… he doesn't 'tutor' Larsen, per se, but the whole family thinks he's helping. Larsen's got cerebral palsy, and Albert doesn't see it or doesn't mind. He helps with lots of things. He even found a way for them to play video games together."

"What - 'they share a controller, somehow?"

"No. Not at all. Albert rigged up something using old nylons and a laundry rack. It stretches out

Larsen's movement, before buttons get pressed. It looks ridiculous, and Larsen gets a workout, but it translates to fine motor skills. It's brilliant. I said it before: my kid's gonna love you. Two peas in a pod."

We can't jump into this, he thought.

Clark spoke quietly: "Do you, like, have work?"

"Mmm. Not till this evening."

He thought for a few moments.

"Actually - I remembered something. Do you know Ms Philson, at the library?"

"Who, the tall lady? short hair? really thoughtful?"

"Yeah. In a few weeks, she and some parents are taking kids on a big trip. They're going to the Metro Museum for a week. They needed more funding, so I supported them. Do you think Albert would want to go? They'd make room for him."

"HAH-haha. A convenient way to keep him busy."

"Well... ya, if we were gonna figure things out, together, I guess that'd give us some space."

"You're a damn genius, Clark."

"N... no, I thought Albert might want to go. It's the last week for that famous dinosaur exhibit, right? They have one of the largest reconstructed T-Rex skeletons in the world. It's frickin' terrifying. To me, 'looks like some ancient, reptilian death-lord. But Albert? He might love it. I remembered he has a thing for dinosaurs. Doesn't he?"

Riley's eyes boiled back in her head. She could

only reach his chest, so she started kissing there.

He exhaled. "What - you have a dinosaur fetish, too?"

She shook her head. "Clark? You take care of me, and now my KID. You're always so good to me. You even watched over me, while I slept."

She pulled away and looked at him dreamily.

"Do you wanna rest, a little? Could I hold you this time, if you wanted to get some sleep?"

He shook his head modestly. "I don't think I can sleep."

"C'mon," she tugged his shirt-sleeve. "I won't bite. Well, I mean, I might nibble a bit."

He gave a quiet puff of laughter. "Couch?"

She stopped him. She looked up. Those were the eyes he saw on prom night - they were irresistible.

"Maybe bedroom?"

He felt that lance through his heart like frigid steel. The most beautiful woman he had ever known was standing here, in his bathrobe, tugging at his sleeve.

Take me to bed, she was saying.

Clark's insides twisted into spiny knots.

"Why haven't we done this, Clark? For years, you wouldn't kiss me. You wouldn't ask me out. Last night, you didn't sleep with me. Now, you're hesitating again. What's wrong with me?"

"NOTHING."

"Clark, you can't put me on a pedestal. You can't treat me like I'm absolute purity. I've been married and divorced. I've had a son. I'm my own little family with him. I'm not some pure-and-untouched maiden. You don't need white gloves with me."

He couldn't respond.

"Is there something else? Some other secret?"

His eyes shut.

She started scowling a little, but then he replied: "I put up walls. This whole house is kinda like that. Walls, to separate me from you. They protect me from the pain of loss. I'm sorry about those walls, but they actually protect both of us. If I let you in, you'll know how I truly feel about you."

She squeezed his arms. "You care! There's nothing wrong!"

His whisper was a wraith. "My love is an absolute savage… and it destroyed my life, when you got married. I'm worried about my self-control. When I'm with you, it's always tapping… ticking… straining to get out."

She stepped back. She looked at him squarely.

"You said 'Us' after our first kiss. I agreed. Clark? We're TOGETHER now. As half of this relationship, I'm gonna get my way some of the time. So, we're going to your room. Then, I'm going to give you a back rub, and we're going to cuddle. If you fall asleep, I'll lie with you and kiss good dreams into your head. That's the deal. Come with me."

She pulled him by the sleeve. She led him past the kitchen.

"Err… where exactly is your bedroom?"

"Right, and along this wall." He directed her past the kitchen. "Now left. Yeah… in here - bedroom. Same windows, same view as the kitchen. Nice sunrise, in the mornings."

Clark's room was large, but spartan. A king-sized bed took the left side of the room. It was covered with a white duvet. Riley didn't see any pictures on the walls or on his nightstand. His bed was close to the window. He'd have a good view of the night sky. There was a huge bookcase opposite his bed. It was weighed down by old volumes, like dusty paper bricks.

Riley glanced at the walls, the window, the books, and the wall closet beside the bookcase. She drew the curtains for him.

"Uhh," she looked down, "I'm just going to turn around, if you feel better. Do you have pajama bottoms?"

"No," he grunted. "Boxers."

She closed her eyes and swallowed.

"I guess that's fine."

She heard him disrobe and slip into bed.

She didn't open her eyes. "Y'know, Babe - I have walls too. No-one's ever been so sensual, but so respectful. I feel like I'm a virgin - not with sex, but acknowledgement or something."

His voice was a low purr: "Hmm - validation." He shook his head. "Has that ever been a question?"

"What, that you validate me?" She turned to him again.

"No - that you always deserved to be validated." He sighed. "It's important. It's vital. So I think you ARE a virgin. I don't think anyone's ever been fair to you, or treated you the way you should've been treated. I didn't kiss you, before, and it was because of that. I never pushed, because it wasn't RIGHT. It really didn't matter how I felt. You deserved better."

Clark lay flat on his belly. He folded his arms above him. Riley watched his shoulders turn to mountains. The strength of his back was a buried landscape beneath his skin.

"So you DIDN'T kiss me... out of respect? as an act of love?" She blushed.

"...Yeah. Definitely."

Her eyes turned. She tried to digest that fact. She climbed next to Clark.

"Holy," she exhaled. "A lot of times, I just wanted to smooch you. I wanted to drop everything and make out with you on the spot. In a hall, or walking somewhere, or anywhere."

He groaned softly. "I can relate."

She shrugged. "But we DIDN'T kiss. We didn't relate, 'cuz of our stupid walls."

"And basic respect. Like, say, if you'd had a few drinks. That got in the way."

She reached for his shoulder. "Hey. What's this cut on your arm? This, by your shoulder, here?"

"Ahh - yeah, that was from work. Back in the lab. Y'know, exploding potions and stuff? That was an ill-fated beaker. A little cut," he lied.

She touched his back. His mass was bred from iron and stone. Her hands were thin leaves, blowing across this statue. They made statues like him in ancient Greece.

"Beaker? Y'know, I'm imagining that funny, skinny, orange-haired weirdo from The Muppets. The guy in the lab. Right? All he says is 'mi-mee-mur, mi-mi-meep.'"

"Mmm-hmm," Clark murmured, sensing her touch. "In the lab. With the potions. Yeah. That was mi-m'me…"

Her hands were both warm and cool at the same time. Her palms pressed a gentle firmness. He felt them slide up his shoulders like butter: long, full slides. She wasn't just massaging him. She loved this. Her hands licked up the muscle of his back. He smiled deep in his jaw.

Mmm, he thought. Riley's enjoying my shoulders… hee-hee-hee.

Her little hands reached along his arms like slow waves on sand. He almost growled back to her.

She looked closer. That cut looked deep. It was a slice along his upper arm, curving up his shoulder.

It was no beaker.

Four years ago, Clark screamed in his lab. Alarms blared and amber lights flashed. Clark turned his head and roared: "You and YOU! Back into containment! ALL of you! Get in there, and seal the door!" He stabbed his finger at 'Decontamination.'

Clark whipped a flash drive from his computer.

He jammed it under his wristwatch. Just then, the sound of gunfire popped from the floors above him, and then the nearby corridor. Black-clad mercenaries rushed through the facility.

POP-POP, went their double taps. POP-POP, POP-POP, as if they were shooting people dead. It was recon-by-fire. It was a scare tactic to flush out anyone who was hiding. Clark saw muzzle flashes in the hallway. There were two secure doors for this lab, but they wouldn't be enough.

He sneered meanly. "No… no, not today. Not today, you STUPID F-"

He grabbed a bunsen burner, tensed his fist around it, and ripped it from the wall. His arm bulked out, and the hose stretched and pinged loose. Gas flooded into the room with its oily smell.

Clark wrapped the wall pipe with hose, hammered his fist down, and cracked it wide open. More gas began whistling into the room.

He covered his mouth with his sleeve. That smell was powerful. He closed the inside security door, but made sure it wasn't locked.

The lab was big enough for six workstations, and could accommodate thirty staff. Today, it was only Clark and his five techs.

He turned fiercely and screamed at them: "SEAL IT, damn you!"

The alarms continued blaring. Five terrified faces hid in the back of the lab. They were wide-eyed, like trapped mice. They jumped back when they heard new gunfire. It pounded right outside the lab's entrance. They shrank back into containment and sealed the door.

They left Clark alone, there, in the lab area. He was in the open.

Clark snarled. The stink of gas was getting worse.

Outside, an armored soldier shotgunned the security cameras. Each camera was protected with a thick plastic dome, but was sheared away with a heavy POOM sound. Then the fire-team leader called for a breach on the first secure door. It only took them a few seconds to get through.

Inside, Clark had what they wanted: the flash drive. It was hidden under his wristwatch. It was the only copy of his research data. The other lab computers had self-destructed by sealing themselves and melting their own hard drives.

Clark crossed over to a containment station. Iso-stations were used for volatile experiments - they were small, reinforced booths with shatterproof windows. They were environmentally sealed.

He grabbed a small canister of liquid nitrogen. He figured he'd use it for self-defence, or maybe as concealment. He crawled tightly inside the iso-station and secured the fume hood. He breathed on the observation glass, gave it a quick spray of nitrogen, and hid there. He was sealed in there, huddled in a ball, behind frosted glass. At least the smell of gas wasn't as strong.

The first secure door thundered open. Soon, the

mercenaries whipped open the second door and entered. The lights from their headlamps swept across the tabletops. Men checked computers, but all the hard drives were melted slag.

"AGHH," the leader growled in his gas mask. "SOMEONE'S got it. Those white-coats, hiding back there? Grab one. Bleed it out of 'em. Make the others watch. Someone's gotta talk. Move!"

The breacher checked the containment door, then sighed.

"Boss?" his voice buzzed. "Yeah, 'gonna need the acetylene torch, here. Thermite."

The leader fumed. "Then GET TO WORK!" He squared his shoulders at the door. His cold eyes wanted to bore right through it. His silenced pistol was restless in his hand.

Clark clutched his knees with his arms. He held his can of liquid nitrogen. He listened to the thugs and the crackling hiss of their gas masks. They were attacking a government-level chem facility, so they each had a mask and a separate supply of oxygen.

He did some basic math. The gas leak was still streaming into the room. The alarms were too loud for anyone to hear it. These mercenaries wouldn't have time to open the containment door; gas would fill the room, first. When they breached into decontamination, they'd ignite the gas. They'd incinerate themselves as well as his colleagues inside.

NO, he thought, MY LITTLE SURPRISE IS FOR YOU. JUST FOR YOU.

He tapped his fingernails against the fume hood.
Someone's ears perked. "Ay. 'You hear that?"

Five soldiers raised their weapons. Two lifted
their squat, tactical shotguns. Three others had
machine pistols like angry metal scorpions - tense and
eager to strike.

Clark listened to them breathing. They listened
for him. He waited. It was cat-and-mouse, but with
soldiers, guns, and explosive gas.

"What the hell WAS that?"

"Who cares. Get them squealers out. Move!"

Clark waited silently. They placed thermite packs
over the locks. They began rigging the primers. The
gas would be thick, right now. They wouldn't notice,
because their masks only fed them safe, breathable air.

With his fingernails, Clark scratched the fume
hood.

Scrit-scritchy. Scritch-scritch.

"Okay, someone's screwin' with us! Fan out!"

YEAH, Clark scowled. FAN OUT. NICE AN'
WIDE.

When they were spaced out across the room and
unknowingly wading through flammable gas, Clark
ducked his head and said a brief prayer.

"I just want to see you again," he whispered.
"Please, my sweet love... I just want to live, so I can
see your beautiful face... just one more time."

He held up the metal can of liquid nitrogen. He
steeled himself.

"I love you, Riley."

He bent his wrist, then rapped the can sharply against the fume hood.

Tap-TAP!

"Who the-?!" A merc panicked. He yanked up his shotgun.

Chik-clack, POOM!

The entire lab bloomed hellfire. Gale-force flames ripped it apart. The men were thrown wildly like leaves in a storm. Then, explosion alarms honked noisily and everything locked down. Gas was cut, fans halted, windows secured. Only the sprinklers hissed wide sheets of water through the air. Alarms honked fat notes and rang like tinnitus.

Clark tried to move.

"A-...AAH-hagh!" A piece of someone's kevlar had stripped right out of their armor, blown across the room, and chopped through Clark's fume hood. It gouged through the barrier and into his upper arm, like a cleaver. He was pinned.

"G-... DAMMIT," he screamed. "You SON-of-a-..."

Over the next minute, he dragged his arm off that kevlar plate. He grit his teeth and tried to pull his shoulder muscle loose. Once he was free, he bled strongly and went limp with relief.

"OHH-ho-ho," he threatened the kevlar. He was wobbly from shock and pain. "You are SO coming home with me, you chunky, ugly souvenir..." He shook his head briskly. He didn't want to be delirious.

It had been a fiery blast, but the concussion knocked the soldiers unconscious. Some of them had been thrown through the air and bounced against walls. If they were alive, they were having nightmares about headaches.

Clark stepped over them - almost politely - and reached containment. He clutched his bleeding arm. He thumped the containment door with his elbow. A little blood crept through his fingers.

"Naveen?" he knocked on the glass. "HEY - Naveen! Get them up. Let's get out of here. NAVEEN? Let's get OUT of here!"

Naveen had been covering the other techs as they all cowered in the corner. They were sealed in decontamination, but he held his white coat over them anyway. Naveen wanted to protect everyone.

Naveen was impeccably tidy, and even had an adorable little pencil-thin mustache. He helped the tall lady from Finland, and the other two Americans, and the fifth pudgy guy from New Zealand.

"Come on," Naveen urged them, "Mr Benjamin says this whole ordeal is over. We really must depart, now. Come on - get up, please."

The six of them made their way out of the lab. Sprinklers plastered their hair to their scalps. They gagged at the smells of unidentifiable smoldering things. They headed toward the secure elevator, but federal guards swarmed them in seconds. The guards also wore black, with well fitted breath masks and tight straps across their body armor. The six scientists were more in custody than safety. Hard gloves seized them, and faceless masks glared. They grabbed Naveen roughly.

"Sirs! We - OWW! Sirs, we are all compliant! We are compl-" He was grappled and muzzled.

Clark didn't make any sudden moves. He held up his hands until they cuffed him. Before they covered his mouth, he stated, "Hey. There's a flash drive here, under my wristwatch. I know what's on it. So does your boss. You keep it safe, my friend - as safe as your own family."

Two guards held him. They gripped his hand and his arm. The head guard peered closely at Clark's wrist. He clicked a device on his armor, and his glove made a slight ticking sound. No explosives or toxins were detected, other than obvious traces from the recent explosion. Nothing radioactive, nothing incendiary, no obvious primers.

The head guard nodded sharply and pulled the flash drive loose. He tucked it into a pocket underneath his belt.

All the scientists were detained and interrogated for two days. Guards grilled them about security, right down to the finest details. Apparently, Naveen had just been dumped by his girlfriend, two weeks ago. The lady from Finland bought her second BMW last month, and was planning on getting one for her daughter. One of the Americans admitted to problems with stress, and neither alcohol nor cannabis helped him.

Afterward, all six were lined up in a dark room.
A man in a smooth suit walked up to them. He was
bald, thick-set and paunchy. His aftershave was
terrible; it smelled like gasoline with a hard-on.

"You and you? FIRED. Get out. You, and you…
and also you? You're, uh… Mr… Mr Josh?"

"Naveen Joshi, sir." He gave a loose nod.

"Boss likes you enough. Walk away. But you?
Benjamin?"

Clark Benjamin looked up. "Yes, sir?"

"We don't have purple hearts for eggheads. We
don't celebrate maniacs, neither, but you're our kind
of crazy. You know what you did. You either got balls
of brass, or you love your country more'n your own
mother. We want to thank you, so we have someone
here you wanna meet."

OH MY GOD, he thought, reeling back. NO
WAY! Did they find her? Is she here? Can I SEE her?

The suit gestured to another person. It was
someone whom Clark easily recognized. It was
someone who was 'never officially there.'

They shared a handshake and pleasant small talk.
He thanked Clark genuinely, and gave another cordial
handshake. Clark hid his disappointment.

"Thank you, Mr Vice President. An honor."

When they were alone again, the bald man
addressed Clark.

"You are NOT cut out for this, Mr Benjamin."

Clark sighed. The man's expression went flat.

"No," he continued. "You're better."

The man's voice dropped to a new level. He extended his hand and shook Clark's.

"My name's Philip Archibauld. I'm conscripting you. You got a brain we value, and a tenacity we need. You're gonna work with us in S.I."

Clark remained still.

"Could you tell me what that is, sir?" he asked quietly.

"Don't feel bad if you don't know, 'cuz it's what we do. It's our business."

Archibauld shifted his weight. He smiled somewhere in his tired eyes.

"You, Mr Benjamin, are gonna be part of Secure Intelogistics. We're the federal department that handles the security and logistics of information. We're the reason WHY you haven't heard of us."

Clark wanted to step back slowly, but he didn't dare. The man's eyes held him in place.

"Knowledge is power, right?"

"Uhh," Clark shrugged innocently. "Yeah. I believe that."

"And this is America, right?"

"Well," Clark smiled nervously. "I mean, yeah. Yeah, of course it's-"

"And AMERICA'S got the damn nukes; everybody knows that. So you bet your bottom dollar, we own knowledge too. Patents? Intellectual copyrights? HAH. That's kiddie stuff."

Archibauld sucked his lip noisily.

"You'll be doing 'research,' as we like to call it.

It's finding out what people know. Later, you'll do field research. You will engineer what people know. You will redefine the field; you will shape the perceived world. You will neither be seen nor remembered.

"You'll no longer be 'population,' Mr Benjamin. You'll be an agent."

Clark wanted to say something, beginning with the words 'I can't.' The man wouldn't let him.

"You'll learn a core set of skills that adapt to many, many situations. You will not fear small arms, physical assault, or most common domestic threats. You'll have a persona that will protect you from traumatic crisis situations. You will not be shackled by the common delusions of 'normality' or 'sanity.'

"You'll learn the science of human inner strength. You WILL stem rivers, because we turn tides. We channel the flow of events."

"Sir," Clark shook his head, "I'm not a soldier. The training? I don't..."

"We can't let you be vulnerable, Mr Benjamin. We can't afford it. So you won't get 'training.' You'll have mastery. You won't learn to fight, or play punchy patty-cake; you're the one who turns off the lights and leaves the room. You get me?"

"But... I'm an academic, sir. I'm not ready for this kind of danger."

"Yeah? Well, it's intelligence. Where do you think we get our agents? our specialists?"

Archibauld stared at him. Clark smothered in the

silence. He tried to break it.

"Uhh... from special ops?"

"No. Soldiers do the heavy lifting. They're the spine. They're Mr Steel."

"Yeah," Clark agreed. "Well, ex-spies, then?"

"No, espionage is just management. Management and sheer balls - you could call them Mr Brass."

"Okay, okay." Clark tossed his head in frustration. "So who's S.I., huh? Are you the alchemists, or something? Wait - are you Mr Gold?"

A spark lit the man's eye. He looked like an old cat who still had some jungle in him.

"No," he rumbled. "In S.I., you are the forge. You mould things. You shape things."

They crossed a threshold.

"You... are Mr Smith."

A mean smile grew on his lips.

"You are a Renaissance man, Mr Benjamin. Renaissance men defined the Renaissance. They weren't born into it. They didn't inherit it. They built it. They WERE the Renaissance. That's who you are. And that's who we are..."

He leaned in close.

"...and on our own terms."

Clark shifted. The man squinted at him sideways.

"Knowing isn't half the battle. It's everything. So we own knowledge. Maybe you never heard of S.I., but fish don't see the ocean, neither. You prob'ly don't realize it, but you breathe sky everyday. Time to wake up, Mr Benjamin. You've earned it."

"Sir?" Clark raised his finger. "As a scientist, I have my strengths. But as a man, I have other serious weaknesses."

Archibauld rasped, "I know what you are."

The room drained; pretense was gone. Archibauld loved every second of it.

"People live on their little stack of sanity, kid. It's all they know. They don't know the rest of the iceberg, underneath. The world is nine-tenths madness. You don't have the luxury of lying to yourself anymore. You're valuable; you're coming with us."

"I can't," Clark started, "I really can't do this. I'm sorry. It's not that I have another job. And I'm not married or anything…"

"Yeah," Archibauld drawled. "And she was a nice girl, too." He watched Clark stiffen, as if Clark took a sudden vow of silence.

Archibauld gave a token smile and turned from the room.

"I'd suggest you think about it, like they say in the movies… but this is real life. You start before the end of the week. Welcome to S.I., Mr Benjamin."

His shoulder wound was so deep, it left a prominent scar. He never guessed that in another four years, Riley herself would be running her fingers over his arm. She traced lightly over that pale line.

"Jeez," she remarked. "That's not the Beaker I was thinking of." She touched his back affectionately: pat-pat.

"Life isn't…" He started drifting off. "Life's not EXACTLY… like The Muppets. I'm not Kermit, and you're nothing like Miss Piggy."

She inhaled slowly and stretched her arms over him.

"I dunno, Clark. I think we're a famous pair. You're the 'Mahna-Mahna' to my 'Doot-Doo Dee-Doo-Doo'…"

He shook a few times from chuckling. She lay down over his back. She nuzzled close to him.

"Clark? Your skin's really warm."

His eyes bolted open. "OH-…"

She pulled up the sheets. Her bathrobe crumpled onto the floor.

"Ya. Ya, Riley… So's yours."

CHAPTER TWENTY-THREE

The Dream

Riley murmured sleepily. She smelled fresh sheets and lavender. Everything was quiet. She smiled to herself. Her eyelids fluttered.

Mmm, she grinned. Oh, I LOVE these dreams! I get to cuddle with Clark in this fancy hotel, and I kiss him lots, and we hold each other, and then we always go dancing every night. And he makes me the prettiest dresses for the royal ball! Aww, I can't wait to see him this time.

...Hmm? Wait, where am I?

She woke. She floated like a cloud in a big, white duvet. The faint scent of lavender surrounded her. She saw she was alone, in a king-size bed. It wasn't a hotel. It was Clark's bedroom. She heard his voice nearby. Things sounded dulled, so she tried to pop her ears.

She sat up and saw him pacing outside the bedroom. He was dressed. He held his phone close to his cheek.

"…No sir, I want cutaway. It's personal, and I'd like to invoke Aegis 20: my rights as an asset, as much as an agent. There is no… No, sir. No compromise or breach of any kind. This is my elective choice.

"To be a civilian. That's right. I can't be available for standby or flash-ops… Yeah, I know what you're going to ask. 'Icarus.' No, it's secure. I haven't decided where it'll… Yes, you can be assured of that. And my portfolios can be reassigned.

"Okay. So close them all. Threat One up to Threat Eight. All of them. Transfer them to whoever's most qualified, whenever you find them. Notify me of any concerns.

"Yes, I want out. I know I'm losing a lot.

"Well… thank you. And y'know, if S.I. Wasn't 'Black-Tier,' I'd be the first to recommend you. Mmm-hmm. I appreciate that, sir, but I have a life, and I have my rights. Aegis 20. Thank you.

"…You're welcome, sir. It's been an honor and a privilege."

Click.

"Athena?" he called quietly, "End Secure Lockdown."

The wall beeped. The white noise of ventilation started up again. Riley's ears must have popped, because she could hear things clearly again.

Clark rubbed his temples, then stood tall. His

head dipped down to look at something in his hand. He closed it in his fist.

He turned and saw Riley looking at him.

"Wait - did you hear much of that?"

She said nothing. He pocketed whatever was in his hand.

"Well," he walked up to her, "it was good news. Umm... look, do you wanna go get some lunch? Or even some croissants, maybe?"

She scoffed lightly and grinned. "You know everything. You must be obsessed with me..."

She saw this sting him, so she tried to recover.

"...because you always seem to know what I want. It's uncanny."

He rolled his eyes playfully. "WELL... I might remind you, you're not the only one who likes croissants. Plus, I have to try the Sunny Side Bakery. By the way - it's a little past one in the afternoon. Albert must still be at Larsen's...?"

She nodded.

"I had my friend Morgan fix a dress for you. She works over at Renner and Scot. I had it sent just an hour ago."

Riley backed up. She thumped against the bed's headboard. She grabbed the duvet and clutched it against her chest.

"W-What is this, Clark? How did you know?"

"What? that you didn't have anything to wear? Last night, you were wearing a 'pinchy, scaly monster,' and I wrapped you in my coat, instead.

Other than that, you only have my bathrobe. You might want something better."

Her head spun. "No. I was just dreaming about this. You, making me dresses."

He pouted thoughtfully, then smirked and shook his head. "Dunno." He shrugged.

He stepped out to the hall and called back to her, "But I'm no tailor. This was Morgan. She's a total whiz. She's almost…"

He poked his head around the door again.

"Almost an artist like yourself." He held up a long, crinkly bag.

"She said lightweight, woven fabric. Yeah. A modern, minimalist floral pattern… it's loose-fitting, and it's smocked at the bodice. 'Should be comfy."

He draped the garment bag across the bed like an offering. She opened the zipper and looked at the dress - it was gorgeous. The colors were playful and summery, like an impressionist painting that was overjoyed to be her dress. It was prettier than anything she'd ever owned.

Her whole expression deflated. "Clark, I have the worst culture shock right now. I don't deserve…"

He sat in front of her, leaned forward, and kissed her cheek. "Morgan grabbed something else at the mall. Jogging pants? Zip-up hoodie? For those 'yoga pants' days? She told me it's a thing."

"Clark, I don't know if I can do this - be your princess. The dresses, dinners, wine, or…" She waved around the room. "All of this."

"Well, I hope you can indulge ME. I might dote on you. If you were all about wealth, I wouldn't bring you little things like dresses. I'd bring you... I dunno, deeds to real estate."

She dipped her brow. He could've brought her land deeds. Easily.

"Riley, if you're going to have a partner, you should have the best partner in the world. So I might..." he chuckled softly, "Yeah, I might try pretty hard."

She whined sweetly and touched his arm.

"Also, I'm cutting some of the complications at work. I hope you don't mind, but I think it's for the best. We'll be losing a bit. Freedom has a price."

She listened carefully.

"I checked my net worth. Yeah, it was at $17.3 million, this morning. After cutaway, we'll be at about nine - or, $8.8 million, more like."

"W-what are you doing, Clark?" She didn't know what was happening.

He rolled his eyes and huffed. "Y'know, all we lose is an investments portfolio. It's just government affiliates. The good thing is... LOSING those frickin' government affiliates. There are under-the-table contractors who do specialized stuff. They're called 'special assets.' There's big money there, because things... can get ugly."

"What, are you worried about men in dark suits?" she joked.

"Actually, no."

His face wore no expression. His silence filled the room.

"Well," she started, then swallowed. "How cloak-and-dagger is this government research stuff? I'm probably not allowed to know, right? Do people get hurt?"

His eyes tipped downward. His brow sank. Yes, people got hurt. Entire households disappeared overnight.

"Wait." She searched him with stern eyes. "What's the worst thing you've had to do? What are you expected to do? Can you even tell me?"

He looked away. He shook his head.

"I just do research. But I've worked under special government funding."

He sucked his teeth, like coming to a conclusion.

"Do you remember Ferdinand Lester? Mr Lester, the gym teacher?"

"Yeah." She sorted the duvet on her lap. "Kinda balding? Never blinked? Creepy, greasy smile?" She looked nauseated. "He always stared at the boys in their gym shorts. What, did you catch him with something?"

"No," Clark grit his teeth. "I used him."

Clark turned to face her. She sat up to listen.

"Not too long ago, the FBI followed a case of child exploitation - online kiddie stuff. They wanted my help. I used Mr Lester, sorta like 'fingerprints.' He led to thirty-eight other men, all of them much worse than he was. One of 'em was even a retired judge living in South America. That was the FBI target."

"Whoa. And you caught them?"

Clark squinted for a moment.

"No. Those guys led to a few hundred others. It was a dark network. There were server hubs hidden in basements, like protected bunkers. Every one of those online servers burned." His eyes shone. "Like, literally, every one of those servers caught fire."

He clearly enjoyed that fact.

"Holy CRAP, man..." Riley's hands lay limp in the duvet. "And you did all that?"

"What, you think I stopped there?"

She suddenly saw a ruthless, brilliant gleam. Something vicious in him was smiling.

"Hell, no. I tracked beyond that. I found common sources. I went further upstream."

Her jaw hung and her brows raised.

"I found the money trails. I followed every possible branch, from street-level 'talent scouts' right up to the filming locations. I found the... producers, and where they lived. Where they slept. And those assholes were NOT expecting our little visit, in the middle of the night."

His face darkened.

"In one week, twenty-three kids were rescued and given asylum."

Riley couldn't breathe.

"Yeah. I did THAT, Riley. Twenty-three kids. And a big, sick money-train came to a screeching halt. And that was the FIRST week.

"When we stormed those locations, there were no casualties and only five men were injured. Later, though, I heard that some judge died in a car accident, somewhere. I don't know details.

"The media loves dirt, right? Well, this wasn't fit for TV. I personally hired the best child psychologists I could find, out of necessity. Do you understand what I mean?"

He looked toward her, but couldn't make eye contact. She stared straight at him.

"But," she started, "there's ALWAYS horrible stuff on the news."

"Yeah. You hear about terrorists. You hear about disasters. You DON'T hear about a lot of things. There are much worse things - harmful things - and we have them sewn up, like they never existed."

"Do you always have to do this stuff? Does it wear on you?"

"A friend of mine handles a lot - Matt. I mentioned him earlier. To most people, he's just a nice guy in a suit. To me? He's one hell of soldier. He changes what people see. Believe me, it's necessary."

"He sounds like a government spook," Riley added, "like in movies. Just - not the worst type."

Clark sat straight. "It's our government. It's our nation. He's behind the scenes, yeah, because he holds the stage up. The show must go on, and he gives it a chance. He's a very pure, very ethical man... especially considering what he fights."

"He must know some insane stuff," Riley added.

"Yeah, well… I'll tell you one secret he's kept forever. He never told anyone."

Riley leaned forward, listening.

"He knows I'm hopelessly in love with someone… and that I'd do anything for her."

"Hah - ANY-thinggg?" she joked, conspiratorially. Mischief danced in her eyes.

Clark kept a straight face.

"Dude," she poked him, "I'm totally joking. I might ask for a croissant; that's about it."

"You realize I just lost eight million dollars this morning; you don't mind that?"

"Actually," she laughed, "you kept saying 'we.' You said 'we' lose investments, or 'we' lose a chunk of money. I liked that." She grinned. "We're really together, aren't we? It feels natural."

Clark's phone bleeped. He checked his texts.

"Great. Now I gotta go in to work tomorrow… consultancy nonsense."

He stood up from the bed. He walked over to his wall closet next to the bookcase. The closet doors folded open to show his pressed suits.

"Someday?" he chuckled, "Someday, I'll go back to jeans and T-shirts." He fished in his pocket and deposited something in a coat.

"No," she pointed right at him, "I've seen you in impeccable suits, dressy clothes… and I've even seen you in your boxers, big fella. I have never seen you wear jeans." She squinted her eyes at him playfully. "I don't think you're a 'jeans' kind of guy."

CHAPTER TWENTY-FOUR
To Leave the Field

Riley worked at a little Greek diner called Dino's. It was cramped and sweaty like an armpit. One rainy evening, it was only marginally less humid than the rainstorm outside. The air was heavy inside Riley's chest.

Riley's boss yelled half-English, half-Greek, and must have been responsible for half of the hot air in this diner. His hands flapped around like startled pigeons. Either that, or he was conducting the loudest orchestra in the world.

"Fest! FEST!" he yelled at the cook. He yelled the same thing at the prep, and the dishwashers, and the servers. The only people he didn't yell at were the customers.

Speed was volume. Volume was sales. Cash was everything.

Riley's shift was almost over. Her boss counted money behind the cash register. He palmed through twenties and fifties. Riley wore a discreet coin dispenser over her black apron. She had to make correct change if someone offered a $3.25 tip.

She ducked back in the kitchen to retrieve someone's order. Her bank called her cellphone, but the connection was weird. Nothing on the other end. She'd have to call back after her shift.

"Fester!" her boss yelled. "New costumer!"

She wouldn't correct him on his English. This was the only job she could find, at the moment... or for the last several years.

Two new customers entered. A third followed shortly after.

The last one was tall. Rain dripped from his broad, black hat. He seemed conservative, like he didn't want to make a mess. He shook his longcoat and hat by the door, but wore them inside. He gestured to the corner, where he'd contain his raindrops. He looked cold and miserable.

Riley almost rolled her eyes. The dark, steamy diner? The late evening? The rainstorm outside? The mysterious, tall stranger in the dark coat and fedora? It was so clichéd, it had an innocent charm. The man tucked into his corner and huddled behind a menu.

The other two weren't as charming. They were Ashvale regulars: Timmy Karnes and Jonno Malick. Timmy was chronically anxious, and Jonno was so chill, it was creepy. She hated how they looked at her.

They came here all the time.

"Hey," Jonno's voice rolled. It was deep and imposing. "Could I get some service?" He scratched the front of his pants.

Timmy giggled to himself.

Jonno had dull brown hair. It was flat and jutting, like Frankenstein's monster. His eyes were as dead as the monster's, but his mouth always had a gross smile hoisting it up. His smile lifted like a pervert's coat - like indecent exposure.

Timmy Karnes had mousy red-bronze hair. He had a smattering of freckles over his face. His eyes twitched frequently, but not toward anything in particular. Riley didn't know what color his eyes were, but she never looked closely. She didn't want to. She wouldn't try to pet a rabid weasel, either.

"Hey. Service?" Jonno repeated, scratching his groin again.

"Welcome to Dino's, gentlemen," she wore a patient face. "What could I get you, this evening?"

"Off..." Jonno started.

There was a sickening silence. Riley just wished that the man in the hat was actually a cop.

"Off the top of my head..." Jonno continued, nodding at her.

He paused for effect.

"Off the top of my head, I dunno. What's special, tonight?"

Riley wore her stupid apron, and recited the same stupid specials, and wore the same smile, and wanted out.

Clark? she thought to herself. Okay, I want out now. Ya.

Jonno and Timmy smiled eagerly as she finished her rehearsed speech.

"And that comes with rice pudding, for dessert."

"Rice PUDDING?" Timmy twitched. He turned to Jonno. "What IS that?"

Jonno shrugged, and gestured to Riley. "You have it at the end. Right, Riley? What's it like?"

"It's just… sweetened rice."

"Like grains? Grains of rice?" Jonno asked.

"No, sorta mashed. More creamy." Riley's teeth closed.

"OH…" Jonno nodded at Timmy. "Right. Creamy and sticky, and it comes at the end. See? She knows all about it."

Riley turned her head. Her boss was staring iron nails at her.

She obliged, and served the idiotic regulars their stupid diner food. They wouldn't tip; she remembered this.

She went to the other man - the last customer, in the coat and hat. He just shook his head. He tapped toward a special and nodded.

"Anything else, sir?"

He whispered, "No."

"And water, to drink?"

"…Yeah," he whispered again, in a hoarse voice.

She shrank away from him. He was bundled tight

in his coat, like he was chilled to the bone. Perhaps he'd travelled a long way, to get to Ashvale? Dino's was robbed six years ago. Was he going to rob the place?

"Are you alright, sir?"

He said nothing, but nodded. There was something wrong with him.

"Hey," Jonno called out again, "Could I get some service, please?" He loosely jangled his belt, like he was scratching his belly button.

Riley's boss glared at her until she served Jonno. She actually had to play along, and help him make yet another asinine sexual remark.

The last part of her shift ended like this: Jonno led the show, Timmy cackled like a seagull, and Riley's boss made sure it all played out. He'd fire her, if she didn't keep up this ridiculous act for paying customers.

"I like your apron," Jonno drawled. "Do you clean up messes with it?"

The hat man snapped his fingers, softly, and beckoned to her.

"If you'll excuse," she dodged away, as Jonno reached for her behind. "Excuse me a moment...!"

Riley's boss sat up straight to stare at her. She stepped quickly over to the man in the hat.

"Could I-" she took a breath. "Could I help you, sir?"

"Quit your day job," he whispered.

"Quit my day job?" She chuckled, and leveled

with him kindly. "Y'know, this mysterious stranger stuff? It's cute, but kinda dated. Are you a detective, under there? Or what - are you gonna recruit me for some once-in-a-lifetime chance? I get to be a superhero or something?"

He nodded at her. "Once-in-a-lifetime… because you only HAVE one lifetime, Miss Riley. So quit your day job."

He looked up at her with his steady grey eyes. He leaned into his hand. His finger crossed his lips.

She relaxed and spoke with quiet calm. "Why are you doing this to me, Clark? Are you nuts?"

His eye met hers. "You wear his childish apron, I wear my childish disguise. You think I'M nuts, but I think YOU put up with way too much. Not that I'd judge you."

She squared her jaw.

"Yeah, this is pretty childish - for you. For me, it's sacrifices I make for my kid. Family. You don't have those worries. You have all your time to work in a fancy lab and make lots of money. That's the difference. It's not my first choice to do this floor-scrubbing Cinderella CRAP."

He moved his hand forward on the table.

"I never had you. I had nothing. Paper money is nothing; all of it is nothing. But an evening walk, with you? That was my life's dream. Sorry if I look like a success. I'm not. I really need you, Riley."

He looked down at his plate. There were extra black olives.

"I'll pay at the till," he said.

"Yeah. Money. You and my boss have that in common."

Clark fiddled with his smartphone and walked up to the till. He spoke for a few moments with the owner. Riley walked past them, back to the kitchen. When she returned, Clark was gone.

The rain pounded outside. The dining room stank. The air stuck to Riley's skin like a drunk that wouldn't stop hugging her.

"Hey - some SERVICE, please?" Jonno chuckled once, but Timmy scolded him with a sharp hiss.

Riley shook her head. "Boss? That's it for me."

"What? What you're saying?"

"I mean, that'll be it for me. The customers harass staff, you do nothing, and it actually ruins the atmosphere for many other good, paying customers."

"But we need costumers. What you thinking?"

"Customers," she enunciated politely. "Yeah. But not PIGS."

She turned toward Jonno.

"Not gross, grabby perverts who come here for their cheap sexist kicks."

Jonno stared vacantly. Riley's boss shrugged.

"You're service. It's what you do."

She untied her apron, bundled it in her fists, and pitched it on the till.

"Nah. I'm a damn good mother, and I'll do the best I can for my kid. This place isn't it, so I quit. G'night."

"But I NEED you! Ms Henwies? Ms Henwies, I need you!"

That's a new one, she thought. Needs me? And calling me "Ms" as a form of respect? Oh, damn… what did Clark do? What, did he BUY the place?

She scowled and stepped out into the pouring rain. It wasn't wet. It was as if a big, black wing unfolded over her, to protect her.

"You brought me an umbrella?" She shook her head at Clark.

He nodded. He joked with her, meekly: "Could I offer you a drive, Miss?"

She grabbed the umbrella by the neck like plucking a flower. She wrenched it aside. It fell in a drain on the street-curb. It sat collecting rainwater. She grabbed Clark's hat, spun it around, and plopped it over her own head. Now Clark was getting drenched, and she looked like a talking hat. She stuck out her tongue and blew a raspberry.

Clark hesitated. "I, uh… can't see your lovely face. Where are you?"

She took away the hat and tossed it with the umbrella. Rain splattered on their faces. She stood with an impish smirk as they became equally messy.

"Oh, this is definitely me, Clark. And I said BAREFOOT. Or in the rain; doesn't matter. It's me." Water ran down her skin. Clark had to take away his glasses because of the fogging and drips.

"I get it," he replied. "I want to help, but I don't mean to insult your dignity."

Her answer was a strong, cheeky smile. She patted her hands on his chest like a bongo drum: patta-pat.

"Barefoot, UNEMPLOYED, in the rain."

He gasped, "Congratulations!"

She waved a cautionary finger at him.

"But we need to be good together, Clark. We need to understand each other."

"I think we're good - and we'll get even better."

"Hey. Your smartphone's blinking, dude."

"Oh, right...! Yeah, do you want to sit in the car? I've got something for you."

"Mmm - just one more thing, Columbo."

She looped her hands behind his neck. She tried pulling herself toward his lips. He lifted her the rest of the way. Her feet dangled above the wet pavement.

The rain pattered around them like so many unfinished kisses. It was the sound of tiny, unsatisfying pecks on flat roofs or cement. They were all kisses that missed... like hitting cheeks or chins. Riley and Clark made up for it.

She'd thrown her past aside, like an empty shell, and he swept down and dipped into her. This was love - this was real - and they savored it like chocolate. She murmured agreement into his mouth. He chuckled deeply.

Breath rushed in and out like ocean swells. They let go of some things, but were instantly caught up by others. Their mouths were heavy; innocent moans fell out.

When she pulled away, their lips were a noisy, wet exclamation mark. She saw his eyes flare hungrily.

Clark settled her in his car, then hustled around to his side and got in. He tossed his umbrella and hat in the back. He closed his own door with finality.

"Okay," Clark grinned darkly. He clicked his smartphone and held it between them.

"Excuse me? I'll pay now."

"Ya, you were in t'corner. With, ah, with Waitress Riley."

"That's right. This'll cover the dinner, plus - I wanted to thank you for the quality of your service, at Dino's."

"...What's this?"

"Your waitress. Riley. She was very helpful; she gave me directions to where I'm going, and she set my mind at ease. She improves your hospitality as a whole. I'd like to be sure she gets an extra tip. This is an extra fifty, and it's for her."

"This... what...?"

"Be sure that gets to her, would you? And I'd STRONGLY recommend you consider her for any promotion, or benefits, or tenure. If she chooses to work here, for any length of time..."

"NO WAY..." Riley's eyes bugged out. Thrills raced inside her.

"...If she chooses to work here, for any length of time, please realize what she brings to your business. She IS the quality, here. She's more than any investment. Without Miss Riley, I think Dino's would be at a loss.

"You keep her however you can, sir. If you do, I'll be sure to recommend Dino's to my business partners. Thank you so much. Have a good evening."

Riley wore a cartoonish, fake expression of fear. She spoke in a pinched, nasal, little-old-lady voice: "You are a very, very bad man, Mr Clark."

She snatched his phone and leaned over to give him a quick peck.

"Ya, I'll need my phone back."

"Why?" she chuckled. "Are you going to crank-call him, next? Make a big order to some fake address? Ooh! Be sure to ask for extra olives!"

"Nah. But thanks, I'll just-"

Riley heard shuffling on the phone's speaker. She heard Clark's footsteps walking out of the diner.

"Uh, Riley? I need that. Need it back."

She eyed him curiously. Then, the phone spoke:

"Jonno."

There was a low ruffling sound like cloth.

"You understand... if you TOUCH her... EVER AGAIN..."

Riley swallowed and listened. Clark froze - paralyzed.

"If you touch her...?"

The recording was suddenly clear, because of closeness.

"...I WILL FIND YOU."

Clark looked away. Riley listened to the sound of the diner's front door chime. Then, sound was dulled by rainfall. The recording ended with a click.

"Clark? That wasn't cool. That was really, really NOT COOL. It felt awesome, at the same time, but you can't do that."

Clark's shame tightened his face. It twisted him painfully.

"What did you mean, when you said you'd 'find him'...?"

"It was just... I think he'll leave you alone, now. Plus, Timmy heard it too."

She looked at him sternly. "You can't threaten people, Clark."

He straightened up. "No, there are assholes in this world. They vilify ALL men. They don't just assault their victims. They attack and terrify women, but they also make monsters out of ordinary men. This is my fight, too."

"Funny," she mused. "Most men don't seem to give a damn."

"Then they have no spines. And cops never take anything seriously. Courts answer to the highest-paid lawyer, and justice is incidental. But I'd still fight somehow, and it's for my own sake. It's redemption."

She tilted her head. "I've done pretty well, so far, without threatening people. You noticed that, right?"

"I know. You aren't a damsel in distress. You hold your own. But Jonno stands for something despicable, and I stand against him. It's partly about who I am, as a man. I am not a 'Jonno.' I'll make that very clear."

She waited, nodded, then looked straight at him.

"Babe, how come you got so drenched? Your hat, and coat, and everything?"

"I went to the door a few times. I was waiting for your shift to end. I just wanted to give you a drive home."

She thought for a moment.

"Right. 'A drive home.' Well, thank you. We gotta decide something, though. When you drive me home, do you mean my apartment with Albert? or YOUR place?"

CHAPTER TWENTY-FIVE
THE PRINCE

Ashvale Elementary was a squat, wide building. It was designed that way, as a school; it was a flat and featureless stepping-stone that offered no real advantage.

In front of the school was a long stretch of roadway. It was lined by old trees with great crowns of leaves. Whenever it rained in autumn, fallen leaves made the sidewalks slick. Little kids went home with bruised elbows and shins.

The trees offered deep shade over the road. One sunny Thursday, a black SUV waited there. It arrived before recess and waited in the shade for hours. It only left at the end of the day, when kids ran around the yard. Two men approached Albert and introduced themselves as police officers. They left with him just before Albert's bus arrived. No-one saw anything.

The yard monitor was out sick, that day - something like food poisoning. The Vice-Principal didn't see a reason to call in a substitute. At the end of the day, no incidents had been reported.

That afternoon, Riley was sorting through her apartment. She moved one thing, but then had to reposition something else. That something-else was broken, so it couldn't be moved. Then her refrigerator cut out again. She had to lie down on the kitchen floor to reach under and shake the power cord back into place. There was a short somewhere, in the cord, and she didn't want her food to go bad.

Sadly, her neighbor was stoned again. He was a drummer in a death metal band. When he was stoned, his drumming was a zoo of noise.

At about 4:45, Riley got a phone call from the school. She saw the school's caller I.D. on the display.

"Hello?"

There was no reply.

"Uh, hello?"

Again, silence.

Riley's eyes tipped side-to-side as she listened.

"Hey, uh… is this Albert?"

CLICK.

Riley ran her tongue through her teeth.

Hunnh, she thought. Some twerp pulling pranks?

Her neighbor's drumming accelerated. The bass drum pounded like a mattress slamming at the wall. Every other noise seemed to trip over itself and fall down a flight of stairs.

This building's owner was never around, and the superintendent handed off his responsibilities to his son, and his son asked Riley's neighbor to take care of things. Riley mentioned the broken refrigerator, and her neighbor promised that he'd call someone to take a look at it. That was two months ago. Right now, he was preoccupied with his drumming.

Riley got a text from Larsen's parents, saying Albert went to visit them. They'd contact her again, after dinner. About 8pm, she got another phone call. It was from Larsen's mom.

"Hello? Hey, Ms McKinnley - I hope he wasn't any trouble. He doesn't usually invite himself over to his friends' places."

Ms McKinnley wasn't answering.

"Hello? Did you call earlier?"

Again, no answer.

"Uh - could you put Albert on? I'd like to speak with him."

The line stayed quiet. Riley's hand went to her hip.

"Okay, I'm not in the mood for games, ma'am. Could I please talk to my son, to make sure he's alright?"

CLICK.

She wanted to call Clark, but she knew he was working in the city. She wasn't sure she'd even reach him. She didn't understand these prank calls from people she actually knew. At least, the caller I.D. said it was the school... and then Ms McKinnley.

She tried calling Clark, regardless. When he picked up, he sounded stressed. There was a tinny squealing in the background, followed by a deep and resonant hum.

"Hello? Yeah - hey, how are things?"

"Clark, I can't reach Albert. I got a text saying he went to Larsen's, today, but I've been getting weird silent phone calls. And from different places."

Riley could hear him grab the phone and hold it tight to his ear. There were sounds like shuffling.

"How many silent phone calls?"

"Just two. Maybe quarter-to-five, and another one just now."

"Only two?"

"Yeah."

She heard him pause and breathe.

"Hunnh," he puzzled. He called back to his coworkers. "Hey, guys? I'm taking a break."

Riley heard his footsteps on tile.

"Okay, uhh," he muttered, "Stay on the line for a sec."

She heard two short bleeps in her phone. Then, it made a rapid series of pops like a tiny woodpecker.

He spoke to her calmly. "Could you check your call history? Don't hang up - just go into your phone app, and look at recent calls. Tell me what you see."

Riley tapped through her phone, went to the recent calls, and told him what was on the screen.

"Umm," she paused. "Yeah, the calls are there, but... but they say 'unlisted.' And there are more of them - not just two. And the times are gone. But I know it was a call before five, and another one just a minute ag-…"

Her face blanched.

"Umm… they all went blank. Just now. All of them."

"Riley? Listen carefully. Do not answer the phone, unless it's me. You give me twenty minutes. Alright? I'll call you in twenty."

"Clark, what's going on?"

She listened intently, and she thought she could hear his teeth grind.

"We'll talk soon," he replied. "I'm going to go find Albert and make sure he's safe. I'll bring him right to you."

"Wait, is this your government stuff? Where is he? What is this?"

"I have to check with someone. Albert's fine, but I really am going to look into this. Okay?"

"WHAT?"

Clark went cold. "He's gonna be fine. I promise you. Alright? Give me twenty-"

Sheer panic: "GIVE ME MY SON, CLARK!"

Hardened steel: "I WILL. I will, Riley, My Heart. On my life, I promise I will. And I'll call you. Twenty minutes."

His end clicked.

"W-what the hell?" She staggered back. "What is this?"

Her arm swung down to her side. She dropped

her phone on an end-table, beside her little couch. She fell on the couch, sitting with her head in her hands. The next-door drumming sounded like guns going off.

She looked around her crappy two-bedroom apartment. It was made of faded wallpaper, worn furniture, and appliances that rattled whenever they were working. The couch she sat on was stained - the springs creaked when they sagged. This was all she could do for her son, but it wasn't enough. Right now, her whole life wasn't enough to keep her son safe. She'd gone from desperate to helpless.

CHAPTER TWENTY-SIX
THE SWORD'S EDGE

Clark was working when he got Riley's unexpected call. After their tense conversation, he walked out of his lab. No explanation; not a word.

In twenty minutes, he had to find Albert. He knew what was happening, and he knew he was already out of time.

Clark's phone bleeped on and speed-dialed with a manic flutter. He strode quickly from the lab area, tearing away his white coat. He whipped the crumpled fabric to the floor. His outgoing phone call buzzed only once.

"Matteo?" he demanded.

"Yeh?" came a smoky reply.

Matteo was leaning back in his chair with his feet up. It was Thursday, and he was finishing this week's paperwork. He was clean-shaven. His dark hair, angular face and pointy chin came together neatly, like the sharp features of a fox. He was so handsome, he looked like he was made for his suit. The gleam in his eye was particularly alert.

"Matteo. NOW. Whatever you're into, drop it. I need an extraction. Authorize it under Secure Intelogistics."

Matteo snapped upright. He tossed his paperwork aside. "CRAP, man... What can I do?"

Clark's voice was low, like a crouching wolf:

"Excessively overreact."

Matteo listened to the grim orders.

"Get a strike team. Local. The best on standby. I need night drones; fit 'em with flashbangs. I need a full assault squad, but this is a clean capture. Extraction of a seven-year-old boy, curly dark hair. Maybe four feet tall. Name is Albert-"

Clark choked. He grit his teeth and forced out the syllables. "Albert Henway."

"Got it, got it," came the smoky voice. "The agents? Equipment, affiliation?"

Clark panted. "I don't know who they are..." He scowled. "Or where. And I don't know how many."

Matteo grinned like a shark. "Ohh, CLARK, my man! This is why I love you. You're the best. I'm all over this, like a new coat of paint." He jumped up with a pounce.

Clark growled, "Yeah, yeah. Sync with my phone. I'm scanning with Athena." Clark tapped a new code into his smartphone. Athena lit his screen.

Other lab techs dodged aside when they saw Clark coming. He ran to the parking garage and stood at the security booth. He stamped his I.D. against the glass, looked at the three-hundred-pound security guard, and then rushed by. The other guards stood at attention without making eye contact.

In the parking garage, his shoes clapped with echoes. He broke into a sprint.

"MATTEO?!"

"We're on it… annnd confirmed. Yeah - we have fourteen guys with boots, body armor, and bad attitudes. We found a mobile crate of drones, and signal-transmission relays for the pilots. We'll pop out lights, rush 'em, and wrap 'em up. Clark, my man? We're a flash fire. We're ready to happen. Where's the op?"

Clark reached his car, thumbed the keyless entry, and leapt in. He waited.

"ATHENA? Address?" He looked at his scan. Athena wasn't finding anything.

Whoever took Albert knew about Athena. They'd somehow blocked her.

"Matt? Be ready for electronics countermeasures. Athena's locked out. Either they're running without electricity, or it must be underground. REALLY secure, like total control of the property. We'll use that. Investigate these property owners and nail them to the wall."

Clark drove out of the garage and onto the street. Traffic was moving like herds of big, dumb, metal cows. His head swam with heat. His pulse thudded at the insides of his skin.

Matteo thought aloud, "They blocked Athena? for a kid? How big is this, man? They really planned it. What are their motives?"

"Leverage," Clark growled. "They hacked telecommunications for recon, and now they're using it to mess with people's heads. They used the mother's phone, probably tracked her, and then orchestrated an abduction. Now they'll use her phone to instill panic. They'll push for a hard deal. It's just leverage, but they're using… they're specifically using him."

"Uhh - Clark? You sound upset. This isn't just the FBI thing, is it? Were these idiots trying to go personal? against YOU?"

Clark didn't answer. He waited another minute. He stared at his phone and watched Athena working. She still couldn't find anything.

His phone lit and started ringing on another line. Clark jumped. A new call was coming in. The caller I.D. said "Clark Benjamin."

He couldn't answer. His ears pounded with his heartbeat. He dismissed the call and spoke to Matteo.

"We're not tracing fast enough. They're just gonna wear people down; they've isolated themselves, even from Athena. I gotta contact brass, okay? This is nuts, but I need to do this. I'll need you to vouch for me."

"Yeah," Matteo said. "Of course."

Clark blinked heavily. He tapped his smartphone

again, put in another password, and scrolled down a list. He selected a rare number. He squeezed his eyes shut for a moment, then pressed dial.

The line buzzed only once. It was answered by a monotone voice which could've been male or female. The voice was dull and colorless, like slate. It asked about third parties. Clark informed them that Matteo Landucci was also on the line. Matteo spoke to confirm it.

Clark asked to relay a message to the colonel. The voice advised him to wait.

There were a few seconds of quiet on the other end.

A deep, rolling voice spoke over the phone, and Clark greeted him cordially. After a very brief exchange of small-talk, Clark made an offer: if he gained their added assistance, just this once, he'd give them Icarus. He'd give them the whole project. It was his life's work. He said that someone else, an independent, was starting to use leverage against him.

The voice rumbled like a boulder and asked for pertinent details. Clark told him about Albert, Athena's blindness, and the likely abduction. He waited on a knife-edge of silence.

On his phone's screen, Athena bleeped brighter, then glitched a series of numbers and letters. It was a complete address. Clark took a screenshot, thanked the voice sincerely, and ended the call.

Matteo jumped in: "Clark? I got it onscreen! The address - some storage site, downtown!"

"GET THERE!" he barked back. "Bring the boys, and get him out SAFE!"

Clark stomped the gas before he even grabbed the wheel. He wrestled his car into control and turned into traffic.

The address was an underground storage facility. It had been a business that suddenly dried up about a year ago.

Clark suspected that Albert would be close by. If Albert was used as leverage, he'd need to be delivered quickly. If things ever went sideways, the goons would need urban amenities and extra collateral. The city's population was collateral; dead civilians were a bargaining chip.

Clark sped through the city, occasionally slipping between the lines of traffic. People swore at him as he streaked by. Many phoned the police.

Intersection, he scowled. Dammit. No time.

He shoulder-checked both sides, looked up and down the streets, and ran the red light. A horn blared angrily. A transport truck squealed and skipped its tires - the metal grill loomed close. Clark ripped his car down to low gear and flattened the accelerator. The truck rumbled to a stop behind him. Two other cars barely kept from colliding.

His smartphone lit again. It was a text. The I.D. said "Riley Henway."

"Hey, Honey - have you seen my son? And what's this 'Icarus' thing?"

* * *

Clark grit his teeth. "Matteo?"

"We're at the site," Matteo answered. "We did lights and sirens to the bank, an' then hustled on foot for a block. They heard nothin'. We got someone cutting their power now, and drones are ready to breach."

Clark prayed quietly. "Matt? Please be careful with this kid."

Matteo paused. "…Oh my God, Clark. This is HER kid, isn't it? HERS?"

"Shut up," Clark grunted. "Get it done. Get him out of there."

Matteo snapped, "Screw it! Clark? I'm going in right now. I'll grab a vest." He popped his phone in his breast pocket. The microphone peeked from the top. It was still a live line.

"Clark? I've got you, man."

Through the phone line, Clark could hear Matteo zipping up a kevlar vest.

At the building, two punks were parked there in a hatchback. Their car stereo thrashed out ungodly noise. Matteo had them disarmed and zip-tied within seconds. They had guns under their seats and in the trunk. There was an assault rifle in the back with armor-piercing rounds - someone could've popped out and ended a car chase abruptly.

Matteo shook his head. "Noobs… Real punks have more friends than that. Lookout guards are posted in pairs."

Further down the sidewalk, a young couple leaned into a wall, smooching… on the most unromantic street imaginable. 'Empty storage facility' is not a date hotspot. She had lots of tattoos. One of them was blacked out for dishonorable discharge. She was quite vocal when she was apprehended.

Another ten seconds, and the building blinked to darkness. Matteo's crew entered using thermal vision. They subdued several mercenaries quickly, muzzling and binding them. Other men rushed out with flashlights or night scopes, peering through the dark, but then drones buzzed overhead and burst their onboard flashbang grenades. It was a dazzling spectacle, to say the least.

Underground, beneath the street, no-one would hear the chatter of silenced gunfire or the sharp knocking of bulletproof vests. Matteo waded through the fracas with a pistol in one hand and a taser in the other. His vest was light, and he was fast.

In the thick of things, in close-quarters combat, he sidestepped someone's knife and flipped his taser to sting down like an electric scorpion. He quickly knelt with his victim to shock him again twice, and then lifted his body as cover. He carried him to advance further, charging at two men with rifles. Again, in hand-to-hand range, he dumped his cover and stepped between their extended barrels. He struck outward with his taser and pistol, crackling sparks under one man's chin. The other bucked backward from a few pistol rounds to his armor, until Matt followed up with shocks to his arms and chest. Then Matt glanced over these three rigid bodies, checked his nearby corners and blind spots, and advanced again.

In minutes, fourteen specialists captured twenty-two thugs. Matteo captured the last two without conflict. One of them had been texting Clark a new message:

"Icarus - or he bleeds."

Clark stood at the entrance, waiting impatiently. Matteo emerged and walked up to greet him. He was panting and grinning evilly - another win.

Apparently, the two kidnappers who'd taken Albert were especially nice to him. Their orders said he was key leverage. He had to be kept in perfect health. Then, during negotiation, his mother could witness the increasing levels of suffering.

This made Clark seethe. Matteo looked at him sideways.

"Clark, are you gonna be okay?"

"Never mind. Do these two main guys have opposing agencies? private bounties on them?"

Matteo whistled idly and checked his phone. "Barnaby Simon... Darrell Vickers..." He gawked at the screen. "Oh yeah. These boys are career. They certainly do. They got boogeymen all over the place."

Clark pondered. "Where's the worst place for them to vacation?"

Matteo chuckled. "Mexico?"

Clark smiled. "Worst place in Mexico?"

"Mexico City, for them. Exposure."

"The most accessible place in Mexico City?" Clark bobbed his head.

"Probably the International Airport. So?"

"Matteo, if you can't get these scum officially deported in the next two hours, cook up some documents. Then, I want you to send a tip to every country that wants their heads. Leaks - EVERYWHERE. I want those countries to race for extradition. China, Russia, Iran, North Korea… I don't care. We deport 'em to Mexico, but they're snatched as soon as their toes touch dirt. Do it."

"D'you want me to process the other twenty?" Matteo asked.

"Nah, I got 'em. Just handle these two. I need your diligence."

Clark felt his knuckles. He stretched his neck.

"I'm just gonna have a quick word with them, first. Y'know. Give my regards."

Matteo sprang forward.

"CLARK… no! I got it. I g-… got it."

He gasped and grabbed at his bulletproof vest. He doubled over like it was pinching him. He stumbled back again.

Clark looked him up and down.

"What, 'got your hands dirty? Have someone check that."

"I'm good. But just wait a…"

Clark stepped past him and found the secured

room. At the door, he showed his I.D. to a straight-spined soldier. He asked for a moment of confidentiality.

"Intel," Clark lied. "Sensitive information. It'll just take a sec."

The soldier rolled his eyes. He knew that type of discussion. He started humming something patriotic and wandered out of earshot.

Inside, the fake-cop kidnappers were cuffed and bound to steel chairs. When they struggled, the chairs scratched against the concrete floor. They were just waiting to be transported.

They spat harsh words. They threatened Riley, whoever she was, and they swore they'd gut Albert slowly. Clark only stood and listened. They snapped random insults at him, nudging their heads up. They bit their lower lips and taunted him.

"Yeah? What NOW, Mr Suit? Huh? Whatcha got for me? 'Whadda you GOT?'"

They spouted the usual tough-guy nonsense. Clark stood patiently.

The oldest one slowed, then looked more carefully. He suddenly went quiet. His face turned as white as his eyes. He hissed to his partner.

"Ksst! Shut up... it's Benjamin - it's HIM!"

Both of them stopped dead.

Were they good cop/bad cop? No, Clark thought to himself, more like mentor and understudy. He could read their criminal roles: a dysfunctional father-son relationship. New bitterness grew inside him.

He stepped squarely in front of them, calmly, and looked each of them in the eye. He paced over to the elder, paused, and stared hard into his pupil. He tunneled into that small, inner darkness where the man lived. This was where he thought about things. This was the safe little room inside him where he could still hear his mother's voice. Clark looked in with a practiced eye, and the man suddenly knew: he couldn't hide anything. His fear was completely naked.

Clark nodded gently. Then he turned his entire torso, bent his tight arm and shoulder, and let his hand cut a mean arc across the man's face. He backhanded him so hard, the man and his chair were hurled sideways across the room. The noise stung the air to ringing. When the man hit the ground, his chair screeched long stripes into the cement floor. The shock left him reeling and wordless.

Clark breathed, and then breathed some more, and then walked over to him and stood him back up. He faced him again. He stared into him, as cold as the reaper's scythe. What did he have, for the thug? What did he have?

"NOTHING," Clark answered. And he meant it. He stared for a moment longer, while the thug tried to chew his face straight.

Then they knew. Clark nodded to them. 'Nothing' was their destination. 'Nothing' was what they'd be... very, very soon. Both men slowly dropped their heads.

Matteo heard the sharp crack from outside. Then he watched Clark stride over to another area, find Albert, and lead him by the shoulder. He ducked Albert safely into his car.

Clark looked back one last time and offered a stiff, surreptitious nod. Matteo closed his eyes and nodded back. In another minute, Clark drove away.

Jesus, Matteo thought. Clark's carrying SO MUCH weight. They abducted the son… of his great love? Those men should be in pieces, right now!

Matteo held his vest tighter. A field medic approached him.

"Yeah," he admitted, "I might've picked one up - under the kevlar, here."

The medic called for assistance and helped Matteo onto a gurney. He looked Matteo up-and-down in disbelief.

"Agent Landucci? Yeah, I heard you took down five of 'em. No wonder you got tagged… Wait. You went in there with a light vest? 'The hell is wrong with you, boy? Those were paramilitaries! Body armor and carbines! Are you frickin' high, or something?"

Matteo jabbed his finger and spoke sternly.

"You did NOT want to lose this one. Take my word for it."

"What?" The medic stretched gloves onto his hands. "His kid? Yeah, yeah, I get it. I've seen all that paternal stuff befo-"

"No," Matteo shook his head. "No, you don't

understand. ESPECIALLY since it isn't his kid. It's someone else's. That 'someone else' means everything to him, and he just failed her. He just failed her SON. He's in a dark corner of hell, right now."

The medic ducked sheepishly and tended to Matteo's wound. He didn't say another word.

Matteo only had one word in his mind: Henway.

CHAPTER TWENTY-SEVEN
IN THE NAME OF THE CROWN

Twenty minutes, Clark said. He'd call her in twenty minutes, and he'd have Albert. He promised.

In fourteen minutes, she got a phone call. The ringtone jolted her. She sat up on her couch. She didn't want to look at the phone display, but she picked it up, steadied herself, and checked.

It was Clark.

"Hello? This had better be Clark."

"Riley? It's me. I've got Albert. I'll fill you in soon. Should I take him to your place? or should I meet you, pick you up, and bring you both to mine?"

She looked around her apartment. Her neighbor started pounding AND singing something unrecognizable - tribal dances for cave-dorks.

"I wanna talk to my son. Put him on."

"Just a sec."

Clark murmured something, and Riley heard "Well, YEAH!" from young Albert.

Then, the phone turned to the sweetest music.

"MOMMM! Holy crap, mom! I had the weirdest day, today! Police an' everything! Is it okay that I talk with that Clark guy? He seems really nice, and, like, you even kissed him an' stuff, so I hope it's okay for me to talk to him."

"Ya," she whimpered, "ya, ya, that's fine. I think he's okay. Are you? Are you okay?"

"Are you KIDDING? I wanna be a cop, when I grow up! They hafta do totally whack stuff, WAY more interesting than TV. Today was craziness!"

"ARE YOU... OKAY... ALBERT?"

"Ya, I'm fine. Clark just picked me up."

"Albert?" she quavered. She had to cross a painful line. "Albert, y-you just stay there with Clark, okay? I need you to stick close to him. I mean it. I MEAN-IT mean it. 'Got that?"

"Sure! Can we hang out?"

Her breath sobbed out of her.

"Yeah, Honey, I think he's okay."

"No - YOU. I wanna hang out with you, Mom. Can we?"

She choked on tears. Her hand held her own face, and she managed two syllables: "Mmm-hmm."

"YESSS," he hissed.

Somewhere in the background, she heard Clark say, "I'ma pick her up now. Jump in the back. She'll sit with you."

"LOVE YOU, Mom!"

She heard plunking, and then the sound of Clark fastening a seatbelt. Then, a quiet moment.

"Okay. Athena wasn't following you. You asked her not to. What was your address, again?"

She tried to build herself back up. Word by word, she gave him the address.

He considered. "Be there in fifteen?"

"Mmm-hmm," she nodded. "And I'll be outside, k-... k-... okay?" Her voice choked. She felt her face drain. It probably turned green; she couldn't feel it. She couldn't tell.

"RILEY. I'll see you soon, and I'm bringing Albert."

"Mmm-hmm," she squeaked.

She dropped her phone and fell on her couch.

Twelve minutes later, Clark's car pulled up outside her apartment. She was waiting on the front step. She grabbed her tan-colored pack (which she'd had since art school), and hustled down to the car. Albert was waving from the back seat. Clark thumbed back to those seats, telling her to join him.

She lunged into the car and hugged him. He was alive, healthy, and excited. Probably in shock.

"Mom! Holy crap - did you win a lottery, today? 'Cuz these police guys showed up, and they said you did. They said they had to keep me safe, in case someone tried to kidnap me. I heard you won a gazillion dollars, so even the cops had to protect me!"

Those weren't cops, she thought.

"We were waiting around for a couple HOURS, Mom. I didn't really know what was going on, but I've never won a lottery before. Have you? I guess they have to keep everything safe."

Yeah, she thought. Clark knows all about safe, doesn't he?

"But then, a bunch of stuff happened. Like, JUST NOW. Noises, and cracks, and buzzing stuff. I still don't really know what was going on."

It damned-well SHOULDN'T have gone on, she thought.

"Two cops were there with me most the time, but then this other guy showed up. He told me Clark was on the way. And then the cops looked real nervous. They tried to say you an' me were fine, Mom - and that they had to leave. But then this guy 'detained' them, or whatever, and took me outta the room.

"It was all downtown, somewhere even safer than the cop station. It was safe, they said, but I don't think they meant it. Even the cops didn't look too safe, on their faces. Not when they heard Clark was coming. They kinda smiled back and forth at each other weirdly. Kinda like their boss was angry. Do cops get fired? I think they got fired."

Riley grit her teeth: I hope they get eaten alive, piece by piece, under a swarm of a thousand starving rats.

"So this guy is there for only a few seconds, and BOOM-"

Riley clutched her heart.

"CLARK was right there! Badda-BOOM, all done! So, I'm guessing these cops made a big mistake about the lottery, right?"

Riley stared into space.

"Yeah, I think someone messed up."

"Where are we going, anyway?" Albert chirped. "Are we going for a burger, or something? I'm actually kinda hungry."

Clark spoke as gentle as silk, "We're going to visit my place, if you don't mind. You visit Larsen, right? Sometimes, you stay over?"

"OH yeah - Larsen's great. Man, he's so good at Space Titans, it's ridiculous. He makes my high score look like the I.Q. of a june bug."

Riley hugged him tight and wouldn't let go. Clark looked at him through the rearview mirror.

"Would you feel okay about staying at MY place, for a while? I've got a smart TV, movie networks, and you can mess with my laptop computer, if you get really bored."

"Mmm - okay. I'm still kinda hungry, though. Do you have any food, there?"

Clark's eyes seemed to deal with something, inside.

"Uh... yeah. I can probably scrounge up something to eat."

The last supper, he thought. And afterwards, she'll leave me forever.

Riley hugged her son as they drove through the city. She stared at the back of Clark's head.

CHAPTER TWENTY-EIGHT
ALL THE KING'S MEN

Finally, they pulled in the driveway. Albert looked up at Clark's house.

"You LIVE here?"

"Yeah," Clark shrugged.

"Do you have kids, and family stuff? Like, are you married?"

Clark sighed. "No kids. Not married. So there's, uh… lots of room, here."

"Well, GOOD, 'cuz my mom smooched you. If you were married, she'd be in trouble."

"Nah," Clark shook his head. "Don't worry. I'm really, really not married right now. 'Probably not getting married anytime soon. So, your mom? She's not in any trouble. Nope. Not your mom, anyway."

Before they stepped inside, Clark went ahead. He held up his finger for 'one minute.'

He spoke to the house: "Athena? Create a new Guardian Mode. Highest level; Protocol X. Subject name: Albert Henway. Keep no records, but inform me of any potential adverse agents."

Athena replied immediately in her composite voices:

"Compiled. Potential agent located: Barnaby Simon, 38, now en route to board AeroMexico outbound flight 403 to Mexico City. Also, Darrell Vickers, 24, now en route to board AeroMexico outbound flight 403 to Mexico City. Note: expedited deportation in progress. Also note: hostile elements on location at Mexico City International Airport. Subjects Simon and Vickers are at serious risk - Threat Level 7."

Clark blew breath out his lips.

I almost feel bad for them, he thought. Sorta.

"Arright. C'mon in, Albert. Riley."

He led them into the kitchen.

"SO… Albert, my man. If you had any choice, what would you want for supper?"

He peeked upward at Clark. "Uh… maybe a cheeseburger, instead of just a hamburger?"

Clark gave him a big, goofy scowl. "Ay! Pretend you're a prince! You had a big day, today. This is your victory. C'mon, it's 8:35 at night! So… what BIG DINNER… is the feast for a prince, after a huge day like today?"

"Could we, like, get pizza?"

Riley nodded to Clark. Pizza was fine.

Clark pretended to write on his hand.

"You like meat toppings?

"Ya."

"You like cheese?"

"Ya."

"You like extra broccoli, and weird Korean mushroom things?"

"Eww," he smiled back.

"Aha," Clark nodded. "Korean-mushroom pizza, it is." He winked at the kid, then stepped away to order.

Riley sat her son on the couch and held him. She tried to listen to Clark on the phone. Again, it was politely quiet. She heard two clear words: "qualità," followed by a warm and satisfied "bene." Clark returned to the living area, and was greeted by Albert's incredulous voice.

"Wait... did YOU have to win a lottery, Clark? This is an awful big place, in here."

"No, it's paid for. It was probably a bit of money, though; good call on that. See, I work for the government - or, I used to. This is a place they have for government people. It's solid. It's a big house, and I don't have noisy neighbors."

Another fifteen minutes passed. When the pizza arrived, it wasn't fancy gourmet. There was no trace of Korean mushrooms. The melted cheese had spiced oils, and the sauce was both sweet and piquant. The toppings were generous chunks that weighed into the cheese. This pizza was so big, they had to split it up at the kitchen table. Three chairs, three people, three sides of the table. It wasn't crowded. It was complete.

"Mmm... so, these police guys came up to me after school, an' said Mom won a lottery. It was so much, they were 'a little concerned for my safety.' They were worried someone would use me for ransom. Like... steal me, and then steal Mom's money."

"Nope," Riley corrected him. "Someone screwed up. I'm not the one with money."

"They showed me some cop badges, and we went in their ghost car - or, it was an SUV, actually. We went to this place downtown, and under a garage or something... and through some heavy, sliding doors. It was really protected! They had people guarding it, and everything.

"Y'know, I wondered why cops would ever have a safer place than their station... 'cuz why wouldn't they just have ONE really safe place, and make sure it was really, REALLY safe? Then just keep stuff there? Like, with other cops?"

"I dunno," Riley mumbled softly. "I guess those men thought it was all under control."

"Well, they just had me sit there. I was busy thinking about that lottery. And all they had was clear bottled water, and it didn't have flavors in it or anything."

"Yeah," she whispered to the table's surface. "At least Clark feeds you. We'll stay here for a bit."

"Well anyways, barely an hour ago I heard guys

on radio walkie-talkies. And then - get this - the WHOLE PLACE went dark. TOTALLY pitch black. It was freaky-awesome! They lost power - downtown, even! Safe place, my butt! And then I heard whirring or buzzing, like little lawnmowers. It was sorta icky feeling, actually."

Clark tipped his head. "Drones, Albert. Drones with infrared cameras, piloted by experts. They flew in to stun the bad guys."

Albert froze for a second. "COOLLLL! 'Cuz yeah, there were really bright flashes, and then there was yelling, but it was all made quiet. Like 'hush-up' quiet. And then the lights came back on. This all happened in a couple minutes."

"It should've happened faster," Clark moaned.

"It shouldn't have happened," Riley said in a level voice.

"Well, it felt like some sports competition thing, where one team tries to go faster than the other. Or when real cops 'rrest somebody. But this was a LOT of guys, in there, and I guess THEY were the ones who got arrested. There were, like, fifty dudes in there."

Riley pursed her lips together. Her eyes scorched the tabletop.

"Yeah, Albert." Clark looked at him sadly. "There were twenty-two."

"Twenty-two is still a lot," Albert argued.

"It absolutely is," Clark assured him with a troubled sigh.

"Well, I didn't feel totally safe. They were wearing more smelly cologne than cops would, so they weren't scent-friendly. Cops should be. And the guns they carried weren't on their hip, but in their coats. They were the square pistols, and they looked different. Like, 'other country' different."

Riley tried to look curious, and not horrified.

"They really had guns?"

"Ya. But I just kept quiet, and stayed still. If they actually were cops, I'd want some lawyer person around anyway. I know that much from TV."

"A lawyer," Riley agreed quietly. "Or someone, at least."

Albert pointed at Clark proudly. "Mom, THIS guy showed up after another minute. Lights came on, guy-in-a-suit popped in, and then there was Clark. Man, I was so glad to see him. We just got in his car, and he's like, 'We're calling your mother.' I laughed out loud!"

"Why were you laughing?" she asked plainly.

"Well, because he sounded really worried. Sorry, Clark, but you looked like you were gonna cry. And he was like, 'Albert, I'm in SO much trouble. I really hope you're okay. I might not see you, after this.' And then he got really serious: 'I'm so sorry, Albert.'

"I don't even get it. What did you mean, Clark? You got rid of bad guys, if there were any. I don't know why you're in trouble."

Riley cut in: "Because he's rich and complicated, and there really ARE bad guys." She held her head in her hands and rubbed her temples. "They follow him around, and today they followed you."

Albert shrank back. "Gah. I'm not grown-up enough for that. You have bad guys after you, Clark?"

He nodded gravely and straightened up. He tried to apologize, but Albert cut him off.

"What - we just met, and now they're MY bad guys too?"

Clark shook his head. "Not anymore. Those two bad guys, themselves, have WORSE guys after them. Now THEY'RE in trouble. Way-big trouble.

"You were incredibly brave, with those dudes… but they're gone now. They're out of the country. Deported."

Riley did a double-take. "Clark…? Seriously?"

"Oh ya."

She thought for a moment.

"Dead-serious?" she asked, over Albert's head.

Clark lifted his eyes, met hers, and he gave a shallow nod.

Conversation slowed over the next half-hour. Riley had two slices of pizza and stared straight at Clark. Clark had a few bites, and he couldn't look back at her. His brow dipped low. When Albert finally scarfed down his fifth piece of pizza, Clark reached over and patted his back.

"Hey - 'you good, big guy?"

"Ohh - I stuffed, Clark," he answered. He crossed his eyes and swatted his little round belly.

Clark spoke calmly. "I bet it was tiring, being so brave."

"Uh-huh. Maybe a little."

"I've got a den, here, so you can stay over. There's a TV, and a nice bed. It's a good, comfy place to rest. Today was a real shocker, man. Let me know when you want to settle in. Okay?"

"Mmm - sure. Not yet," he said.

Little Albert sat with them on the couch. He leaned into Riley's side for a few minutes, till his head fell on Riley's lap. When the day's shock wore off, and fatigue hit, and five slices of pizza weighed in his belly, he was breathing deep. Soft air rushed through his lips. He was asleep.

"You want to carry?" Clark asked.

"I'll come along. I'll supervise." Her smile was patient.

Clark lifted Albert up and rested him against his shoulder.

Albert mumbled sleepily, "Mff... but it's quiet here. And that was the long-style pizza..."

They reached the den and the small bed. Riley took Albert in her arms and laid him down.

"Thanks, Clark." Her smile was ice when she waved him from the room. She undressed Albert down to his undies and wrapped him in blankets.

Clark went back to the kitchen to tidy up. Plates clicked in the silence. He wiped the kitchen table where they'd eaten. He slowed, then polished it with care - with reverence. He smiled wistfully. Most likely, they wouldn't have dinner ever again.

Several minutes later, Riley emerged. She climbed the stairs and walked over to him.

"C'n I chat with you, for a sec?" She indicated the far window past the kitchen and living area. It was the farthest from the den.

He nodded - worried. He walked with her to those floor-to-ceiling windows. It was late enough at night that the windows were black mirrors. They stood together at the edge of a darker, outside world.

She faced him there and smiled up. She nodded slightly. She touched the front of his shirt and gripped it in her hand. She felt her other hand up his shoulder. She smoothed it dearly over his neck, and then across his cheek.

She looked up at him with glistening eyes.

Her whole shoulder winged back and she slapped him sharply across the face. His glasses ejected from his nose. Her deathly smile remained and her furious eyes burned him. Her teeth bared, and then she slapped him again. She slapped hard enough to tilt him to the side. She whimpered painfully and struck again, and again - hard, ringing claps in the night air. He stood there to receive her. He stood red cheeked. He was there to listen.

Again and again she slapped, as she grunted in pain and effort. Then one final CLAP, and she panted and sobbed a few words.

"Never, never, EVER, EVER AGAIN..."

"No," he agreed.

"NEVER." She stabbed her pointer finger at his face. "NEVER. You hear me?"

He nodded humbly.

"NEVER AGAIN." Her finger was a knife to his eyes. Her teeth hissed at him, "Pawn your OWN child, next time."

He closed his eyes and made a vow.

"Riley, if even a shade of this falls near you, ever again, I make you two promises. ONE, I will destroy any possibility of threat. I'll root it out, and I will annihilate it, even if it kills me. And TWO... I will sign over my assets, including this house. Then I will get you a gun, and you will shoot me. Could we agree to these terms?"

Her eyes narrowed. "Don't patronize me with your arrogant, puffed-up melodramatics, you rich JACK-ASS!"

He looked at her clearly. "I'd want you to kill me, Riley. Threats to you would end immediately. Besides, I couldn't live with myself anyway. I'd want you to kill me."

She jabbed her finger again. "This is my SON, and you dragged him into your sick, corrupt life. This isn't just you and your whining, anymore. It's not even messing with me and my feelings. This is the life of a seven-year-old boy. Don't promise your grandiose self-sacrifices, pal. If I EVER think this is creeping up on us, I am OUT your door and I'm never seeing you again. You will NOT endanger my family with your twisted games!"

Her steel smile came out again: "Oh, you're pretty tough... but dammit, SO AM I."

His voice was smooth and low. "They're gone forever, Riley."

She wasn't impressed. She glared with wide-open eyes. "I'm not kidding."

"Neither am I." His eyes bored into hers. He met her fire with fire. "Those men? They're GONE. They're probably being flown to an unnamed island south of Vladivostok. Do you get it?"

Her eyes sagged. "What. They have some kinda vacation bonus, now?" She nearly spat.

"NO. Probably one of North Korea's damned black sites... someplace that doesn't exist. Think about what that means - what they'll DO to them, over there. Yeah. Consider it my personal grudge."

He could picture them clearly in his mind: Muzzled. Weeping. Screaming.

She paused and shook her head. "What do you mean, grudge?"

He looked at her like an attack dog. There was a coldness in his eye... something inhuman.

"What grudge? W...? ALBERT!"

His pain began to surface. This had been personal to him from the very beginning.

"Those guys? They were deported. Then, they were briskly extradited to some other country that'll eat them alive. Their worst enemies fought over them. We just tossed 'em overboard, and some BIG friggin' sharks were waiting. THAT'S my grudge."

She found guilty pleasure, here. She smiled weakly.

"That's genius. They were hot-potato, tossed to hell? Okay. You have some scary friends, man, but I think I like them. A little."

He was strangely quiet. Then she knew.

"…You arranged that. You deported them. You set them up. Didn't you."

The gleam in his eye was hellfire.

"No-one will DARE harass you or your son, because I made an example of them. They signed up for life-and-death contracts, but not this. Not this. No agents anywhere want to go near you. Or Albert."

She asked meekly, "Did you kill them, Clark? or is it worse?"

He replied without expression, "I don't know. WE don't know, and no-one ever will. But I guarantee you, they won't be seen again."

There was a morbid quiet in the room. It was sweaty and uncomfortably close.

He clucked his tongue. "They just got kidnapped in the worst possible way. If North Korea had their sights on 'em, they won't be staying in a five-star hotel… Pff. They won't be able to COUNT to five, on all their fingers.

"They won't betray American secrets. They were just high-end mercs paid by some asshole, and they're very, VERY sorry right now."

"I think I'm gonna be sick," she muttered.

"Well, the big bad wolf just got eaten by bears, or

dragons, or something worse in the forest. My friend in the nice suit dropped a couple breadcrumbs, and that's all. But it's the end of their little story. So, yeah. Never, ever, ever again."

He waited for that to sink in.

"Umm," she paused. "This is so inappropriate, but…"

She shut her eyes, leaned forward and embraced him. She squeezed lightly. He tentatively hugged her back.

"Also," he added wearily, "there's no reason for anyone to come after us. After today, I have nothing of value."

CHAPTER TWENTY-NINE
A Shining Kingdom

Riley stuffed her face into his chest.

"Y'know, I think your brand of crazy matches mine. At least with protecting my son, anyway. But what did you have to DO?"

He spoke low. "I have a great friend. Matt's known for extraction as much as security. Today, he-"

"NO," she interrupted. "What did you do, to get this shadow in your life? Did you make a new bomb, or something? Do you really kill people?"

"It's aeronautics, mostly. I could explain, if you wanted."

She stared at him. Knowing too much could endanger her life.

"You could give me the short version." She looked away, sighing.

"Okay. Aircraft, as we know them, will be obsolete in fifteen years. Power generation will experience a renaissance. Those are just two things on the horizon. The world is about to change."

The words stewed in the air.

"Like, a new era?" she asked.

"Yeah," he said quietly. "Probably. A step forward."

She stared at him in fascination and terror.

"Aeronautics? But a new era? Like when electricity changed everything? Thomas Edison stuff?"

"Close, yeah. Nikola Tesla might smile and nod. This is pretty big, Sweetheart. But a couple rich jerks will probably buy it out, like they always do. Progress threatens monopolies.

"Soon, we may not depend on world resources. Materialism will fade. World poverty will be abated. Great minds will rise from everywhere - from every country. A lot of things could change for the better, and of course that has complications."

Her breath felt too light. Something strange was happening. She panicked. Her girlish fantasies were taking a very real shape. Clark would invent a new time.

Her eyes fixed on him. "Who… ARE you?"

He studied the floor for two minutes. To Clark, it felt like decades passing.

I'm a monster, he thought. I'm a freak, and a monster - so much that I endangered your family.

"We had the park," he said weakly, "my

confession of love, our first kiss… a nice dinner… and I had your company."

His face flushed red.

"And then there was Albert's abduction, and armored mercenaries, and an extraction. Prides and shames. Right now, I wish I'd never been born."

"Well," she quipped, "all three of us just had greasy, late-night pizza. You, me, and my son. That's who I want. Are you still in there?"

He couldn't answer. She took his hand.

"We need to lie together and look at the stars for a while. I'm serious. We need perspective."

She led him by the hand through the hallway, then pulled him into the bedroom. They pushed the bed close to the window and lay on it sideways. The floor-to-ceiling windows showed the universe like a giant aquarium. She took his hand again and rubbed it like a rabbit's foot.

"You love… more than men can love; you think more than men can think; you're beautifully fit, and you're sweetly caring with others… and you just saved my son, Clark. Today. And now, I'm hearing that you're going to revolutionize the planet.

"I want you to tell me the TRUTH," she said. "Because it's okay, either way. Don't feel any pressure. I will not judge. I'm open."

"Okay," he agreed, curiously.

"And I need you to take this seriously, because my world needs a better answer."

"Okay."

"Clark? You're intense. And you're a genius. You're not like any other man. Are you actually from somewhere else?"

They lay quietly for a moment.

"You're asking if I'm a frickin' alien?"

He paused, then turned his head away from her.

He exhaled sharply. "Pff! My mom has Asperger's. There's this 'other planet' feeling, which is symptomatic. She was actually afraid of being from another planet. She was ashamed of her own abilities. But she's just a total brainiac, and a sweet lady, and I'm proud that she's my mom. I love her. She's nutty, and she's wonderful.

"So, no. I might have inherited some of my mom's wits, but neither of us are from another frickin' planet. Or moon. Or dimension. Okay? Arright?"

She held his hand and played with it.

"I'm sorry, Babe. You're just, like... like a different instrument. We've got drums, and bells, and cymbals..."

She looked straight at him.

"Like my neighbor, for instance? He's got drums and cymbals, for sure."

She looked up again at the stars.

"I'm probably the little metal triangle. All I do is 'ding.' That's it. But you're an 18th-Century violin. You're MADE for different purposes. We all still belong to the same band, but you kinda stand out a bit."

He chewed on his lip angrily.

"So maybe I'm a psycho."

"There's no such thing, Clark. There are no psychos. There's just a bunch of deluded, boring people who don't take time to understand. It's another in crowd, like from high school; that's what 'normal' really is. And that's ALL it is. Humanity is too small to see its own beauty."

"Sometimes," he confessed, "I feel like a write-off. I shouldn't even be here."

"No." She squeezed his hand. "I love you, even if I don't understand what you do, or how you do it. All I know is, you're brilliant. It's even jarring, sometimes. Could you ever tell me about... this new era thing?"

He turned to her sharply. His eyebrows wrenched up with irritation.

"Wanna know?" he snapped, irritated. "Alright. I'll tell you."

He looked up at the walls.

"Athena? Secure Lockdown."

The house went silent. The air felt close and muffled.

"Riley, I'm creating co-resonant energetic vector fields, in pre-geometric foci. Okay? 'Got that?"

He narrowed his eyes at her.

"It's like magnetism, but it affects all matter... not just metals. And we control it. We can actually control potential and kinetic energy in matter. We control physics.

"Here's the deal. If you have enough energy, it actually changes space. Sort of like 'warp' from science fiction movies... but this is real. And now, it doesn't take that much energy.

"See, not too long ago, someone set up magnets differently in electrical engines. All of a sudden, those engines were four times more powerful, or four times as efficient. I've done something like that, but with energy fields instead of magnetic fields."

"Yeah," she nodded eagerly, "You were experimenting with magnets."

"Well, my energy field can be more powerful, because it's so efficient. As long as that energy field is there, matter and space can have different relativity. We can control physical interaction and forces. It's kinda a 'lite' version of the space-time warp thing. It's just like a magnetic field, but it's a field of force. Physical force."

"Wait... did you say a forcefield?"

He waited for a breath.

"You could call it that. We're stepping outside thermodynamic laws. We're changing the rules a little."

"You're changing physics?"

"Controlling, more like. Now imagine using that control, but backwards. Imagine absorbing ambient force, like the Earth's spin. We could tap the Earth's momentum for power. That is a LOT of power. That could easily power my energy field."

"Whoa," she stopped. "That's big, man."

"But we're siphoning energy from the earth, and then using the field to pump it back in. We control physical interactions, right? So we can keep things stable! Net-zero. Even if there is a minor screwup, meteorites always fall here naturally. They affect the Earth a tiny bit. My system would affect it even less."

Riley held out her hand to slow him down, then droned flatly, "Did you seriously make a perpetual machine-thing, this time?"

"Yeah. It's safely piggybacking energy off the Earth's spin."

She tried to follow.

"Uhh... so, how do you make things cooperate? You had the word 'co-resonate' in there, somewhere."

"Co-resonance is the efficiency. It's how I aligned the fields to reinforce themselves. Think of echoes, but they create their own echoes. They resonate in themselves. 'Co-resonant.' The energy field is easier to create, that way. So... in the end, it doesn't take that much power. It's safer."

"Safer sounds good." She didn't want to blink.

"We can project this field, or focus it, or use it anywhere. It could be used in flight, or industrial machinery, or even protective suits. And THAT'S where the military came in."

"No kidding!" she chuckled nervously. "Forcefields? Yeah, they'd want that."

"The U.S. Military wanted protective suits, like armor. A suit that controls kinetic energy would be impervious to bullets. It could fly. It could punch something from a distance and utterly destroy it. It could even fall from space, and land like a cat… and it'd be perfectly fine. That's why I called it 'Icarus.' The military got pretty interested in this research."

"Have you already tapped into the earth, with this thing? with the suit?"

"No. The suit's solar, actually. The fields channel ambient light directly into energy. It looks weird; the suit doesn't reflect light at all. It's the world's first artificial shadow." He chuckled vaguely. "It really is the shadow in my life, apparently."

She kept playing with his hand. She squeezed his fingers and knuckles. At length, she turned to him with a worried look.

"With all this, will you still have time for me?"

He didn't move.

"I only had time for this because I DIDN'T have you. Besides… they're getting Icarus, now. Everything."

He waited, then his brow fell heavy over his eyes.

"Wait a sec. What's wrong? What is this, right now?"

"Shame," he answered. "It kills me that Albert was dragged into this Machiavellian crap. But they have Icarus now, so it should be all over."

Riley squeezed his hand.

"Did you sell Icarus to them?"

He shook his head sadly, but with a smile.

She hesitated.

"Why do they have Icarus?"

"I traded it," he muttered. He turned away from her. "Look, they came after me because of the Icarus Project. I survived. No big deal. But when they came after Albert, they hid him in a place that Athena couldn't reach. Whoever they were, they were smart. It was well planned. So I made a call, and I signed over the Icarus Project to the U.S. Military. I traded all of it for Albert. I made the military find Albert on the spot, and then my guys sprung him out."

"Y..." she stuttered. "W... you... TODAY?"

He shrugged and nodded. "Yeah. They wanted Icarus for years. I mean, it's even protected by dual keycodes, like nukes are. No single person can steal it. But yeah. I gave it to them, and they found Albert. I have no idea what they used to find him. Satellites? Coordinated traffic cams? Speech recognition, using cellphones? Airborne DNA sampling? I don't know... and I didn't care.

"Yeah," he smiled with a twist, "they got Icarus... but dammit, I got your son back."

She stopped rubbing his hand. She held it, instead. He tightened his fingers on hers.

"Now, the Icarus Project is off the table. Everything backfired on those kidnappers."

"But... that was your life's work, wasn't it?" She tightened her brows. "Everything you just told me?"

"Worth it," he declared. "Besides - it kinda makes sense."

She turned to him curiously.

"How? What do you mean?"

A faint laugh puffed from his nose. Again, he looked into her eyes. He lifted her hand up to his dimply smile. He smooched the tops of her fingers.

He swallowed, and then took great care in his words.

"I gave up Icarus to get your son back. That was simple. But Icarus? It came from you, Riley.

"See, a long time ago I had this 'feeling.' I wondered what it would be like to fly without wings. That feeling came from you. That was how you made me feel. I found my way into aeronautics, and electrodynamics, and all that... but you were my inspiration. The beauty. I owe everything to you."

She didn't even look at him.

"I'm a screwup, Clark. That's my claim to fame. I don't inspire. And whatever I've earned in life, I can easily throw away. In fact, the only power I truly have is your Protocol One clearance. And on that note... Athena?"

Composite voices answered. "Yes, Miss Henway?"

"Athena? End Secure Lockdown, thank you." The air seemed to clear, like doors opening.

Clark turned and held her chin. "Genius isn't about a couple patents on glorified kitchen gadgets. It's not about some snotty résumé. Genius is, by definition, something that can't be understood. That's its fundamental nature. So of COURSE people don't give you credit. You're brilliant in ways they can't comprehend."

"Oh yeah?" she snapped. "Then why are YOU successful, and I'm not?"

"Because the world is wrong!" His face squeezed like a lemon. "All this millionaire crap is wrong! Your career should have the millions, not my idiotic zappy-field science tricks!"

"Except, you'll change the world. Cure world hunger, and stuff. That helps a little. Better than ART, I'd say."

He shut his eyes. "Riley, your art is misunderstood. Sure, I'm different from the rest of the orchestra, but you do NOT play second fiddle to me."

That night, she went to cuddle with Albert. She left Clark alone in his room, watching stars. Again, she was down a simple flight of stairs, resting in a safe place. Again, he had to protect her from himself.

CHAPTER THIRTY
COVERED

Around two-thirty in the morning, the wall console beeped.

"Hmm? Athena? Update?" Clark asked.

She answered with her many voices. "Regarding subject Albert Noble Henway: Darrell Vickers, 24, no longer a threat."

Clark set his teeth on edge. He wanted to ask about the cause of death. It must've been in Mexico.

"The other one. Tell me."

"Barnaby Simon, 38, location unknown; last seen at Mexico City International Airport. Was intercepted by Song Jin-Woo, former officer in the Korean People's Army, Special Operation Force. Mr Simon was then taken by private helicopter at..."

"Thank you, Athena," Clark interrupted. He rubbed his temples wearily.

He lay in bed for a moment, then went to his closet. He folded open the doors and looked at his pressed suits. He slid his hand in a pocket and withdrew something small. He held it like an old wedding ring, or like a small pet that had died.

"So what's that?" Riley startled him. She stood in the doorframe with her arms crossed.

He couldn't answer her.

"Alright," she stepped forward, "Wanna help me out, here?"

He turned to her.

"Fine. Love me or hate me, this is the truth. This is what I did for a living."

"What?" she asked. "Research? Changing the world? I'm actually okay with that."

He held out his hand. In his palm, there was a tiny white thing like a plastic worm. It was an earpiece with a coiling wire.

"No, Riley. Field research. Knowing what others know, or keeping things quiet. It's how the government rigs the game. It's like a casino - the house always wins."

She looked at the earpiece. Her mouth fell open and couldn't close.

"How far down does this go? What did you do?"

"Actually, I need to ask you." He dropped his head. "What does this make me, to you?"

She reached past him and shut the doors of his closet. She pressed them till they clicked. She kept her hand there, like putting all his suits to rest.

She took the earpiece, left it on the bookcase, then stood in front of him and clasped his hand. She closed her eyes like wishing.

"Clark, I know who you are. I know who you are."

They had a moment of quiet before she led him back to bed.

Above them, the night sky watched. It was wider and colder than she'd ever seen.

"So… you were a man in black? a spook?"

Clark said nothing. His silence confirmed it.

"Are you CIA?" she asked curiously.

"Actually, no. 'Man in black' is closer."

"So you really ARE the guy in the park, with the black suit. Is your scientist stuff a cover? or are you their expert on planes?"

He confessed quietly, "Mostly, I do theoretical dynamics. You've heard about aerodynamics, and thermodynamics, and electrodynamics? They're all about a 'flow.' We compare that flow to lots of things, including macro-cultural psychology and public information management."

"Information management? Oh - you mean you know things," she huffed. "Things I'm not allowed to know. Alien cover-ups and stuff. Great."

He gazed upward. His voice fell to a drone.

"Humor me: 'first contact.' You heard about Christopher Columbus, right? What about Leif Ericson, or Piri Reis, or Zheng He from China? or even St Brendan the Navigator, from Ireland, back in the 6th century? No-one knows who made first contact with The New World. It's academic."

"Uhh... not all those 'visitors' came in peace, Clark. Some of them invaded. That's pretty friggin' important to know."

"But WHEN?" he turned to her. "The 6th century? or 1492? There's a thousand years of uncertainty, and that's with old, wooden sailing ships.

"If aliens have space travel, they might've been here last week, or maybe back in the stone age. Heck, we can't even figure out the history of boats."

She chuckled once. The room went still.

"In North America," he added, "I think the First Nations peoples have a right to know... but damn, it'd be a call to arms. And while the actual truth about extraterrestrials wouldn't matter, people's reactions would. Facts are nothing; reactions are the world. Things need to be censored."

"No respect," she grimaced. "People deserve the truth."

"Well, how about this: I love you. Someone just leveraged that, using your son. That made me the worst thing that ever happened to your lives."

She stared off into the distance and mused, "Maybe it shouldn't have been a secret, big guy. Too bad you didn't save me from Jeff, back in high school."

Clark couldn't breathe.

"You know, Jeff Anders? My snotty boyfriend?"

He asked her, weakly, "What'd he do to you?"

"You know - Jeff! And that thug, Jonno. Those creeps. Too bad you couldn't make them 'disappear,' or something."

They're gone, Clark thought. By tomorrow morning, they're gone. Not a trace.

"Jeff always treated me like crap. Jonno was a total slime-ball. All the gross leering?" She elbowed him. "If you'd just smooched me, it would've scared them off. You would've been the BEST thing to happen to my life. That would've been truth, and it would've been pretty awesome."

"Mmm," he nodded. He swallowed his rage back inside.

"Come to think of it, Mr Spooky-Secrecy… you did magnets, then aeronautics, then electric fields, and then changing laws of physics. And you made an Athena-computer, too. Do you have a Batmobile somewhere? Is that you?"

"Please stop," he begged quietly.

"Well, why don't YOU stop? Huh?"

"Maybe 'cuz it's all the same thing," he grumbled, "and there really is one grand equation that explains existence. Da Vinci started covering the bases. Call it the 'flow' of things, or unified field theory, or karmic law, or whatever, but it's the poetry of God. It's the mechanics of destiny, and I'm a teensy bit obsessed with it because I can't handle losing my…" He fumed. "Losing again."

She saw his wounded heart all over his face. She didn't even need his new tears or his clenched hands.

He refocused. "Government conspiracies are just intentional futures; they're destiny-by-design. They wanted my insights."

"You don't need to know all the secrets of the universe, Clark. And you haven't lost anything." She stroked his hair with her fingers. "You saved my boy, today, and that had nothing to do with government plans. That was you. I think THAT'S who you really are, okay? Maybe you're not a spook. You're more like a knight."

He sighed. "Well… thank you."

"You wear dark suits, you INVENT dark suits… but you're the good man, underneath. You saved my son. That's who I really know."

He leaned against her warmly.

"Well, it was Albert Henway," he added. "So they had no idea what they were doing."

CHAPTER THIRTY-ONE
BROUGHT TO THE TABLE

Around 7:30 in the morning, Riley woke. Her duvet was wrapped awkwardly from her shoulder to half-way around her head. She felt a little drool on her cheek. She realized she was in Clark's bed. She groaned happily.

She wiped the drool. She rolled over and swatted out her free arm.

Empty space.

She flopped it farther, and felt nothing. She reached outward again, and still felt nothing but sheets.

It was Friday. She was hoping to find Clark. He wasn't there.

She heard a blender whirring in the kitchen. Then, a pause. Then Albert let out a long, emphatic "EEWWWW!"

Clark hammed it up like a game show host.

"Whaddya mean, 'eew?' This is superhero stuff. This is a World-Saving Breakfast."

Albert was not impressed.

"It tastes like a bunch of wet cardboard, upchucked into a bucket."

"Bahhh…" Clark dismissed him. "You add a little bit of milk, and carob, and then some honey… and maybe a TINY bit of chocolate syrup."

Another pregnant pause.

The little voice resumed. "Okay, that's not as barfy. I could survive that."

"Dude, you survive everything. That's why I have to make you superhero breakfasts. 'Cuz you are one."

Albert leveled with him, "I'm not really a superhero."

Clark plunked his smoothie back onto the countertop, expressing his disbelief.

"Ya, you are!" he sang out with utter shock. "You're MY hero! Look at the facts, man. Look at what happened yesterday, and how brave you were! And look at how smart you are! And you're really handsome, too; that's good, if they make comic books about you.

"I've known some great people, so believe me. Even better, believe it yourself! Believe that you're a hero, an' you'll prove it. Start with school, and then build from there. You'll see what I mean."

Riley got in her housecoat and walked closer to the kitchen.

Albert whined: "Are we going to school today?"

"Yahh, sadly. You have school, and I have work."

Albert paused.

"Clark - what do you do, anyway? What's 'work,' for you?"

"Research - sorta. Finding out what people know. People have boring jobs, and I'm a secretary. Pencils, papers, blah blah blah. Records, and charts, and predicted outcomes. That's why I need you and your mom around. Otherwise I'm the boring-est person in the world."

Riley listened. She could tell that Clark was making a weird face.

Albert chirped back, "You're not boring! You have freaky friends in the government, and you know about those special night-vision drones, and you found ME when I was down in some secret base with bad guys, underground. That's cool! I'm even telling my friends about you."

Clark reared back in surprise. "You're pullin' my leg."

"Nope. And my mom? She even kisses you. She doesn't kiss anyone else - not even my dad. Not since MILLIONS of years. She doesn't give mushy-kisses to anybody. She only kisses me on the cheek."

Albert shifted. Things got real.

"Ya know what I think? My mom's a boss of everything - 'cuz she does everything. She does it all the time. Dad's gone, right? I help, but otherwise she's a whole family all by herself. And then she picks you, out of all the guys in the world. Better than Dad. That's gotta say something."

Clark smiled at his promotion.

"Ya, 'cuz Mom's still kinda pretty. Even if she's out of shape, and her bum got wide."

"Hey," Clark corrected him. "Your mom's absolutely beautiful, not just pretty. And she has a gentle figure, and…"

Albert listened tensely.

Clark whispered: "…and she has a cute butt. You'll see someone's cute butt, in another five or six years. Trust me."

Albert squawked with revulsion, "You think her BUM is cute? What's WRONG with you? Do you even know what those are for?"

"Look," Clark shrugged, raising his palms. "I like her butt, and I cannot lie."

Albert peered up curiously. "Clark? You don't, do you? You never even lie. I bet you don't."

Another short quiet.

"No. I respect words. I won't waste them. Do you ever lie? It's just a choice, y'know."

Albert must have been staring. Riley listened carefully.

"I don't wanna. Nehh."

"No?" Clark prompted him. "It's your choice, man, but that's good. That's integrity."

"I won't lie," Albert concluded. "Dad was a liar, and he never helped anything. He wanted to have a bunch of other moms with… WHOEVER. He wasn't much family, because of that. I'm not gonna go there.

"Then, with you and me? We just met. And you helped me, and you're not-a-liar. I think being not-a-liar means something. Maybe I'll end up like you, but… it's 'cuz I wanna. 'Not-lying' is better."

"Hey, dude? Albert?"

"Ya?"

"You grew up a bit, just now. You did. You made a man-decision, and you're more of a man, now, than you were a minute ago."

Clark let that sink in.

"That was really cool. I'm glad I was here to see it. Your mom would smooch you on the cheek."

Riley listened carefully, smiling. She didn't want to interrupt. She couldn't ruin this.

"Dude," he said to the kid, "there are invisible things about people. You have to guard those, like guarding the real people.

"Remember when you told me about your dad, and Naomi, and Monique? I bet that was hard. But you told me anyway."

"Ya," Albert rolled his eyes, "Well, I didn't hurt Dad any more than he already did himself."

Clark paused to think.

"You're probably right. But that day, I also told you about me and your mom, and how I loved her. Remember all that?"

Clark leaned closer.

"Holy moley, I was nervous! But you listened. You understood me, and that really helped. You sorta guarded me, man... and you guarded my invisible stuff, because you listened to me. You let it be real. I appreciate that so much."

Albert pondered.

"Invisible stuff," he thought, "Not lies... right. Like Larsen has 'srebal palsy, but we don't talk about it. He's my best friend. An' sometimes his jokes are downright hilarious."

Again, Albert sat for a moment, then shrugged.

"I won't say anything to Mom, that you like her bum. I'm not gonna say anything at ALL. You guys and your weird grown-up stages - pff! You think kids are bad? Well, look at you and Mom! I won't lie, but... liking butts? I'm definitely not gonna go there."

"Well, she already knows I love her, from head to toe. It's all good."

Albert twisted up his face. "Even bad breath? Huh? What if she has really bad breath?"

"Yeah, Albert. I'd kiss her bad breath. She's more important."

A few seconds passed.

"Wait... you love my mom, right? Like, live-in-a-house love?"

Riley had to get closer. She padded up the hall toward the kitchen. She watched Clark. He snuck a wink at her.

"Albert, you're a great man. Okay? I know this. I really like you, and I could learn lots from you. But you can make a choice here, and it's totally your choice. Do you like this house okay?"

"Yyyyeah, I guess…"

He wasn't clicking with the message, yet.

"Alright. Do you think your mom and I get along? No, wait…"

Clark's thoughts were fussing in his head. His eyes and brows had to straighten themselves out.

"Albert? Am I a good enough guy to be with your mom? Please think carefully, because this matters to me."

Clark stood attentively. He held his breath. Riley bit her lip.

Albert didn't take long to answer.

"She probably knows more about dating stuff than I do. She'll have to make some decisions on her own. Y'know, even BEFORE Dad ran off, she was basically the 'man of the house' - like old people used to say. Mom decided important stuff. Moms do that, so I think she'll be alright.

"See, I think your cooking is pretty good. You make weird milkshakes, but your breakfasts are okay. And I like how you always know everything. You're like a dictionary. Like… old, but full of important words."

"Thanks," Clark chuckled.

"If you're with my mom, we'll probably see each other a lot. You an' I could be friends. If you an' Mom do your kissy stuff, it's got NOTHIN' to do with me, anyway. So… just be sure to ask her."

Albert looked up toward Clark, then looked straight at him. It clicked in Albert's head.

"You did, didn't you? You talked about 'live-in-a-house' stuff?"

Clark dropped his eyes. A thoughtful moment passed. He looked up at the kid again.

"Yeah," Clark admitted. "A bit. She's thinking. I needed to ask you, though. It's partly about you and me getting along. Us two guys."

Albert added, "An' we just met, too… but you and Mom knew each other back in YOUR school, when YOU were kids. Now you're old, and doing jobs… so you want a house together?"

"Yeah," Clark sighed. "And I think she already quit her job. They didn't pay her enough for all the hard work she did. She deserves better."

Albert sat up. "Wait - she quit? What about our apartment? How are we gonna get food and rent? Why can't she work?"

"She deserves better, Albert. So do you. She worked really hard at a terrible job. You should thank her for putting up with it."

"Well," the kid looked confused, "how do we keep our place? All our stuff is there! It's noisy sometimes, because of the neighbors, but I have my dinosaur collection…"

Riley winced at Clark. She shrugged sadly.

Don't break my son's heart, she thought.

"Ya," Clark said. "Of course you can keep that place. I'll keep it FOR you. You can still live there, or you can just go there whenever you want. But - if you feel like it - I'll make room for you here. You can keep anything here."

"If Mom doesn't work at Dino's, what's she gonna do? Is she gonna start knitting socks, or something, like grandmothers?"

"No," Clark's voice lowered, "she's an artist. You know about that, right? I hope she'll focus on that."

Albert sat still, but his eyes scanned through dozens of thoughts. He leaned forward.

"Clark, don't tell her this, but… she's not just a 'pictures' artist. She's an artist that's, like… really SMART. Do you know what I mean? Like those museums with actual real dinosaurs? They have art there, too. And she's like those guys."

Clark spoke with quiet strength. "I know. So maybe someone else should work at Dino's. Maybe some teenager who's sick of delivering newspapers."

Clark stood tall. "I've thought this for a long time, Albert. I really want her to do art."

"Does she have to go away somewhere?" he squeaked.

"HECK NO," Clark grinned at him.

"Do you do art? Is that why you love her all that much?"

"I don't do art at all."

"…You're kinda weird."

"Y'know what?" Clark propped his hand on his hip. "Your mom isn't like other artists. She's better than this whole town. She's the most beautiful woman I've ever seen, and there's no-one like her anywhere. And you? You're a hero, and a fantastic guy. You and your mom… are you two weird? 'Cuz you two are really different, just from being awesome."

"No. You're weird. She's an artist. I'm gonna be a specialist on dinosaurs."

"I know…" He sat next to Albert with a gleam in his eye. "Look. There's this field trip you gotta go on. Not because I want you to, and not because your mom wants you to, but YOU'RE gonna want it. Talk to your mom about this, okay? I can help. It's a whole week, and you'll get to see dinosaurs at the museum.

"Wait… think about this: what if you could go to any school you wanted, further down the road? Big schools, that is. What if… you could go to the best school for studying dinosaurs?"

Riley walked in.

No bribing my kid, she thought.

"I'm gonna do that," Albert declared. "If I have to study stuff, I will. I don't care what classes."

"I want to see you do that."

Clark saw Riley looking at him. He sat at attention. He dropped his hands on his knees and braced himself.

"I'd make your school lunches, if it makes things easier."

Riley padded forward wearing her robe. She was royalty, and the guys both knew it. She tousled Albert's hair.

"Hey, little monster… 'sleep okay? Listen, Clark and I have stuff to figure out, and he has work, and you've got school. I'm gonna get dressed, borrow

Clark's car, and I'll get you to school on time. Okay? Hop to it."

He grumbled and started getting ready for school.

Riley and Clark sat at the table. They had a light breakfast and didn't speak much. They made plans to contact the school about security, though Clark assured her that 'his people' had taken care of it.

"My friend Matteo? He's on it."

Riley raised her brows and pressed her lips. She wouldn't look Clark in the eye.

"Nah," she said, "I'll have a chat with the school anyway. There's a weak link, somewhere, and I don't care where it is. Someone's not doing their job. I'll do it for them, until they shape up or get replaced."

She nearly spat. "Albert's my son. He will NOT suffer because of some overpaid slacker."

It didn't take long for Albert to get ready. Riley soon joined him. When they left the front hall, Albert called back to the kitchen.

"Thanks, Clark! I gotta go to school, and then prob'ly get home."

The kitchen was suddenly silent. Riley paused.

She poked Albert's shoulder. "Hang on for a sec, little monster."

Back in the kitchen, Clark folded his arms on the table. He laid his head down. In front of him, in the middle of the table, a tall glass of breakfast smoothie stood alone. Albert hadn't quite finished it.

Riley touched his arm. "Babe. 'You gonna be okay?"

He nodded to her. She stroked her fingers in his hair.

"Hey. I gotta check on my apartment today, but I'm coming right back."

ARE YOU SURE? Clark thought. OR DO YOU WANT SOMEPLACE SAFER?

His voice was weak. "For a few minutes, I was part of a table. Do you understand? It was almost like breakfast... you, and me, and Albert."

"It was," she said. She smiled curiously.

"No, I mean... a table, like Thanksgiving. A table to come home to, where we talk, and we can be..."

He opened his hands with his fingers strained out. Then his hands relaxed and fell. His palms lay open. He stared straight ahead.

"We had that, for a second. I felt it." He closed his eyes.

She rubbed his shoulder.

"Hey - big guy? That's what we're looking at. The first steps are gonna be strange. Hang tight. I'll be back soon. Promise."

She smiled for real, kissed him on the head, then turned and took her son to school.

Riley spent the afternoon sorting through her apartment. It was rickety furniture and a sagging couch, but lots of Albert's colorful drawings. They were proudly displayed in dollar-store picture frames.

This apartment was everything she'd cobbled together over the years. It was everything she'd achieved. It was nothing like Clark's place; it was a hole. The floors smelled bad because of something damp under the carpets. The overhead light hummed and crackled in the ceiling. At 3:30 in the afternoon, she could hear her neighbor snoring through the wall. No, this place didn't have charm, but at least it was familiar... and for several years, this was where she raised her son. This apartment still had meaning.

At the end of the day, Riley went to Albert's school to wait for him. She sat on a bench near the front entrance. She watched for shady-looking people in suits. She only saw paunchy school administrators with their ugly ties and over-stressed teachers in pastel skirts and blazers.

She sat on that bench in front of Ashvale Elementary, remembering when it was her school. Back in those days, she was the little girl running around with hopes in her bright eyes. The future was so big and so near, there was no time to sit down. The world wouldn't wait!

Now Riley waited there for Albert. She was there for her son. She smiled at herself - she'd greet him noisily and throw her jazz hands in the air:

"Annnnnnd, HERE HE IS, folks! It's the guy you've ALL BEEN WAITING FOR! The MAN... the LEGEND... You know him, you love him - it's ALBERRRT the GREATTTT!"

And she'd imitate crowd cheers before running up and hugging him. She'd give him a good squeeze.

"Heyya, monkey-boy. 'Learn anything good?"

No-one ever did that for her. Why? Her dad

wouldn't, because he was drinking at the bar. Her mom was always scrambling to keep the household together, or looking for an escape. Granny Faye cared, but she didn't get around too well.

No-one ever waited for Riley. No-one hoped to see her. She knew this.

She sat there on that bench for almost an hour. Sometimes she felt a breeze in her hair, or a draft through her coat. She bundled closer to keep warm, and she waited for her son. She was alone.

CHAPTER THIRTY-TWO

LYNCHPINS

"No," Clark fumed. He gripped the phone against his cheek. "This is how it is. I'm cashing in and retiring. You got what you wanted; I'm giving you ICARUS, for God's sake. You don't even care about my work with S.I."

He leaned into his smartphone.

"There are time-locked releases. You'll get tech advances regularly, like clockwork. This isn't stuff you can invent, by the way. I had to invent technology just to…"

He listened to the phone.

"Yes."

He listened again.

"Yeah - like Newton, when he had to invent calculus. But the proofs are all provided. 'Co-resonant energetic vector fields in pre-geometric foci.' It sounds whack because it doesn't exist yet - or it shouldn't. The method will come in time-released installments, and you'll have the only copy in the world, along with the prototype."

And then, he thought, no-one gets to ruin Albert's life. Icarus is YOUR problem.

"BUT," he continued, "if anything happens to me or people I love, I wouldn't be able to stop it from being sent to your rivals. It's a lynchpin that only I can keep in place. If I don't check in on time, and give my code, ALL the data automatically goes to the Chinese AND the Russians... both. Simultaneously.

"You heard me right. The golden goose IS held hostage. You gotta protect me to protect your interests."

Dead silence.

"The U.S. Government has to keep me safe. But then, you boys gain big time. It's well worth it."

Brief chatter on the other end of the phone.

"No, it's extreme because no protection program OR assassination ever carried this much weight. Icarus is one of the biggest investments in world history."

Babble on the other end.

"I get my freedom, and you change the face of the world. Or make untold billions of dollars. Whichever suits your fancy. And that, my good sirs, is that."

There was further babbling on the other end. Clark hung up. Somewhere, old rich men popped champagne. Clark didn't care.

I'm out, he thought. Enough is enough. No more S.I., no more Icarus... I want a life.

Clark closed his eyes. He prayed softly.

"I'm coming back to you, My Love. I am."

At that same moment, twenty-four hands lay motionless. They rested on a long, black table. The table was like a gravestone - hard, cold, final. It was the cutting board where world events got sorted.

Cigar smoke steamed out from tight, angry lips. An ugly fact hovered in the room.

"He still has everything in his head. And now we have nothing."

"We need him."

"He could leak to anyone else; any nation. Not just the American government, or the Ruskies, or the friggin' Chinese. What about Iran? or even Syria? or any half-assed private military? Anyone could make a move and steal Icarus. Clark Benjamin is a loose end. He represents too much imbalance."

"We agree."

"We agree, also."

Heads turned to Mr Jeffrey Stewart Anders.

Anders spoke. "The Icarus Project is worth billions, but so is his brain."

"Yes, we know."

"Look," Anders flopped his hands together, "the usual government hit is only a few - pff - thousand dollars. Doing it right? Hundred thou, tops. But that didn't work, even up close. The man is stubborn. A few years back, he even repelled a strike team at his research lab. Their op was blown to hell. Clark David Benjamin is unbelievably... He is NOTORIOUSLY difficult to kill."

"We know."

"Mmm-hmm. We saw."

Anders wore a sickening grin.

"So, gentlemen, he's with this lippy little skirt named Henway. Riley Henway. Perhaps you've heard about her? or maybe her son?"

Everyone knew. No-one wanted to respond.

"Okay. So when twenty-two paramilitaries capture her seven-year-old boy, Clark Benjamin turns into Mr White Knight. He charges in with cavalry and rescues the kid. They planned for days, with location assets, but he nullified them in minutes. MINUTES!

"Yes - be sure you heard that right, gentlemen: twenty-two high-end mercenaries can't successfully ransom a seven-year-old child."

The room soured in silence.

"We lost those soldiers. No contact since. And not just the two face-men - ALL OF THEM."

Faces drained; they went as cold as the table.

"Those first two? He made them human sacrifices. We lost any semblance of authority, after that... spectacle. But the other twenty? WHERE ARE THEY?"

No-one breathed. Where were the other soldiers?

"Those other twenty mercenaries? I'll give you the answer: they're ashes, gentlemen. THAT'S Benjamin. That's who we're dealing with."

The air weighed heavily. It solidified. The men were trapped in it - a dozen fossil bugs in amber.

"Who is he?" someone grumbled. "Affiliations? Is he CIA?"

"We don't know."

Anders mocked them: "Do you feel safe, gentlemen?"

No-one answered.

"Do you feel SAFE? Are your families safe? or this little 'focus group,' here? We need control."

Someone reluctantly spoke. "Our options?"

Anders's fist boomed on the table.

"I'm gonna own Ashvale Plains. I'll be mayor, shortly. Real estate, local government, banks... I'll have the whole county by the balls.

"I'll go after Clark with a personal touch, because the tried-and-true methods have all failed. Hits, raids, ransoms - all failures. I'll handle this myself, because it needs tact. Oh, and also because NO-ONE ELSE DOES ANYTHING."

Somewhere in the room, a man cleared his throat.

Anders rolled his eyes. "Also - Agent Landucci? That little punk? He'll never see this coming. This won't be conventional warfare. He won't be ready."

A few hands turned to knuckles and rapped the tabletop.

"First, I'll send in this bimbo from my PR staff, Colleen Dietrich. She's just a banker, but she has some attitude regarding Clark and little Riley. She'll find dirt.

"Then we'll create some generic world catastrophe, wear him down, and then hit Benjamin on the small scale: family. It's always family. It's the chink in his armor, right? Then when he's weak, we'll own him. We'll own him HARD.

"Either we'll own him, or no-one will. He really is Icarus. It's time for him to fall."

Many knuckles rapped on the black tabletop.

Jeff Anders never revealed his true plans. Any government project could be bought or stolen, then eventually owned. Clark could not. Clark was a factor that had to be removed completely.

CHAPTER THIRTY-THREE
THE EVIL QUEEN

As time passed, Clark's house became a regular hangout. Albert and Larsen spent a lot of time there; Larsen called it "Albert's BIG place." He never saw Albert's apartment anymore.

At first, Larsen was surprised at Clark's height. He reared his head back with huge, shocked eyes. At the same time, Clark was surprised to actually MEET Larsen. Was he the real Larsen? that guy? the man who'd mastered the 'Space Titans' video game? When Larsen confirmed the rumors, he knew he was welcomed. Clark was honored to have him visit.

One bright Saturday morning, Albert and Larsen were in the den. They babbled excitedly about a school trip. Clark was checking Athena on his laptop because she'd been acting glitchy. There was a sudden, sharp knocking at the door and the doorbell rang. Clark got up to answer it; he was moderately dressed, whereas Riley was wearing a big sweater, pajama bottoms, and reading socks. She was cocooned in her favorite blanket with a mochaccino and a glossy magazine.

"Got it," he grunted to her. She blew him a big, dramatic kiss.

Clark tightened his belt and smoothed out his shirt. When he reached the door, he looked at the figure in the monitor. A woman stood there in a pressed suit. Was that Colleen Dietrich? from Ashvale High School? 'Little Miss Popular?'

He slowly pulled the door open.

"Uh - good morning?" He blinked his eyes as if he'd just gotten out of bed. Maybe she wouldn't recognize him. Or maybe she'd buzz off.

"CLARK?" Colleen gasped. "Clark BEN-jamin, aww, Ashvale High! D'you remember me?" Her voice jumped like a circus poodle.

"Yeah, Colleen. I remember." He spoke gravely. "Oh, I remember."

"Aww, it's been too long!" Her tone slung around in loops like a yo-yo trick. "Is this you? Is this you?" She gestured at Clark's tall, well founded house. "I always hoped you'd make it somehow, Clarkie. Nice digs. Well done."

Colleen swatted playfully at his midsection. Her little hand patted his abs.

She continued, "Listen, Handsome, I'm just out canvassing. I get to be part of the PR department for

Jeff Anders. You remember Jeff? Well ya, he's running for mayor!"

"Mayor?" Clark feigned surprise.

"Yes! I know, I'm really excited for him. So now I'm checking with… you know, keeping in touch with, like, 'the people,' and whatever."

"Mmm-hmm," Clark grumbled. "Maintaining his high public profile."

She hesitated. "Yyyeah… and you know me, Clarkie, so I can count on your vote, right? I mean… Mr Anders can count on your vote? for the proud Anders family?"

"Oh," he waved in the air, "It's already been decided."

He'd decided within fractions of a second.

"EXCELLENT." Colleen faced him with her most photogenic smile. That was when she heard Albert and Larsen.

"Oh, Clark… you're a family man, too! Oh, I'm so happy for you. Big house, and little tykes, and…" Her creeping smile slid toward him. "Who, may I ask, is the lucky lady?"

Clark breathed deep and straightened his spine. He stood taller than he'd ever stood in his life.

"The artist, Riley Henway. And I'm the lucky one, believe me." He glowed; his glory met her like the heavenly host.

He watched Colleen's blood die inside her face. Her little world ground to a complete halt. Her smile was soulless plastic.

"Really…?" she smiled emptily. She finally blinked to keep her eyes from falling out of her head.

"Yes," he purred, with a nod. "We're very much in love."

"Well, um… when it comes to ballots, be sure Riley gives it a LITTLE extra thought." She pinched her fingers in the air to demonstrate 'a little' extra thinking. "I'm sure she'll be onboard." Colleen's fist made a shallow swoop of encouragement. Venom boiled in her eyes.

"Uhh… voting? for her ex? Colleen, did you even hear how Jeff dumped her, back in grade twelve? It was positively savage."

Colleen's mouth hovered open for a moment.

"I'd hoped bygones could be bygones. This election is about Ashvale moving forward. She'll remember the Anders family, right? She's met them, so at least she's MET people with integrity…"

Clark resisted slamming the door on her face. It would've left makeup stains on the door.

"Uh-huh," he droned. "I'll definitely remind her."

That was very unlikely.

"Great, then! Seeya around, Clarkie!" She winked, waved, and strode off.

Clark's eyes rolled like measuring infinity. He turned back inside and met Riley. Her expression was pure shock.

"Was that…?"

"Yeah. Colleen Dietrich." Clark's feet flopped over toward her. He stopped, leaned into her arms, and nuzzled her cheek.

"SAVE ME," he whispered.

She snorted, and they snickered together.

Albert called up from the den, "Hey, who was at the door?"

Clark kissed Riley on the cheek, then turned to Albert. "Nobody!"

Colleen didn't hear "nobody," even if Clark wished she had. She was walking back to her car when she fished her tiny smartphone from her purse. She tapped in a number.

She sang into it, "Hi, it's me."

There was a brief silence. Her smile dropped like the gallows.

She clarified: "Dietrich. Colleen Dietrich. You know... in PR? Your BOSS? 'Kay, never mind the hard questions, since you're obviously not qualified.

"I need information. 'Clark Benjamin.' No, I don't even think he has a middle name. How should I know? Am I s'posed to be his frickin' bio-lographer? He was, like, the biggest nerd in high school. Bound for greatness and wealth... and he frickin'-well got it.

"A friend of mine? Are you cray-cray? He was the bottom of the cow pile. He's nothing. He's one of the worker bees - he brings home the honey. But now it's gonna be our honey. Err... money. Whatev's. But trust me, Anders wants a piece. It's about real estate, so he'll want in."

She listened to her phone.

"Because of his house. No nerd gets a place like

this. YOU'D never get a place like this, even if I DID give you that raise. And another thing, this house has never been on the market, before. How did he get this property?

"No, he doesn't have family. I dunno. Maybe he had a mom and dad somewhere? Children, ya. Definitely. And… no, wait. Forget all that. His little wifey isn't just collateral. She's, like… make her a damn target, or something.

"RILEY. Riley Ann Henway. Ya, I said 'target.' Like a smear campaign. You're going to destroy that little tramp. I don't care how you do it. Put a hard squeeze on these two. We'll get that house."

Colleen put her manicured finger against her chin. This property was never up for sale. It had to be a family thing.

She pressed her phone close to her cheek. "Look. Jeff Anders is gonna own this town. He's got interests, and it's not just being mayor. Got it? You aren't gonna stand in his way, not even with your giant pile of stupid. So pass this on to Mr Anders, direct. You breathe a word of it to anyone else, and you won't have that little raise to take care of your kids. You'll be FIRED. Got it?"

The phone was meekly quiet.

"On second thought, pass this on right now. Right now. And then, you're actually fired. For reals. You're so dumb, it's causing me pain."

Colleen shoved her tiny phone back into her purse. She walked down the stone path from Clark's house. Her heels clicked like tiny, sharpened hooves.

She smiled to herself. "Bust up Riley, snag a property for Anders... too good."

She walked four steps and her phone rang. It was Jeff Anders.

"Hello? Hey, Jeff! What can I do for you?"

Her shoes clipped along the stonework and then went silent. She halted. She stood stock still.

"Oh. That was quick. How'd you...? What, the house? Yeah, it's really nice; I didn't know you had an interest. Yes, Clark's there with that little skank, Riley Henway. Your ex. Gold-diggin' little skeeze..."

She listened to Jeff. Her eyes widened in fascination.

"Wait. You want the property, AND you want Clark gone, AND you want Riley out? That's, like, LITERALLY three birds with... with, like, LITERALLY one stone, here."

Devils danced through her mind.

"If you want his house... maybe call him away for work? You've got connections. Send him someplace far away, and then push her buttons. Really sting her. What? WHY? 'Cuz Riley's his weakness, Jeff. I could tell. Hurt her, and it hurts him. When Clark loses his nerdy little mind, and his job gets shaky, Riley loses everything. Nobody else cares about her. When they're broken, you can snatch up the property cheap. That's a win-win situation, with a couple more wins sprinkled on top.

"Jeff? This time, we play it smart and we follow

through. We're not pulling high school pranks, here. Dig under their foundations. When you hit her, you dig down to her roots.

"And you remember me on payday, mkay Jeff? Bye-eee." She grinned her pointy teeth. Her heels ticked the flagstones as she trotted away.

CHAPTER THIRTY-FOUR
WHERE THE HEART IS

A few days later, the house was quiet. Albert and Larsen were away. They'd both gone on the week-long trip to the Metro Museum.

Albert saw one of the largest reconstructed T-Rex skeletons in the world. A gigantic past stood right there, right in front of him. His far-off dreams of wonder and terror now stood inches away - he could see them; they were REAL. He stared, and they stared right back.

He looked at the T-Rex and its giant, clawed feet, but then its massive skull leered down at him. He craned upward again to see its huge, hollow eyes, but then its whole body loomed - tons of skeletal trap, tensed to grab him.

This museum was Albert's cathedral. He was thrilled, but humbled; he'd never thought he'd see it, but it really was HIM. The T-Rex... The King. Albert stood right there, at the foot of The King.

Somewhere in his mind, his mom was waving to him from the shore. She and Clark both waved at him as he floated away in his dreams.

At home, in Clark's house, everything was strangely quiet. Things were peaceful, with Albert away. Riley found herself completely alone with Clark. She found candles lit with her dinners. She discovered rose petals in the bedsheets. Nothing ever disturbed that beautiful quiet... except at night, and a few random times during the day.

Riley had never woken up to mornings like these. Coffee was an old friend that ushered her into newer, brighter days. Her cheek woke to warm, meaningful kisses. Everything had changed. She'd never experienced so much eye contact in her whole life.

Of course, it couldn't last.

Late on Wednesday evening, Riley got a call. She'd been waiting for Clark all afternoon. He'd only gone out for more chocolate ice cream.

"Umm... Clark? Where are you? Are you okay?" She stood with her phone in the hallway.

Silence on the other end of the line. Cold.

"I'm fine," he crackled, on the other end. "Just... some overtime, at work."

None of Clark's words were 'fine.' He wasn't at work. He never had overtime at work, either. He couldn't tell her what was wrong, but he couldn't hide his fear.

Riley stopped. She held the phone with two hands; she knew what this meant. The military. Something classified. Something he couldn't talk about.

"Will y-... can I get you some dinner? Like, we'll have something together, later? Maybe?"

He said nothing.

"Maybe? Sometime tonight? Honey?"

He stayed silent. His answer finally arrived, after a few seconds of pain. His voice shook.

"...I'm not sure."

He wished he could be in her arms - more than anything. He would've given anything to feel her warmth, and her touch, and to smell her hair. He ached for her.

She swallowed. Had he been taken hostage? The other end of the phone call was muted. Distant. He was trapped somewhere. Her arms begged to touch him.

"Clark?"

"-Ya?" He was quick to answer.

"I-... I love you. Honey." She pressed the phone tight to her ear.

"I know," he whispered. "I love you too. I love you. I love you, Riley - GOD, I love you..." He sobbed quietly: "I love you so much..."

A harsh beeping and squeal came through the line. Riley choked.

She heard his breath. It streamed close against the phone.

"I love you, so, SO-"

The line clicked.

"...Clark?"

She stood there and listened for a few minutes. Nothing. She hoped he'd pick up again, but... nothing. She waited. She kept perfectly still.

"...Clark?"

She stood straight-spined in his hallway. There was no answer.

There was a chill in the nighttime air. He was out there, somewhere. She wasn't allowed to know where. He could've been in another country, for all she knew.

She waited on the dead line.

"Clark, please pick up...?"

She bit her lip. She couldn't leave the phone. She needed to hear him. Just one word. She heard nothing.

"...Clark?" she rasped into the phone. Her lower lip trembled.

She whispered, "Honey?"

She closed her eyes, struggled to lift her arm, then slowly pressed the red hang-up button. She was alone in the house.

After an hour, she tried to find some answers.

"Athena?"

The chorus of voices replied, "Yes, Miss Henway?"

"Where is Clark Benjamin?"

Athena stayed quiet. She wouldn't answer that question.

Clark wouldn't come home that night at all. Riley cuddled a pillow in bed. Every other night, she lay on her side while his warm chest supported her back. She'd sit her thighs on his lap, and his great arms would wrap all the way around her. He always held her. He guarded her every single night. He wouldn't let the world have her. He kept her safe, like in a treasure chest, until the morning.

Riley woke with the pillow by her belly. She'd kept trying to hug it closer.

Clark didn't come home in the morning, either.

Riley paced. She worked at her art when she could. She picked away at some projects in her studio. She called Albert a few times to see if he was okay. He didn't have much time to talk. He assured her that everything was "not just alright," but "mind-blowing and awesome." Albert sensed her worry as pure mothering instinct.

"Mommm," he whined, "There's adults all over the place. Ms Philson from the library is here, an' she has her niece along to watch us. She studies social stuff in a big school, and I think she's studying kids, or something. So she keeps track, like documenting. I feel like one of those monkeys on TV when some old guy is talking about behaviors."

Riley had a brief laugh.

"How's Clark? Are you two bored, back there?"

She steeled herself and replied, "No. Clark's okay. He's busy working, and I still have my art. We'll be okay. Ya. We will. We'll be fine."

Albert had to rush off for lunch. Riley smiled, saying goodbye, but stood in silence afterward. Even the air of this house had scents, in it: Albert's room; Clark's cooking. Her two guys were gone, and she felt it. The hollowness inside her ached.

She tried not to turn on the news. She gave in, around 1pm. She snatched the TV remote and flicked through the channels.

"Some claim that the company is responsible for alleged price fixing, including large-scale real estate deals, but representatives from the bank's legal department declined to comment on any-"

Click.

"WELL, I don't know about you, Jilly, but I say this kid has TALENT. You, kiddo? You're going to the FINALS in-"

Click.

"...whether the airport provides adequate security. It's an emerging factor, given the growing popularity of private jets and rotorcraft. The current rash of politically motivated-"

Click.

"...only twenty minutes from Krakow, one of the

largest cities in Poland. The majority of the industrial complex was engulfed in the blaze, and there have been serious public health concerns over the toxic gases released into the air. The dispersion has been compared with modern-day aerosol chemical weapons.

"Meteorological analysts have projected the approximate range of contamination in the lower atmosphere. Response teams have been dispatched to the most vulnerable populated areas.

"Within hours, there were even reports of blackouts in surrounding power grids. A spokesman for Tkane Złoto has assured that all precautions are being taken for the greater interest of the Polish people, in-company staff, and valued investors in their textiles production. In addition to eighteen crews of firefighters, a detail from the Polish government has continually overseen containment concerns. The fire is not being considered suspicious at this time."

The remote slipped from her fingers.

Aerosol chemical weapons, she thought.

Where wind meets energy, she thought again.

Clark's research. Militaries. Aeronautics. World powers. Where is he? Who took him?

"That was no fire," she said out loud. "That was an attack."

That afternoon, Athena bleeped at her loudly. She couldn't get an answer why; supposedly there were no new updates.

Another two days went by. She couldn't create art. She lost her appetite. She didn't know how she'd pick up Albert after his museum trip; she didn't have Clark's car. She was stranded, worrying, trapped in Clark's house.

At night, she lay in bed alone, hugging a pillow. That didn't help; it smelled too much like clean linens. It didn't smell warm and gorgeous like Clark. She'd even settle for that raggedy old stuffed bunny, from when she was a kid.

"I'm sorry I lost you, Louis… I really wish I had you here. You always helped me get through stuff."

Clark returned late Friday evening. He hadn't shaved, he was grimy, and the smell of burned plastic fumed around him. His blazer had sweat-stains.

Riley covered her mouth. She was shocked, but deeply relieved.

"CLARK! OH… OH, HONEY!"

He pushed out his hands. He was exhausted, but furious. His eyes made him look like an old boxer. He stumbled into the bedroom and muttered about being alone. The door closed in her face.

Her heart withered. Her insides shrank away to a lonely corner. Her hand raised to the bedroom door; it wanted to knock. It wanted to tap on the door, just so she could step inside, touch his shirt, and pull him close.

She couldn't even close her fingers to make knuckles. She withdrew her hand. She stood outside the door for a minute, but she knew he'd decided.

She stayed close, that night, in case he needed her. She rearranged some couch cushions, put on another sweater, and slept in the living room.

This wasn't the first time she was displaced from bed and had to sleep on a couch. This time, though, it was Clark's couch. She was rejected by Clark. That hurt differently.

She had no blanket. She curled up with a pillow and squeezed it tight against her. She squeezed and squeezed, and she knew over and over again that she wasn't hugging Clark. He was in their bedroom, and she couldn't see him. She sucked in long breaths, and they jerked out of her silently. She cried as quietly as she could.

Oh, no, she thought. Am I turning into my mother? Is that what this is, now?

Halfway through the night, she got up and walked to the coat closet by the front door. She flung through a few blazers on their squeaky hangers and found his longcoat: charcoal grey, wool, with hints of cologne. She brought it with her, and slept with it in the living room.

He's here, she thought. He's safe.

She reminded herself of this, over and over. He slept till 10am on Saturday.

As soon as she heard him, she tried to fix him a breakfast. She jumped up, hustled to the kitchen, and tried to cook eggs over-easy. They ended up scrambled. Hash-browns would take too long, so she chopped up some french fries and tossed them in a skillet with oil. Toast was simple. She was proud of the bacon; that turned out pretty well.

He said nothing; he just dropped to the table, ate, and wouldn't look at her.

"Clark?" She was afraid to speak. "If you need anything, you KNOW you can ask me. I'll do anything I can, okay?"

"I'm getting a shower," he muttered.

He chewed a last bit of toast-and-jam, looked up, and looked into her eyes for the first time in days. He had a hard time holding contact. He'd eaten everything but the scrambled eggs. He wouldn't touch them.

"Darling? A shower. And then I need you to hold me." Everything in his gaze was weakened. "Please, Riley? Could you?"

"Of course! Yeah, of course. Of course."

He closed his eyes with relief. He tidied up and shuffled to the washroom.

He shaved like he was shedding an old skin. He was comforted to see the man underneath; yes, he was still there.

He twisted the shower on and ran it hot. He inhaled the steam to cleanse himself. He peeled away his clothes, and then separated his belt from his slacks. His leather belt was all he kept - the rest, he bunched into the garbage.

He stood there, naked, and tied the trash bag tight. He felt like he was man-versus-monster: bare chested and primal. No clothes, no loincloth; just grime, after so much endurance. He strangled a few knots into the plastic bag. He cinched them and yanked them bitterly. His chest twitched. His whole body growled at this little bag of clothes. He tossed it by the door. He'd never wear those clothes again. HELL no.

When he stepped into the shower, the water was holy absolution. It was a stream of glassy lava that melted him. He could feel it taking all the poisons away; it washed them from his shoulders and back. It scoured his skin.

He inhaled deep, and let out a long, purifying sigh. For a moment, he wished those other people had such luxury. Just… clean water, to make their bodies right. Something to purify them, and wash out the toxins. Something to stop the bloating and hemorrhaging.

He knew Riley meant well, but he couldn't eat those scrambled eggs. Not after what he'd just seen.

The shower continued hissing. Water pattered against his muscle like wet sparks. He let it snake down, rippling past his shoulders, chest, and belly. He didn't care about the water; he wanted Riley's hands. He wanted the touch of her fingers across his arms and behind his neck. He wanted to see her eyes. He was starved to feel her love again.

Ugh, he thought. She deserves a cleaner me. She deserves a BETTER me. My life is madness.

Crap, he thought again. It's been days. No time with her. Does she miss me? Does she hate me?

After vigorous scrubbing, the froth of soap finally swished away. Clear water twisted down his front and trailed along his features. He emerged from the bathroom with a billow of steam and the scent of cologne. He was clean-shaven. His jaw was one smooth color. He was wearing only his bathrobe.

He cleared his throat and called out to her.

He padded toward her usual haunts.

Is she gone? he worried.

He looked in her studio. He hoped to see her there - but no. She wasn't there. There were several charcoal sketches, but no Riley. Sun poured through the skylights to greet her newest works. He was about to leave, but then he saw a three-faced chimera hidden in the sketch of city hall. He recognized Jeff Anders as mayor. He was ugly, but in the goofiest way possible. Clark chortled. He had no idea what she was up to, but it belonged in a gallery of 'commentary architectural design,' if there was such a thing. He paused to admire her other works. One was darkly shaded, but it looked like a statue or a figure from a commemorative coin. She'd drawn its lines over and over, like trying to find its true definition. Another one looked like an artist at an easel, but the lines were light and it looked alone in the centre. It was so empty, it looked hesitant... lost.

Always creating, he thought. So talented.

He looked in the living room. No. Her books and magazines were there, and also her reading socks, but no Riley. His coat, too... weird. The TV remote was under a couple days of junk mail.

"Riley?" he called. "Are you here?" His voice started to tighten.

Kitchen? No. He thought she might be doing the daily sudoku at the kitchen table, drinking chai. Her brunette beauty and the scent of chai seemed to go together naturally. He always wondered at that.

Sunlight brightened the windowpanes... the rest of the kitchen was quiet. Only the fridge hummed to itself distantly.

"Uhh," he called out carefully. "Honey?"

Oh, no. Did she really leave me? I deserve it.

When he opened the bedroom door, he saw darkness... then little candles singing everywhere. They were tiny love angels, singing light to him. The bedroom didn't smell like burned plastic; it was scented with vanilla. Clark couldn't place the other scents, like ylang-ylang. The bed was clean, and its sheets were folded aside. Riley sat in the middle wearing her nightgown. She leaned against the headboard. Again, he met the fey beauty of her modest curves, slowly lifting while she breathed.

His eyes couldn't stray, nor could they blink. They lit brightly. They were the gleam of a starved wolf. He walked toward her weakly... though he wanted to grab her body, dip her in chocolate, and gobble her. Instead, he lay back against her, with his head on her belly and hip. Her hands made spirals in his hair.

Several minutes passed.

"Uhh," he began, slowly. "A lot of…"

She looked aside. This would be it - this would be the explanation. He wouldn't abandon her, but there was some reason why she was alone for days.

His brow dropped. "A lot of people almost died. A lot. Like, hundreds of thousands. This wasn't military. I was part of a response team, like triage. It was still classified.

"The whole time, I kept thinking of you. I just wanted to leave, and come back to you."

Riley's face bent to sad shapes. "This can't keep happening to us, Clark. I'd move, you know. If you wanted to."

He shook his head slightly. "I don't think that would change anything."

Her breath came as an angry gust. "I don't know. It might. I DO know that I can't deal with my kid getting abducted, and you vanishing for whole days at a time, and… I'm really sorry to say that. I can't do it."

He reached up, took her hand, and kissed it. "I'm sorry I have strings attached. I thought I cut them."

"Yeah, well, okay." She nodded curtly. "THANKS. I guess."

He turned his head with frustration.

"About 770,000 Poles and Slovaks are grateful for your sacrifice."

She furrowed her brow. He lowered his head.

"I know," he backed up. "I know you didn't deserve that. But look - I called in some favors to get

Albert. Actually, I sold the Icarus Project, to get him back. I cut major ties and lost eight million dollars, all for the sake of our freedom. I'm REALLY trying. I don't even know who enlisted me, on Wednesday. It was weirdly sudden."

He grit his teeth, then closed his eyes.

"I don't want any more of this, ever. Not after what I saw."

He lowered his head.

"It was Poland. It was large-scale terrorism. Chemical warfare threatened Central Europe. I saw what it did to people. A dozen factory workers - they, like... curdled, inside their bodies. It's something I don't want to see again.

"We tracked the chemical with satellites and aerosol binding agents. They needed me for that. The fire at the plant was intentional. I made them start it. It lifted most of the chemical into the air, where we contained it. Well... where I contained it."

"Yeah," she added, "I saw the fire on the news. Wait - what do you mean, YOU contained it?"

"They needed me. I'm sorry." He cringed from her. "The fire lifted the chemical. We tracked it. I tightened it in projected fields, and then I contained it. Containment drew a lot of power from the local grid."

"Poland? You were actually THERE?"

He went still.

"Did they fly you to Europe for this?"

"Not enough time," he said quietly.

Then she understood.

"Did you actually use that project, yourself? Icarus? Is that how you got there?"

He remained quiet. His brow sank.

"Clark, please answer me."

"Yes. I used the prototype. Three hours' flight time. I kept to about Mach 4, so I wouldn't scare anyone. Portuguese airspace got nitpicky, anyway."

She leaned forward tensely. "You flew there, with that suit-thing you made?"

He blew out breath. "It's just a test suit, Riley. Only big-wigs care about it. I just wanted to come home."

She tried to find the right words. She hugged him closer.

"You really are gonna create a new era. Your mind is…"

"FORGET IT," he snapped. "I just scare people away, alright? And I know this."

Her soothing touch stopped.

His voice softened. "I'm sorry about how I am, as a person. I know I'm intense. There are things I still can't fix. I know it hurts us."

Thoughts flashed in his mind.

"I wonder if somebody's planning something."

Riley blinked.

"Huh?"

Clark swallowed, then said, "I heard there were some legal issues with the bank and real estate. Big money. There have been businesses bought out and left abandoned, like that place where they held Albert. That was downtown! That's pretty valuable land. And now Jeff Anders is gunning for mayor? That's 'Mr Real-Estate,' himself.

"Colleen Dietrich is his PR, and she was eyeing this house funny, and then I'm suddenly called away for days at a time."

"They can't take your house, Clark."

"I know," he said sadly. "But it looks like 'all roads lead to Anders.' I think moving away might give him an opportunity."

Riley rolled her eyes. "Jeff? Naw, I don't think you need to worry about Jeff. You're ten times the man he is. He's ASKING people for votes, just so he can be boss of Ashvale. What do you do? You literally fly, Clark. I could make superhero jokes, right about now."

She poked him. He chuckled weakly.

"I am not Clark K-..."

There was a weary silence.

He spoke sadly, "I wanna call my mom, soon. Then I want a new life. I want a home with you."

She spread her fingers through his hair.

"What if work needs you? What about the greater good?"

It was a new, pressing question for her.

"Y'know, I can't get in the way of human lives," she added.

"No," he stated. "I want OUR lives. I'm not the only one in the world who can... who can..."

A few seconds of silence dragged by.

"What?" she blurted. "Engineer force technology? Ya. You're the only one."

"But my past work should mean something. They need to recognize it and just be content."

His head sank. His voice fell to a whisper.

"I just want to be with you."

She played with his hair idly.

"Yeah," she added. "I hope we can do that."

CHAPTER THIRTY-FIVE
A Return to Home

When Clark woke up, Riley was stroking his cheek. She'd been staring straight ahead, pensively, looking at his bookcase. His whole complicated life was collected right there, right in their bedroom. Those huge books symbolized something - a deeper, darker Clark that she didn't know. His life had another level.

She saw his eyelids open. She smiled down at him.

"Hi," she breathed to him.

He immediately asked: "Are we okay?"

She nodded a bit and played with his hair.

"Ya."

He really wanted to believe her.

"I gotta go to the bank," he said. "Will you come with me?"

She looked at him quizzically. "The bank?"

"Yeah," he answered, confidently. "One last form. It's about our retirement package and Albert's college options. I didn't get to this, a few days back, so I rescheduled. I figured you might want to be part of it, this time."

She shook her head. "Maybe you should have the satisfaction. You'll come BACK this time. I wanna feel that."

He sighed. "You're sure? I'll be right back, then - within the hour." He paused. "Are you okay to be here, for a bit?"

"Mmm-hmm."

"It's still Saturday, right? Albert's back from his museum trip, tomorrow. It's gonna get busier around here."

"Oh ya." She smiled a little.

He lifted up. He leaned over and held his cheek into hers.

He whispered close to her ear, "We're together. We'll have this evening for us, okay? I want things to be good with us. So don't do anything naughty... 'least, not until I get back."

She chuckled with mischief.

He wrapped his arms round her. He smelled her hair and sensed the warmth of her cheek. He kissed her one final time and pressed close. His lips met her ear and passed a message: "Mmm... 'Love you!"

She whined sweetly. Her brows pinched upward.

He collected himself and set out on his errand. She heard the front door close. She sighed.

She ambled out of bed and found her jeans and a loose blouse. She made herself a latte. She paced around the house for a while, then found herself in the backyard with Clark's garden. She settled on a bench there. She sat, drew her legs close to her, and stared vacantly. Here she was... at his place, alone. Clark was busy taking care of HIS money, with HIS bank. Somehow, she was supposed to fit somewhere. She didn't understand his household. She'd never even had a garden before, and Clark had tidy, well tended rows of tomatoes and greens. She hugged her legs and gazed ahead at nothing.

She finished her latte and wandered into her studio. She looked around her works-in-progress. She didn't like them. One was simply too dark; she'd worked on it for so long, it had turned murky. This other one? Nah, the form was weak. There was nothing there.

She crumpled them both and threw them to the trash. They had no future.

She pulled on her smock and patted her hands together. Maybe she could still accomplish something? She puffed her bangs away from her brow. She was just about to pick up the charcoal when there was a knock at the door. It wasn't Clark. It wasn't Colleen. It was some joker, banging away - a 'bro' knock.

'Shave-and-a-haircut... shampoo.'

She rolled her eyes.

"Who the hell is THAT? Agh... 'Know what? Forget it. I quit. I quit art."

She bundled her smock in her fist and tossed it over her chair. AGAIN, there was a familiar knocking.

"KNOCK-knocka-KNOCK-KNOCK... KNOCK KNOCK."

Riley stalked to the front hallway. She was unimpressed.

Jeez, she thought. 'Ever heard of a doorbell? Or are you a frickin' doorknob, yourself?

She looked in the monitor.

"...JEFF?"

Her mouth hung open. She was stunned. Jeff Anders? Really? She had to know why he was here. She swung open the door.

"Jeff Anders - SERIOUSLY? What the heck, man?" She half-smiled from the irony. They had an uncomfortable moment.

He kept his hand pressed inside his pocket. He had a .38 pistol hidden there under his belt. Did she hate him? Had she heard about the rape pills, back in school? He'd know in a second.

"Dude. 'Haven't seen YOU in a while."

She shrugged at him with raised palms. He used that: he quickly stepped forward and threaded his arms through hers. His spontaneous hug shocked her.

"RILES! Hey! Just the person I was hoping to see!"

She was still spinning. "Well, what is this? Yeah, I haven't seen you for..."

He stared at her with his strong grin. He'd aged, and lost some hair, and his arms were flabby, and his gut hung over his belt buckle. His black tie was a little loose, and his shirt was partly untucked to cover his belt. His thinning hair was still brown with bits of grey. His blue eyes looked murky.

"Yeah, I looked you up. I heard about this 'artist' thing you were into - but REALLY being an artist, not just kid stuff. I had to pay you a visit and wish you well on your... venture."

"Ahh. Maybe Clark talked about my art. Did he?"

Jeff spoke with practiced confidence, "Yeah, he's the man! But it was Colleen Dietrich who told me that you two were out here... 'cuz, y'know, we had to hire Colleen. It wasn't even about that equality hiring crap, either. My election actually needed a strong PR department."

He gave a funny sideways look to Riley. Riley smirked back. Her shoulders dropped. She tipped her head back and forth, and Jeff joined her.

"Yyyyeah," they both drawled together, "Colleen Dietrich." They almost laughed.

"The world's biggest busybody," Riley concluded.

"So, hey," Jeff straightened himself. "Is Clark in? I thought I might wanna... well, congratulate you two."

Jeff faked a little blush. "That's all."

Riley took an easier stance.

"No, not at the moment," she said. "He's out taking care of an errand. He'll be back soon. Maybe stop by in a bit?"

"Aww, yeah. Absolutely. Y'know, I haven't seen the guy since HIGH SCHOOL. I'd love it if I could say a quick hello... especially since you guys settled in so well." He looked around the house. He spoke gently, "You guys made it. It's awesome. I gotta say, I envy you a bit."

Jeff stepped into the doorframe.

"Actually, is there any way I could wait for Clark? C'mon, it'd be like a tiny... hah... like a three-person reunion. You, an' me, an'... well, three buds from Ashvale High. Right? We could have a drink, maybe."

"Well," Riley reached over to the door monitor and bleeped the keypad. She activated Athena to admit him, but also to record video.

Added security, Riley thought. Why is he even here? Maybe Clark can make sense of this.

"I dunno. Okay," she shrugged again, "I mean, he'll be back in a few."

She opened the door to Jeff. She reflected on how many years it had been.

"So what is it, Jeff? Fourteen, fifteen years? 'Cuz yeah, my life's looked up since then. And yeah, I'm working on my art. And you're gonna be mayor, I hear."

Riley walked ahead of him. As she walked down the hallway, Jeff's jaw went loose. He followed her from a polite distance. He looked her up and down, slowly, like wiping her with a greasy sponge. His eyes stopped on her behind. He stared at it. He remembered having this woman. He remembered her body.

His head pumped idly; this would be a cinch - just like a play in football. As easy as 'running interference,' but between Riley and Clark.

"Uh, yeah," he said. "Me an' the boys were talking. We were planning a get-together. A couple of us. You know - have a drink or two, chill out somewhere." He lifted his hand vaguely.

"Right," she smiled dryly. "Like reminisce? Have memories?"

He paused, then answered earnestly, "Maybe, yeah. But then we heard about you and CLARK, of all people..."

Riley's head tilted with exasperation. "Wha...? Clark's a good man, Jeff."

"Oh yeah." Jeff looked around, admiring the house. "I see that."

She hesitated, then walked into the kitchen with Jeff. She sat him down at the head of the dining table and found two cans of beer in the fridge. She sometimes stashed beer for herself, since Clark didn't drink.

"I'll listen, Jeff. It's been enough years, I'm genuinely curious about what you have to say." She nodded.

And if you're trying to scam Clark's house, she thought, I have Athena watching you.

Meanwhile, Clark arrived at the bank. He swung open the doors and smiled to himself.

"CLARKIE!" Colleen cheered.

Colleen Dietrich spotted him immediately. She worked there, but it was almost like she expected him. She was there like clockwork.

"How's everything? How's work?"

Clark was caught off-guard. "Uhh… work? All good. Yeah. Same old, same old."

She grinned at him like an evil lawn gnome - something weakly decorative, but full of malice. A lap dog with pointy, smiley teeth.

Clark played along with her politeness act.

"How's everything going for you guys? 'Everything going according to plan?" he asked.

"The-" she stuttered, "Sorry, what?" She looked panicked.

"You, the PR, and Jeff's election?" Clark prompted. "You know, the whole election campaign?"

"Oh, THAT…" she flapped her hand down and tossed her golden mane. "Oh, it's in the bag, Clarkie-boy. You know me. And Jeff? He has everything figured out."

"Yeah," he agreed. "Jeff has a keen mind for plans."

"He DOES, he does." Colleen turned her head with a blank expression. For a moment, it looked like she wanted to run away.

The bank manager emerged from his office.

"Mr Benjamin? Right on time." He and Clark shook hands. Clark waved a quick 'seeya' to Colleen.

She watched the bank manager usher him inside. They'd be busy for half an hour; maybe forty-five minutes. The manager was booked for more appointments immediately afterward.

Colleen tried to edge closer to eavesdrop on their conversation. The white noise filter stopped her. It wasn't high-tech muting like her noise-cancellation headphones. It was just a hushing, blanketing noise.

Clark was here; time to act. Colleen grabbed her miniature phone and started texting.

As Riley sat at the kitchen table with Jeff, his phone bleeped. He answered a text message.

"Oh... ya, see what I mean? I just got a text from one of the guys. He's at the bank. He just saw Clark go in for an appointment. An'... I'm just gonna write: 'Got in touch with Riley Henway - she's an artist now. Hoping she might come with us.' Aww, man, they'd love to see you. The old gang."

She looked back dubiously. Jeff's expression turned humble.

"Okay, wait." Jeff sat back. He put on his friendliest face. "You and Clark. You both know what I'm talking about. Do you two ever get nostalgic about the good ol' days?"

"What?" she shook her head, confused. "Do either of us miss being bullied in high school? Do we miss the cliques and social warfare? Nope. We live in the now." She gave a lop-sided smile. "All the 'old days' weren't the best, if I remember. And you and I didn't part on the best of terms, either."

He blushed red again. "Young and stupid - that was me. Now I've got the election, and everyone's so busy. That's why I won't take friends for granted. Did Clark tell you about the gym? about our antics?"

She was quiet, then shook her head.

Perfect, he thought.

"Ya," he smiled back at her, "Clark and I have some history. Some old stories. And see, I've missed that guy. 'Tried to catch up with him a few times, over the years, just to see what he was up to. He's always been so busy. Busy-busy, right?"

He looked down at his beer humbly. He folded his hands.

"C'mon," he raised his brow, "You don't miss it? school? all the ridiculous stuff we got away with? Sorry to bring it up, but... even us? Having your companionship, back then, is something I'm grateful for. I'm grateful now, as an adult."

She didn't budge. He took another drink of his beer.

"I really have to thank you, Riley, for being this forgiving. You're very understanding. I wanted to visit you and Clark, just to say 'hi,' but also to congratulate you. You found each other, and it's like some kinda fairy-tale. A real fairy-tale ending."

"We did," she agreed. "So, what's your plan with the guys, anyway? What, you basically wanted to have a pub crawl, or something? Since high school, nobody really kept in touch. I thought people were happy to get away from Ashvale."

"Oh, come ON," Jeff flopped backward in his chair. His beer can rapped against the wooden table. A bit of froth slopped on the table's surface.

"The golden days of youth? I've had time to think about it. I'm really glad you two made it, but I think high school was my golden era, period. To me, that was the best part of my life. And Mr Gray, and Timmy, and even Colleen… and you, of course! You're part of that. I think you know what I mean."

She turned her head. "The past. And that's about it."

"For a lot of us, that's all life IS, Riles. All you've got is what you survived through, and the people you were with. The rest is meaningless scrambling and juggling, just trying to FIND that again… trying to find MEANING. We don't have anything, except where we're from."

Riley was silent.

"Yeah," he continued. "It's like childhood memories, only it's your young life. You remember high school? You remember figuring things out, as a teenager?"

"I remember Mr Gray being a jerk. I remember Colleen's friends bullying me. I remember struggling."

Jeff's eyes were uncommonly kind.

"But that was you, at your most real. That's the last time you were YOU. Your friends knew you. And they were your real friends. They accepted you for who you were. And they loved you."

Yeah, he thought. That usually works.

"Back then," Jeff shook his head and opened his eyes wide, "we actually had freedom. Believe it or not, but we teenagers didn't have mortgages or bank loans or stressful jobs. We were free to be ourselves, and we weren't enslaved by money or bent out of shape by obligations. Being a teenager was being real. That's why I wanna help people, as mayor. To ALLOW them that freedom. To express. So they can be their real selves."

She stood from the table.

"Jeff, I have my life, now. My son. My partner. My art. I graduated from high school, and I moved on. And that was a long time ago. Things have grown, since then... and that's the real me. I haven't just changed. I am the change, and it's by choice."

She stepped over to the work island. The openness of the kitchen gave him space to leave. Jeff eyed her backside again.

Soon, he thought.

Riley shrugged, "I know it looks like a step away, but it's my step forward. This is where I'm going. I can't run with you wolves, now. I'm no sheep, but I can't be one of your pack. I can't go running crazy under the full moon, at night. No beer-soaked parties. I've got a kid. And I have Clark."

He looked at her flatly. "Riley? You're the same person. You have the same family. You have a GOOD family: it's us."

"...What."

Riley was most assuredly not smiling.

"Listen," he continued, "it's like what they said about a village, raising a kid: it takes everyone. 'It takes a whole village to raise a child.' We were the village. You were a kid, like us kids, and we all survived together. We were kids, but we were more than that. We were, like… kin."

Jeff drained his beer. He walked up to stand beside her.

"It's like family," he said softly, "but I mean 'real family.' The ones who know who you really are. Yeah, I know you struggled. I know that, and your real friends know that. Ashvale knew you way back, and it hasn't forgotten."

"Uhh - everyone has their youth, Jeff. But most of us grow up."

"Well," he spun his hand in the air, "Y'know, the 'golden days' were the ONLY good days. You remember them, like nostalgia, because this is TRUE. It's as simple as that."

She could only look at him.

"A small town, a few kids who stick it out; you never have friends like you did when you were young. It's like… no-one ever loved you, that way, since. 'Sucks to say that, but it's true. We spend a lot of years trying to fool ourselves afterward. We try to pretend we're happy. Some 'big career' is pretending you're happy. And some 'big house' is pretending, too, like hiding in a really big closet."

"Nah," she stopped him. "You can't live, if you're always staying in the same place. You need to keep going. Walk your path. You can't go backwards."

He smirked at her. "To what, Riles? Walk WHERE? to something you don't know? to people you don't know, or can't trust? You know who you are." He made his point by quietly thumping his fist onto the counter.

He looked at her steadily. A smile brewed under his surface. She watched him.

"You can't escape who you are, Riley. And why would you want to? Don't let Clark hear this, but... I know how beautiful you are. I knew you then, and you're the same person now, and you're one of us. We're always gonna be your people. You can't forget that. We remember, and we're just gonna hang out, together, because we know the truth. It's family. Real family."

He kept smiling at her. He quickly glanced at her lips. She noticed. She didn't move.

"Hey, I dunno. I remember you struggling back then, but at least things were real. And you?" He chuckled frankly. "You were the LAST person to be a poser. That's one thing I know about you for sure: you are the genuine article."

Her brow softened. She looked at him again... and he was someone she knew. He talked about dirt, but he meant solid ground. Ashvale was where she came from. High school sucked, but it was her life... and he was there. This was still Jeff, even if he'd aged. He was the personality - the character - that she'd dated as a girl. Despite everything, he and his friends welcomed her back. She was welcomed, even after all these years.

Meanwhile, the bank manager concluded business with Clark. Through the fogged glass, Colleen could see them rising up from their chairs. She hurried back behind the counters, grabbed her phone, and started tapping.

Clark smoothed out his clothes. "SO - I might not see you again in the near future."

The bank manager shook his head humbly.

"Visit anytime you like, Mr Benjamin. She must be very, very special to you. I've never seen such commitment to family and future generations. Speaking man-to-man? My hat's off to you, sir."

The bank seemed smaller as Clark walked out. It was cute like a dollhouse. It seemed quaint and familiar. Even Colleen was out of sight.

He swung open the outside door and stepped into the autumn sunshine. The air was pure and cool, like a splash of fresh water.

He stood tall. The entire town was smaller, now, but it was good. He'd just built a foundation. He'd created a future for his family.

My family, he thought. For the first time, I can say that.

He had a few happy gusts of laughter. Then he stopped, closed his eyes, and grinned to himself. A few tears squeezed out. He clutched his hand to his heart.

"I gotta celebrate with someone."

There was no question who that would be.

He remembered their restaurant, *Rosa della Città*, and that Sauternes she liked. He'd never tasted it, but she seemed to like it a lot. Clark stopped at a liquor store and asked for the best 'sweet' white wine they had. The woman at the cash was bewildered. No-one at the store recognized him. He left with a tall bottle under his arm.

"Ahh," he thought aloud. "Roses. Definitely. Everything today is Riley and me, so it's roses." He drove to a florist, looked around, wasn't entirely satisfied, then drove to another. He insisted on golden-ink script.

One dozen long-stemmed roses, and a tiny perfumed card:

*"Just So You Know - YOU *ARE* LOVE."*

Yeah, he grinned to himself. Today's our first day, and my best day ever. From now on, there are only bright tomorrows. I love you SO MUCH, my sweet, sweet Riley.

Clark started for home. He set the wine and roses in the passenger seat beside him. They were safe.

Riley looked up to Jeff's eyes. He shrugged at her.

"It's just... truth's truth. I know where I belong, right? I'm even hoping to be mayor! I'm devoted to my people, and I love them. And, like, I know who you are. I know what you've been through, because I've been through it too. You and me? We're kinda the same, Riley, because we both... belong."

He looked to the side, as if nonchalant.

Her brown eyes were caught in hesitation. She sensed something that she needed. She needed more of it. She caught a glimpse of something that really mattered; something that was absent from her life. She stared straight ahead.

Jeff let her eyes sink. He let the doubt do its work, to weaken her. He'd seduced her this way before. He let her eyes wander. He let them lose their certainty.

Then he set his hand on hers for a moment. That could be a friendly gesture, or it could be that one spark they needed.

She didn't move away.

In his mind, he growled with satisfaction. He was pulling her in. It always worked after this point.

"You know, Riles, we all know who we are. We don't need 'out,' if we know who we are. Sometimes we find ourselves in some high-and-mighty palace, like this, but we're Ashvale... born and bred. Dyed in the wool. It's like your human nature; you can't fight it. If you're real about it, though? You can embrace it."

He watched her chest rise and fall. He'd finally gotten through.

Ahh, he smiled. There she is. Got her.

"It's just honesty," he whispered. "It's a deeper loyalty. Be true to yourself. You deserve it."

She closed her eyes for a second, then opened them again. She couldn't move. He was right.

Jeff leaned forward and kissed her lips.

She exhaled suddenly, like releasing a burden. She inhaled again, and it became frightened panting. She couldn't tell if she was afraid of the kiss, or afraid of an inner truth. Truth was unavoidable.

He pushed harder. She didn't know what was happening until it was happening. She knew how Jeff moved, and that was both the best part and the worst. She thought of Clark… but Jeff's hands were steady and familiar, and they took away her fear. She knew them well. They were a comfort. She wasn't afraid of anything, anymore.

Clark turned through the last intersection and had a clear road ahead. He took a new, deep breath.

Yes, sweet Riley - I'm finally coming home to you. For real. This will be us. All that money? It works for us, now. We can do what we want, with no worries. We can really be a family.

So much in Riley swelled. Ashvale was an irritated blister, and it rose up inside her until it couldn't be contained. Something popped.

As he kissed, Jeff steered her past the kitchen. He found the laundry room, then kissed her again, and kept guiding her with his kiss until he spotted the bedroom.

Pathetic, he thought to himself. You're a pathetic little girl. You could never marry an Anders. You and Clark? BOTH pathetic.

Riley's eyes hazed over. She thought she smelled cheap cigarettes, beer, leather jackets, cold pub food, broken plaster walls, and her old couch... everything she knew from her rotten past. She remembered trying to get away from her dad, or get away from Jonno's leering, or just get through school. It was what she knew. Running.

Running was where she belonged. And THIS, with Jeff, was definitely running. Maybe she ran with the wolves because it was in her blood. Maybe she was meant to.

Jeff laid her onto the bed. He stood over her - kind of stupid, kind of unattractive now, but someone she knew. She knew Jeff, and his idiot friends, and all their stupid jokes, and she knew it by heart. She stared up to his blue eyes. He was the same person SHE was. The two of them were together in life: not caring, not trying, but just scratching by in the crappy town of Ashvale Plains.

He unhooked her jeans and pulled.

Clark cruised down that final stretch. This was like the end of a nightmare, and he could finally rest. He and Riley had a golden life to live - the two of them, with Albert.

He slowed his car, like he was deep in thought.

Yeah. Albert. I love that little monkey. He's the perfect son, as long as I can be a good provider. I'll offer home-schooling, or just tutor him if he needs it. We can go to movies, or go hiking, or we'll do sports together, or chess, or go to... to...? It doesn't matter where we go! It's not the journey, or the destination - it's the company! And I love him!

My God, Clark thought. I can be a good dad...! I'll always be there for him. Ohh, I'm gonna make Riley so proud of me!

He parked his car in the driveway. He opened his door and quickly swung out. He snorted, because he almost forgot the wine and roses. He grabbed them in his hands and tapped the door shut with his foot. The door didn't close all the way. He leaned into it, so it'd latch. The car door didn't thump; it closed quietly. He walked eagerly up his stone path.

"Ohh, will I ever kiss her...!" he mused. "Tonight, we celebrate. Tomorrow, we begin our future. I'll prove myself. I'll be a good father, and a good partner, and a good man, and..."

He used Athena's keyless entry.

Inside, he heard a soft murmur.

Hunnh, he thought, smiling a little. She couldn't wait for me?

He walked into the kitchen. That was when he heard two voices, and they were coming from the bedroom.

He set the wine and roses on the kitchen table and noticed the pair of beer cans.

More murmuring. Her voice - her moans - not really excited, but in the mood. And... someone else?

He walked to the open doorframe of his bedroom, and he looked inside.

Something in his chest broke apart and fell.

CHAPTER THIRTY-SIX
THE FAMILY TABLE

Clark stared. Years and years ago, he'd heard that Riley got married. Then he couldn't love and couldn't smile. He couldn't live. For years, he gave up hope. His soul had nothing to hang on to. It was Riley's love that finally brought him back to life. She found his soul, and she helped it live again.

This time, Clark didn't just die. Something else took his place.

He watched a man in his bedroom. The man shuffled in his pants, bent himself downward, and shoved into Riley. She lay back with her pale thighs spread like wings and her naked butt open to the air. She lay back on Clark's bed, moaning, as this man entered her.

Her eyes flashed bright when they met Clark. They looked up at him - the tall figure standing in the doorway. Her eyes turned moon-white with terror.

Jeff turned, covered himself with his hand, and said one word:

"Whoa…"

That was when Clark changed. Something else stood there - something born of dread and hate. Riley felt a frigid stab inside her chest; she didn't see the man she loved. Clark was gone.

The tall figure spoke.

"NO, NO…" he waved at them in false encouragement. He looked blankly in her direction.

"NO, GO AHEAD, JEFF… GO AHEAD AND… FINISH… SCREWING MY LOVER."

Riley's breath seized. Either it was her blood drumming in her ears, or the air itself… something was a roaring silence.

Clark's eyes only held ground; they wouldn't look at her.

Jeff's pants hung loose around his waist. His tiny .38 pistol was there, on the inside of his belt. He'd planned ahead for this.

"YEAH, GO AHEAD, JEFF…" The voice wasn't calm. It was rising lava. "BUT, UH… WHENEVER YOU'RE… 'DONE'… SHE AND I NEED TO HAVE A LITTLE CHAT."

The air stank with rage. Riley's eyes widened to pure, glassy horror. Tears made a sheen over them as she stared at Clark. But that wasn't Clark anymore. She'd killed him. This man was ice, and he clearly hated her.

Still worse, Jeff waited a moment and then half-shrugged. He turned back to her and decided to do as Clark suggested. He tried to continue mating with Riley, right there on the bed.

Something in her chest sank down to her guts. She knew her true worth to Jeff and to all of Ashvale. She wasn't even worth dignity; she was nothing but a plaything. She was nothing but a bedroom toy. She really was nothing.

Clark - or what used to be Clark - stared in her direction. It looked like he was staring at nothing.

"Nn-... NO," she whimpered and kicked. She shoved Jeff away with her feet and legs. Jeff tried to recover his balance. He pulled up his pants and kept his hand near his pistol.

It was a deathly quiet.

"NO?" said the tall man, still waiting in the doorframe. "THEN GET OUT."

He stepped aside to make room in the doorway. He didn't take a wrestler's stance. He stood aside like a soldier in defeat: tall, strong, and solemn.

"OUT." His voice was dark like a smoking barrel. "JUST... OUT. BOTH OF YOU."

Jeff clipped his belt together. He remembered this man, and remembered the score that was unsettled. He listened, but couldn't hear Clark breathing.

He was going to make that permanent.

"Well," Jeff smirked, looking back and forth between them, "She doesn't care much about you either... does she, Clarkie-boy?"

Clark's stare was titanium. It drilled easily through Jeff's skull. Jeff twitched his chin upward in defiance. Clark's knuckles ticked. His fists hardened.

This is it, Jeff thought.

"Yeah," he grinned at Clark. "So whaddya gonna do now, loser? Did you lose your woman, too? Did you actually lose this... this low-life whore?"

Clark was motionless. He watched Jeff's upper spine. He mapped out major nerve bundles. He was deciding the most painful way to cripple Jeff for life.

Jeff hung his thumbs from his belt line. "Well, I mean, she's good for one thing, if nothin' else." He popped up his eyebrows and tugged his belt suggestively.

His fingers were ready beside his pistol. He looked to Clark, then to Riley, then to Clark again. He knew the biggest threat - it had always been Clark. So it was Clark first, and then Riley. Yeah... Riley could be later... 'after.'

Jeff smiled. Today, he concluded business. This was REAL business. Winner-take-all. It didn't matter if Clark and Riley had kids. Orphans were easy to sweep under the rug.

Jeff turned to the side and pulled his pistol. He grinned with bared teeth like a pirate skull. He jammed his gun right up to Clark's face and there was a hard, meaty clap. Clark's hand denied it. His grip crushed Jeff's arm.

Riley saw the gun and scrambled backward. She panted through her open lips.

Clark guided Jeff's hand. The little gun slowly lifted until it was pointing straight into Clark's teeth. A cruel smile tightened there. Something demonic grinned back at Jeff. It welcomed this deadly dance.

Jeff's arm was caught - snared. Tendons couldn't move; Jeff couldn't use any of his fingers. He couldn't muster the strength to pull that tiny trigger.

"YOU GOTTA BE JOKING," the tall man growled, with the pistol hovering an inch from his mouth. He twisted his grip and Jeff's arm fell slack.

Jeff panicked. "Why can't I...? What'd you do to my ARM?"

Clark retrieved the gun gently, like tending to a child. Jeff's arm sagged at the elbow. A neural block had put his arm to sleep. Soon, Clark's hand took an easy, familiar hold on the pistol.

"No," came a tiny squeak. Riley watched everything happening. "No, no, no..."

Jeff flinched away, jerking against his own arm. He couldn't get free. It was like his arm was part of a cement wall, and he couldn't yank it out.

Clark slowly raised the gun higher, above anyone's reach. He tipped it down at Jeff like a stinger. The little barrel was a dark, round "O" shape, like a mouth shocked to silence. His thumb smoothly clicked back the hammer. The cylinder turned, and a shining-new bullet aligned in the chamber.

"CLARK...?" Riley squeaked.

Jeff's eyes blazed wide open. He yanked himself violently. He wished he could yank out his own shoulder, and maybe escape, and maybe survive. He flapped like a loose flag on a steel pole. Clark turned his arm like a simple lever, then plowed him into the side of the doorframe. The stiff frame knocked with his bones. All Jeff could do was whimper.

Riley gibbered. "CLARK? Clar-... Clar-...!" She watched the gun in his hand.

"MA'AM?" the tall figure spoke to her soothingly. "STAY WHERE YOU ARE, MA'AM."

The pistol settled on the back of Jeff's head.

"CLARK!" she cried. "Honey? This isn't... this isn't like..."

"MA'AM?" he purred quietly.

"Clark?" she sobbed weakly. "Wh-... Who are you, right now?"

He didn't look at her.

"MA'AM... ELVIS HAS LEFT THE BUILDING."

She noticed his squared shoulders and perfect posture. He looked like he should be wearing a pressed suit.

He stood over Jeff, there, for a few final words.

"REMEMBER THIS DAY, JEFF.

"TODAY IS THE DAY YOU DIED.

"YOU REMEMBER THIS... FOR THE REST OF YOUR WORTHLESS, PATHETIC LIFE."

His thumb slid the hammer back into place. He flicked open the cylinder and let tiny bullets tap onto the floor: tap tap, tap tap. Something squeaked and pinged, and the cylinder itself clattered down by their feet. Clark reached back and flung the remains of the pistol down the hallway. It slid long across the tile.

He spotted a light on the wall console. Athena had been set to monitor the house; she'd captured everything.

"SURVEILLANCE," he seethed. "CAPTURED VIDEO OF HOME INVASION AND RAPE. I'M SURE YOUR RIVALS WILL LOVE THIS FOOTAGE, 'MR MAYOR.' TODAY, YOUR CAREER DIES FOR REAL."

One hand held Jeff's shoulder, and the other gripped the back of his skull.

"BUT YOU'RE OUT OF WARNINGS… RAPIST."

Jeff discovered one last card to play.

He smiled back at Clark, "Oh, but your little pet hooker didn't resist. You saw her. She lay wide open. You heard her, too. Her moaning. 'Oh… Oh, JEFF…' She tells the REAL story, here."

He grinned wide, "And it's a happy story."

He watched as Clark wilted. He broke free, then fell against the doorframe. He scooted across the hallway like a rodent, trying to keep out of reach. He made for the front door.

On his way out, Jeff glanced around for valuables - briefcase? Laptop computer? No matter. He'd accomplished what he'd set out to do. Riley and Clark were split, and Clark was an emotional mess. He hurried out the front door.

In the bedroom, an exhausted man leaned against the doorframe.

"YOU," he said. "HERE..."

He dug in his pocket. His breathing was growing deeper and stronger, like a storm brewing. She cinched her clothes back on.

"HERE," he said quietly, fishing in his wallet. "HERE'S... SIX-HUNDRED DOLLARS. TAKE IT. GO AND... GO STAY AT A MOTEL. OR WHEREVER."

"Clark," she squeaked. "I, uh-"

His voice didn't rise. It was lethally calm.

"JUST FINISH IT, THIS TIME. WALK AWAY."

He stood motionless. She slipped past him as quietly as a ghost.

Riley managed to grab her purse. She walked through the front hall, trying to listen for Clark. He was still behind her, somewhere. Her head felt light and floaty as she walked out the front door. She stopped on the front step and turned back. The door slowly swung shut. She wanted to put her hand on it. She wanted to touch the house. She wanted to apologize to it.

Jeff stood a few paces down the driveway. He stood back and watched her. Ten seconds later, he asked, "So, uhh... Well, d'you wanna come to my place?"

She closed her eyes. Her teeth sharpened against themselves. She could feel her mouth grinding a murderous hatred.

Jeff added, "You could, like... stay over, tonight. If you really want."

Riley tilted her head. She turned around to face him. Her expression was the gate of hell.

"Jeff?" she gritted her teeth. "You get off this property, Jeff."

He took a step backward.

"If you don't leave RIGHT NOW, I will legitimately murder you. You stupid, stupid boy... If you aren't gone within thirty seconds? That MAN in there..."

She pointed into the house.

Sobs and growls fought in her voice. "I know that man. I know what he does to people. And I would murder you, Jeff... but he will do things that are a million times worse."

Jeff read her eyes - she was real. She'd kill him. He could run, but she still knew too much. Plus, there was the surveillance footage. Could he send hitmen to silence her? He'd have to send them quickly, unless he did everything himself.

"Riley, wait. I really need to talk with you. Things are so screwed up. There's these guys who really want Clark's work, okay? It doesn't even have anything to do with you, or me... or even Clark, actually. So NONE of this has to happen. I'll explain it to Clark, even. I just need to talk with you someplace quiet. Just hear me out; it'll only take five minutes. Just some private place, where I can explain everything..."

"Did you need a gun for that?"

She wouldn't blink. He couldn't answer.

"Jeff?" She fished in her purse. A thick pencil and a big gummy eraser fell out. She flung away a small roll of tape. She found a pair of steel scissors.

"Jeff? ONE..."

She opened the scissors, then bent them a full 180 degrees. She looped her fingers in the handles and held the scissors like a dagger. The blades were jammed back-to-back, with both cutting edges out. They trembled in her fist.

"TWO..."

Jeff raised his hands, watching her like a wild animal. She was definitely real about this.

She squinted, then looked at him sideways.

"TWO-AND-A-HALF."

He stepped back, then stumbled when he bumped into the hood of Clark's car. He skipped around the side and began running. He ran till he was out of sight.

Riley was left on the doorstep. The autumn air was clear and chilly. She dropped the scissors in her purse and wobbled back to face the house. She listened; she didn't know what else she could do. Her guts felt hollow.

Her hand raised to the doorframe, like trying to touch it with sympathy. She couldn't hear Clark at first. Then, she heard a pained wheezing. Every breath was a burden to him.

She listened, trying to know where he was. He was in... she could tell by the echoes, that he was in the kitchen...? Why the kitchen? He was wheezing, like when a runner pushes too hard and tastes blood.

Riley's hand went to her shirt, tugging at its front. She pulled it closer around her.

Clark's wheezing intensified. It was a waking giant. His vocal cords ripped like the teeth of a saw. His gasps were a hideous, gulping "EEEEH" sound, followed by a deflated "h-hough."

"Eeeh… h-hough… Eeeh… h-houghhh…"

Then Riley heard a wooden thump.

He lifted his kitchen table, and his low grunt roared up to an anguished, broken howl. He screamed raw, spun his whole body, and hammer-tossed the table through the tall windows of the kitchen. It flew from the house in a noisy burst of glass. Broken shards bashed down onto the tile floor; Clark reeled, wobbled, and then fell with them.

There could be no family table in Clark's life.

Riley's fist gripped white on her shirt. Her arm clutched it close. She would've given anything to help him, or soothe him, or kneel by him, or speak to him, or whisper anything, or comfort him in any way, but she was the worst person in the world to even try.

Of all the people in Clark's world, she had the ability to hurt him the most. That was exactly what she did, and she knew it.

Clark lay in the fetal position with his arms and legs shaking. A broken bottle of white wine now spilled across the floor, silently bleeding itself to death. Scattered around him were a dozen long-stemmed roses. They were strewn wide as worthless gestures of love. They all lay together on the floor amidst broken shards of glass.

He could barely feel the chill air rushing in. Glass from the window had nicked him in a few places, and drops of blood lay with him on the kitchen tile.

He had no idea where to turn; he'd focus on work again, but he'd given it up for her. His house? He couldn't stay there; he'd wanted it to be for the three of them, like a family home. His past ties? His commitments? No. He'd broken away, hoping for a shared future with her. His losses, or his battles…? No - he'd fought everything for her. He'd fought his demons for her.

All his years of praying to be with her… to find her, to be true to her, and to love her… it was his heart's devotion over a long and lonely lifetime.

All of his love… all of it for her…

…all for nothing.

She showed him it was nothing. She made it nothing, right there in front of him. She'd opened their bedroom to another man. It was a man they both knew, and a man who did not care about her. She'd opened herself and her intimate love; she showed Clark that a sniveling weasel deserved as much closeness as he ever did.

Clark understood, now, that he was a stranger. To her, he was a stranger. At most, he was equal to that other man - the one who didn't belong in his bedroom. So he, himself, was a stranger.

Riley took the first painful step away from the

house. That was when reality hit her: this stone pathway was smooth, and easy to walk, but it led her away from Clark's home. She was leaving, now, and she was turning a corner in her life. She had to live this new life. No home. No job. No support for herself or for Albert.

The noon sun shone brightly, during this wounded calm. She had no idea what sort of day could follow a morning like this.

I've killed it, she thought. My heart's secret... my life with my dear, dear Clark.

She walked along the smooth stones. They looked back at her blankly, like slates that were wiped clean. No words, no lines, no expression. Just empty. Her life would be hard again; she knew this. But what had she done to his?

Could she just run in, now, and throw herself at his feet? Could she just cry there in front of him, and maybe he'd hear something in her that he'd understand? Would he ever understand? Would he ever want to?

Would he even look at her, ever again?

CHAPTER THIRTY-SEVEN
Knock on Driftwood

Soon, Riley panicked. She had no place to go, and only so much money, and not many friends.

"Umm… Granny Faye?" She held the phone to her ear. She tried her best to be brave. "Gran, could I visit for a bit? Some things went upside down. I need a place for myself and for Albert, maybe for a few days. Would that be alright?"

Her feet drew close together. She pinched her toes up like praying.

"No, things aren't okay… no… yeah. No, not with Clark… that's the problem. NO, he wasn't doing anything stupid. I really messed up… yeah, we can talk about it. Can we? Yeah? I'll be there in an…"

Her throat tightened.

"I guess an hour or so… yeah. I'll take a cab."

She wouldn't be going to Clark's tonight. She

couldn't go back to her old apartment, since she'd moved out. She had nowhere to go and she needed a place to stay. Later, she needed a place for her son.

"Gran? I need to pick up Albert tomorrow from his museum trip. But I'll find him some movies… something to keep him busy. I definitely need to talk to you. And, uhh… I really, REALLY need a shower right now."

Granny Faye responded with silence.

When her cab arrived at Gran's place, she didn't say much. She paid for the thirty-dollar cab ride, and that was all she could do. Riley's eyes were blank with shock. She quickly excused herself to the bathroom and showered for fifty minutes. Later, Granny fed her some reheated casserole and sat with her. They spoke very little.

One of the cats, Vincent, was restless. He watched her with wide eyes. Later that evening, Riley showered again before going to bed. Vincent slept beside her room until the morning.

The next day, Riley got another cab to pick up Albert. That cost another thirty dollars. Riley had five-hundred-and-thirty-four dollars left, and some of that would have to be food. Then, she'd probably need some new clothes for Albert. She only had eighteen dollars of her own, in her purse. Her credit card was maxed out.

"When's Clark coming?" Albert asked. She couldn't answer.

At Granny Faye's, Riley and her grandmother

wore sad smiles to protect Albert. As soon as he was safe there, busy watching an old movie, Gran sat with Riley at the kitchen table and held her hand. The three cats lounged on bookshelves and on the windowsill.

Granny spoke softly, "In your own time, Love."

"I really screwed up," Riley began. She looked down to the floor with wide eyes. In a few moments, she was stifling sobs. Gran listened to her patiently. "I... this guy came to our... Jeff. He came to Clark's house, and..."

Gran's face twisted in fear.

"...and he was talking about Ashvale, and the old gang, and the friends I used to have."

Gran was sour. "A lot of them were ruffians, me dear. You know that by now, right?"

Riley looked at her with pained desperation. Gran went quiet.

"He just talked about stuff... all the stuff that I knew, and treasured, even though it was trash. Stuff like ripped jeans that were your good clothes, and sneaking cigarettes in school like they were valentines. Getting out of trouble by lying, and then getting drunk to celebrate. All that crap that I forgot about. Everything I left behind me; he made it feel so simple."

"Mmm. Lulled you, did he?" Gran watched with careful eyes. "Gave you a sense of security? Where is he now?"

"He's gone. He'd better be. I threatened him,

because of what he… what Clark saw us…"

Gran closed her eyes sadly.

Riley summed up: "Because of what I did to Clark."

Her face went red. She sat silently at the table, trembling. In the background, they heard Albert's movie. Riley gasped and held her tears in.

Gran asked gently, "When things settle, after a while, can I help you talk to Clark?"

Riley shook her head doubtfully.

"Just… stupid JEFF, and on Clark's BED, for God's sake! And all I could think of was where I really belonged. I was safe in my past, where I mattered, and that's all I cared about!"

Granny Faye lowered her head. She struggled, like trying to swallow something before it choked her.

Riley blubbered a few syllables. Tears leaked down her face. All Gran could do was hold her hand; she knew this was one of those cornerstones in life where things happen for better or worse. This was a cornerstone, like a turn in the road.

Vincent was a well fed tabby cat. He had a plump, wise face like the Buddha. He sauntered over and sat at Riley's feet. He looked up and yapped at her. It was a single utterance, like "quack." Riley sniffled, then hefted him up onto her lap. He was so thrilled at the attention, he put his tail on display.

"Mmf," Riley said, getting a face-full of tail feathers. "Yeah. Great. Thanks, Angus." She scratched his back and neck.

Granny said, aside, "Ehh - that's Vincent, dear. He's looking out for you. I know he is. See, Vincent has so many stories to tell... but he keeps them, and he just listens. Cats are REAL therapists. They listen. They let you find the answer in your own words, and in your own time. And they wait, and they're warm, and they're usually purring.

"BELIEVE that they understand. Their hearts certainly do. It helps to know this."

Vincent nudged Riley's arm. If she petted him, she'd feel probably feel better.

"They harbor so many secrets, me dear. And look at him - still smiling."

Riley looked up.

"Gran? Clark WAS my secret." She went quiet for a moment. "I got through school, and I loved him. I got married, and I still loved him. I had Albert... and I still loved Clark. He was my REAL. He was my secret, underneath. You know - the dream that keeps you going? the soul?"

Gran offered a respectful silence.

"Clark was my Meant-To-Be, but he never happened. And then he..." Riley sniffed. "He actually, miraculously happened, Gran, and somehow I threw him away. My DREAM. He's gone, now. I ruined everything. And Clark? Yeah, I definitely ruined Clark, himself. The man broke, right in front of me."

Granny Faye lowered her head. This one would be tough.

Vincent looked up at Riley, turned, and settled

into her lap. He was warm, and his purr engine was idling.

The women were silent. The arrival of a new voice dropped them into an even deeper pit.

"Are you guys okay out here? Mom? What's going on? What's wrong? Mom?"

Gran called him over. His voice turned quiet.

"Is something wrong with Clark? Why won't you tell me?"

"Albert, son..." Gran hugged him.

"I'm your grand... wait. I'm your GREAT-grandson."

"Well, Mr McSmartie-Pants... things went unspoken with your mum, and now things are spilling over. Clark and your mum have some big talks ahead of them. We need to patch things - all of us. It's family, me dear."

"What aren't we talking about? Did I do something? Am I in trouble?"

"No, Honey." Riley shook her head. "No, there are just things that are hard to talk about, and now they need to be talked about."

"Oh. You mean, not trouble? So not lies... but just grown-up stuff. The hard-to-understand stuff. Right?"

Riley paused. "Umm... sometimes that's lies," she admitted. "Sometimes things that I don't even know. Sometimes it's secrets we keep, even from ourselves. You understand. You probably know about secrets."

"Well, yeah." Albert stared at the floor.

Gran turned to him. Muriel flicked her tail; she was sitting on a bookshelf across the room. She looked intently at Albert.

"Albert." Riley tipped her head at him. "Are you okay, little monster?"

"Ya." He pursed his lips.

"Are you sure?" Gran asked. "How was your museum trip? Was it okay?"

"It was great - yeah, everything was good." He nodded.

"ALBERT." Riley leaned forward a little. "Is there something here - anything - that you're not telling me?"

He didn't answer. He couldn't. He didn't want to lie. His eyes scanned aimlessly while he thought.

"I don't wanna lie. Not for anybody."

Gran leaned on the table to brace herself. Riley stared.

Albert backed up a little. "I like Clark. I don't want anything bad to happen, so I want you to fix things."

Riley didn't show her surprise. "What do you mean, Honey? You can tell me anything. I'm your mum - I'm always on your side. What is this about Clark?"

Granny Faye's eyes lit. Red lights flashed in her mind.

"ALBERT, me son… would Clark ever hurt you?"

There was quiet in the room.

Albert shook his head wide and answered loudly: "No way. Clark's like one of my best friends, just only he's a big person. An adult. He's like Larsen, but wise and stuff."

Riley turned to Granny Faye. "Gran, you'd have to meet him. Clark's on the other side of that scale. He'd give his life to protect Albert. And those old-school values? honor and chivalry? Clark's the grandmaster."

"YA," Albert nodded rapidly with big eyes. "Ya, Clark's CRAZY, but like the good way. The 'man' way, like strong and honesty. You can't get us guys in trouble!" He tucked his chin and stared angrily at the floor. "I'm not one of the bad guys, and Clark is definitely one of the good guys. So nobody's going to jail, or anything. You have to promise!"

After about five minutes (or barely one-and-a-half), Albert unravelled. He told everything he knew, but the whole story was this:

It was a movie night, and it happened recently. Riley needed a break, so Clark took Albert out for the evening. He promised he'd take Albert to 'some guy flick,' and that they'd have some quality male bonding. Except, without the beer.

Riley spent the afternoon working on one of her sketches. She wasn't sure about it, at first, but then it started to breathe. Then, after a few hours, she threw it out entirely. She wondered why she'd taken up art again.

She ordered some Szechuan Chinese food. She

meant to have a light dinner, but she ended up with a sprawling heap on the coffee table. Some hospital show was on TV. The music kept ending with a dramatic clang, and then characters gave each other the hairy eyeball. Riley fell asleep with smoky flavors swirling in her head.

Meanwhile, Albert and Clark were in the theatre, watching the end of *Rad Rangers 3: The Pact of the Kroom*. Clark crunched down in his seat. Albert sat on the edge of his.

Albert had always been a huge fan of Rad Rangers. He wanted to wear his Rad Rangers onesie, but his mother said it wouldn't be warm enough. Clark suggested he wear it secretly, under his 'normal' clothes. Riley agreed, as long as no-one else knew… because he couldn't run around in his underwear. This was acceptable to Albert.

On the big screen, Doctor Morgendorff stood with his silver boots wide. His legs made a broad V-stance, and he crossed his arms arrogantly. His glassy neuro-helmet made a lightbulb of his head; it even showed his big, insectoid brain clicking.

The volcano behind Doctor Morgendorff boiled out acidic green smoke. He laughed at the Rad Rangers and their feeble quest. He bragged about how he would now demonstrate TRUE power, and how he would vanquish them this time. He would soon destroy Dino-World, and all five dimensions with it. Then he laughed some more.

René was the smart-alecky girl otherwise known

as Black Shadow. She did, in fact, wear a lot of eye shadow, but it only sharpened her brassy remarks.

"Oh yeah, Doc?" She crunched her knuckles and yelled defiantly, "Well, BRING ON THE HOT SAUCE!" She was mouthy, she was bad-ass, and she was clearly one of Albert's favorites. Albert flapped his hand on Clark's arm with excitement. He grabbed Clark's sleeve as the Rad Rangers did their trademark slow-motion panoramic flex, and the climactic battle began.

Clark wondered how they sorted their laundry. They had SO MANY colored suits. He also noticed that overlords had a pretty good sense of humor, when it came to destroying existence. Universal annihilation seemed pretty darned funny to them. They'd laugh about it for quite a long time.

Ten minutes of acrobatics and special effects later, the movie ended. Clark shifted in his seat. His legs were stiff. Albert was so psyched, he couldn't wait for the NEXT sequel, and then the sequel after that.

"Ya," Clark tipped his head and admitted, "I can't say I've seen that kinda… film… recently. But y'know what? It was pretty fun!" He rubbed his jaw and reflected on the gratuitous, color-saturated fracas he'd just watched. It spun his head like a giddy carnival ride. He looked over at Albert. The kid's eyes were huge and shining.

"WHAT?" Albert hooted, "Naw, that was WICKED! Man, I'd give a million bucks to see that again sometime."

Something in Clark's chest turned over. 'A million bucks.' There was a time when Clark didn't know what a million bucks really was. Back then, the world was bigger. Skies meant forever. Dreams were beautiful back then, and a million bucks could buy anything.

"We can see it again," Clark said. He nodded down at his little friend, whose head craned up.

Albert was breathless. "Like… like, can we see it again this weekend?"

This was the perfect moment. Clark was fully alive. He beamed like moonlight. He glanced around furtively, and whispered to Albert:

"CAN YOU KEEP A SECRET?"

Albert was frozen stiff. He said nothing.

"Don't EVER tell your mom… but we can watch it again NOW, if you want."

Albert almost lost it. "You gotta be KIDDING me! And I'm s'posed to be the KID, here! Can we really?"

Clark nodded and stood straight. "It's getting really late, though. We gotta take care of things. YES, I'm serious… so c'mon. We'll get tickets. And you need to use the can, too."

"No, I don't."

"Ya, you do." Clark raised a brow.

In the men's washroom. Clark stood a distance away while Albert took care of excess drainage.

"I didn't need to go that bad. I coulda waited, Clark."

"Nope. That's not how this works. It's getting late, and we're drinking some cola. Cola's a diuretic. We're like ninjas, preparing for a mission."

Albert squawked back at him, both skeptical and amused: "Whaaat?"

"No, really - caffeine is this little powder. Sometimes they put it in drinks. It's like a secret ninja powder for energy. It's even in coffee. Trust me, adults use it for survival all the time.

"The problem is, it makes you wiz. So we're not going to fall asleep, here. We'll prepare... with cola. I'll get more tickets, and popcorn, and some of those cola drinks. You already took care of the wizzing part. See? We're a team. We're TOTALLY gonna watch this movie again." He smiled broadly. "And don't tell your mom. Us guys? We're going just an eensy-bit wild."

They walked through the darkened corridors outside. Muffled booms shook the nearby walls. It was like a cave surrounded by other primal caves, with strange shadows of people filing through. Albert hung onto Clark's sleeve.

"Clark? You're kinda weird, but in a really cool way. I can see why Mom likes you."

Clark smiled. He hoped that she liked him.

"Did you do stuff like this with YOUR dad? Clark? Wait, why are we stopping?"

Clark stalled. No, he never did this with his dad. Ever. And he couldn't be Albert's dad, no matter how hard he tried. He'd never deserve that honor.

Then everything took a nosedive. Colleen Dietrich stood in the entrance to the cineplex. She was surrounded by her usual gaggle of hand-fluttering, skinny-legged flamingos. All they needed were cocktail glasses and frilly feathers in their hair.

He prayed that she wouldn't see him. He got as far as the ticket booth.

"Caa-LARKIE!"

He tried not to be seen, and he failed horribly.

"Here, Clarkie!" she waved. It sounded too much like calling a dog: 'Here, Sparky!'

When Clark was obligated to turn to her, she swooned and clapped her hands together.

"Oh, hi again! Fancy meeting you here!"

Ugh, he thought. Not as fancy as you'd like, ya preening twit.

"Oh, and is this your young one?"

Clark's irritation glowed like a hot iron.

"Y'okay," she recovered, "I was just talking about you with a few friends - you remember Jessi and Jenny from Ashvale High?"

He nodded vacantly. "Ya. 'Course."

"We're so happy to see how far you've come, Clark." She leaned up against him. She was chummy with him in front of all her friends. She leaned close, her hand touched his chest, and she sighed a tiny breath that only Clark could hear.

"...Oahh."

She was only joking - with them. She entertained her friends by schmoozing with 'Clark the Nerd.' She showed off her skills of manipulation, right there in front of them. She flipped her hair again, shone her glossy smile, and began casting her poisonous spells.

"You have such a lovely home, out there, with all the stonework and glass. I was really surprised - impressed, I mean. You must be pretty secure, to have that place. How'd you ever manage that?"

He tried to defuse everything. "Investments. Now I'm retired. Riley and I are very lucky."

Jessi and Jenny sighed and shook their heads with disapproval.

"You're retired?" Colleen acted surprised. "Already? And no commitments? What if your work calls you back, or calls you away? Trust me, I know; ties of the past can come back to haunt you."

"Nah. It's pretty much settled. We're good. A little banking, now and then."

"Well, I certainly hope your little friend… Riley… is alright by her lonesome, whenever you're away. 'Cuz maybe you have something actually important to do, right?"

He turned to her dryly. "Meh - you don't know her. Tonight, she's busy preparing for a new exhibit; we're just keeping out of the way."

Nobody knew what Riley was doing with her art, but an upcoming exhibit was a good red herring. Clark could throw that at them.

"Hmm. 'Glad things are good between you two. You've always been higher profile, Clarkie-boy. I hope she can respect that."

Wait, he thought. Does she know what I do? Or is that simply a 'higher-profile-than-Riley-is' jab?

Behind her, Jessi and Jenny whispered something.

Clark leaned his head a little. "How about you, Colleen? Have you met anyone who can keep up with you? Elections? Public image?"

He said 'keep up' with you. It sounded like 'put up' with you.

"Nah," she grinned back. "I'm totally career." She paused. "Wait a sec - are you actually going to see this flick? Oh, Clarkie, why WOULD you? It's a little immature, isn't it, big fella?" Her disbelief was a stage production all its own. Her lower lip hung loose. Something like laughter fell out.

Clark clamped his jaw tight. ENOUGH, Colleen.

He reached down and hoisted Albert into his arm.

"Albert, do you want to see this movie?"

The kid lit like a firework: "I'm DYIN' to see this movie!"

Clark punctuated by sliding him back to the floor. Colleen's friends split with laughter. She tried to recover, but her friends drowned her out.

Clark grabbed the tickets and the extra-mega deal of popcorn and cola. He gave a courteous nod to Colleen and the rest of her flock. Then he tugged Albert back to the theatre.

Albert squeaked up at him, "Did you know them? I didn't. Were they being mean or something?"

"OH yeah. But she was just getting started. And then you were my hero again."

"What?" He grabbed Clark's sleeve. "Tell me what you know! You always know more, even more than usual adults." He scowled oddly.

"Ninja mind control," Clark growled through a wicked grin. "A social victory. I lifted you up, and you flexed your enthusiasm. Nobody looked as good as you did. Everybody loved it. You were so awesome, they laughed their heads off."

The kid squinted thoughtfully. "Except for the really blonde lady. Her head looked sorta clobbered."

"Exactly!" Clark gleamed. "That lady, Colleen? She couldn't keep up. You were my secret ninja… my secret weapon. Your enthusiasm drowned her out completely. That's why we won. Man, I tell you - we really are a team."

Clark stopped and looked straight at him.

"Thank you, Albert. I mean it. You stole the spotlight, even from Colleen Dietrich. That was epic."

Colleen Dietrich, he thought. Your mom would be so proud!

Albert's head spun. They glanced around the theatre and picked better seats this time. Albert handled his soft drink, but spilled about half of the popcorn. Clark bent down to clean up.

"Agh… okay, stay put. I got it. Hang on to your drink, dude." He slid his feet across the floor, trying to scoop the popcorn into a pile. Albert watched him taking care of the accident.

"So, are you ever going to be my dad? Like, my mom and you? together?"

Clark was glad to be occupied. He didn't have to make eye contact.

"I can't be your dad, Albert." He stayed busy, cleaning up the mess. "And it's not because you already have a dad, somewhere. It's because I know I'd screw it up."

"What?"

Clark sighed. "Did you ever meet your grandfather?"

"Grampa Duke?"

"No. Your mom's dad."

"Grampa ROGER...!"

"No, actually; Roger just married your mom's mom, Kim. Roger became your grandfather later... he's pretty cool. But I'm talking about Morley. Morley Henway. Your mom's real father. He wasn't nice to your mom. My dad was sorta like that, too. Even my mom was a bit distant, when I was young. I don't want to be like them."

Albert looked up at him. "I'd take care of you. I'd make sure you're okay."

Clark shook his head. He crushed the spilled popcorn in his fist and dunked it into a waste bag. He stuffed the bag briskly, like taking care of unwanted business. He rose up and tied the bag tight.

"It makes more sense if you and I are friends, man. 'Cuz you're a great friend."

"But you COULD be a dad..."

Clark knew he'd missed popcorn under the seats. He stood straighter and took a moment to explain.

"Albert, it's actually a good thing that you don't know about bad parents. I'm sorry about your own father, and I bet it was hard. But some moms or dads… man, they shouldn't have had kids at all. Their own problems spilled over."

"So the truth is, I'm afraid."

"But you're NEVER afraid," Albert argued.

He faced Albert and answered: "I'm ALWAYS afraid. I'll admit it. Being a dad is huge, and I'd screw it up. You're too important, and… believe me, I'm just really afraid."

Albert sat in his seat. He didn't settle in; he watched Clark and hung on to his drink with two hands.

"Look, you're seven years old. You don't have to worry about this right now. And besides, tonight isn't father-son stuff at all. We're just two dudes, watching a great movie. We're being ridiculous and spontaneous. Seriously, don't tell your mom. She'd say we're irresponsible… staying out really late, dosing on soft drinks. But - it's classic 'guy stuff.' It's sorta life-affirming."

"Well," Albert concluded, "then you're not a screwup."

Clark tried to smile. He couldn't.

I can't lose you, he thought to himself. I can't scare you away.

The second viewing of *Rad Rangers 3* was nearly as good. The caffeine wore off in the last quarter. Albert didn't need to see the credits at the end.

"Can we see another one?" Albert spun his head in the dark corridor, outside.

Clark's eyebrows shot up. "Ahh… no. We'll be late getting home, as it is."

Albert's feet clumped heavily. "Oh, come on. If we're late anyway, Mom won't even care."

"Hey. We're trying to stay OUT of trouble, man."

They found their way to his car.

"I don't even wanna go home. Can we go someplace else?"

"Man, I'm not trying to be a jerk… but we both have to get home. Hop in."

Albert plunked into his seat and slammed his door. "That sucks. This all sucks."

Clark leaned his head to the side. "You won't even believe me, but that powder is wearing off. Your liver and kidneys are working overtime. If you get some rest, we can go out again soon. I really mean 'soon.' But ONLY if we both get some rest."

"I'm FINE," Albert huffed. "I can stay up. I'm not a little kid anymore."

"Yeah, but we both want to stay out of trouble. It's late. It's, like…" He checked the time. "OH… Aww, man, it's a quarter-to-twelve."

He leaned over to Albert.

"Here. Buckle in." Clark made sure the seatbelt was secure. "I'ma turn on the seat warmers. And you can have my coat for a bit. I'll open the window for some fresh air, too."

Albert grumbled again.

"Albert, you're fighting that powder, caffeine. That stuff is legal, but it really is a drug. People use it because it's mostly safe. If we hadn't, we both would've conked out in that second movie."

Albert turned on him with a look of alarm.

Clark reassured him, "And right now, you're crashing. You feel cranky, and so do I. That powdery caffeine stuff is a drug, so it has a bad side. Like a nasty aftertaste. But you can fight it by getting good rest."

Terror flashed on Albert's face. "Wait… I'm on DRUGS? What the HELL, Clark?!"

"…And that's okay, to feel like that. It was just cola: caffeine and wayyy too much sugar. Take a few deep breaths. It's good for you. Deep breaths."

Albert pouted and flopped on his side, away from Clark.

"This is all crazy-nuts," he moaned. "And YOU'RE crazy. No wonder you don't have kids."

Clark paused. He was relieved that Albert couldn't see his face; it twisted painfully. His finger jabbed the window control. Albert's passenger-side window cracked open for fresh air.

It was only a half-hour drive through the city, but Albert slept through most of it. The streets were a werewolf, after midnight. Traffic was chaotic. People were out for more than just movies. They proved how cool they were by harassing random strangers. Clark closed the windows to keep out the noise.

He saw things that only happen at night: three police cars flashing lights outside a little restaurant; half a dozen teenage girls on hillside, screaming the lyrics to a song; a guy wearing a cape and football helmet, running down the sidewalk carrying a torch.

At one intersection, some boozy pedestrians crossed the street while drumming the hoods of cars. They were very spirited, celebrating their festival of Holy St Obnoxious. They pounded and shook the car in the adjacent lane, and it looked like the elderly driver was traumatized. Clark leaned forward to catch a drunk's eye.

NO, Clark stared at him. NO, YOU WILL NOT.

The drunk man staggered backward. He was more afraid of Clark's eyes than actually being run over. He had a sudden, sobering moment of caution and crossed the street quickly. The traffic light switched to green. Clark revved with slight satisfaction and carried Albert through the night.

Outside, it was chilly and black. Clark navigated that strange realm of emptiness and sudden, glaring lights. He checked his passenger again. Dear Albert was there with his light whooshes of breath. Clark's coat was a shield for him.

Here, Clark was ennobled. He was so, so proud. He had this honor of safeguarding Albert; it was a duty and a higher purpose. He kept Albert perfectly safe.

At home, Clark didn't see lights on. He carried Albert inside, took him to the den, and settled him into bed. His Rad Rangers onesie doubled as pajamas.

Riley had fallen asleep in front of the TV. He knelt down to her and woke her gently.

"Honey? Do you want to come to bed?"

"Oogh…" she stretched groggily. "Ya. Howza movie? Mmm - how's my guys?" She blinked a few times. She smelled like Chinese food.

"It was a fun flick," he muttered, nodding. "Albert's already flopped in bed. He's good."

"Mmf," she pawed at his shirt. "Wanna tuck me in, too?"

"Of course," he smiled. "It's dark, though; you should hold my hand."

Much later, Albert recounted the whole thing.

"I'm really sorry if we lied, but we had a heck of a lot of fun, even if I got really tired, after. It's still an awesome movie - you gotta see it. And Clark said we were irresponsible, but he was still like CLARK. I mean, I can't imagine him being like Dad in the 'bad' way. Right?"

Riley's face went bleak.

"So… you boys had fun, and you snuck a second movie into movie night? and you stayed out late? You were worried I'd be upset…" She closed her eyes and spoke softly. "THAT was your secret?"

He nodded sheepishly. "And I drank an extra-mega cola. I don't know how much caffeine they put in it, that time. But I hope I'm not addicted, or anything. It was actually a drug. Are things gonna be okay with you and Clark?"

He looked back and forth between Granny Faye and Riley. Gran's little feathery arm reached out to his shoulder. Her smile tried hard, and he noticed.

She pulled another chair to her table. Albert joined them. All three of them sat together, worrying about what was going to happen.

"Is Clark gonna be alright?"

Gran looked down and shook her head. Her neck was tense.

"We don't know, yet, me dear. I'm sorry to say."

CHAPTER THIRTY-EIGHT
LOST

Days went by. Every evening, the sun fell under the edge of the world and disappeared in darkness. Riley's six-hundred dollars ticked away rapidly. She lived skinny like she did before; she only ate before going out job-searching. She watched her spending as best she could, but she was down to two-hundred-and-eight dollars.

There weren't any jobs in Ashvale, not even waiting tables. The local telemarketing call center wouldn't look at her application. They got a weird, anonymous tip saying Riley Henway was impulsive, hot tempered, and verbally abusive. There was no way to convince them otherwise. Someone, somewhere, hated her.

The only job available was cleaning washrooms at a club on the far side of town. It had a stylized sign in script: "The Gentlemen's TEA Room." It was for male customers only, and they never served tea. The "T" stood for something else - something more like "T-shirts off." It was spelled "T-&-A" because it was a strip club.

She considered the job anyway; she'd clean washrooms. She looked at the costs of food, and the cheapest housing... she could maybe afford a place in a rooming house. She'd take the floor, and Albert would sleep in the bed. She'd have enough money for his basic food, but she'd have to find other income to pay for anything else. She didn't want to moonlight, considering where she'd have to work.

She was shunned by other places, even where they had high turnover. The only recognition she got was a pat on the behind as she left a paper-shredding office.

Ashvale had nothing for her, so she had nothing for Albert. It was possible that she couldn't provide for him as a parent. She had to face the ugliest fact in the world, and she had to turn to something she never, ever wanted.

Around 8:30pm, one night, Riley stood outside Gran's place and pulled out her phone. She edited her phone settings and unblocked a number. Her finger dipped over the keypad, like a tiny bird drinking poison. She hadn't dialed this number since the divorce. She made her finger dunk down and connect. The call began. The dial tone made her wince. It rang three times.

"...'Llo?"

"Hello, uh… I'm looking for… wait - Monique? Is that you?" Riley's neck corded tight.

"Hyahh."

She felt like a mouse wiggling cheese from a trap. "Yeah. Well, I'd like to speak with, uh…"

"Ah-whoo's this?"

She sighed. "It's Riley Henway. We actually met a few years-"

"A-HA-ha-ha-ha…!" Monique's bony teeth were shining in her skinny face.

Riley stood there and endured Monique's laughing. Monique really was a hyena; her rabid cackling made her stand out from other anorexic women. She even had a tired, over-bleached mane that used to be hair. Riley didn't know if it was her lineage, but she seemed to have a lot of 'grinning skeleton' in her.

"Look," Riley leveled with her, "It's about his son, okay? It's about Albert."

"Awyeah. So what, izzy dead?" Monique squished her nicotine gum in her teeth.

"NO, he's not dead! What's wrong with you, you f-… Look, it's best if I just talk with his dad. Could you put him on?" She was losing patience already.

Silence.

"Ah-why? You got your divorce."

Yeah, Riley thought. And he got you. Talk about strings attached, you scrawny little sleaze…

"And I'm happy for you both, Monique. Still, I'd really like to talk with him." Riley knew she had to speak her language. "It's about the extended scholarship that Albert just won. It's unprecedented; he really has his dad's brains. And there's co-signer benefits, here, so it's something he'd be interested in."

More silence.

"Not interested in your benefits. Y'know, Rye, maybe you should clean up a little. You don't sound so great. You can't look so great, either, if you're all strung out like that."

"I'm okay. I'm fine. I just figured I shouldn't be the only one gaining from Albert, what with him being a prodigy."

Another thoughtful silence.

"Ya, well, he's YOUR progeny, isn't he? Your progeny, your problem, Sweetie. Anything else? 'Cuz some of us have a life to get back to." She smacked her nicotine gum.

"Is he even HOME?"

Those words hit Monique; they hit squarely, like a boxer's knock-out punch. Riley listened carefully as Monique held silent. She was prone to these quiet, philosophical musings whenever she had to connect two or three dots.

WHACK, went her phone. The noise stabbed Riley's ear. There was the sound of chewing gum, then two more sharp whacks, then Monique hung up.

Riley dropped her arm. She didn't look at her phone. She leaned back against the cold, outside wall of Gran's place. She turned and let it support her back and both of her shoulders. Then she slumped down to the ground.

Thank you Mr Wall, she thought. When my back is against you, you're there for me. And you remind me of how warm and caring people are.

She curled herself into her knees. Her breathing nodded her head. Soon, her cheeks were shining and her lap was wet from tears.

Did she have to send Albert to a foster home? Would she, herself, be homeless? Was she working in a strip bar, now? Would she try for promotions, in a place like that?

Nah.

This was nothing. She'd vaulted off stone walls before, and she'd hit the ground running. She'd make this work. Maybe another town? It didn't matter. There was no such thing as 'fate.' Human spirit is everything. She'd find that town. And she'd find a way. She and Albert were family.

She stopped.

Family?

Her chest whined. New tears flooded down her face. Her cheeks shook. Her head folded down into her crossed arms. Her ribs jerked with sobbing.

"Clark? I'm so sorry… what I did… to us…!"

She'd made him alone. She had un-loved him, right there in his own house. All the un-love that she'd ever been, her whole life, she'd just given to him. Her worthlessness finally caught up with them both.

She sniffled. She slowly lifted her head and tried

to plan the next month. On weekends, bus service around the Gentlemen's TEA Room ended early. Cabs would be too expensive for that distance. She'd need to stay overnight at the club, or find someplace to sleep nearby.

At that moment, twenty-four hands thumped their black table. Palms were dusted off. Cigars were lit. There were grunts of approval from the shadows.

"He'll come to us whining and begging for a job, or he'll kill himself."

"Both good."

"Landucci?"

"Ah, he knows nothing. He couldn't help, now, anyway."

Jeff Anders puffed up his chest. "Thank you for the opportunity, sirs. I would say I delivered."

"Yes. Well orchestrated. You are a man with initiative."

"Agreed."

"Agreed."

"What about the tramp? Henway?"

"Trash to the gutter. As always."

Anders lifted his hands evenly.

"Gentlemen? I have plans for her, first. Benjamin's either dead meat, or he's in our pocket. We'll buy out the government research as usual. But Henway? She needs to know who wears the pants around here. She'll get a special nighttime visit - and I got an old friend who wants a piece of this pie. We'll have some quality time with her before she disappears."

"Henway knows more than she should."

"Agreed. Tick that little box, Anders."

Jeff waved his fingers. "The 'Anders Personal Touch' seems to work. We'll take care of her right now. My old friend's on South Street."

"Very nice."

"Well played, gentlemen."

CHAPTER THIRTY-NINE

EMPTY SHELL

Clark crawled. Broken glass clicked and scraped against his skin. He moaned, rolled onto his back, and gave up.

He lay there for… hours? A day? He stared up at his clean, white ceiling. Either he'd died, or something terrible and cold had been born into his body.

Clark rose from the floor. He wiped the shards and blood from his skin. He turned and admired his broken window. It was broken right through. It was wounded and ugly, and the view was perfectly clear.

He poked his smartphone. The autodial fluttered. The call went through immediately.

Matteo Landucci was at home tidying up his kitchen. A dishtowel was flung over one shoulder while he scrubbed the last few plates. His phone buzzed. He grabbed it to answer.

"Hello? Clark? Ya, it's Matt… what's wrong, man?"

The line was silent. Clark couldn't answer that question.

Matteo went cold.

"Fifteen seconds' silence, Clark, and I'm coming to you. What's wrong?"

The voice was low and smooth. "Matt? I need your help."

"Anything," he replied, tossing his towel. "Need me to cover something? Need the boys? What's the op?"

His voice turned grave. "Matt, I need you."

Matteo's ears perked. His eyes narrowed. He stood straight.

"Call's secure, on my end. Tell me what needs doing."

He listened to Clark breathing for a moment. Then, Clark spoke flatly.

"Give me Icarus."

Matteo gaped in silence.

Clark panted, "I need the… you have to give me your codes, Matt. For development. Builds. Everything."

Matteo sputtered. "Wh-… My codes? The dual keycodes?"

"Yeah. The codes. I need your codes."

Matteo kept quiet. He held the phone at a safe distance. He felt like a living flame next to a very short fuse.

"MATT. GIVE ME THE CODES." Breath thundered through the phone's speaker. "GIVE THEM. NOW."

Matteo felt his adrenaline jump. He realized he was speaking with Dr Hyde, again.

He tipped his chin down. "Clark? Work with me, okay? I'm here with you. You and me, bro. We can-"

The phone crackled.

"NO. THE CODES. ICARUS."

He could almost hear Clark's bared teeth.

"Clark, you and I both know... what that thing could do. It's not an answer. Please, let me help you."

The plastic on Clark's phone creaked tightly.

Matt tried to ease him into talking. "Please?"

He wouldn't answer.

"Alright," Matteo soothed him. "I know this is your persona, and not you. I know something must've happened. You're in crisis mode, and you're protecting yourself from trauma. So listen to my voice, okay Clark? We're gonna get through this."

Clark scoffed on the other end.

"Now... I'm sorry for what I'm gonna say, but we gotta reach into the fire. Just stay with me. Please. Stay with me, here."

The other man listened impatiently. Hot breath steamed from his nostrils.

"Clark? WHERE is she?"

The breathing stopped. Matteo thought he heard a dull, steady tapping. He realized it was Clark's pulse. He'd just tripped a wire, and these were the final ticks before the explosion.

"I'm really sorry to upset you, man, but I can't give you the codes. I have to help you some other way. We're gonna talk this through, okay Clar-"

CLICK.

Matteo listened to the dead phone line. He closed his eyes for a moment, then flipped his phone face-up and speed dialed.

"Hello? It's Agent Landucci. Matteo Alessio Landucci. I need a lockdown."

He bit his lip.

"A former agent. Agent Clark David Benjamin. He worked Field, S.I., Black Tier. He worked three-hundred-and-seven portfolios, to my knowledge. Just lock it all down. All of it. Mainly, secure the military project known as 'Icarus.'

"The Icarus data transfer is set up like a damned grenade. He's holding pins in place. He gives his authentication on schedule, or it leaks to other world powers. We can't afford to lose that data."

Brief objections on the other line.

"But you CAN'T isolate it all. It has dual security keycodes - Clark's codes and mine. We're like a toll booth for a bridge, but he's holding the entire bridge up. We don't have enough access to save it."

Matteo's phone bleeped. He'd received a text message:

"Agent Landucci: I have no further use of your services. - C Benjamin"

Matteo jammed his phone against his cheek.

"No. Contact brass. He's gonna rescind my authority and take the damn codes. Shut everything down right now. Cut power to the entire building - I mean it. If you hear ANYTHING activate over there, get the hell out. Get everyone out. Do NOT engage Benjamin, don't approach him, don't…"

Matteo paced, then stopped.

"What? When? Just NOW?"

He chewed his knuckle.

"Did he give a reason?"

Matteo learned that the Icarus Project had been signed over completely. All necessary authentications were given, with no conditions. The U.S. Military now owned all the data. There were no time-released installments. There were no lynchpins. Clark added a memo, which simply read:

"The original inspiration is lost to me."

Matteo sighed.

Another call came in immediately. Matt reared back, then refocused and answered. A tired, drawling voice addressed him.

"Agent Landucci? Philip Archibauld. You worked closely with Clark Benjamin, right?"

"Well," Matt paused, "Yeah. He was with S.I., a while back. But he just fired me, sir."

Archibauld snorted.

"What, with your service record?"

"Apparently so, sir. Uhh... you know about my work record?"

"Yeah, you're hired. Welcome back."

Archibauld waited a beat.

"Look, I'm sorry about this, but we need you to fully close his S.I. contract."

There was a horrid silence. One of Matteo's worst nightmares turned and looked him in the face.

"Did you hear me, Agent?"

"Yes," Matt answered. "Yes, sir, I heard you."

"You know him better than most, Landucci. We need you to finalize closure."

The blood drained from Matt's face.

Archibauld continued, "He's a genius, but he's still just a man. Someone could compromise him in the near future. That would make him worthless to us. You'll prevent that future from happening. There can be no compromise. You understand."

Matt closed his eyes. "Yes. I understand."

"Just do your job, Agent. His departure from S.I. has already been contentious."

After a few moments, Matteo asked one final question.

"Sir? He's a good man. Even outside S.I., he's a strong asset. What if I remove the compromise? I mean, that's the threat, right?"

Archibauld chuckled. "What are you thinking, Landucci? 'Gonna charge in and save the day, again?"

Matt scowled. He set his jaw.

"No, sir. You're talking about someone breaching S.I. through Clark Benjamin, even AFTER he's cut ties. Clark's a tough nut, and we both know this. If someone tries to go through him, they're taking a long, hard road. They'd have deliberate plans. Traceable plans. And they're the real problem, here."

"Yeah, that's a slightly bigger problem, son."

"It's what I do." Matteo slapped his thigh and exhaled into the phone. On the other end, Philip Archibauld stopped and listened.

"So just let me do my job, sir."

Matteo heard amused chortling on the other end. It was followed by a thoughtful silence. Then the drawling voice came back.

"…Mayoral Candidate Jeffrey Stewart Anders. The real estate guy. 'Gotta hunch that little dickhead has been after Benjamin for years. He's been pulling strings at all levels - legal, political, criminal… If you can shut him up, none of us will complain. And while you're at it, keep an eye on Riley Ann Henway."

"Henway," Matteo mused. "Henway… Her son is Albert Henway, right?"

"Well, well. Someone's takin' notes. He wanted to keep her clear of all this… which makes her pretty obvious."

"He never told me anything about her."

"For damned good reasons, son - attacks, the kid's abduction, and now some kinda incident?"

"Yeah," Matt sighed. "I was just speaking with his persona. Clark's buried pretty far down."

Archibauld chuckled once. "And you're his personal security advisor? You gotta full plate, kid."

"Wait a sec." Matt poked at his phone. "They're all FROM here. Anders, Riley Henway, and Clark. They're all from Ashvale. And they're the same age. The same high school class, even!"

"Bad blood," Archibauld rumbled.

"Wait wait wait…" Matt's eyes flicked through his thoughts. "Anders? The 'Mr Real Estate' Anders, you said? That secure storage facility, where Albert was hidden - it was so far underground, not even Athena could hack it. If someone dodged Athena and threatened Clark using the KID, that's deep knowledge! And it's also land ownership in the heart of the city…"

"Bad blood," Archibauld repeated. "So. 'Got the scent?"

Matt kept reading his phone. "Back in high school, Anders's buddy went to the hospital. Reports were conflicted. A few years later, Anders's phone records stopped completely… the same day Clark had a stab wound. Yeah, right, as if THAT'S not suspicious…" Matteo rolled his eyes.

"You sound hungry." Archibauld's wrinkles pulled around a devious smile.

"I'm gonna have Anders on a silver platter," Matteo muttered through his teeth. "Or maybe I'll just eat him alive."

"Attaboy," Archibauld growled. "One last question, Landucci. The Icarus Project? The files, the backing theory - everything's signed over to us. We're all real' happy about that. Except, where's the prototype?"

CHAPTER FORTY
The Shadow

That evening, there was chatter on the local TV news:

"Strange weather conditions were reported today over the local industrial park, suburban areas, and nearby air force base. The skies were described as orange and flickering. A meteorological expert at the airbase claimed it was 'leftover static charge' from a very brief, very intense lightning storm that occurred sometime the previous night. While this storm wasn't witnessed by most, local authorities and consultants from the air force base stated that it was a rare but natural occurrence.

"The real estate market took a surprising turn, this morning. Owners of twenty-six apartment complexes were served by legal representatives from

Ashvale Town Hall. All apartment buildings had been found to have fundamentally unsafe wiring, as demonstrated by an independent auditor from-

"Uhh, we have breaking news: a leading Ashvale mayoral candidate, it is reported, has just suffered a car accident at the downtown intersection of Main and South. Eye-witnesses claimed they saw a tall man in a coat and hat standing in the intersection, when Mr Jeffrey Anders collided... his car collided with the...

"Sorry, details are still coming in, but it seems witnesses saw a tall man in a coat and hat standing in the intersection, who was then struck by Mr Anders's car. We don't have reliable reports on any injuries sustained, and much of the footage was obscured by some kind of electrical interference. Mr Anders's vehicle was extensively damaged, and allegedly caught fire shortly after impact."

Another station had the same story.

"Two traffic cams and an ATM security camera recorded the crash. All videos have the same static.

"The ATM camera shows a human-sized figure dropping from above and crushing into the pavement. As you can see, this is where the video has sudden interference. The figure appears featureless and very dim, compared to everything else. Some suggest it looks like amateur CGI effects. The shading doesn't match the ambient light.

"And here you can see the crash, where Anders's car collides full-on. Note how the vehicle deforms around the humanoid figure. Obviously, this can't be real. It doesn't even look like actual physics. This has to be fake."

Another station debunked everything.

"Some have made references to the Hat Man, an urban myth akin to men in black or the 'shadow people.' The figure here is hazy, dark, and featureless. Still, this footage doesn't suggest 'supernatural creature' as much as 'computer-savvy teenager.'

"Naturally, the image gets distorted by static... because no-one ever gets a clear photo of bigfoot, right?

"There have been unconfirmed reports that Jeffrey Anders suffered spinal injuries during the incident. He was ejected from his car, or was possibly pulled from the wreckage shortly after the crash. He was not admitted to the Metro Central Hospital. His location is still unknown.

"Mr Anders's car was crushed inward, at the front, then somehow ripped in half right up to the driver's seat. Only the machines at a junkyard could do that kind of work. The car caught fire after the crash, making a detailed analysis difficult.

"Was this meant as a publicity stunt? Was it meant to discredit Mr Anders, during his election campaign? Why does the video go fuzzy, just when

we need a clear image? What did Anders REALLY hit, for his car to suffer that damage?

"I have one main question: why is no-one from the Anders family available for comment? No phone calls have been returned, and no-one answers the door at their main residence.

"The purpose of this footage is as hazy as its recorded content. Like most other paranormal and conspiracy-related media, it is obviously a hoax."

PART THREE

The Real

CHAPTER FORTY-ONE
DEAR RILEY

At first it was the kitchen table. A happy family life was just sitting there in his kitchen, mocking him. It reminded him that he was unlovable. He'd hurled that table through the windows. He banished it from the house. Family could never live with him. Broken glass and cold air were the truth. He needed truth.

There had been a six-pack of beer in his fridge. Only four were left, still stuck in their plastic rings. He grabbed them by the plastic and whipped them all against the edge of the sink. Again, and again, he bashed them till they dribbled and bled. They died as crumpled metal, leaking froth down the drain.

She'd shared those… with him.

There was more in the fridge: there was cheap Chinese food that she'd ordered in. It was all spices, and syrup, and liquid smoke. He crushed their little square boxes when he dunked them into the garbage.

HMM... he thought. WHO ELSE DID SHE SCREW FROM CHINATOWN?

He knew this kitchen wasn't everything; she'd lived here. She was everywhere. Albert had lived here, too.

They had all tried, hadn't they?

Clark blundered away from the kitchen. It was too much. His legs thumped heavily, and his arms swung like they were drunk. Then he saw the front closet and her coat. He saw her scarves and her little shoes.

Clark fell backward. His back thumped against a door, and it swung open like a trap. He fell reeling to the floor.

He landed in her studio.

His arms reached out for balance, but then they died. Her charcoal sketches - they were gone, just like she was. Had she planned to leave him? Why were these easels empty? He'd always loved her art.

They left him, too.

His chest quaked. Finally, he pulled in a long breath, and a short, twisted cry escaped. Her art - the soul that he'd loved so much - was all gone. She was gone. Tiny sounds trembled out of him. They squeezed out, like through cracks. His eyes flooded tears, and his mouth and nose drizzled. His face was drool and sweat.

Riley was gone. Everything was broken. She was gone.

Clark had no immediate neighbors. No-one heard that house screaming. Day and night, it stood tall and strong - white stonework, alone, with something from hell inside it. Anyone who witnessed those sounds would keep them as scars.

He couldn't understand what had happened to the world. It was hollow, but ringing with madness.

WELCOME HOME, CLARK.

Several days later, he staggered across his home office. He fell at his desk again. By sheer luck, he fell in his chair. He still tasted the blood in his mouth from weeping and screaming. The pain in his heart had left his body ragged. The walls of his house rested in this temporary quiet.

He couldn't get the images out of his head; Athena had recorded video, and Riley had set it up herself. The video showed Jeff strolling into the house, drinking a beer with Riley, talking... and then the two of them were kissing. They kissed in the kitchen, and kept kissing, and they fell into the bedroom together.

RILEY set up this recording, as soon as Jeff arrived. Why would she want her own video of Jeff Anders? Why would she want her own little sex-tape of the two of them? Her, and her ex-boyfriend from high school, in bed together? He seemed to arrive shortly after Clark left... like it was planned. Were they having an affair? Had it started when he was in Poland? The video also detected Jeff's pistol. Had Jeff been carrying that to defend himself? It didn't seem to make Riley nervous, if she knew about it. Maybe

Riley and Jeff BOTH wanted his house and assets, and then someone would shoot him. No more threats to her, or Albert… or Jeff. Maybe she chose Jeff. Again.

Clark's arm swung up over his desk and he clicked on his computer. Sweat and tears dribbled from his chin.

He meant to write to her. Maybe he'd ask her something. Was she okay? Was she safe? And did she ever love him?

He didn't have the chance. He scrolled to his emails and saw four new ones, all from his aunt. The subject lines said everything:

"Need to talk. Please call."

"Clark, please call us."

"No connection?"

He'd turned off his phone for a few days. He didn't want it harassing him, and there was no way he could work anyway.

Then, just two hours ago:

"Clark. So, so sorry."

He read the last email, and didn't need the others. They were from his Aunt Stephanie.

Aunt Steffie was his father's sister. After his father

split, she stayed in touch. She still cared for Clark and his mother.

"*Dear Clark,*

"*I'm so sorry that I have to tell you this through email.*

"*Your mother Bernita had a sudden fall last night. She was talking with someone at the front door, and they say she just dropped.*

"*She was taken to the hospital around tea-time. A doctor saw her in a few minutes. Another doctor checked her and still couldn't tell what was wrong.*

"*I was the only family they could reach. I went there and waited at the hospital for four hours. Another third doctor came, and he seemed to be in charge. He told me Bernita had an aneurysm. He said a 'ruptured aneurysm.' He took me aside and told me that even with a specialist, they wouldn't have had time.*

"*He told me to go home at about ten at night. He and a really nice Chinese nurse sat with me, then. She told me that your mum, Bernita, had passed. It was quick, I think, if they couldn't do anything. They were doctors, right? If they could've, they would've.*

"*I asked about autopsies, but that third doctor said it wouldn't even be necessary. He was certain.*

"*Clark, dear - your father didn't have much to say, and if you want to talk to him, you might want to reach out yourself...*"

"He can rot," Clark growled. "He wasn't there for her. Not in life, OR in death."

"We hope we hear from you soon. She was a sweet, cheery sister-in-law, and I was so happy to meet her in this life.
"She had funeral plans, and I guess you decided on these as a family - you and Bernita did. I'm here for you, and I really hope I can see you sooner.
"I'm so sorry, dear Clark. Call anytime.
"All my love -

- Aunt Steffie"

He sighed darkly.

"Ahh, good ol' Aunt Steffie. I should call her - except, she's been talking to Mr Spineless Scum-Suck. He'd better not be there, at her funeral. That'd be a crappy time to start showing... loyalty..."

He paused. Sick bile pumped in his veins. Evil grinned inside him. He looked upward.

"I LOVE YOU, MOM."

He clicked to compose a new email. He raised his hands and started typing:

"Dear Riley,
"I know we have our differences, but perhaps you'd like to attend a reception for my recently departed mother. I recall that my mother thought highly of you.

"The time and details of the church service are listed below. The invitation to you stands open..."

Clark wrote bitter acid across the final words:

"...unless you have another wedding, that day."

Clark sat back. His blood pounded in his ears. He stared at those words. He thought of deleting them.
DON'T DO IT, CLARK.
DON'T YOU DARE DELETE THOSE WORDS-
Clark clicked. He slowly dragged his cursor across the words.
CLARK - SHE IS A...
He dragged and highlighted the whole line.
...A BETRAYER. A LIAR!
A WHORE.
He stared at that bitterness. Did she deserve it?
RUIN HER, misery said.
His misery wanted her company. The text sat on his screen, highlighted. Black turned to white, and white turned to black. It waited for him to decide. It was all lit in negative.
"Who am I?" he asked aloud. "Would I hurt her?"
He stopped. He thought of her and her choices. She married someone else, had a child with someone else, and even in their own bed... she had sex with someone else. What did he mean to her? What was 'Clark' in her world? He didn't know.

He knew Riley by who she was, and how he'd always felt about her. His heart knew her. On this, he was certain.

Click. His backspace key banished the insult. Pure, glowing white remained onscreen. The cursor blinked at him patiently.

"Who am I?" he asked again. "I'm me. I am CLARK Benjamin. I am not my persona. I am not my father. I'm me. I tell the truth; I do what's right, no matter the cost.

"Just because she doesn't love me, it doesn't mean she's a bad person. And I'll always respect her. I hate myself for it, but I'll always love her - whether I want to or not.

"Besides. She's real life. She's still alive, and she's still with us. I have to contact her. It's more important than how I feel."

He quietly thanked his mother for teaching him another life lesson.

"The invitation to you stands open, Riley. If you'd consider attending, it would be a comfort to me.

- Clark"

He clicked the send button.

CHAPTER FORTY-TWO

The Departed

Riley walked in darkness. She wore a black dress lent to her by Granny Faye. It was the dress Faye had worn, herself, when she lost her husband Everett. Today, Riley wore black out of respect, but also for her own loss. This would probably be one of the last times she saw Clark.

Earlier, a smoky voice phoned her and requested that she attend. She confirmed that she would. She'd wear black, but it wouldn't be a damned black suit. The voice kindly asked her to speak to Clark, or to reach out to him. He needed her. Riley stated that things seemed final, and Clark probably wouldn't acknowledge her at all. Then she hung up.

She stepped through the church doors with the slow grace of a dancer. Inside, people spoke in small groups. All of them wore black. She was shocked at how few people there were… maybe eight or nine? Eight, total. The church itself was sad, this evening.

She crept forward with her head bowed. A tall, red-haired man stood next to the coffin, paying his respects. Riley trailed after him. When he turned to leave, she moved up to where he'd been standing.

There she was: Bernita Lynn Hale-Benjamin. Compulsive scholar, enthusiast, and mother to Riley's greatest love. She was the kindest, most generous angel. She brought Clark to this world.

Riley wanted to speak to her. She wanted to apologize for how she'd treated her son. If she could, she'd lie down in her own coffin. Then she'd apologize to Bernita personally, in the afterlife.

A man spoke beside her ear.

"Hey. I don't think we've met. You were a student of hers?"

The red-haired man stood behind her. He was as tall as a viking. He had a short, fiery beard sending flicks of red from his chin. His hair was brassy with bits of ash-white. His eyes were plain blue. They had no spark today. He had an imposing stature; he was almost as tall as Clark. His voice was deep and resonant.

She answered him. "No, I just knew her a little."

"I'm Al," he said, offering his hand. "I was her husband."

She shook his hand. "Hi - Riley. Henway. I'm actually with Clark."

She caught herself. With Clark? No she wasn't.

The man stopped. He seemed surprised. "Oh. What, 'some friend of his?'"

Okay, she thought. I've heard about you, pal. You think I'm just Clark's FRIEND? and you're introducing yourself to young women at a FUNERAL?

"No," she replied. "He's my partner. So I know who you are, and that's prob'ly why we haven't met. Your reputation precedes you, Mr Alexander F Benjamin."

Yeah, you dickhead. Now you know who you're dealing with. You owe him - both Clark AND his mom. I'll break your creepy hand, instead of shaking it.

Alexander Benjamin slowed, dropped his arms to his sides, and let a smile tug up his face. He looked amused.

"Ma'am, let me just say: I've always admired him. I know he and I never got along, and I know it really hurt him when..." He stalled and looked at the carpet. "When I split. From the family. I know that changed him, as a boy. But that MAN? Clark? I've known him from a distance. I know who he is, and who he's become. As his partner, you should count yourself real' lucky."

Riley shook her head, bemused. Lucky? This, coming from Clark's DAD? What was he saying?

He tipped his head at her, like getting down to brass tacks.

"Look - Bernita's doing fine right now, I can

guarantee you that. Why? Because of her son. He has grit that'd strike terror in the devil's heart. Angels are taking especially good care of Bernita, because of him. NOBODY messes with his family or loved ones. I don't know if he learned from my mistakes, or what... but you have a solid guy, there. More than you know, I'd wager."

Alexander nodded, but watched Riley's head hang low. He could see her throat choking up.

"Yeah," he set his hand on Bernita's coffin, "Y'know, her passing hit us all pretty hard. Lemme tell you - it's rough, losing a partner. You make a few bad choices, and then you wake up and suddenly it's too late. I wish I coulda just talked to Bernita. I just..."

Riley's tears streamed down and patted the floor. They were loose pieces of her breaking heart.

"Well, I dunno. Find some solace in this, maybe: Clark seems like a nerd, but he's more like a knight. You're lucky to have him. Especially if you're together, like family."

He reached to gently touch her shoulder. She looked up - her eyes stopped him. Her tears were silver, but her eyes were steel.

You wouldn't dare, they said.

Alexander smiled and huffed lightly, then turned toward the exit.

"Arright. Well. Seeya around, maybe." He gave a final wink.

He was a tall shape striding to the door. An

equally tall shadow stood in his way. The new shadow took up the entire doorframe. It was just as powerful as its father.

CONVENIENT, the shadow thought, tightening its fists. YOU'RE ALREADY WEARING FUNERAL BLACK.

The shadow said nothing. It only stared.

Alexander saw him. He lowered his head slightly and kept walking toward the door. It took forever to get there. Everyone stopped talking and watched the slowest, hardest ten steps ever witnessed. It was like seeing a disaster happen in slow motion. Giants were destined to collide. The weight of the entire church shifted as the two men came face-to-face.

Alexander slowed. His lips parted to speak. The two hadn't shared a kind word for decades, and now Clark might listen. Could he reach over this wall? Could he reach out to his son, and maybe shake his hand?

Clark stepped neatly to the side, offering the perfect exit.

His face said it all: TIME TO WALK OUT AGAIN... 'DAD.'

Alexander paused. He bit his lip, bobbed his head loosely, and then resumed pace. He stepped out of the church and was gone.

Clark's face lowered. He might have been staring at the church floor. Riley had never seen him look so alone.

CHAPTER FORTY-THREE

ALONE

Albert was left alone with Granny Faye. He wouldn't settle in with a movie. He started pacing.

"No-one tells me anything," he moped. "What's going on? Why can't I visit with Clark?"

Granny Faye tried to answer as best she could. "He's in a really rough time right now, Sweetheart. And your mum is trying to put patches together. It's for the two of them. It takes time. It's worth it."

"Well," he stomped, "hasn't it taken TIME, yet?"

"It's a big job, Albert. It needs care. It may take more time than we think. Right now, your mum needs to find her footing. She needs some… some security."

Albert stopped. He heard something he understood, and he didn't like it.

"Is Mom gonna be okay? Are we gonna be okay? All of us?"

Gran couldn't answer that one.

"Wait… Is Clark gonna leave us, like Dad did? He is, isn't he? Is that what this is all about?"

"No," Gran replied, "that's not quite it."

"Well," Albert sputtered, "Clark doesn't cheat on people. And CLARK DOESN'T LIE!"

Gran's lips stiffened. "I know, Albert!"

"He DOESN'T! So I don't see what the problem is. And he always loved Mom, and not anybody else. I see him looking at her all big-eyed, all the time! Dad never did that! Mom's not just 'little love' to Clark - you can tell. And it's bigger than 'mushy' by a long shot. He loves her CRAZY-BIG."

Gran sighed.

"An' I think he loves her like 'live-in-a-house' love. It's like I'm the kid, and Mom's the mom, and Clark's the real dad. An ACTUAL dad, this time. This is where things are supposed to work out, Granny! Things don't break them apart!"

There was a tiny 'mew' from across the room. They stopped and looked over at Muriel. Muriel's eyes were wide and her tail was stiff and bushy.

"So if Clark doesn't lie, and if Mom loves him, and if he loves Mom, what the hell is the deal?"

Muriel stared at Albert with big moony eyes. Albert noticed and stared back.

"What?" he shrugged at the cat. "Granny, that cat is staring at me again. Make her stop it, will you? She's weirding me out. She thinks she's my spirit watcher, or something."

Granny sat him down at the table again. She sat with him and leaned forward. "Albert? Bad things happen, sometimes, but there's always a reason. We don't always know that reason. In fact, sometimes the reason is bigger and smarter than any of us. We just have to continue on. We just need to keep walking our path, wherever it goes. The reason is always with us. THAT'S real."

Albert wouldn't lean on the table. He sat apart, like a little post with messy hair and red cheeks.

His voice rose from desperation. "But I really LIKE Clark… can't he still be MY friend, if he isn't Mom's?"

CHAPTER FORTY-FOUR
Goodbyes and Forever

Evening dimmed the skies. People departed from the church. They offered Clark their condolences. In total, there were fourteen people. They filtered by and left him there. Except her. At the end, she was there next to him. She remained silent.

They were on the front step of the church. Clark stood there in his longcoat, watching nothing. His coat was the only thing that held him or comforted him. Riley tried to stand at his side. She didn't dare look in his face. She watched the ground and crunched her toes inside her shoes.

The city air wafted past them. It was white noise to their cheeks. It passed idly, like hours or years drifting by.

Finally, she took a breath. Then, another. Then, she spoke.

"Will you walk with me, for a bit?"

He didn't reply, but he didn't argue.

They left the front steps and walked in silence. Clark's shoulders hung from his frame like dead animals. His face looked broken - wrecked, and hanging from loose springs. In exhaustion, he moved to a bench, leaned down to it like an elderly man, and dropped. He sat there, blank faced.

The bench was at the edge of a park. It was a bus stop. Green grass lay behind them and rushing traffic was ahead. Riley sat near him. The two sat alone.

In front of them, buses growled to a halt. Strangers crossed between the buses and the sidewalk. All these people were real lives, and they all had one thing in common: they meant nothing to each other. They passed by without a thought, and then the buses coughed fumes and roared away.

One girl got off a bus, poking at her cellphone. Whoever 'Tyler' was, he wasn't answering her. She couldn't get through. She bared her teeth in frustration. After she stalked away, a young man emerged. He carried his wife's luggage in one hand. Neither he nor his wife spoke, but he held her carefully with his free arm. He tried to console her. Her face was numb. She'd lost something very important. She stared ahead without focus. Then, a guy wearing a backwards ball cap and headphones strode past them. He swaggered onboard and flung himself into a seat. Wherever he was going, he didn't care. Another dozen people followed after. Finally, there was a mother carrying her young daughter. She had four extra pieces of luggage. Tote bags and daypacks flapped like useless wings. She climbed on after the rest.

Riley watched them. These people all had hopes, and stories, and they were still strangers. They'd always be strangers, and she'd never see them again. She realized that she was one of them.

She sat straighter. Well, this is it, she thought. Time to face the music. I can't take anything back. I'll apologize, then I'll politely listen, and then we'll make plans for me to collect my stuff. At least... maybe I'll hold his hand one last time, before I have to leave. Before I have to start over.

She wanted to reach out to him, but it was like surgery with cement. He was inches away, but it felt like crossing an ocean. She slowly reached over toward Clark's arm. Her weak fingers touched his sleeve. Fingertips scratched along the cloth; they begged to be forgiven for touching him.

He didn't move. Even his arms were exhausted... or perhaps they didn't care. Clark knew she was right there, beside him, but he wouldn't respond.

He stared down to the cement sidewalk. That path was made of flat, square blocks, measured over a worthless patch of ground. No-one cared how many squares it took to reach a destination. The journey was always forgotten. In the end, the journey didn't matter. Worthless squares were the foundation stones of Ashvale.

His dad left him, and Riley left him, and now his mother was gone.

We all walk, he thought, and we walk alone. And we're alone, because our dreams are in our heads. That's all life is. That's all it can be. We can only be ourselves with our own little dreams. That's why we walk alone.

I've lost my whole family, and I've lost Riley. I'm alone. This is the most real that life ever gets.

A breeze crossed their faces. It wandered invisibly past them and slowed to nothing. When it stopped, it disappeared completely.

Then, Riley slipped her hand down to his. Her fingertips crept inside. They slowly weaved between his fingers, and he didn't pull away. He didn't respond.

The sidewalk has cracks, he thought. The road is cracked and broken. Some things can't be fixed. Sometimes, the road disappears. People wander, because they have no road. Who are they then?

Riley cupped his hand and looked over to him.

I want to die, she thought. Clark? I wish I was dead, and I wish your mom was still here. She was sweet, and lovely, and she was your family. And I'm absolutely horrible to you. I'm sloppy, and I'm difficult, and I'm ungrateful, and I'm HEARTLESS. And I'm lazy, and...

He held her hand sweetly. The warmth startled her.

Cracks, he thought. Of course. Sidewalk cracks?

Broken roads? They grow flowers. They do, don't they? Broken roads are still real, and they grow flowers, and they're beautiful!

She looked up to him hopefully. Her eyes widened. She squeezed his hand gently, trying to wring an answer out of him.

Please, her eyes begged. Please, my dear Clark... could you ever forgive me? ever? Just so I can live with myself? I can't go on if you hate me, Clark. Could you ever love me SO MUCH, that you could still care about me? even a little? after what I've done?

He clasped their hands tight. This was their bond. He smiled at it; THIS was real. This mattered. This endured. THIS. Always.

Clark? her eyes pleaded to him, Would you ever... EVER... love me again? Would you EVER love me?

"Forever," he declared out loud. He nodded at their hands. "Forever, Riley."

Of course, he thought. Who am I? I can only be me, and I can only love you. SCREW the sidewalk. Let's break roads together. Let's walk through weeds and flowers! I'll even go barefoot, if I can walk with you!

He clasped her hand with both of his. He looked at her face like looking into the sky, or looking into the future. Nothing could make her not-beautiful. When he was without his father, she was there for him. When he lost his mother, she was STILL there for him. Riley meant Everything to him, because that's who she always was.

She turned pale. Her breath rushed out and swept in again. Another torrent of breath escaped her body. They were long gusts of relief. He shrugged away his longcoat and gathered her inside it. He cupped her head against his chest.

WHAT? she blinked. How is he doing this? Why does he love?

They leaned against each other on that bench. Another bus stopped in front of them, but no-one got on. It waited for a minute, then rumbled off. Empty. Disgruntled.

His voice was flat. "We can talk about things soon… but I think I need you with me tonight. Really. So, will Albert be okay?"

"Umm… he's expecting me back at Granny Faye's… probably in an hour. Should I call?"

"Mmm. Granny Faye. I want to meet her, sometime, if that's cool."

"She'll adore you," Riley whispered.

Clark almost laughed.

She dug for her smartphone. It fell from her hand and skittered onto the sidewalk. Clark kept holding her there, but he reached out his long leg and tapped it back toward them. He twisted his body, stretched downward, and picked it up for her.

"Mmm - here," he grunted. He handed her the phone.

Whiffs of laughter blew from her nose. She took the phone, but she couldn't dial. She held it in her hand and looked at it. It was her link to real life: work, obligations, and day-to-day things. When she handled real life stuff, he was right beside her. Clark was there beside her, and that never changed.

Her cheek felt his warm chest. His breathing was her favorite song in the entire world. Her head moved with it like slow dancing.

Just one more minute, she decided.

He hugged her shoulder and smiled distantly. Something nameless and unfinished had been solved. They strayed far from the beaten paths of Ashvale Plains, and they still found their way.

"Hey," he smirked. "Thanks for the walk."

For about an hour, they sat on that bench beside the park. Then Riley started to notice things: the cool air, a kid playing with her dog, and the sweet smell of grass.

CHAPTER FORTY-FIVE

LAST JOURNEY

They rose from the bench. Clark steadied her.

"Gotta call Albert," he reminded her.

"Ya," she agreed.

They walked back to the church, where Clark left his car. He looked at her meekly and opened the driver's side door.

"Dear… would you mind driving? I'm pretty exhausted."

She nodded quickly. She was tapping her smartphone to call her grandmother's place. She put it on speakerphone as they drove out to the highway.

"Uh… Yeah, Granny Faye? It's me. It's Riley… and I'm good. I have you on speakerphone, here."

Granny's voice was thin and trembly: "Ohh, dear Riley, m'child - are you okay, Honeysweet?"

She sighed. "I'm better than okay. Uh, I think

Clark and I can talk, now. 'Good talking,' that is. I think we're okay."

There was an indistinct whooping sound in the background.

"Gran, is that Albert? Is he acting up?"

"NO, Silly-Head, that was ME! You and Clark? You're okay? Is he alright? Wait. You're on speakerphone, you said?"

Clark leaned closer: "So - you're Ms Faye McEwen, yes? Such a pleasure to finally hear your voice, ma'am. You brighten a dark day."

Riley watched his gentlemanly manners. She grew a lop-sided smile.

"OH! Well, Mr Clark, it's a meeting long overdue. Though, I am very sorry about your loss. My heart goes out to you."

He smiled faintly. "Thank you. She'll be missed, but I have faith that my mother's in good care now."

"Well, we're very grateful to have you with us, Clark. You've been missed on many occasions, yourself. Not just recently; I missed you at Riley's wedding. I know she did, too."

Riley recoiled.

Clark balked, "Uh - I couldn't attend, sadly." He pursed his lips.

"It was sadness all around, me dear Clark. Very mutual. Your present company is most welcome."

Clark puzzled over this.

Riley spoke up, "Hey, uh, Gran? Could Albert stay for a while longer? Clark and I have some catching up."

Gran rolled her eyes: "Oh, me - do you want to speak with the young rascal? Wait, here he-"

"HI MOM! It's me, Albert! Did you know Ed Wood made 'buncha movies a long time ago? They're SO FUNNY! I wish I could do stuff like... hey, are you okay? Did you ever get to talk to Clark? Can I see him sometime? I wanna see him."

Riley felt a glow. She almost spoke, but Clark leaned in again.

"Hey, man - it's me. Are you alright, over there?"

"Oh, hi! What happened? I didn't see you for, like, DAYS! Did you starve to death, or fall in a hole, or something?"

Riley made a 'sorry' face.

Clark considered. "Basically, YEAH. I fell into something like a hole. It was a bad one. I thought I lost everything. I can explain later; it's complicated. But, uh... hey, Albert?"

"Ya?" he perked up.

Clark waited. The seconds were long and heavy.

"Your mom rescued me."

Albert went quiet. Riley inhaled, set her jaw, and lowered her brow a little. What the hell was he doing?

"Your mom saved me, dude. You should know that. I think she might even be a ninja, like us." He looked over at Riley, who gripped the steering wheel and focused on driving.

"No she's notttt...! She's just Mom. She just takes care of everything."

Even over speakerphone, Clark raised his finger. "That's skills, Albert. And the fact is, NOBODY knew she was a ninja. So that means she's a natural."

Albert winced. "You're pullin' my leg."

"Nope. When people are silent, they always say 'Mum's The Word.' Right? So she's your mum, and she knows things that are unspoken. Totally mystical. Totally ninja.

"Look, your mom saved me. And your mom and I really love each other. Okay, buddy? That's not an unspoken secret anymore. It's bold-faced truth. I love your mom, and I always will."

The kid whined back, "Bahhh, you're always telling me this mushy stuff. Then Mom smooches you. And then she looks at you funny. And then I gotta stay overnight at Larsen's. You guys have some kind of habit."

Riley turned away, smirking.

Clark leveled with him. "Are you okay with staying at your Gran's? For tonight, anyway?"

"Ya, I guess. Clark? I miss you too. It's not JUST my mom who misses you. We gotta put patches together - maybe like one of Gran's quilts. Those are warm, like campfires and cottages. They must take a while, but they're totally worth it. We should be like that."

"Yeah," Clark agreed, "Campfires. I think I get it. So, seeya in a bit?"

"Ya. FINALLY," he sounded exasperated. "Don't get lost anywheres."

Clark nodded. "Deal."

Gran took the phone and added, "Imagine all that, but turned up to ten. That was Kim, first, and then you, Miss Riley."

Riley froze for a second. She thought she remembered something from when she was a kid. 'Miss Riley?' Did Gran call her that?

"Ma'am?" Clark asked her. "Perhaps I could help with things? Then, maybe you and Riley could spend more time together. You know - Girls' Night?"

Riley slowed the car a little.

Wait, she thought. Girls' Night? What? Like mom and I used to have? I never told Clark about that stuff. And I'm 'Miss Riley,' and he even brings me dresses like in my dreams? How do we fit together so well? Is this chemistry? No, bigger than chemistry. Astrology, maybe. Hmm... astronomy?

She steered toward Clark's place, thinking of his house. She thought of the kitchen, and the couch, and their warm bed. That house was waiting for her - expecting her. It was too big for just one person. It was planned for something bigger than Clark. Their fit was greater than the single pieces, alone.

"Ms McEwen, I know a bit about strained families, and how hard it can be. If I could help, you could spend more quality time together."

Gran spoke with royal dignity: "We'd welcome you as part of that, dear Clark. You seem a true gentleman. I'll be overjoyed to finally meet you in person."

"Thank you," he said. "Likewise."

They ended their call.

Clark said aside, "Your grandmother? She's enchanting."

"Mmm," Riley nodded back, absently. "Yeah. She does that."

The car was quiet for a while, except for the hushing sound of tires. Clark watched Riley's hands as she guided the wheel. He built himself up and finally spoke.

"Look, I gave up a lot from my career. It was tough, but I don't regret it. I did it for us. But now, I need you to do something for me."

"Yeah," she nodded. She looked over to him. "Anything."

"I need you to pursue your art. I want you to MAKE yourself in this world. Get out there. Be known. Forget carpe diem - seize the FIRE. You are Riley Henway... and this world has it comin'.

"I had my day, and now we're financially stable. But that's just a foundation stone. Let's do the real stuff, now."

She hesitated. "I'll..." She shook her head. She couldn't finish.

He turned to her shyly. He looked over her face, and to her eyes, and to her lips. He watched her whole profile as she focused on driving.

"I always wished I could be as smart as you."

He faced something monstrous inside. He looked in several different directions. She saw fear on his face when he closed his eyes and committed to these words:

"My dad was an asshole… but could I help care for your son, so you can do art? Can we do a trial period, where I could be a dad? Would that be okay?"

Riley bit her lip. Her hands tightened on the steering wheel. She drove straight. He continued.

"Your call. You wouldn't have to be a single mom so much. I'll still do grocery runs, I'll get art supplies, and I've already got most of the household figured out."

"Babe?" she replied, letting her head drop, "You already are his dad. And we're perfect, as things are. We can just be together. Just being 'us' will make me perfectly happy. We don't have to push my art. I want to be there for you, too. The art thing can rest. It had its time."

He paused. He chewed a little.

"NO," he stated firmly. "You LISTEN to me. You are a phenomenon. Something held you back, but this is where everything turns around."

She thought something flashed in the windshield. She felt a warmth spreading like wings around her.

"Your art is next-level. Your brilliance deserves to be widely known. We focus on your art, now."

Well, she thought, Clark just proved that it's never too late. Could I still do it? My art? A career?

"You will claim it," he growled softly, "and there's nothing more glorious than the comeback fight." He gazed ahead with a wolfish gleam.

She laughed once, smiled a little, then started to wonder.

Inside the car, they could see the whole world rushing by. She held the wheel and sat back to take a better look.

CHAPTER FORTY-SIX
THE VIGIL

Riley parked, and they both slowly walked up the driveway. She still didn't know if this stone path would welcome her, or if the door would be open to her ever again. She smelled the thyme growing between the stones. Somehow, this felt like another funeral. She grieved the life they'd had together.

She stopped half-way up the path. He held her shoulders and brought her the rest of the way, guiding her up to the doorstep.

"I don't know if I can cook a good dinner, right now." Clark slumped against the doorframe. His eyes were downcast. They looked like former residents of a strong face.

Riley held onto his arm, steadied him, then helped him inside. The sound of her shoes echoed from the tile floors.

"Uh - yeah," she replied. "No problem. I'll make something. I'll try. Just sit at the tabl…"

The glass window had been replaced. A potted plant stood in front of it; it was a nasturtium. Its little orange flowers were edible, so Clark had gotten it for his kitchen. It was a band-aid of home decor.

The same table was right there. It was back. Two of its legs had been repaired, but a long scar streaked across its surface. It looked like 'happy family' had been crossed out. The table looked aged and sad. Riley seated Clark there, but then she needed to sit down, herself.

"It's fine." He waved at the air and passed her his phone. "Cheap pizza. Just call this number. Say 'the usual.' They'll know by the caller display."

She tapped dial, and a surprised man answered. "The usual?" she requested.

Clark touched her arm: "…but no black olives, this time. They're gross, right?"

They waited in the kitchen without speaking. The order arrived. Clark made his way to the door, paid, and returned to see candles lit.

Candles. He hadn't seen candles in a while. Something inside him blushed to see this romantic gesture: dinner with Riley, with candles… again. They were such a sweet reminder of the past. He didn't know if those candles were there to torment him, or to greet him again faithfully.

Perhaps not 'faithfully.'

He sat down beside her.

"The good thing about MOST junk food," she said, "is that it can be eaten with one hand." Clark watched her open the box, lift a slice, and then take his hand. She held his hand the whole time.

For many lonely nights, he was a bachelor eating this pizza. He was reminded of being alone, in the quiet, missing her, with a swelling ache in his heart. But was she really here, tonight? or was she just passing through, in his bachelor life? He didn't know, but at least she held his hand.

That night, Clark kept a candle lit. It glowed on his nightstand. Riley thought it was for his mother; it wasn't.

Clark knew his mother was in good company. She followed every family elder who'd gone before. Wherever she was, she was surrounded by people who loved her, and to them, she'd finally come home. She'd never feel alone, ever again. This made Clark smile inside.

Their candle was a single flame that would keep burning all night. He wanted that light for Riley - for his sweetheart. They lay in bed together, in darkness, with that one candle watching over them. They lay in bed again, as they had many times before. He pulled her close and clasped his arms around her.

"Clark?" she whispered. "You know what I did."

He closed his eyes solemnly. He nodded once.

She braced herself. "I cheated on you, Clark."

The air seemed noisy. It felt like an angry, milling crowd around them.

He asked, "Can you talk to me?"

Her head wobbled slowly. "This house has been a shock. You and I weren't really... I mean, this has all been new, and strange, and we weren't... sorry, but it wasn't making sense. And then HE showed up, just that day. And it just reminded me of stuff."

Clark waited.

"Like, not good stuff, either, but something I knew. Not strange; not scary. Kind of stupid and idiotic, but familiar. Like a small town. The devil I know. Maybe if the devil was a whiny, overprivileged piece of..."

She sighed. He waited.

Clark finally asked, "Do you love him?"

She wheezed out breath. "I told him I'd murder him, Clark. I don't want to see his face ever again."

"...Do you LOVE him, Riley?"

She turned up to face him.

"I never loved him. And I said I'd kill him, if he didn't leave. And I meant it. And YOU - I said you'd pretty much eviscerate him. Wait, do you think he'll come after us? as mayor? He'll have lawyers."

"Nah," Clark answered confidently, "If I suffered that kind of disgrace, I think I'd leave the country. Or maybe I'd fake my own death and disappear. Cook up some fake evidence."

"Really? Like a cover-up?"

"Yeah. Politicians do it all the time. Why - did you hear about him on the news, lately?"

"Actually, no."

"That probably says something, in itself. So he only showed up that one day?"

She nodded sadly. "Mmm-hmm."

"And he only showed up to… what, chat? He was fishing for a booty-call?"

Riley looked up strangely.

"Ya, pretty much. That's pretty accurate, I think. How did you know?"

He squeezed her.

"We're both from Ashvale Plains. We both know these people. There are jerks, there are scum, and there are even a few predatory sociopaths. Some of them pretend they're popular."

He looked at her in the candlelight.

"But this guy… it was still Jeff, right? from high school?"

She nodded slightly.

"And somehow, umm… this wasn't rape?"

Her throat tightened.

"Okay. How did…? You don't love him, but… why?"

Clark's neck tightened. She clenched her teeth, and couldn't respond.

His chest went tight. "Somehow, he offered you comfort? Was that it?"

She nodded very faintly.

"Something I couldn't do." His teeth went on edge. "Is there anything else, here? Talk with me. I'll listen. I promise."

She took a few shallow breaths.

"It was just something I knew, and I slipped. Like trying to quit smoking, but then falling back into the habit. He pushed me off balance, and he grabbed me when I fell."

She turned to Clark.

"I was uncertain about this house. He shot me down, using that weakness. And then he caught me. I think he conned me."

"Mmm," he pondered. "The video surveillance, though? You set that up when he came in."

"I didn't even trust him, when... OH GOD - you saw that? Everything?"

"I saw your face change. I saw it go blank. I saw him chip at your confidence, wearing you down, till he edged in with his comforts."

The room went darker.

"And then you two kissed."

"It wasn't..." She choked. "It's a past I'm trying to leave behind, okay? Please understand that."

"...Sorry."

He dipped his head and swallowed pride.

"I have to know something. Is there anything you need, Riley, outside our relationship? I'm not really comfortable with this, but we could still talk, as adults. I could take care of you, as a partner, even if there's something I can't do for you. Maybe there's something another man CAN do.

"Uhh... am I competent enough, in the bedr... Do you... I mean, for your sexual health, do you need to see other men?"

"CLARK!" she yelped. "HELL no! That's the stupidest thing I've ever heard you say! You're more than I could ever hope for, and usually it feels like you're more than I can... mmf."

She shifted her hips. The corners of her mouth were shy to smile.

"Look, big fella, you're a force to be reckoned with. And some nights, I get pretty reckoned. And then really glowy."

"So," he continued, "you're mostly content with our bedroom life?"

"Clark, you're passionate. I am thoroughly content, and frequently. Believe me, this other crap was entirely different. It wasn't love. It wasn't like what we had, before. It was doubt. It was MY doubt. Then I flopped back in the gutter."

He held her head to support her.

"Well, what would anyone else do? You had an abusive father, you were treated horribly by your boyfriends, you had a crap marriage with a cheater, your artistic ambitions were shot down by everyone... you were lied to, cheated, and abused for your whole damn life. And here? Okay. So, I think you made a mistake. You felt something like comfort, and belonging, and you were drawn to it. You said it felt familiar? like a small town?"

She nodded. "Mmm-hmm."

"Yeah," he tipped his head. "Those are words for 'home.' I know how important that is. It's something we haven't totally worked out yet, you and me."

She didn't want to admit that fact. Words refused to happen.

"Jeff used that," Clark nodded, "or, he tried to." Satisfaction settled on his face.

She smiled vaguely. She breathed in small gusts.

He spoke steadily. "I want you back here with me. You and Albert. I want you both in my life, and you have to know that."

"You…" She scoffed lightly. "You want me? Somehow, you STILL want me?" She was quietly incredulous.

"You have to KNOW this, Riley." He slowly, solidly kissed her brow and rubbed her shoulders. He tried to press the meaning into her.

"Look, you made a mistake. You felt an old attachment, even though it was a bad one. It was like an abusive relationship, and a continuing cycle. So, maybe it's not your fault."

She couldn't move. He was right.

"Also, I can't change. Even when it's agony, I still love you."

You actually want me? she thought. Even now? Still?

"Look," he spoke softly, "When I held you at night, and you slept, your brow was clear as sky. Nothing but peace. And you were happy and grinny when I hung out with Albert… and he's your SON, for God's sake. You've loved me."

His eyes were still. He spoke low and held the back of her head.

"I need you to know. Allow yourself. Know that you're loved. KNOW that you're trusted. Just… be with me? Please?"

She looked up and asked, "And… you S-STILL… want me?"

He closed his eyes. They settled like warm blankets.

"I want you back. Come home to me, Riley."

She turned pink and red in her face. Her limbs fell loose. Her eyes seemed stunned.

"Are you alright?" he asked. He knew she wasn't.

Her lips parted and breath snaked out. She went still. First tears, then shaky, shivering breaths. Then sobs. Her feminine voice bent into tight, wrong shapes. Lumpy sounds fell out. Her breath jerked inward several times and a long cry flooded out.

She tried to curl into a ball. She just wanted to hide from everything she'd done. She crumpled like trash.

Clark gathered her in his arms. Warm tears fell onto his skin and ran down his shoulder. His face twisted, and his neck turned. Her crying tortured him inside. It was the worst thing his heart ever heard.

The candle was their only light. They lay together as dim shapes in the darkness.

Riley wept: stuttering gasps and long, broken wails. They were terrible, falling sounds that buckled at the end. Her inner child was hurt and alone. She pawed at Clark with feeble arms. Her cries rose, then fell back again into loneliness.

She seemed to choke, then struggle with gasps. Her face turned hard red. She tried to stop. She pushed out her palms, like 'enough.'

His voice was deep, like the ocean.

"No - it's okay. You can. You're with me."

He pulled her close.

"I think you need this, and I'll keep you safe. So... you can cry with me. You can. I just want to be with you."

A muted squeal built inside her, and she collapsed. Her breath stacked up like broken bricks, then tumbled back down again in sobs.

He held her, kissed her head, and rocked her gently. He tried to steel himself by clenching his jaw, but her sounds crippled him. Everything strong inside him crumbled.

She pulled air in her lungs and howled it back out. Her cries lurched at the end. He continued rocking her in his arms.

"I..." she wept. "I..."

She couldn't finish.

"Shh... no," he whispered to her. "No, it's okay. Tell me later."

"I d-..."

"Shhhh," he hushed. "No, Sweetheart. Shhh... shh-shh-shh... Let's take care of you. Talk another time."

"How? ...did- didn't know?"

His arms kept her close. Didn't know what? He wouldn't ask.

"I did- didn-..." she panted. "I didn't know. I can't believe I didn't know... how much..."

Her face tightened and shook like a fist. Her words were strangled before they could escape. Her eyes shone wide.

"Shhh..." he soothed her. "You're with me. Okay? Just rest."

He continued cradling her. Her head fell on his shoulder. Beads of tears ran down his neck.

She slumped. "I don't deserve... I just wanna die."

"No," he said firmly. "GOD no. I need you."

She tucked into him.

"I'm the worst person I know. I'm filth, and you treat me like treasure. And I don't deserve this, Baby. I'm a terrible, terrible person. How do you still care about me?"

"I know who you really are."

"Then you're crazy," she sobbed. "And you proved it. After all this time, after twenty years, and I got married, and even after what I did, you STILL somehow love me. JESUS, Clark. You must be insane."

"Well, is that okay by you?" he joked. Then he looked away.

"Clark," she squeezed her eyes shut. "Your mind is golden. And your body is, well... rather drool-inducing, to be completely honest. But your heart? I'm afraid your heart is nuts. Your heart is a madman."

She sniffled.

"Your heart is insane, and hell-bent on one, sole purpose - no matter how stupid that purpose is, or how much of an airhead, or how much of a broken, pathetic, absolute screwup."

He held her still and looked her in the eye.

"No. It's not madness. It's you. How do you do it? You reach inside me, and you reach impossibly far. You touch the REAL me, inside, and it's terrifying. Are you partly me, somehow? Are you my soul? Or are you an angel?"

His brow tightened and his eyes begged for an answer. He whispered close.

"The way I love you... did you create me? Are you an angel?"

His thumb stroked her cheek. He waited, but she said nothing. He touched their heads together.

"All I know is, you make 'me.' You make TRUTH, inside me. That doesn't even make sense, to hear it, but I mean it. You're Truth, not madness. You're royalty in my world.

"You do NOT belong amongst frail beauty."

Her chest released. Her breathing swept in and out slowly, but easily. She breathed for the first time in a new part of her life.

He stroked the hair of the broken, abused, scarred girl who constantly struggled. He watched, as something was pulled away - something like a blockage. Her arms drooped off his chest. She went restfully limp. She had no need for walls; she was very loved, and very strong. She knew, now… and nothing prevented her from sleep.

"Shh," he hushed gently. His fingers sifted through her hair.

She was surprised at herself. Where was her father? Where was Jeff Anders? Where were her teachers? Where was Colleen Dietrich? Where was Jonno? Where was her boss, at the Greek diner? She could remember their faces, but she couldn't hear them. They couldn't hurt her anymore. They were like the TV, when it was turned off.

The candle stayed lit all night. It reminded Riley of campfires and stories from her childhood. She couldn't really remember the stories, but she remembered the fire. Those memories meant something, because of it. Tonight, the two of them huddled beside their own little fire. They borrowed from an ancient tradition.

As she was fading into dreams, she remembered being five years old. She'd tried jumping over a ditch somewhere, but fell backwards and bruised her leg. She'd started hobbling home, but her mom found her, lifted her up, and carried her by piggyback.

She had no idea that her mother was so strong. She admired her for that, but she felt something else. It was something even stronger, and it couldn't be put into words. Back then, she thought her mom would always be there to hug her or carry her. It was her mom; this was what moms did. This was what she believed as a child.

Many years later, she slept in strong arms. A candle watched over her. She breathed easily all night; she rested on Clark's heart.

CHAPTER FORTY-SEVEN

STARLIGHT

The next night, Albert watched a movie with them. He sat next to his mom and checked on her often. Clark hugged her with one arm, but he also reached down to hold her hand. Albert still didn't understand how adults got lost from each other.

By the time the movie was over, Riley yawned and stretched like a cat. It was getting late.

"Hey," she looked up to Clark. "I think it's prob'ly bedtime. 'Wanna throw some blankets on monster boy? Just dump clean laundry on top, till he can't move. We'll dig him out tomorrow."

Clark's eyes wrinkled with smiling.

"…You love him to the moon and back, don't you?"

She nodded happily. Her lips said "Oh, ya."

"Hey, Albert?" Clark turned to him.

"I don't wanna go ta bed."

"It's bedtime, pal."

"I don't WANNA go ta bed!"

"Okay, kiddo," Riley sighed. "But you gotta get some sleep sometime. Lie dormant now, so you can terrorize the planet tomorrow."

"I don't wanna. I wanna stay up and see this movie."

Albert pointed at an upcoming movie. It had zombies, cannibals, and tentacled aliens. All the heroes wore short skirts.

"Why?" Clark said. "You'll know what's gonna happen every single minute. It's THAT kinda movie. I bet you could write a better script in your sleep, dude... I bet you could prove it."

"I don't wanna go to bed. I'm not even tired."

"No, kiddo. You have to," Riley sighed again. "And I have to get some rest too. Everybody does."

"Then YOU go to sleep." Albert crossed his arms. "I'll stay up. You two go fall asleep an' snore at each other."

Clark shrugged. "Alright, but I was gonna tell you about secret stuff. Powers that get embedded in your mind. Old-school passive meditation. I was hoping tonight would be the night."

The kid went stiff. "What?"

Clark's hand wafted dismissively.

"Whatever. Watch tentacle movies. Your mom and I can learn psychic meditation. Seeya in the morning."

"Wait. You're trying to trick me, aren'tcha Clark? What are you talking about?"

He turned to Riley. He stroked his jaw.

"We need a quieter place than here. A safer place. Someplace where we can practice the more secret arts. Away from... you know... HIM."

"Mmm," she agreed cryptically. "Well, there's the den. He's not going to bed, right?"

Clark stood and helped her up.

"That works. Well, ANYWAY... G'night, Albert."

Albert sat up.

Clark took Riley's hand again. They headed toward the den; this was where Albert slept at the time.

Clark muttered to her, "I'm thinking of making an addition to the house. Maybe near the kitchen area. A room for Albert? He needs better windows."

Little feet snuck behind them. Clark heard, but didn't let on.

"Yeah. He needs to see constellations, if the akashic knowledge is going to take root in his brain. Right now, when he sleeps, he only gets a third of the psychic power. I want him to absorb more."

"Aww. You're always looking out for my kid." Riley squeezed his hand.

Albert squawked, "I HEARD THAT!"

"Jeez LOUISE!" Clark flinched. "Ya almost gave me a heart attack, ninja-stealth boy!" He scowled back at Albert, who beamed with pride.

"Look, bedtime doesn't mean SLEEPING. We're

just gonna sit and have a man-talk. Secret wisdom. It's the foundations of a ninja clan, you know. Oh - your mom can listen in, too. She keeps secrets for decades."

Riley's nails dug into Clark's hand a little.

At the den, Clark waited outside. Riley tried to fit Albert into his pajamas, but he wouldn't budge.

"I'm STAYING UP, Mom." He pouted sideways.

Clark spoke back to him from the doorway.

"You need to be comfortable to absorb all this. You can't have distracting, pinchy clothes. This is why ninjas dress the way they do - black pajamas, right? Did you ever see a ninja wearing a big, bulky, three-piece suit?"

"Maybe that GUY. That friend of yours. Is he in on this, like you are?"

"Oh yeah. He is. He's a ninja, too. But that's his disguise, right? Suits. He texted me today, 'cuz he caught some more bad guys - like those thugs who weren't really cops. He had to use 'fake clothes' to do that, to blend in - his suits. Not his... you know, his black pajamas."

Riley looked to Clark, who still stood patiently in the doorframe.

"Was this your friend Matt? the guy in the suit?"

"Yeah," he replied. "That's him. See, we don't even hear about it. He was a shadow - just another fella with a nice coat. You'd never know, would you? But that's ninja stealth, for ya...

"So Albert, you need to get your jammies on. Be a

real, committed ninja. We'll find some AUTHENTIC black pajamas for you soon. Black pajamas for night-time meditation."

"I'm not going to sleep, but maybe we can talk about stuff. Did ninjas ever use an uzi gun?"

Riley winced. She tugged his pajamas around him.

"W-... An uzi?" Clark asked.

"Ya. There's this gun that sounds like 'br-br-br-br-br,' really fast. It's way better than ninja stars, and it's bullets, instead."

Clark turned his head. "Actually, Albert, it was the other way around."

Albert paused, then jumped down into his sheets. He needed to hear this.

"Yeah," Clark continued. He walked in and sat next to Albert.

"See, in later years, ninja clans were absorbed by the Japanese special forces. So, ninjas didn't use modern stuff. Instead, today's militaries used THEM."

Riley listened. She wondered how in the heck he'd turn this around. Clark talked about special ops teams and what really made them strong. He talked about brotherhood, and unity, and how it was a team's greatest strength. Warriors have always been about fellowship and honor.

He looked carefully at Albert.

"So, you and I get along, right? And your mom loves you to bits. We're on the right track."

Albert rolled on his side.

"Ya. But you and Mom aren't warriors, or anything."

Clark looked over his glasses skeptically. He nudged his head toward Riley. "She survives everything, just like you. Trust me - your mom's a warrior. She's a forever guardian, like a guardian angel. She's like… 'bring on the hot sauce.' She really is that tough."

He looked Albert in the eye.

"Dude? Moms are hard core." He leaned in and fussed with Albert's pillow. "Here - get comfy."

The kid gave him a funny look.

"Do you tuck my mom in? or is she YOUR guardian, too?"

Clark stopped for a second. No, he always guarded her. He wrapped his arms around her and held her close, every single night. He clasped her to his own living heart. In the mornings, he only snuck away to make her breakfast.

The kid beamed at him.

"Wait a sec - Clark, do you? D'you tuck her in, and sing her lullabies? Do you read stories to her? You're probably a pretty good dad, but she's WAY too old for that stuff."

Clark tried to keep a straight face, as any 'pretty good dad' would. He finally peered back at him.

"First: your mom's not old. But lullabies? Yes and no."

Riley glanced up at him.

He closed his eyes solemnly, "I'll tell you the

truth. I don't sing it, but there's a lullaby for her. It's hers, and nobody else's; she's special."

"Whaddya mean, it's HERS?"

"Hmm?" She was genuinely curious. "Wait, I have a lullaby?"

Clark shrugged and nodded - of course Riley had her own lullaby. Albert, naturally, needed to hear it.

"What is it? Sing it!" By now, he'd completely forgotten about tentacle-alien movies.

"What?" Clark protested. "You want to hear her lullaby?"

"Uh-huh! What is it?"

"Ya, Clark," Riley grinned. "Maybe we should hear it."

He shook his head at the kid, hesitating. "I dunno... I'd sing this to you, man, but only because YOU might be special, like your mom. I wouldn't do this for anybody else. I haven't sung it before."

"What?" Albert was mystified. "You didn't sing it to her?"

"Ya, Clark," she blinked up at him, "You didn't sing it to her?"

"Will you two just...?!" He fumed in comic frustration. He pouted like a cartoon bulldog.

"Arright, you two. You're both ganging up on me. Not fair at all! This was meant for your mom, because she's special. But you, Albert?"

He tipped his head back and forth. He squinted at the kid. He was gauging Albert's special-ness.

"Well... yeah, you're special enough... I GUESS."

Clark flashed him a twinkly eye. The kid giggled. Riley's lips rose; they swelled right up to the brim.

Albert listened carefully while Clark explained:

"Okay. When I was just a bit older than you, I'd look up at the night sky… and I'd really miss your mom. With my hand over my heart, sometimes I'd even pray a little. You know the song *'You Are My Sunshine,'* right?"

"That's not a lullaby!"

"Ya, well, I sometimes sang this version at night, when no-one else would hear it. It's different. I hoped the stars would be listening, and maybe they'd tell her. Do you really want to hear this?"

"Mmm-hmm!"

Riley leaned back beside her son and added, "Ya, I prob'ly wouldn't mind." She looked up expectantly.

"Okay." He sat straighter. "Don't laugh! And I can't sing, so don't expect perfection."

He took a few breaths. He closed his eyes. In that quiet room, his song was like a prayer.

"You are my starshine,
Belovèd starshine.
You are my angel
In sacred night.
You have my heart, and
All that which was mine…
You are my love,
And my soul,
And my light."

* * *

The room was silent for a moment.

"That's not so bad," Albert said quietly. He puzzled a little. "What do you mean, light? How can someone be light?"

Clark held his shoulder. "You're a light. A light is something that's so clear to us, it guides us. It's something truly good. It helps us find the right way.

"You guide me, because you really are that important. Other things aren't. Because of you, I know what matters. And your mom's a light, also - so I'm really lucky, because I have TWO!"

There was no way Albert's arms could reach around Clark. He sat up and hugged his arm, instead. When he flopped back down on his pillow again, his brown eyes shone happily.

Riley looked at them as they continued talking. She couldn't quite smile. She watched them and played with her hair. She watched as Clark sat with her son - making him feel safe, helping him go to sleep.

According to her son, Clark was 'probably a pretty good dad.'

CHAPTER FORTY-EIGHT
What Lies Beneath

Months passed. They were bright days, cool nights, and mornings of new sunshine. It was a rhythm of healing.

One morning, Clark leaned over Riley's pillow and kissed her brow. She smiled, cooed softly, but didn't open her eyes.

"Love?" he whispered. "Albert has a history quiz today. I'm going to make sure he's all set, and then I'll take him to school. I'll be right back. I'll bring you something. And a coffee."

"Mmm-kay, ya..." she sighed. She yawned, reached, and stretched. He gazed down at her. He pulled the blankets up and tucked them around her back. She made happy whining sounds, like a puppy.

He warmed her shoulder with his hand. He stood there and admired her lips for a moment - the most beautiful lips in the world. He decided to visit them.

A higher voice sang from the kitchen.

"CLARRRK! Do I gotta go to school? Can't I be sick, today?"

Mid-kiss, they both chuckled. He rose up, winked at her, then strode toward the kitchen.

"NOPE! Put on your rock star pants, big guy - today you conquer."

"What?"

Riley heard them fussing in the kitchen. Clark grabbed some things in the fridge.

"Your big brain, my man, is gonna tell the world who you really are. Yep! Today's a big battle, and you're gonna WIN. Man, oh man... I can't wait to hear all about it, this afternoon."

A glass clinked. Something thick poured into it.

"Clark, I don't even drink that smoothie healthy stuff. It has green-grass in it."

"WHEATgrass. No, don't drink it. It's vitamins. 'Same reason you don't put nitro in your family car. Right? 'Cuz then it turns into a speed demon."

Albert was puzzled for a second.

"...Whadda you talkin' about, Clark?" Riley could even hear Albert's hands flapping down onto the table.

He spoke furtively to Albert, "You want to share another ninja secret? Sneak some of these vitamins into your chocolate milk, here. Today is the mission, young master. Prepare. You will vanquish your history quiz."

"That's not ninja stuff," he squawked. "That's just your smoothie stuff in my chocolate milk."

"This is how secrecy works," Clark told him. "It's an art form. It's why ninjas are so powerful; they want other people to THINK this is just chocolate milk. But you and I both know that it has secret vitamins that make you stronger, and faster… even faster in the mind! Do you think ANYBODY else knows this? Nope. Secrecy. Drink this, and you're learning the true art of the ninja."

Relative quiet. Then, Albert slurped his glass.

"Why do you know so much? You must've done really good… done really WELL, with school. How come you know all this?"

"I was preparing, Albert. I hoped that someday, maybe, I might get to meet you. And maybe your mom, if I was real' lucky."

"No! Real-LY lucky." The kid shuffled his backpack on.

"Ah, right," Clark opened the door. "Really, REAL-LY lucky. Thanks, man. See, I need you around to help me with this sort of-"

The door closed. Riley turned over and bunched the blankets into her face. She was smirking so hard, she had to press into the duvet, and the sheets, and she nuzzled with that happiness till she dropped off to sleep.

Maybe half an hour later, she woke again. She'd been dreaming about her old home, when she was a teenager. She had chilly nights, sleeping on that old couch. She'd wear two sets of socks to keep her feet warm. The clock always ticked like a stern, ceremonial march, or like the slow drum at the gallows.

She woke and opened her eyes. She heard a tick. Then another. It came from Clark's bookcase, across from the bed. It was no clock. It wasn't a timer. It was like a radiator, or something heating and cooling.

She scowled a little, then sat up. All was quiet.

Yet, there it was again.

"Athena? Is anyone else in the house?"

Composite voices replied, "Good morning, Miss Henway. No, you are the only one currently on the property."

Riley hesitated. "Umm… Athena?"

The guardian's response was immediate. "Yes, ma'am?"

"What's that ticking?"

Athena stayed silent.

Riley sat straight. "Athena?"

"Yes, Miss Henway?"

"I asked you, what's that ticking?"

Athena wouldn't answer.

Riley got up and found her bathrobe. She scratched her head, then turned to listen. Nothing. Then, another tick. It was coming from the bookcase.

"Athena, what's that TICKING sound?"

Athena wouldn't answer.

Riley walked forward, closer to the bookcase. She stopped and listened. Two more ticks.

She froze in place with her ears straining. It ticked again.

She glanced over the books, taking several off the shelf. He had some weighty old volumes, up there. Some were classics, some were poetry. Some were old scientific works, including many studies on Leonardo da Vinci. They were actually written in Italian. Clark must have studied Da Vinci from the source.

A few books focused on a single poem. A whole book was dedicated to William Blake's poem, *The Angel*.

The bookcase ticked. *The Angel* ticked. Riley very slowly touched the dust jacket. It was surprisingly cold. She tried to pull out the book, but couldn't.

"Athena - what the hell is this? Frickin' ANSWER ME, dumb robot!"

No answer.

The dust jacket ripped. Underneath, it wasn't a book. It was a steel block welded to the bookcase.

"Athena, I have Protocol One clearance. I demand to know what's going on with this bookcase. Is it a safe, or something?"

The guardian voices replied, "I'm sorry, Miss Henway. Insufficient security clearance."

"It's Protocol ONE, dammit."

"I apologize, Miss Henway. You do not have sufficient security clearance."

Riley's pulse rose. She thought she heard Clark's car pulling in. Then, she recognized the car door slamming. He was home.

Riley set her jaw. "Hey Athena? Okay, bot-head. You protect the house, right?"

The voices replied, "Yes, Miss Henway, I do."

"I'm Protocol One. That means I have full access to this house, don't I? You give me access."

"Correct, ma'am."

"And YOU'RE part of the house, right? So I have access to you, in this house... So, Athena? With my Protocol One clearance, I want you to access yourself. Access Athena. Open up a new userbase entry. I'm Riley Ann Henway, Protocol X."

She'd heard Clark mention Protocol X once or twice.

Athena beeped loudly.

"Granted," the voices said. "Welcome, Angel."

Just then, Clark opened the front door. He called out to Riley. The wind from the open door ticked the bookcase rapidly.

"Athena, LET ME IN THROUGH THE BOOKCASE."

Steel and concrete clanged from the wall. Riley jumped. Her hand clutched her heart. Two more massive booms followed, like Stonehenge falling onto train tracks. The bookcase split and hummed open. She faced a dark, open passage, and a series of concrete steps leading down. It was a spiral staircase - a hollowness in the foundations of their home.

In the kitchen, she heard a paper bag fall. She heard a coffee cup crunch onto the floor. She heard the splatter of coffee on the kitchen tile. Clark panicked and came running.

"No, no, NO NO NO, RILEY! RILEY! RILEY, NO!"

He ran to her, but stood at the entrance to their bedroom. His eyes were wild. His hand clamped over his mouth.

Riley stood there, shocked. She was trapped between a frantic Clark and this yawning, black stairwell. It was a hidden underground... right next to his wall closet full of black suits.

"Oh, sweetest love... no." He collapsed. He fell to his knees. His voice shook, like it would fall out. "Please, My Love. PLEASE, My Heart... please, no..."

She watched Clark wither. She looked back at the dark passage. She knew it wasn't going anywhere; she carefully started walking over to Clark.

"Clark?" she asked meekly. "W-... What'd I just do?"

His hand gripped his mouth. Tears bled down his face. He sucked in air and wobbled forward as if he'd vomit.

"Clark," she began quietly, trying to soothe him. "Clark? Can you tell me what this is? Can you tell me where this goes?"

He took her hand and held it lovingly. He bent his head right down to her feet.

She asked gently: "Clark? Is this a government safe-room?"

At her feet, he shook his head.

She asked sadly, "Is this a fallout bunker, in case of war?"

He slowly shook his head.

"Clark." She rested her hand on his shoulder. "I love you with all my heart. You know this. But if I see where this goes… will WE be okay?"

He sobbed. She felt his hot breath on her toes, and sudden, trickling tears.

Would they be okay? He shook his head 'No.'

He rolled onto his side. She sat close by and stroked his hair.

"I love you, Clark."

He shook his head.

"Babe, can you hear me? Can we take this slow? Please? I'm gonna need to understand. Alright?"

He breathed long and deep. It was forced, like through a mask.

"We can do this," she started. Her lip trembled. Her voice rippled. "I love you, big guy."

She had a strong feeling that this was the end. She tried to save their relationship anyway.

"I love you, Clark."

He lay there and shook his head 'No.'

"I LOVE you, dammit! I mean it!" She took hold of his arm and shook it. She tried to convince him.

He shook his head 'No.'

She sobbed, "Sweetheart, I don't understand now, but I love you and I trust you. I love you, my sweet man."

His throat wheezed like a death-rattle. He held on

to her hand with humble reverence. He held her fingers like they were the silk that became the light that created the universe.

It exhausted him when he tried to speak. His face was the portrait of loss. Finally, he whispered words. They were thin like cobwebs:

"PLEASE DON'T LEAVE ME…"

For the next ten minutes, that was all he could say.

Riley's face fell further and further. She sank into this realization: everything was over. They were finished. Their dream was broken. She'd really loved it, while it lasted.

Life is short, and all good things come to an end.

She stroked his back - up and down, up and down. The open stairwell gaped at them. It was a strange darkness, and it wouldn't go away. It was a cold mouth yawning open from its black heart.

Wait, she thought. This might be worse than breaking up. I might actually have to run… REALLY run. But I'd never escape the government. I can't get away from Athena. And I don't think I could run faster than Clark. I know Albert couldn't. If this is worse than a government safe room… and if it's worse than a nuclear fallout bunker…? Either of those could get me killed!

It's not a safe room, and not a fallout bunker, but something even worse? and I found it? I'm a loose end, now. Does Clark have to silence me? Is that how I 'leave' him? Am I going to die?

She shivered. The thought of Clark killing her was the worst thing she could imagine. She had to face this terror now.

Maybe he'll be kind, she thought. Maybe I'll beg him to make it painless. If I begged him, he'd do that for me… wouldn't he? And could he find a place for my son? He's still Clark; would he raise my little boy?

She sniffled, wiped her nose, and tried to be brave.

"I'm sorry, big guy, but I need to ask: is this one of those government things, where *'you could tell me, but you'd have to kill me?'* Is it a black suit thing?"

He curled up and hid his face. His jaw clenched. His whole skull tightened.

"Your career had some serious stuff." She took a breath and refocused. "So right now, do I have reason to fear for my life?"

He went still. He had barely enough breath for these words:

"You'll run, anyway. You will. It's just instinct." His hand tightened on hers. "For what it's worth, I am deeply sorry."

Riley squeaked. Her face went sickly pale.

"I know nothing, Clark. Nothing at all. I just heard some babble about Icarus, and I didn't follow. I don't know anything! And I didn't say ANYTHING to Albert - NOT A THING! If you ever loved me, you can't hurt my little boy!"

She tried to pull away, but his hand tightened again. She couldn't escape.

His voice took a sudden clarity.

"No, this... IS A LOT WORSE THAN ICARUS." He swallowed. "It's worse than government. It's worse than military. I'd never, ever hurt you, My Love... but you'll still run. We're, uhh... yeah, we're finished. Please know that I'm very, very sorry."

She puffed a quick laugh. She shook her head rigidly. She was bewildered.

"No...!" she scowled at him. "What is this, then? Can you walk me through this?"

He rolled his head, stared at nothing, and finally answered, "I have to. You deserve the truth. I really, really can't do this, but I will. For you."

She slowly stood. He rose up on his knee, tried to balance, but then pitched sideways. His elbow boomed against the floor. His hair whipped and stuck to the sweat of his brow. He panted and crawled. He swallowed, like trying not to be sick. He staggered up, swung about drunkenly, and finally managed to stand on his own.

The two stepped toward the blackness. The cold air of the stairwell shocked her. He took her hand and looked at her.

"I'm so sorry, my darling." He offered her one, final smile.

Together, their feet found the first concrete stair. He turned to her again.

"ATHENA?" he commanded.

"Yes, Mr Benjamin?" the chorus answered.

He stood tall and bitter-faced. "Athena, OFF."

The room hushed. New round lights glowed above the stairwell, lighting the passage.

"Huh? Is she actually gone?" Riley asked.

"Unless you call her, she's asleep. Would you feel safer with her around?"

She hugged his arm and shook her head.

"Good," he said quietly, "because she's not allowed down here."

The spherical lights trailed downward, down this rabbit hole to the unknown. Riley noticed that the steps were swept clean. The stairs spiraled down a full circle, and then another. It reached a large, underground room that was softly lit. Riley slowed. She saw how well decorated it was; it had the same taste and thoughtfulness as a museum, or maybe a gallery. A wealth of red silks bathed it in luxury. Light played upon works of gold.

"Riley? You are walking through the darkness of my soul. I never thought I'd tell you about this in our lifetimes. This is my-…"

The strength of his eyes shattered. Two tears tapped the floor.

"This is your shrine."

The floor was laid expertly with cedar and decorated with huge, thick, rich rugs. The rugs reminded her of something - something from an old movie about the East. Ebony, gold and glass made clean displays and furniture.

Her brows pinched oddly. Her voice hopped:

"M-My... what did you say?"

He knelt down to the floor again. His face twisted with soul-gutting shame.

"I have ALWAYS loved you. And I've always missed you, and longed for you. And those aren't so bad, but the intensity...? It's just wrong."

Riley looked at tidy displays of photos. All of them were familiar. She wandered over to one of them. He lifted his hand toward it.

"Dear?" he started. "That? It's your grade three photo. You were a cute kid. Of course."

He gestured to the glass case where she was standing. It was air sealed and well lit inside. A red, silken background held a golden picture frame with Riley's school photo. Next to the photo was a cut negative. Back then, the photographer used real film. The photos came from negatives.

That photo - and all others like it - came from that single negative. Somehow, Clark found the absolute origin of her school photo. It was the actual film material that Riley's light had touched, twenty-five years ago.

"And, uhh... so that's up through high school." He pointed at a series of other glass cases. They all had silken couches. They had similar golden frames and negatives.

"Some are from yearbooks. One was a valentine for Jeff Anders; that one's kinda hard. He, uh... threw it out. But I found it, and I kept it."

She wandered among the glowing displays.

"That one's from the local newspaper. Remember after high school, when you got that art commission? Do you remember that?"

Her voice was thin as a ghost. "Y-yeah... I was proud of that. Do you really have that newspaper?"

"Yes, I do. I have the original text and graphics they used. There were other photos and comments, though, and I found that material in their archives.

"Do you remember Professor Piersen? the older fellow? He was still old, even back then. He said a few things about your art, but the paper cut it for saving space. That was really stupid of them. Read about it there, if you want. It's what Professor Piersen said. It's what was SUPPOSED to be printed in the paper about your work."

Riley approached a carefully preserved document and read aloud:

"She is true, artistic talent, and she deserves recognition. She will be significant; she will be known. Young Miss Henway has strength, identity, and incomparable depth-of-insight. Appreciate her work now, and you'll smile proudly in the future. That future is hers. This, I promise you."

Clark half-smiled. "For an old guy, he was pretty excited."

Riley laughed, amused. "I remember him; that was very flattering."

Clark stopped her. "No, he was a prof. He's professional about the truth. He was excited because of your genuine talent. He wasn't kidding.

"And over there? Same thing. More clippings. People who acknowledged you. They didn't get 'officially' quoted, either. Total media fumble. Ashvale sucks."

She paced ahead a few steps. "What's this paper here? The display with the chair in front of it?"

It took him a moment to respond.

He whispered, "Oh, Sweetheart... that's a little note you wrote to me in French class. Grade eleven. September 23rd. Someone was picking on me, but you took my side. Yeah, I kept the note. See?"

She approached it. She read her own handwriting - something she'd written back in her teens:

"Hey - don't worry, dude. She's a TWIT.
No-one likes her.
But I like you!
One point for Team Clark!"

He smiled a little. "Riley, you're adorable. And that made me glow like a lightbulb."

"But what's with the chair? Something about school?"

"No. I just love your handwriting. I looked at those words a lot. I was appreciating the hand that wrote them."

"Oh." Her eyebrows jumped.

He mumbled, "Yeah. I might have spent a few hours appreciating that paper, and wishing I could hold that hand. So I needed a chair."

When she wrote that little note, she'd also been drawing portraits of Clark and deeply enjoying it. They'd both been in their separate worlds, each of them dreaming about the other.

"We were ships passing in the night," she mused.

She stopped and stood straight. "Wait - is that picture..." She pointed at a larger photo. "Oh, no, Clark. That's my wedding." She stepped backward.

Clark managed to smile. "And you were beautiful. Everyone knew it. And that's your grandmother, right? Look at how she's hanging off your arm. You were enchanting! Look at you."

Riley turned. "No, Clark - she knew about you. She was there beside me for EMOTIONAL SUPPORT."

The air died. He turned to her in that frigid silence. Something like shock and terror rushed through his face.

"At your wedding?"

Riley nodded to him. "She knew about someone else, anyway. It really WAS you! C'mon, this is Gran... she knows everything." Riley exhaled through a smile. "She didn't know your name. But she could read about you, in my eyes. You and I loved each other, and she knew about it. Even back then. Even on my wedding day."

She did a double take.

"Wait a sec. When did you collect all this? I mean, we LIVE together. You're actually a father figure to my son, now. How did this whole collection…" She flapped her hand aimlessly. "How'd this happen?"

He scratched his head. "This IS a government fallout bunker; I just use it for what's really important. See, after high school, I missed you terribly. I found a photo or two. Then I found another photo. And another. I admit, I was obsessed with you. Athena never had any role here, just so you know; I kept her out of it."

He lifted his palms and spoke matter-of-factly. "It was just a love that never, ever went away. I couldn't deny it."

"Oooh, I tried," she sighed. "Dated people, got married, etc. That's pretty big denial." She elbowed him. "Y'know, if I hadn't been in such denial, I'd have a few scrapbooks under the bed, myself."

This was more than a few mementos. There were several textbooks she'd doodled in during math class, a few rejected applications for student bursaries, and even the can of root beer that she'd been drinking at a Christmas party.

Riley's eyes looked left and right. She tried to sort her feelings like warm, fluffy laundry; things were tangled, but very cuddly.

She tugged his arm. "Hey, what's that box? The huge one, there, with the remote thingie on it?" She pointed to a five-foot-tall plastic container.

"Uhh…" he stalled. "That's a shipping crate. The last crate from a manufacturer. Remember that shampoo you used back in high school? The company discontinued it. The manufacturer shut down their line completely. So it wasn't available in North America, but I tracked down one last crate of it in Denmark. That's a few dozen bottles, right there.

"You sat next to me in some of our classes, so I kinda knew what your hair smelled like. It took me a while to find the actual shampoo, but I did. This was what your hair smelled like a long time ago - grade eleven or twelve."

Her eyes bolted open. Her jaw fell.

"Oh my God! Are you serious? SERIOUS serious? I loved that stuff! I was so bummed out, when the stores stopped selling it! Can I… could I, like, have a bottle? to use again?"

He reared back.

"WOULD you?" A sudden thrill raced through him. "Yes! Please! Definitely! Uh, that'd be… 'Riley's Hair,' just like in high school…"

He hid a giant sigh. His pupils dilated.

"Holy crap," he smiled. "Yeah. Nostalgic."

"Clark? Back then, I twiddled my pencil in my hair when I was thinking of you. Now I'm staring my dreams in the face. You get that, right? This shampoo is gonna remind me of the young, dashing gentleman from my teenage years."

They shared a blushy smile, and she broke down to snickering.

"Seriously, man? Fate played a mean joke on us for SO LONG."

She stepped forward again. Clark stood at her side.

She smiled at the crate. A few dozen bottles? She could go down memory lane and revisit high school - revisit youth. One's hair is one's identity, and she had a chance to be a teenager again. She could be gutsy, punky, smart-alecky… ready to take on the world! This time, though, she would NOT be shy about kissing her high school crush. Heck no. She'd kiss the living bejeezus out of poor ol' Clark.

She stepped closer and picked up the stereo remote from the crate. Clark blushed even worse.

"Yeah," he muttered. "Memories of your hair."

Her brow twisted dubiously. "A stereo remote?"

His smile peeked. "Hmm. Press play."

She clicked the button. Soft piano music followed - tones winding and mysterious, like perfume. Music rose from stillness only to offer its hand, and to lead her heart in its slow-circling dance.

He tipped his head. "Chopin's Nocturne, in B flat minor, Opus 9, Number 1." He shrugged. "Your hair. The elegance; the shine; shapes like an autumn wind. How it sweeps behind you, as you walk. Beauty's aura - it follows you wherever you turn."

She stood there, in that chilly space, and listened to Chopin. They were sounds of brief, meaningful caresses; the feel of almost-kisses. It was the melody of terrible, agonized longing.

He stepped behind her and touched her arms. He folded her bathrobe closer around her to keep her warm, or maybe to protect her from something she might not understand. The music drifted up to her innocent ears. She stood with Clark and experienced what HE felt. The music pulled them closer... slow ribbons, winding around their hearts with such lonely beauty.

Her hair was like music, to him?

Her words blurted out frankly. "Clark, that's the most beautiful thing anyone has ever said about me, ever, in my whole life. No-one ever said my hair was like Chopin."

He paused, then shook his head.

"I'm not SAYING it is," he corrected, softly. "I'm not flirting. No, it IS. Really. You're music. You are beauty."

A small huff escaped her chest. She cuddled against him.

"I don't really know what to say, Clark. I knew you cared, and not just on good days. You even took me back after that 'Jeff' thing. I've hurt you, bad things have happened, and you've always loved me. But this, though? It's new to me."

He cringed. "I know... I know, I know. I can't tell you how sorry I am."

I'm so sorry I'm a freak, he thought. Riley, please don't leave me.

She continued, "I always knew you were some kind of genius, but I never thought your mind was set on ME. It's pretty intense. No-one, anywhere, is so adored that they have memories collected, framed in gold, and preserved someplace that's safe from nuclear war."

She looked around at dozens of artifacts and memories. Old photos, pictures of her smile, articles on gallery exhibits… every exhibition of her art and every achievement. Every piece symbolized her. She felt a rush when she truly realized something: there was nothing here about Ashvale. He loved everything about her, and nothing else. Her art, her words, her smiles. Her glory. Her dreams. In HIS heart, her dreams were very, very alive.

"Why wouldn't you tell me about this?"

"I didn't want to scare you."

"You protected me, though."

He was quiet for a moment, and then thoughtful.

"Yeah. I guess so."

"Everything here is just protecting me. You protected memories from being forgotten. You guarded them from Ashvale, and from time itself. All you've ever done is care for me."

She had a final question. "Is there ANYTHING else I should know about? Is there anything you don't tell me, other than your workplace 'classified' stuff?"

"I…" he started meekly, "Well, sometimes I really want to join you, when you're in the shower. I want to be in a place that's just us, and nothing else.

"And y'know, I actually saw you, a few years ago. I didn't have the strength to talk to you. You were with Albert, walking. You just felt… so far away.

"Also, I should've said: there was an attack at work. There was an explosion. That's how I got that scar on my arm. It wasn't a beaker. It was sorta complicated. Some guys tried to jump me in a parking lot, too. Same sort of thing.

"Umm… there was also that one time, when Albert and I stayed for a second viewing of *Rad Rangers* in the theatre. We just bought another set of tickets, and watched the whole movie again. We both had a lot of fun. It was one of those ridiculous things that guys do. Not sensible. Not responsible at all, really…"

"You're totally his hero, Clark." She smirked at him. "You're the best father he could ever have."

This weighed heavily on him. He slouched forward.

"I could be his tutor, at least. I've thought about home-schooling Albert. I could really teach him things, especially what he loves. I could help him with the other stuff, too. One-on-one help."

He tried to build up courage.

"And since I'm letting it all out? Sometimes, I hold your coat up to my chest. In the front hallway, I steal your coat for a minute, and I think of dancing with you in a big ballroom. And I look like a complete idiot, in the front hall, dancing… and I still do it anyway. Why? Because you make me THAT happy. You're my princess, and I could be your shining knight."

His smile was wistful, then it dropped to cold death.

"And I have to tell you something else."

She looked at him with concern. He held her carefully.

"Back in grade twelve, Jeff, Timmy Karnes and John Malick... you know, 'Jonno,' with the deep voice...? They, uhh... I heard them talking, once. They talked about drugging you. Pills. They were going to..."

His face turned stiff as iron.

"They really were. They were planning to..."

Magma rumbled through his veins. Riley breathed quickly and uneasily.

"They were going to rape you. All of them, at once." He gritted his teeth. "I confronted them. They wanted to keep things quiet, so they attacked me. They didn't get far. I tore out... I dislocated Jonno's shoulders. I ended that fight. It was so fast, it was gross. They still deserved worse."

Riley stood motionless.

"A few days later, Jonno's dad apologized. He said he'd send Jonno to reform school. For his family's sake, though, he asked me to stay quiet. And I guess Timmy and Jeff backed off. I hope they did. Jeff didn't say anything, afterward."

"Was there a report to the police?"

"No. I didn't go to the cops about this. Ashvale cops don't take rape seriously; everyone knows that. So I made it serious to Jeff and his friends: if they touched you, I'd cripple them for life."

Riley's feet shifted. "Both of Jonno's shoulders? That was your warning?"

He tried to explain. "Their crime against you would've been unbearable to me. I faced them with the same thing - permanent, lifelong damage. I made sure Jeff had the picture. I made him watch as I ripped Jonno apart. I made him watch what real pain actually looks like. Then, they reconsidered their plans."

Riley's eyes bulged, like boiled eggs. She spoke faintly. "Clark, nothing like this came up. He was a piece of crap, but... well, actually, Jeff was kinda stand-offish, around April or May. The end of grade twelve?"

Clark shrugged at her. "No-one talked about pills, right? No families gave up their sons. And now you know why I hate Jeff."

Riley stepped backward. "And then HERE, in your house, when he... oh, no. Oh, Clark!"

She hesitated, then pulled him close and nuzzled into his chest. His heart was banging inside him. He sighed uneasily. His memory released these things; weights dropped from his body. He closed his eyes with finality.

"Those sorts of people don't care about law, so you can't use law against them. Shame kept them quiet. They were small men living on borrowed time."

"But you didn't tell ME? I mean, it was about RAPING me, Clark."

He seethed. "That's right. No-one wanted to say anything and face criminal charges. They wouldn't. But I stayed silent, too, and they knew why.

"I kept it hidden, so it would've been a cold case if something 'happened' to Jeff. He knew I'd get away with murder. No-one would guess motives, their families would cover it all up, and there was nothing Jeff could do about it."

The bunker was especially quiet at that moment.

Riley closed her eyes and thought: I really shouldn't adore you right now, but I do.

Clark continued, "So maybe this is why Jeff Anders dumped you. It may have been my fault. I don't know how I feel about that."

Riley shook her head. "Not your fault. I'm fine with it. He'll get what's coming to him, someday."

"Well, I don't think he'll be mayor anytime soon," Clark concluded. "And, y'know, Matt just uncovered some things about the Anders family, and now it's all unravelling. There were arrests, even."

Riley braced him with her arms and looked up.

"Yup," he shrugged his brows. "Market control, conspiracy, and power plays big enough to get noticed by the government. They even had criminal ties and drug possession. And there used to be a pharmacist named Anders - maybe that's where Jeff, Jonno and Timmy got those rape pills...?"

"Yeah, well," she muttered, "if it's cowardly, and two-faced, and some kinda upper hand, it's probably an Anders thing."

"They're under federal investigation, now, and Matt's on it. I bet it'll make his career."

Clark didn't know what really happened. One night, at 3am precisely, silhouettes appeared in the Anders mansion. Every doorway loomed dark with a pair of black shapes. They were always twinned - shadows, with their reflections. In doorframes, then archways, and then halls, they came in silence... and then stood. They waited, watching, like black ghosts or messengers of the devil.

In the parlor, then the stairwell, and then in the bedrooms, the shadows stood and watched while the family slept.

Mrs Anders stirred in her sleep. She sensed looming shapes in her bedroom. She moaned, unhappy with her dream. She tossed her head to wake up. The shapes stood by quietly.

She fully woke and looked: the black shapes didn't fade. They weren't a dream. They were real - dark men standing in her door, by her window, and right beside her bed.

Her jaw dropped. Her voice caught in her throat. She dragged in a breath and let out a wavering shriek. Other screams followed, from other bedrooms.

One of the shadows spoke: "Ma'am? You'll have to come with us."

In minutes, evidence was secured and the Anders family was collected. Everything went by the numbers. Still, a smoky voice was impatient: "Boys, can we wrap this up? I gotta date tomorrow night..."

Clark knew nothing about this. He had no idea. He was retired, after all.

"I wanna meet him - Matt." Riley peered up at him. Clark smiled affectionately.

"Yeah, I know. And it's worth it. Maybe someday he'll ditch all that secrecy stuff, and you two can have a beer together. It's so overdue."

Clark paused.

"Oh. One more thing. This belongs to you; I guess I should've kept it with your shampoo."

Clark reached past a display case and produced a small, pink, sparkly backpack.

"Yeah," he continued. "I could've returned this, but... if I'd used Athena to find you, it'd be creepy. I didn't want to be a stalker."

She gingerly took the backpack. Her jaw hung loose.

"I mean, I would've gotten it back to you earlier, but then you'd wonder how I'd gotten it, and where I'd kept it, and..."

Her eyes were dark pools. She unzipped the pack. Her hands lifted out the hair-dryer and passed it to Clark.

"Umm... 'cuz it's personal items, right?"

She handed him the hair brush.

He gave her an odd look. "I'll put these with the Chopin, 'kay? your hair stuff?"

Her hands delved into the pack and took hold of something. She reached in with both hands, and the little pink, sparkly bag fell away. She stood there silently and held a small stuffed toy. She held it for the first time in ten years: a childhood keepsake. She'd had it since she was a little girl - a white rabbit wearing a necktie.

Her dear friend, Louis. He was back. He wore an air of quiet confidence.

Clark returned and stood by her side. He told her that he didn't know, but he thought this might be important. She didn't answer. She couldn't tell him how important it was.

This was about her being the little girl with stars in her eyes. She and Louis were the only ones who really believed in magic. And now he was back, despite the passing of decades - because he was a time wizard, of course.

Yes. He was a time wizard… and she was the heiress to The Hidden Kingdoms.

She felt something sweep around her. It passed over her shoulders and down her back, like a royal mantle. It was warm and loving, but so beautiful it frightened her.

She gazed down at her long-lost childhood friend, Louis-the-Rabbit. She preened his proud white ears. She straightened his necktie for him. She squeezed his little paw gently and stroked his soft fur.

She gaped in disbelief.

Louis? How did you do this? You're ACTUALLY a wizard, aren't you? How did you make this happen? with you, me, and Clark, all together? and all my dreams, in this hidden palace, here? Are you REAL?

He looked back at her in smug silence, as if saying, "Ha-ha. 'Told ya so."

There was no such thing as magic, and yet… here he was.

Clark touched her arms and bent closer.

"Hey," he said softly. "Are you feeling okay?"

She turned to Clark, but she couldn't see him. She felt the warmth of his hands, but she couldn't see his face. Her head rolled to the side. She opened her mouth to say 'Fine.'

He squinted. "Babe? You're starting to… OH, CRAP!"

He hugged her to keep her from falling. He crouched, then hefted her up into his arms. Her legs dangled loosely. He used his lips to nab the little rabbit by the ear; he'd never let it fall to the floor.

He carried her to the back of the room and laid her upon a small cot there. He checked her pulse at her wrist, listened for breath, and felt the temperature of her brow.

He knelt there beside her, at the cot, and let her come around. He settled the stuffed rabbit in the crook of her elbow.

When her eyes cleared, she looked up at him.

"Hey," he asked quietly, "Do you have a headache? weird balance? problems seeing? or… maybe you fainted?"

"You found Louis," she replied. "I only feel maybe a little woozy, but that's because… found Louis again. Everything's… it's overwhelming."

His face fell. A moment passed.

"Overwhelming," he repeated.

He turned dark.

"Yeah," he confessed. "Well, there's the reality. Look around you. I'm a geek, and I'm creepy, and…"

"No, you're a GENIUS."

He waited for the word 'but.' He waited for the other shoe to drop. He was 'a genius, BUT…'

She continued: "And you're handsome, and you're sweet, and you're loving, and…"

He slipped: "I'm a psycho."

He stopped. A hateful word trapped them.

"Like my dad said, when he left: I'll be a psycho. That's what he told me. It turns out, I really am psycho. And I'm truly, literally crazy about you. Do you understand me? You get it, right? All this, around you? This is obsession. It can't be normal. Look at this place."

He hung his head sadly. He was a broken-hearted little boy.

"It's overwhelming, and I'm ashamed. I wish I could be more for you. I wish I could just… be better."

She watched him falling, inside.

His breath squeaked out, "But this is what I am. I was always terrified of losing you, because of this place."

He took a few breaths. He tried to strengthen himself.

"But I have to listen to you, now. Forget secrets.

You know what I am. You see it, all around you. Now you know how PAINFULLY I love you. Now you know how… HORRIBLY… in love… with you, I truly am. Because I'm horrible."

His legs were shaking. Hope was gone, and naked courage was all he had left.

"I'll throw this out, or I'll move away. I'll go to the police and I'll register myself, if you think I'm a dangerous predator. I promise you, I will."

His lower lip twitched. Her eyes followed him carefully.

"And I'll leave this house to you and Albert. I'll sign it over, and make the government honor it. You'll never hear from me again. Just tell me how you want to do this. I swear to you, I'll do as you ask."

He knelt down lower. He bowed his head to her. Lines pulled across his face.

"All you have to do is tell me… but I need to know. I SWEAR, I'll follow every word. I SWEAR to you, right now, on my honor and on my life."

She looked around at all the things he'd kept safe. They were sacred to him, yet he'd hidden everything in fear.

"No. Don't change things."

He glanced up at her again, like taking his last breaths.

"Don't fix stuff. You don't have to. You've never scared me away."

Something clicked in her mind; something made sense. She looked at him steadily, so that their eyes had connection. She wanted him to understand something. She spoke as gently as she could.

"Clark, you didn't make your father leave."

His eyes widened. His throat lumped. His face swelled red.

He croaked, "WHAT."

"You never did anything wrong. You don't need to fix things all the time."

His voice crackled, "I'm a psycho, so he left."

"No. You didn't do anything wrong. You were a young child, Clark, and he was an angry, small man."

Years towered over them like a gloomy mountain.

"Why did my father..." His jaw trembled. "Why couldn't he love me? Why can't I be better?"

"No, Clark. It was just him. His weakness. I love you; you're beautiful."

"My own father hates me. Who could I possibly be, if that's true?"

"You're you, Clark. To me, you're the world."

The weight of his head dropped. Truth fell out.

"Riley? You've always been... You're my only real f-... For all my life, you've been my..."

She cradled his head in her arms.

"I know. Me too."

He slumped down to the floor. She held his head and rocked him sweetly.

"This is the river, Clark - what Gran talked about. The beauty of still rivers. What WE have, as 'us,' isn't something we can speak. And it's very real. We were meant to be."

It surrounded them, like the quiet depth of a river. It was unseen.

He slowly raised his head. His brow creased with concern.

"Have we gone mad, together?"

"Maybe," she replied. "I guess I'm 'Alice Through The Bookcase.' I finally followed a white rabbit down a dark passage. You and I WERE late - late for our very important date."

She shook her head, smiling.

"But no, this is real. I stepped through your final wall - your last piece of armor. This is the sacred realm where your passion can live and breathe. Now I can walk with you, and match your steps. You live in such great, powerful strides, with a heart of vast love… and yet, you choose to walk beside me. To know me. You dance with me."

He looked back oddly.

"THIS is our enchanted waltz," she said. "It's about acceptance and grace."

He growled softly, "How could you possibly take this shrine gracefully?"

"Because I know who you really are. And I know that I'm your princess, no matter what. I married another man, and I had a son with him, and then he divorced me. Then I ran to you, and I lived with you… and then I betrayed you in your own house. So what am I?"

"You're my princess," he stated. "You're golden."

"Right. That's how you hold me, as we dance.

And YOU... make advanced weaponry. You silence mercenaries. You're a man-in-black. But you're noble, and beautiful, and strong. You're my true knight. I know who you really are."

He looked to the side, thinking.

"Who we really are," she continued. "It's how we hold each other. It's how we look at each other, as we step through life. We're dancing."

His eyes strained in desperation. "How can we be together, after you've seen THIS? How do you still care about me?"

She poked him. "Because I've felt unloved my whole life, and only you could change that. You aren't consumed or obsessed. You are UNDEFEATED.

"That's who you really are, Sir Clark: my true knight, undefeated - the guardian of my dreams. I've never been so safe... that I could be so loved."

He shook his head sadly.

"Yes you ARE," she argued. "This is the treasury of your castle. I'm very honored to be here."

"This," he grumbled weakly, "was a fallout bunker."

"No, it's more. And I can prove it again," she declared. "I know this little bed, and what it means. It isn't just a cot. We both understand that, right?"

Clark hesitated, but they both knew.

"What is this cot, Clark?"

"Prom night," he admitted. "You were 'Sleeping Beauty.' It's where I tried really, REALLY hard to not kiss you. It was meant as respect."

"Pff," she scowled playfully, "That was your knightly code, Clark. Don't try to tell me any different. We BOTH know this. Proof."

The cot smelled like an antique - like dust and memory. It smelled like a favorite old book, or the familiar scent of Louis-the-Rabbit. It smelled like something Granny Faye knew about, from years long past. Now Riley and Clark had their own story. This little bed was part of it.

"Okay," Clark looked up, "so this isn't just a cot. And what - alcohol was the evil spell over you, that night?"

She gazed at him. "Yeah. See? It's the truth underneath - the meaning. And what about Louis? I mean - my stuffed rabbit, here, Louis? How did you find him? How did you KNOW?"

"I didn't," he confessed. "I waited at a bus station, one day. I was only waiting there because I really wanted to... to..."

He paused. His eyes searched left and right.

"I needed to see you."

He rose up, then knelt closely beside her. She was right; he had no idea, back then. He certainly had no plan. It was something else. Something else had a plan.

Her voice warmed him: "If you still love me, after all this time and all that pain, that's proof. It's not madness, and not obsession, but something deeper. It's enchantment, and it's real."

Clark began to surface from his gloom. His grey

eyes focused.

She said gently, "Your love still accepted me, after everything. I can accept your love, Clark."

She lay back on the cot.

"There's no evil spell now, because you've WON. So, I must lie on this bed of memory, in our treasury of dreams, and you have to kiss me. Wake us both from any doubt, Sir Clark. You are my true knight, and I am your princess. This is our fairy tale. It's real. We've lived it."

The corners of her mouth tugged.

"In this moment, Truth is our witness."

She slowly closed her eyes. He sighed happily. His face glowed like a strange new dawn.

There, in the inner sanctum of his castle, he bravely leaned down and touched his lips to Princess Riley. He kissed her the way he never could, but the way it was meant to be.

With that kiss, Princess Riley saved him. She freed his heart from the weight of so many years.

A summery smile blossomed on her face. She opened her eyes and turned to him. Their faces were so close, they nearly touched.

"Clark, whenever something's not supposed to happen, it usually does. Things need to happen. They say fairy tales are never real, but they totally are. Something makes them real.

"I think 'something' was happening, all this time. We didn't have any say in it, did we?"

"No," he replied softly.

"This was destiny - written in our stars?"

"Yeah," he whispered.

"But there's still one thing I gotta try again."

He bent closer. "Mmm? What's that?"

She sat up and spoke clearly.

"Well, there's this big wedding. We're both going. You really can't skip out on this one, okay? I wanna get it right this time."

His dimple grew with the silence. As their eyes met, their sparkles danced.

He was already kneeling on one knee.

He placed his hand on his heart, as knights do when taking an oath. His single nod was a noble bow.

"Yes, Miss Riley. Yes. It would be my greatest honor."

CHAPTER FORTY-NINE

EPILOGUE

A couple decades earlier, a bus squealed to a stop. It was a brighter bus - bright like a sunflower. Inside, there were dozens of little faces. They were gabbing, and laughing, and jumping everywhere, like the inside of a popcorn machine. It was the school bus headed to Ashvale Elementary.

A little blond boy passed through the folding doors, climbed up the steps, and got on the bus. It was the new kid. He and his mother just moved to Ashvale Plains; his father left them, so they had to start over.

He looked down the long aisle, which was lined with expectant faces. As soon as the children saw his nerdy glasses, they all pointed and laughed.

Almost all of them.

The bus started again, and he stumbled to regain

his balance. He had a heavy backpack and a blue lunchbox with pictures of space robots. He staggered down the long, straight walk, with walls of eyes staring at him.

A sunny voice called out, "Hey, you!"

He looked up to see a little girl calling to him. She had a ponytail. She had brown hair, and a pretty smile, and dark eyes.

"Sit here!" She flapped her hand inward. It reminded the boy of his mom, when she flapped her hands from 'nerves.'

"Here!" the girl said, hopping into the aisle. Her shoes clapped against the floor. "Sit on th'inside part, so you don't fall out!"

The little boy swung in. All the other children saw this and stopped staring. They went back to talking.

The girl jumped up again and bounced on the bus's seat. Her little legs swung happily from the edge. The boy held his backpack and lunchbox. His legs couldn't swing; they'd grown so long, his feet skimmed the floor.

"What's in your backpack?" she asked.

"Math. Some books."

"D'you need lots of help with math?"

He looked at her. "No, I kinda like it. And I like science, too."

Her face twisted like she'd discovered worms. He shrank back timidly.

"Wow," she squawked, with a curious voice. "I've never heard of anyone who LIKED math. Cool!

Are you gonna be famous, like those science-people on the news?"

"I don't think so." He smiled a little. A young dimple poked on his cheek.

"I'm gonna be famous," she said, staring forward. "But not on the news. More like 'on TV.' I'll have my own art show, on TV, where I teach people how to draw stuff. My dad says don't bother, but I'm totally gonna be famous. Does your dad like science, too?"

"I don't really… I don't think so."

She looked at him for a moment.

"Well, y'know what?" she smiled. "I like that YOU like it."

Things changed inside him. She changed things.

"Hey, wanna see a picture?" She stuffed her hand into her pink, sparkly backpack. She whipped out a big wad of folded papers.

"This one's a long, wooden-log fence. It's on a farm outside town. I saw it once, driving by, so I went back on my bike to draw it. It looks like the big, grey bones of an animal. It's like a dinosaur snake!

"And this is a picture of Louis, my stuffed rabbit. He's a time wizard. You should meet him! See? Here he's casting a spell, putting dreams in someone's head. He's magic; he does that."

The young boy watched her. He wanted to smile, but couldn't. Something felt sad inside him, but beautiful-sad. It was warm, and heavy, and it made him stay still. Every time he breathed, he was pulled toward her on invisible strings. He couldn't stop feeling this, and he couldn't stop looking at her.

"And this is… this…" She turned to him. "What?"

"You HAVE to be an artist." He didn't want to blink. "Those pictures? They're really, really, really, REALLY good. I don't know what your dad said, but you gotta be an artist anyway. Like, you're supposed to be. Those are serious. Those should be in books, AND on TV!"

She flashed a grin. His world exploded with joy.

"I AM an artist!" she stated. "I see things, and I teach others with pictures. But when I'm grown up, I'll do it on TV. Then everybody can see stuff."

The blond kid watched her as she explained things. The bus ride wasn't long enough for her to explain everything - not as much as he wanted. Their journey, that morning, was far too short. He loved every minute. It broke his heart to see those minutes pass.

When the bus stopped, all the other kids rushed out like noisy ants. The blond kid panicked; he was terrified that she'd leave him. Everybody else scrambled to be first. They ran, and scrabbled, and fought to get inside the school. But the little girl lagged behind and walked with her new friend.

"Is your family new here?"

"Uhh," he slowed. "No. Just me and my mom."

"Oh," she said quietly. Then she turned to him. "Well, can I sit with you tomorrow?"

His glasses slipped down his nose. His eyes widened.

She tipped her head. "And what's your name, anyway?"

"I, uh… my name's Clark."

Her feet stopped together. She stood straight. "Your name's CLARK?"

He tensed. "Y-yeah. Is that wrong, somehow?"

"No WAY! It's a great name! To me, it sounds really 'a-stablished,' like it's not running off anywheres."

"Thanks," he blushed. "But what's yours?"

"Me? I'm Riley."

That feeling swam up inside him all over again. He felt like he knew her somehow. Or maybe he was supposed to know her? Maybe he was supposed to be her friend? It felt so strong, there wasn't a word for it. If 'Everything' was the words, she was what they meant. She spoke to him with the same quiet as starlight.

"Riley…" he smiled, like finishing a poem. "That's perfect."

"What?" she chirped oddly. "Why perfect?"

They walked together a little more.

"Because it's such a pretty name."